SIN CITY

Jennifer Samson

First Printing, 2016

ISBN: 978-0-9952777-8-6

Published by Twin Crowns Press
twincrownspress.blogspot.com

www.arieswriting.com

Cover by J. Caleb Design

This story includes references to smoking, gambling, underage drinking, violence, sex, assault, illegal activities, cheating, natural disasters, hospitals, gun violence and more.

For Dawn

1

Ruby Gordon stared out the window of her half brother's El Camino as the desolate landscape passed by. It was as different from Abilene as could be, and worlds away from her birthplace in Mobile. It was like no one lived here and nothing could survive.

Buildings rose in the distance like cacti, and she shivered at the dark clouds forming behind them, hoping it wouldn't storm. She glanced over at her brother, Everett "Rett" Gordon, who was behind the wheel.

"There's the sign." He gestured forward.

Welcome to Fabulous Las Vegas, Nevada.

She frowned at the sign as they approached. She had no idea what she was being welcomed to, since there wasn't anything there.

Ahead, a hotel called the Hacienda came into view. Small motels dotted the road, but soon other large hotels appeared—the Tropicana, the Aladdin, and the Dunes. It was all so strange. Bright signs lined with neon lights beckoned, promising a flashy show at night.

She glanced behind the El Camino—the horse trailer bobbed along behind them. Her daddy had hauled it behind a thirty-six foot trailer the entire way from Abilene to Phoenix, and Ruby was terrified it'd fly off and kill her horse. Everett had picked her up in Phoenix early that morning, hitching the trailer and reassuring Ruby nothing would happen to Bella. But she still worried even though he drove the speed limit.

She looked forward again, seeing an almost-finished building in a construction site on the left side of the road.

"That's the new Caesars Palace," Everett said. "It'll open soon. That's the Flamingo. It was Bugsy Siegel's place. Well, 'til they killed 'im.'"

Ruby glanced over at him, his hair kicking out behind his ears, and Everett shifted the cigar in his mouth, a grin on his face.

"Mob had him killed out in Los Angeles, about twenty years ago. You ever hear about that?"

"I don't make it a habit to monitor the mob," Ruby said.

He chuckled. "Well, you'll make it a habit here. You can't throw a rock without hitting a wise guy."

Everett kept up conversation about Las Vegas as they headed downtown. He turned off Las Vegas Boulevard and onto South Main, heading north until they reached Fremont Street. There were casinos everywhere— McLaney's Carousel, The Mint, the South Seas, the Calypso, Golden Nugget, Binion's Horseshoe.

"You won't be able to gamble—unless you get a fake ID. You're what, nineteen now?" He didn't wait for her to answer. "I ain't gonna boss you— told our old man that—so if you wanna go back to school or not, that's your deal."

Ruby nodded. "I'll think about it." She had no intention of going back to finish high school. It'd probably be the same here as it was in Abilene.

Leaving Abilene was a mixed blessing. She was glad to be away from the high school and everyone in it, but it was like a knife in her heart having to leave the ranch. But her father wanted to go on the road full time. He'd been driving a truck since Korea, and he wasn't going to change.

She'd gone with him on the road sometimes in the summers, keeping his paperwork and looking after the money, but there was never enough money. The sleeper cab barely fit two, and her father would make a bed for himself out of furniture blankets in the trailers. She always felt like an interloper on those trips, try as she might to make herself useful. They'd sold off as much of the land as they could, but the bank still came knocking.

Her father had called Everett, his son from an early and short marriage, and asked him to take Ruby in since there was no way she could afford to live on her own at nineteen. She had no high school diploma, and the most she could do was cook and ride horses, so she didn't have much of a choice in the matter.

Rett was nine years older than her, and the most time she'd spent with him was the occasional week or so when she was a kid, and his mother and step-father would have her visit El Paso. She and Rett had nothing in common then, and she wasn't sure they did now, despite his talk about having a ranch.

"You can go and look over the ranch," Everett said, interrupting her thoughts. "You can do what you like with your horse. She a rodeo horse?"

"She's a trick horse," Ruby said. She still wasn't sure what kind of ranch Everett had. She'd never seen him on a horse in her life despite the western shirt and bolo tie he wore. "Will I look after your horses?"

"Got someone to do that. Jake breaks 'em and trains some for stock companies. Wick looks after the stable and barn." He must've seen her expression because he pushed his hat back on his head. "But maybe you could take care of the foals when they come. Got two mares expecting."

"Any money in it?"

"In foals?"

"For me. Looking after the foals."

She knew her father gave Everett money for her room and board. She felt like one of those orphans in an English novel, like the ones Sue Ann Price liked to read at school.

"Well," Everett said. "I might be able to find something for you to do outside of the stables."

He kept his gaze on the road. She glanced at the plaid shirt dress she wore, wishing she was in her blue jeans. She didn't feel like herself. None of this felt like her.

"You sling a drink alright?" Everett asked a moment later.

"Depends what you want."

"Whiskey highball."

She laughed. "Whiskey and ginger ale."

"Whiskey sour."

"Rett, you ain't even trying. Lemon juice, sugar, whiskey. Come on now, I come from a long line of drinkers, just like you."

"Alright, you're hired," he said. "I ... I might be having some people in tonight, you can help serve drinks."

"For money?"

"We'll see how good you are."

"Rett!"

"Alright, alright, I can toss a dollar or two your way for helping."

She was going to be a waitress. She wanted to cry for a moment, but remembered her life savings consisted of thirteen dollars. She sighed instead. If she wanted a new saddle—or anything for that matter—she'd have to pull up her britches and do it.

The houses they drove past were in disrepair; chain link fences were ratted with tumbleweeds, and there was no one around. Commercial buildings were butted up against houses. Everett turned back onto North Main and pulled off into a dirt lot pressed against railway tracks. Boxcars sat nearby, and the metal train cars screeched and thudded as they lumbered forward.

She looked around in confusion when Everett cut the engine. Across the tracks was a junkyard and the only thing nearby was a white three storey building, the paint flaking off the concrete, and a lopsided sign faded in the window.

"Where are we?" Ruby asked.

"My place." Everett placed the straw cowboy hat on his head. "Yours too now, I suppose."

"Here?"

"'Course here, you see anywhere else?"

She looked around helplessly. "I thought you had a house?"

"I do." He walked toward a set of concrete stairs and gestured at the building.

There was a broken window covered with plywood, and she saw no barn and no stable nearby.

"The ranch is out of town some," Everett said sheepishly.

Of course it was.

She stared at the white building, the tall rectangular windows looking like empty eye sockets. A neon sign was in one window, and she took a breath when she saw it. She had a bad feeling about this.

Everett disappeared inside, a ripped screen door banging behind him. She grabbed her suitcases out of the truck bed and set them on the dusty gravel, leaving her boxes of riding gear. She carried her train case and record player up the concrete steps to what could barely be called a patio and inside the front door.

She paused—it was so dark inside it was like being in a coal miner's lunch pail. She couldn't see a foot in front of her.

As her eyes adjusted to the darkness, she saw the end of a wooden bar in front of her stretching to the far wall, bar stools dotted along its expanse. There were tables and chairs off to her right, and a jukebox in the corner of the room. To her left was a room that looked like it wanted to be a kitchen but didn't know how. The air was stagnant, and Everett turned on a fan that only succeeded in pushing hot air around.

"Jesus," she breathed.

"You like it?" Everett grinned. "I spent a whole year finishing that bar out and fixing this place up."

"It's a bar ... in your house?" She put the record player and train case on a table. "You run a bar?"

"Well, technically speaking just on the weekends and beer only," he said slowly. "I don't exactly have a proper license. But I got assurances from Sam Wyatt it was okay on the weekends and such."

"Who's he?"

"Runs a few casinos downtown, the South Seas and the Calypso. Texan."

"Beer only? Didn't you just ask me if I could mix a drink?"

Rett shrugged. "I'm not gonna be taking any business away from Sam Wyatt, so what he don't know won't hurt his bottom line, and it'll sure help mine."

Ruby couldn't believe her ears. She was going to be living on top of an illegal roadhouse. Somehow, she didn't think their daddy knew about this.

"Come on, I'll show you upstairs to the living area," Everett said.

She grabbed her things and followed Everett up a flight of stairs to the second floor. Doors were shut up and down the hall.

"What're all these rooms?" she asked.

He paused as he reached a second flight of stairs. "Sometimes folks like to stay over if they've had a bit to drink or need a place to stay."

"Paying folk." Ruby didn't pose it as a question this time. She was also sure the city of Las Vegas didn't know this was a hotel. She shook her head as she followed Everett up the rest of the stairs. God only knew what kind of room she was headed for.

She swallowed a lump in her throat the size of the Alamo and wished she was back in Texas. Tears pricked her eyes, and she did her best to hold them in.

Everett opened the door, and she walked in after him, her heart hammering in her chest.

It was a little apartment, complete with a kitchen, eating area, and living room. The doors looked like they might lead to actual bedrooms. She let out a breath. The place was clean and had plumbing. That was all she needed to know right now.

"This'll be your room," Everett said, walking to the bedroom on her right. "Bathroom's just down this hall here."

She looked into the bedroom.

There was a homespun rag rug on the floor, and a small dresser was nestled between two windows. A double iron frame bed sat against the wall to her right. There was plenty of light, and although the room was sparse, it looked clean. The bed was covered with a plain blue bedspread and she hoped clean sheets. Some tension left her shoulders.

She raised her eyebrows at the beer bottle with yellow desert dandelions in it on the dresser. Rett had really tried.

"It's real nice," she said, meaning it. She set her record player on top of the dresser and skimmed her hand over the worn wood.

"Well," Everett said. He shifted from foot to foot, crushing his cowboy hat in his hands. "I figure we should go and get your horse settled at the stable."

"Okay," Ruby said, smiling.

Tim Kelly strode out of the Clark County Jail and took a pack of Pall Malls from his pocket. He struck a loose match with his thumb, watched it flare to life, then lit the cigarette and enjoyed the first taste of freedom.

He hadn't been in jail long, but the moment his fist connected with the head of that asshole from Nevada Southern University, the siren blared. Arrested for assault and battery and waiting to see the judge, he was turned out of the jail that morning with no explanation.

The sheriff glared at Tim on his way out, and Tim only knew one thing that would make a lawman look that way.

He looked around and spotted the blue and white Chevy Bel Air at the curb. A muscular guy with greased black hair and sunglasses lit a cigarette as he closed the door with his hip.

"Thought they'd decided to keep you for good." The man extended his hand.

"Those boys know better." He shook hands with Bill Pearce. "I take it you paid that kid a visit. I owe you one."

"You owe me more than that." Bill's knuckles were raw. "I even dropped off the little weasel this morning to recant, and I'm sure you know how much I hate parking outside a sheriff station."

Tim shrugged. Small price to pay.

He opened the car door, studying the glass-etched flowers on the rear passenger window. Not many guys in a town like Las Vegas could get away with pansy shit on their cars, but most guys weren't Bill Pearce. He tossed his leather jacket into the back seat and got in the passenger seat, waiting for Bill to start the engine.

"Those two guys from Los Angeles are coming in tonight," Bill said as they got on the road. "Our phone got turned off, so they called Rett's two days ago looking to set up a meeting. I figured you wouldn't be too interested in seeing a judge, so we're meeting at Rett's tonight."

"Good," he nodded. He could always count on Bill to make the right calls. These Los Angeles guys needed someone to move merchandise for them. He used to have a nice set up going on the Strip, him and his boys placing bets for guys who got kicked out of the casinos—until the Chicago Outfit got wind of it.

He was ambushed at the Flamingo Wash before Christmas, two sets of headlights shining on him in the middle of the night and a wise guy with a voice like a meat grinder telling him to stay out of their business or else. Tim chose "or else" and came out with a physical reminder and a bigger chip on his shoulder.

His father hadn't been happy to get the call from the hospital he was bloody and barely breathing. The old man spent his whole life trying to weasel into the Chicago Outfit, and Tim spitting in their eye didn't do his father any favors. Tim respected the downtown guys like Benny Binion and Sam Wyatt, both Texans with places on Fremont. He respected them enough to ask permission when he wanted to work something. The Chicago Outfit ran the Strip and his old man, and that was enough for Tim to decide the Chicago boys could eat it as far as he was concerned.

So could guys like Bobby Tafani, a hood with aspirations. He cozied up to the low level guys in the Chicago Outfit, and the last thing Tim wanted was a cocky Tafani thinking he was the shit because he was associated.

The Outfit didn't let street gangs run around the city, but he kept things quiet with his boys and stayed downtown. As long as no one interfered with the Outfit's casino operations things were okay, but without something big to catapult him into the big time he was low man on the totem pole. This meeting might make it otherwise.

He watched the scenery speed by, blue sky stretching over pale, dusty scrub as far as you could see. If all went right with these Californians, it would put him on the map in Sin City.

Bill dropped him a block from his place, and he walked up the street to the yellow row house. He cut through the dirt patch that served as a front yard and opened the screen door. The front door wasn't locked, and when he pushed it open hot air assaulted him. It was quiet inside, no television blared, and that meant his father wasn't home yet.

Frank Kelly had moved from Chicago before Tim was born, chasing some kind of flimsy association with the Chicago Outfit. His Irish-American father always chased after the Italians, hoping some of their association would rub off on him. The only thing his father had going for him was the bottle.

The air in the house was stagnant, and he propped open the front door to let the air circulate. He tossed his jacket onto the couch and headed for the icebox. There were a few bottles of beer inside, and he cracked one open and took a long, satisfying drink.

"Oh ... you're out."

Tim turned around and saw his little sister Diana in the kitchen doorway. She wore white go-go boots, a tight blouse and a short skirt—shorter than their mother would let her wear, he could bet on that—and she looked bored and disappointed at the same time.

"Thought the old assault charges would stick this time," she finished.

"Where the hell are you going in that?"

She glanced at her outfit. "Out."

"Out where? You're sixteen, there's no place for you to go in this town, especially not dressed like that."

She deftly rolled her eyes and flipped the ends of her brown hair over a shoulder. Tim suspected she'd tried to lighten it over the last few weeks. "I'll find some place. And I'm seventeen in August."

"Where's mom? She won't let you out in that."

"Third shift at the casino tonight, she won't be home until past midnight," Diana said. She moved toward the front door.

"You better stay out of the casinos," Tim said. "I hear you've been in there I'll—"

"You'll what?" Diana countered. "You don't do shit as it is. Living in some abandoned building and pretending you're living the high life. All I ever hear is how you're 'working on' getting me outta here. Well, you're lousy at it!"

He spied the red marks on her wrist as she crossed her arms and tried to hide them. He walked over to her, her gaze looking everywhere but him, and he pulled her arm free.

"Ol' man do that?"

"No, the Pope did." Sarcasm was one of Diana's greatest talents.

"He do anything else?"

Her eyes rolled like slot machine reels. "No ... he was just normal drunk, mean and ornery. Not like that. I would've gone to Grace's if he was like that."

Tim huffed, then paced the room, nursing his beer.

"There's a baseball game over at the high school tonight," Diana offered.

"And you gotta dress like a prostitute to watch?"

Diana stared him down. "I dress like every other girl out there."

The only girl he knew that dressed like that was Carolyn West, and it unnerved him to think his own sister dressed like her.

"Are you staying here tonight?" Diana dabbed lipstick on her already red lips.

He shrugged.

"You should," she said. She stowed her compact. "It'd make mom happy."

She slammed the screen door on her way out, and he sighed. He needed cash, and he needed it now. Maybe those Los Angeles boys would be a windfall in more ways than one.

2

Ruby was pleasantly surprised by Everett's ranch, even if it was a ten minute drive away. The stable was well kept, the horses happy, and the barn tidy. Everett's stable man, Wick, was a bit crotchety, but he knew what he was doing. Ruby didn't miss the fact he'd stuffed a bottle of something under his bedding in a small room in the barn, though.

She let Bella out of the horse trailer and into a paddock, where she danced around until settling and seeking out shade. She stowed her gear and set a stall up for Bella, making sure she'd be comfortable. She felt better about everything once she had Bella sorted.

Rett had a handful of horses in the stalls, and he took to telling her all about the dough he was going to make selling the colts and fillies to stock companies and rodeo riders. His horse trainer stable hand was nowhere to be found.

The drive back to the house didn't take long, and Rett said he'd give her use of the El Camino if she wanted to go out each morning.

"Folks'll start arriving soon," he said. He pulled out a Smith and Wesson revolver from below the counter. "You know how to use this?"

"I'm from Texas, even the mosquitoes know how to use that," Ruby said, giving Everett a sidelong glance. "Been awhile since I shot a pistol, though. Daddy kept ours in the truck and had me keep the rifles when I was at home, I'm better with those."

"Well, this is a .357, might be a bit much for you to handle. It shoots .38 Special too, so I'll pick up some cartridges when I remember, and I'll see how you are shooting it. Double action and it's loaded. Someone comes in to rob this place, blow their head off."

She raised an eyebrow, but said nothing.

She followed Everett out from behind the bar and into the room that didn't know how to be a kitchen. There was a wash basin, a bunch of cabinets, and a locked pantry. He opened the pantry to show her aluminum tubs filled with ice and beer.

"The good beer's back here. I'll give you the keys since Jed won't be here tonight. Watch that door, guys like to walk off with the good stuff, so make sure you lock it up. You don't give them one of the good ones unless they ask for it by name, otherwise it's from the keg behind the bar, got it?"

She nodded.

"Gin, scotch, bourbon, and mixers behind the bar, don't let no one back there but me, Jed, and Irene," he said. "Jed's out of town, so you won't meet him tonight. Irene'll take care of washing stuff, but nobody that comes here cares much about how clean the glasses are, I'll tell you that."

He handed her a set of keys and walked toward what he called the back room.

"This room stays locked unless someone needs it," Everett said. "And I don't mean need it for anything like . . . well, you know. They want *that*, they rent a room upstairs. Anyone wants to rent a room, you tell 'em to talk to me."

Jesus, she was gonna be running a bordello.

The room past the stairs held a pool table and two slot machines, along with a few tables and chairs.

"Best get dressed." He looked her up and down. "It's a tough crowd. You wanna make some tips you'll have to dress for it."

She threw him a dirty look—she *was* dressed. She looked at her jeans and t-shirt. They were new ones her daddy'd let her order out of the Montgomery Ward catalogue, and apparently it wasn't good enough for Las Vegas cowboys.

She sighed and went upstairs. All her shirtwaist dresses made her feel like she was headed to school or church, and she had none of those shorter skirts the girls liked to wear. She put on a western blouse instead of the t-shirt.

Music and loud laughter drifted from downstairs, and she prepared to head into the fray. She passed a couple arguing on the stairs and tried not to stare—the girl had more makeup on than any human she'd ever seen, and she wore a fitted bodice covered in sequins with a pair of blue jeans pulled over it, like she was half in costume, and maybe she was.

"Who's that?" Ruby asked her brother.

Everett glanced at the couple on the stairs. "Darla, she dances at a casino on the Strip. And that's Jake Wheeler. He's the one breaking the horses."

"*He* is?"

She stared at the guy who argued with Darla. He wore jeans, a tight black t-shirt, and an aviator jacket, his dark hair military short. He looked like he didn't know what a horse was.

10

"Come on," Rett said.

He introduced her to Irene, who looked to be about a hundred years old, though Everett said she was only in her late thirties. She was the type her father would've said was rode hard and put away wet.

"Holler if you need me."

He weaved his lanky frame through the party-goers. Ruby didn't think she'd ever seen a group so strange. There were older blue collar men, used to hard work and hard living. There were some cowboy types, and a group of bearded bikers had arrived on motorcycles and commandeered a handful of tables.

What surprised her most were all the young people. There were girls there that couldn't have been any older than sixteen, all wearing too much makeup and too little clothing. There were lots of teenage boys, but most were in their twenties, with slicked greased hair and leather jackets. They were smoking, playing cards, and making no move to hide their admiration of any half-decent looking girl that walked by.

She was so busy staring around the room she didn't notice the guy approaching the bar until he was right in front of her. He had a knowing smile on his face, and his dark hair and eyes were a bit of a dream. She noticed more than one girl staring at him. She took in a breath as he approached her.

"I'll have an Old Milwaukee." He tapped his fingers on the bar. "Locked up in back."

He gave her a winning smile, and Ruby figured he was a regular since he knew about Rett's stash.

"Coming right up," she smiled. She went into the kitchen, opened the pantry, and grabbed the beer, hurrying back. She paused before she went back into the bar room, took a breath, then smiled and walked toward the bar.

He was leaning against it, watching her approach, and her nerves jangled. She put the can down and searched the bar for something to open it.

"I got it." He pulled a church key out of his pocket.

She blushed as she slid the can over to him, hoping he didn't think she was a complete idiot.

He winked and held out some coins, touching her hand with his fingers as he gave her them. He locked gazes with her, smiling.

"I'll catch you later?" He winked again, and moved into the crowd.

"Who was that?" Ruby asked, a little awed.

"Name's Ray," Irene said. "He's a sleaze ball. Of course half the hooligans in this place are sleaze balls."

Irene disappeared into the back with a tray of dirty glasses. Ruby tried to spy Ray in the crowd, but he'd vanished. Her night was looking up if the guys around here were like him.

Bill pulled the car into the lot at Everett's at seven-thirty. It was already filled with motorcycles, souped up cars, and people.

"Tell the guys to keep their eyes open," Tim said. "I want eyes all over in case this goes south. Go get some drinks when we get in there, I'll find a table."

He got out of Bill's car and walked inside.

He thought the decibel level might have dropped slightly when he walked in, but he wasn't sure. He glanced at the bar, then looked toward the back corner, past the jukebox, and saw some people crowded around the table he liked. As he walked toward it, people moved out of his way.

He stood at the table, a round one tucked into the back near a window. The folks there looked at him for a moment, then the two couples moved out of the seats quickly.

Tim sat with his back to most of the room. He could see everyone reflected in the window. Most people might think he was stupid for sitting with his back to the door—you never did that unless you wanted to get jumped from behind—but they'd be surprised if someone tried it. He'd see them coming easy.

He lit a cigarette and took a long drag, then slowly looked to his right, appraising the crowd around a raucous poker game. He hadn't been to Everett's in a couple of months, spending most of his time at the Lucky Lady, an Irish bar off Fremont run by Jimmy Lewis's old man. Not much had changed at Everett's, but the girl behind the bar was new. He could see her reflected in the window, busying herself serving drinks. She was small, with almost-black hair, and he'd never seen her in here before. Things might be looking up if Everett had decided to hire waitresses that looked more like her and less like Irene.

He spotted Darla huffing towards the door, half in costume and half in a rage. That meant Jake was probably nearby since he was usually the cause of her temper. He didn't spot Carolyn West, and he was both relieved and disappointed. He didn't like mixing business with pleasure, and her ripe lips and dangerous curves were definitely pleasure. It sure would've been nice to have her waiting upstairs when he was done with his meeting.

Bill came to the table and handed him a beer, and Tim sat back and lazily watched everyone. He liked to tune out the noise and the people and observe. There was a lot you could tell by looking at people, even their reflection in a window.

Pamela Kingston was hard up for Jimmy Lewis, but he was so thick into his poker game he wouldn't notice until he lost, which he was going to with a hand like that. Tony Cochrane was worried his girl Elaine was stepping out on him from the way Tony was watching her chat up Eddie Demarco by the jukebox. Ray Roth was hitting on a girl near the hall, and from the looks of it, striking out. Through the window, he could see his cousin Jesse Lennox outside in a scrap with someone. Carl Hamilton and Adam Barnes were arm wrestling at a small table nearby. Carl put Adam down twice in a row.

Tim glanced at the clock above the bar. Quarter to eight. He cracked his knuckles in anticipation. His boys better be on their toes and ready for trouble when those LA boys showed up.

Ruby handed two beers to a chatty guy in sunglasses, and as he took off into the crowd, Everett handed her a pad and pencil and told her to go see if anyone needed more drinks. She figured that was what Irene was for, but he made her go anyway.

She circled around, taking a few orders, and earning more than enough wary looks from some of the girls, even the ones younger than her. She hoped it was because she was new. Looks like that were why leaving high school was a relief.

She approached a table at the back where the chatty guy sat, the sunglasses now in his pocket. Her gaze was on his friend, a guy a bit older than her with brown hair.

His hair was darkened from the hair oil he used. He had a sharp profile and gazed out the window every so often, as if he wasn't in the room with everyone else. She had the unnerving feeling he was watching her as she approached.

He turned his head slowly, tilted his chin up to look at her, and she inhaled sharply. The right side of his face was as handsome as she'd anticipated from his profile, but something was off about the left side. It looked uneven, one cheek a little off, and she could tell his nose had been broken at some point. Scars danced along his hair line and circled toward his eye, another trailing around his nose. A deep scar started below the left side of his lip and curved like a crescent moon along his chin. She locked gazes with him and swore she saw mirthful amusement in his, as if he'd expected her surprise. She recovered quickly and put on a smile.

"Can I get you boys anything else?"

The one with the scars stood slowly, only inches away from her.

"Can we talk?"

She backed up, nervous about how close he was to her, but she managed to nod. She inhaled sharply, afraid he was angry she'd reacted to his lopsided face. He was so close she could smell his aftershave, and butterflies swirled around in her stomach.

He moved away from her swiftly, cutting through the crowd, and people parted like the Red Sea to let him through. Ruby looked around, watching everyone watch this guy. He stopped in the hallway and turned around looking for her. She hurried over.

"I need that back room," he said. "For a meeting."

"Oh, well . . . um, you should talk to—to Rett," she said, her face hot at how awkwardly the words tumbled out of her mouth.

"You've got the keys."

She looked at him in surprise and followed his gaze. He was looking toward her right hip, the keys nestled in her right back pocket. She wondered what he'd been looking at to notice them there. She picked the keys out slowly and looked up again. His eyes were large and moss green, holding a hint of malice along with amusement. He held her gaze without breaking it, neither challenging nor pressuring.

She walked past him to the locked door and it took a minute for her to find the right key and open it. He walked into the room, and turned to face her.

"My buddy's gonna bring two men in here with him around eight. You follow them in, take drink orders and bring them right away, then don't so much as breathe on the door."

He faced her, like a general giving orders. She wasn't sure she liked it.

"And if I happen to breathe on the door?" she asked archly.

He stepped toward her and bent his head close to hers. She shivered in spite of the warmth.

"You're not gonna wanna do that," he whispered. She took in a sharp breath and backed away, but relaxed when she saw the hint of a smile on his face. She was about to smile back, but he shut the door on her, and she was standing in the hallway alone.

"Hey Rett?" Ruby asked, wandering behind the bar where her brother stood counting change. "Who's the guy with the scars?"

"All on the side of his face? That's Tim Kelly, and you'd do best to stay away from him," Everett said. "Chicago mob gave him that, and he probably deserved it. He's in jail more than not. A pile of trouble."

"He's using your back room," she said, watching the door.

"Nothing unusual about that," Everett said. She watched him clumsily move around behind the bar and figured he was pretty drunk. A lot of good he'd be in a pinch.

"Tim Kelly runs with that kid Ray that was hitting on you, if you could call it that," Irene said. "All a bunch of hoodlums. Dunno why Sam Wyatt let's them run around like they do."

Ruby kept an eye on the front door, and soon she spotted two men come into the bar and figured these were the ones Tim Kelly was waiting on, since they were too well dressed to fit in at Everett's. One wore a big cowboy hat and a fancy belt buckle, while the other wore a tailored western jacket and bolo tie with a silver clasp. Despite the outfits, they didn't look like cowboys to her—just men playing the part. The chatty guy shook hands with both of them and walked them to the back room.

She skimmed her fingers over the gun under the bar, then grabbed a pad of paper and a pen and followed them.

The two men from LA came into the room introducing themselves. The dark haired girl had followed, and she looked more than a little nervous. The gun sticking out of the holster on one guy's hip was probably the reason. When she met his gaze, he nodded slightly to encourage her to get on with it.

She pasted a smile on, asked for their orders and sashayed out, returning a few minutes later with a bourbon and soda for the one with the big cowboy hat who introduced himself with the ridiculous name of Insane Wayne Booker and a Budweiser for his henchman, who introduced himself as Roy Sykes. Tim already knew the score between these two, just by looking. Wayne carried no weapons, while Roy had at least two guns under his jacket and likely a knife in his boot, if not two. He assumed Wayne coasted by on reputation, whether it be earned or not, and relied on Roy to enforce any beefs.

Always be willing to do yourself what you ask of your men, Tim thought. It'd be a cold day in hell before he'd arm Bill to the nines to watch over his ass instead of doing it himself.

They sat around the big table and spent a few minutes shooting the breeze. Tim's old connection Marty had moved out to Los Angeles last year and was dealing in grass. Marty would've been a decent addition to his gang, but he was older, used to being on his own, and didn't want to set foot back in Las Vegas after he saw what the Chicago Outfit had done to Tim's face. Instead, Marty ran his own deal in LA and was turning out to be good at hooking Tim up with the things he needed to get to the next level.

"You heard, I guess, that we need a guy out this way with a truck, a rig," Wayne said. "At least a forty-eight foot trailer."

"You've come to the right place. I got one." Tim leaned back in his chair, doing his best to look bored and uninterested.

Wayne nodded. "We need someone to move some stuff for us on occasion. Nothing into Vegas, just through, places like St. Louis, Kansas City, things like that. We lost our last driver, got pinched speeding by the highway patrol, and he had a warrant on him."

Tim nodded again. "I don't got any warrants, so you don't have to worry there. What kind of stuff are we talking?"

"What you ship isn't important. We need someone we can call in a pinch and have him there, ready to go. It might be a couple weeks before we can get you a run. Might not be anything until the beginning of May, even. That alright?"

Tim nodded. It was more than alright.

They discussed a few more details about payment and finished their drinks, then Bill went to show the men out. Tim leaned against the door frame after they'd left and let out a low sigh.

He couldn't blow this. A trucking run didn't sound like much on the surface, but it was what you could get with it that was important to Tim. A run meant making connections with people in different cities, which could help him get established here. It'd be a fine line to walk between building things up and not stepping on mob toes, but he never figured on owning a casino. He could broker something letting him run street level stuff and leave the casinos to the Outfit. If he could get a bigger foothold in Vegas, there was no telling where it could lead.

Bill re-entered the room and paced, a nervous trait Tim rarely saw from his right-hand man. The staccato raps of Bill's boots were giving him a headache.

"Don't start," Tim warned.

Bill sighed. "You had to tell them you already had a truck and trailer. Jesus, Tim! How on God's green earth are we gonna find a truck and a forty-eight foot trailer? They don't leave those hanging around, you know."

It agitated him when Bill paced. He was a pretty easygoing guy, but when he got riled up . . . he got riled up. It took a lot to shake Bill, and it was making him nervous to see how ill at ease Bill was. There were deep lines furrowed in Bill's brow, and he resumed his pacing, walking around the poker table like he was aiming to cut a channel in the floor.

"I'll think of something," Tim said.

"You'll think of something?" Bill ran a hand through his hair. "Well, that's great."

"I ever let you down before?" Tim asked. He pulled a cigarette out of the pack and struck a match on his thumb nail. He lit the cigarette and took a drag, hoping it would calm the nerves Bill was causing. He felt like an elastic band pulled taut, and he hated that.

"How are we gonna pull this off?" Bill asked. "You think those chuckle-head delinquents we got out there are gonna be able to find a semi-truck? They can't find their own dicks."

Tim smothered a smile. "I told you I'd think of something. For now I'm not telling them what's going on. We'll figure out the truck. Go grab a drink and calm yourself down, we got some time. Wayne said it'd be a few weeks, maybe a month before they'd need us."

"Yeah," Bill said. "And in that time you gotta find a truck, find a trailer, *and* learn to drive it."

Bill opened the door and the music from the jukebox assaulted Tim's ears. Bill shut the door behind him, and Tim frowned.

Dammit.

He had to learn to drive it, too.

Ruby watched the fake cowboys go, wary as they moved through the crowd. She stayed near Everett's gun as they made their way out the door, shaking hands with the chatty one and getting into a big truck out in the dirt lot. She watched their tail lights disappear down the street and turned her attention to the door of the back room. The chatty guy had gone back in and shut the door.

"Hope you still got some beer nice and cold."

Ruby looked over to see Ray standing there. After his disappearance ear-lier she hadn't seen hide nor hair of him, and she figured he'd found a girl more interesting than her. She grabbed the can of Old Milwaukee she'd brought out front just in case, popped it open with a church key and put it on the counter.

He closed his hand around hers and the beer and didn't let go.

"What's your name?"

"Ruby," she answered. "Ruby Gordon."

"Related to Everett?"

"He's my brother."

He looked her up and down. "Don't look much alike."

Everett had blond curls he tried to keep cut close, but they always ran a bit wild, while her own hair was dark like her mother's. She didn't take after the Gordon side of the family in the looks department.

"Name's Ray." His hand was still over hers. "Ray Roth."

She looked at his practiced smile, a little too perfect, and felt a moment of wariness. She tried to move her hand, but he didn't move his. A second later he let her hand go, his fingertips sliding over her own.

She wasn't sure whether to feel excited or relieved.

"Are you working all night?" He downed half the beer in a few gulps.

"Yeah." She wiped the bar with a damp cloth. He was gorgeous, she'd give him that. He had dark brown hair and chiseled cheek bones that would have looked harsh on him if it wasn't for the full mouth. And it was a nice mouth.

"Get off early." He downed the last of the beer and followed her as she walked to the end of the bar. He blocked her way as she tried to head out onto the floor with her tray.

"I can't do that," she said. She tried to move past him, and he blocked her movement again. Her heartbeat sped up.

"It'd be a hell of a lot more fun than hanging around here." He leaned close to her. She could feel his breath on her cheek and smelled beer, Old Spice and cigarettes. "I can promise that much."

"I'll have to pass. I promised Rett I'd stay."

She looked to get past him, but he had blocked her way so she couldn't move without sliding past him, and she wasn't sure she wanted to do that.

"Rett won't care," Ray said, his voice in her hair. "Come out with me later. You ever been to the Pussy Cat A Go Go? I can get us in tonight."

"No. Now please let me go, I gotta work."

He clamped a hand around her arm. She tried to back up, but he held her tighter. Fear blossomed in her stomach.

"What's one date gonna hurt?" he asked.

"Ray, you wanna get your greasy hands off my sister?" Everett stood near the bar, telling, not asking.

"This isn't your business, Gordon," Ray said, his gaze still on Ruby. She looked at Everett, pleading with her eyes for him to get this guy off of her. Everett weaved a little as he approached.

"My sister, my business. Get your hands off her and get the hell outta my place, you're not welcome." Everett grabbed Ray's arm and tried to yank him off of her.

"Like hell," Ray snarled, dropping his grip on Ruby so quickly she stumbled against the bar. Before she had time to right herself, Ray hauled off and punched Everett in the face. Ruby gasped at the blood.

"Rett!"

Ray grabbed her arm, preventing her from getting to Everett.

"Let's get outta here," he said, pulling on her.

"No!" She struggled against him. "I wouldn't go with you if you were the last guy on earth!"

His grip was a vice on her arm. She tried to yank her arm away, then pushed against him. No one made a move to help her. She cried out as Ray tightened his grip, then she looked him in the eye and spat right in his face.

"Dumb bitch!"

He let go of her arm and she stumbled, not seeing his open palm coming until it was too late. He smacked her across the face, and she staggered backwards, her jaw snapping shut and catching her lip. Her cheek stung from the force of his slap, and she tasted blood. She touched her lip, already swelling, and her fingers came away smeared with blood.

The crowd quieted.

"What the hell's going on out here?" an even voice said.

The jukebox changed songs, and it was quiet enough to hear a pin drop.

Everyone turned toward the hallway. Tim Kelly walked slowly toward them, looking at Everett, then Ruby and Ray. He tucked an unlit cigarette behind his ear and stood facing Ray, who didn't answer him.

Tim Kelly hauled off and punched Ray in the face with no warning. Ray spun around, hit his head against the edge of the bar, and slumped onto the floor.

The bar was silent as the jukebox began to play Fontella Bass. The chatty guy hauled Ray up off the floor and outside as people got back to their drinks.

Ruby shook as Tim approached her. He stood in front of her for a second, studying her face with his cool, green eyes, then pulled a handkerchief out of his back pocket. She stared at his hands, the knuckles red, and he tilted her face up. He wet the end of the handkerchief with his tongue and pressed the cloth to her lip gently.

"Keep pressure on it 'til the bleeding stops," he said, his voice low, as if it was meant only for her. "Then ice it down so it won't swell too much."

She nodded, and swallowed hard as he took her hand with his free one and brought it to her face, making her press the cloth to her own lip. Tim glanced over at Everett, who had a napkin to his nose, dark with blood.

"Ray won't be bothering you anymore," he said.

Tim walked outside into the darkness, and Ruby stared at his silhouette, his face softly lit as he struck a match and lit his cigarette before walking into the black.

3

Tim turned over on the mattress, his face tangled in a mess of Carolyn West's hair. He sat up, his eyes closed against the light shining in from the small window. His head pounded, and he felt sluggish and half-dead.

"What time is it?" he mumbled.

"Nine." Carolyn sounded awake and sober. "Go back to sleep."

After leaving Everett's he'd run into her at the South Seas, so he ditched Bill and took her back to the warehouse. It'd been months since he'd had the pleasure, and Carolyn was willing and more than capable of exhausting him. They'd had a few drinks, had sex until the wee hours, and fell asleep in a room he kept an old mattress in. Despite the draft and the mattress on the floor, it was a lot better than the house with his father.

Carolyn got out of bed and wiggled back into her clothes. Her hair, usually teased and flipped within an inch of its life, was hanging loose and straight around her shoulders. Tim could see her dark roots growing in, and mascara had smudged under her eyes, making her look tired and sad.

That was the thing with Carolyn. She *was* tired and sad. He couldn't spend more than a few hours with her without seeing it, remembering it. It made him sad for her, and was one reason why he was never going to be in her bed permanent-like.

"You wanna come over for Easter dinner?" she asked. "My mom's making a ham."

"No," he said. "You go on home."

She pouted, then rolled her eyes. She'd stick to him like a starfish if he let her. She had other safe harbours when times were tough at home—he knew that—and he didn't begrudge her them. Fate had saddled her with a bad situation, but he wasn't any white knight.

She said a soft goodbye, kissed his temple, and slipped out of the room.

He rolled over in the bed, closed his eyes against the light, and tried to shake the hangover. It did no good to think of Carolyn. He couldn't save her. He was barely saving his own sister.

He opened his eyes and studied his bruised knuckles for a moment. Roth had a pretty hard face. He hadn't had much choice but to knock him out last night; Roth knew better than to beat on a girl when he was around. The last thing he needed was Everett refusing to serve them.

The girl behind the bar surprised him. He'd come out to see Ray yanking on her arm, Everett on the floor with a busted nose, and he got the gist— Ray was drunk and dangerous. Instead of crying, the girl had spit in Roth's face, and it was all he could do not to laugh about it. The chick was lucky he'd been there.

He thought someone said she was Everett's sister. They looked nothing alike, and he was surprised Rett had a sister. Tim couldn't remember hearing one word about her.

She wasn't his type—he liked blondes—but there was something about the way she looked at him, her lip bleeding, her silver dollar eyes staring, and her chest rising and falling with each breath that he couldn't get out of his head.

He climbed off the mattress and stood, cracking his back and neck, then used the can in the factory next door, quiet and ghostly on Easter Sunday. He'd forgotten. That meant he'd have to be at home for dinner or his mother would raise hell.

He looked into the mirror and splashed some water on his ruined face, studying it in the mirror. He remembered the smell of the hard pan desert in the Flamingo Wash, his blood soaking into the dry earth and the disturbing feel of air slipping through his shredded face. Metal plates, surgeries, and stitches later, it didn't look any better than it had felt that night.

He scrubbed his hair with some tap water, then grabbed the tin of Dixie Peach from a room he called his office and greased his hair.

He needed a truck.

Jake Wheeler was on the rodeo circuit, and there were always a lot of trucks around rodeos. Tim figured he might be someone to ask.

It wasn't his first choice—Jake had a mouth on him, and everyone from Fremont to the Strip would know about it if he wasn't careful with what he told him. But he was sure Jake would know someone who knew someone, or something like that. It had to be done.

Tim stopped at the house, aiming to take a shower and change before hunting Jake up. The old man's car was gone, but he recognized the one outside his house. He found Ray Roth sitting at the kitchen table with his mother and Diana.

"Hey, Tim." His jaw was bruised where Tim had hit him.

"What are you doing here?"

"Here's your sandwich." Diana placed a plate in front of Ray, and his mother deposited a bottle of beer in front of him.

Tim took in the scene, speechless.

"What the hell is this?"

"Tim, your friend Ray dropped Diana off," his mother said, her lips clamped around a cigarette. She got up to baste the ham. "Where are your manners?"

"Ray's gotta go," Tim said. "He has an appointment."

"I dunno, Tim," he said, swallowing a bite of his sandwich. "This sandwich is pretty good."

Tim circled around and clamped a hand on Ray's neck.

"And he's late for his appointment."

"Thanks for the sandwich, Di," Ray said. "Mrs. Kelly, a pleasure."

"You're sure you can't stay for dinner?" his mother replied.

"He's sure."

Tim guided Ray, beer bottle still in hand, straight out the front door.

"What the hell are you doing?" Tim asked. "You need me to hit the other side of your face, too?"

"Whoa, whoa, calm down there, Tim," Ray said. "I was doing you a favour. But if you wanna bring it, bring it."

He stood back, smiling. Tim pulled back to hit him.

"Tim!" Diana screeched. "What are you doing? You better not hit him!"

She rushed out the door and between them. Tim lowered his arm.

"Gimme one good reason," he asked Diana.

"How about he stopped that goon Marshall Fairfax from hassling me at the Round-Up this morning?"

The Round-Up was a local drive-in restaurant between downtown and the Strip.

"What were you doing at a closed restaurant on Easter Sunday morning?" Tim asked her.

"Meeting friends, not that it's your business. Anyway, you know Fairfax? Red hair, bulging eyes? He followed me when I walked to the bus stop."

"And I stepped in and saved the day," Ray said, grinning again.

"Ray pulled up, popped Fairfax right in the face, and gave me a ride home," Diana said, smiling at Ray like he was the one that had risen that day instead of Jesus.

"I think I'll be on my way," Ray said. "Thanks for everything, Diana. I'll see you around."

Before Tim could school him on why that wasn't going to happen, Ray hurried to his car, got in, and drove off.

"You stay away from him, you got it?" Tim asked. "He up and hit a girl last night, Diana."

Diana crossed her arms in front of her and tilted her head, the picture of defiance.

"So he's not the nicest guy on the planet, but he's handsome, and he was there!" Diana said. "Unlike you. I asked you if you'd stay last night and you didn't."

He had nothing to say to that.

"And how bad can he be if you're friends with him? You can't tell me what to do. Especially if you're not going to be around to take care of things like you always promise."

She turned and went into the house, slamming the front door behind her.

He took out a cigarette, lit it, and took a few drags to calm down. He could deal with Ray later. What he needed to do was focus on a truck—that was the only way he'd make enough money to help any of them.

He walked along the main drag and thumbed a ride toward the Strip. Jake crashed at any number of cheap motels in the area, but he put his money on the Cabana Inn, a motel off the Strip with a gaudy rotating neon sign. He was headed toward the manager's office when a voice called out.

"I heard a rumour you were out of jail," Darla asked. "I'd bet good money there were some shenanigans involved. Think I can get a decent reward if I turn you in?"

"They wouldn't pay more than a nickel for me," he said.

She gave him a sidelong glance. "Oh, I don't know about that."

"Saw you leave Everett's the other night."

Her face clouded over. "Yeah . . . have you seen Jake?"

"Looking for him myself," he said.

He followed her toward the office, and he let her go inside and get the room number—strictly speaking motels weren't supposed to give it out, but men gave pretty much anything to Darla when she asked. She nodded toward the rickety stairs when she came out. He saw a dark bruise circling her upper arm as she reached for the railing, and she pulled her sleeve down, covering it, without realizing he saw.

She was about to knock on Jake's door when it was flung open.

Jake Wheeler didn't look the part, but he was an honest-to-God rodeo rider. He looked more like the Air Force washout he was, shorn hair and bomber jacket. He didn't work for the New York Syndicate or the Chicago Outfit or anyone else for that matter, scraping by on the rodeo circuit, training horses, and betting on races at Thunderbird Downs.

Jake's gaze went from troubled to worse as he saw Tim standing there near Darla.

"Don't this look cozy," Jake said. "What are y'all doing here?"

His Alabama accent was as thick as pea soup.

"Does what look cozy, Jake?" Darla asked, hands on her hips. "The fact I've had to hunt all around town for you? Or the part where you never called me after Saturday?".

"Kelly, what the hell are you doing here?"

"Don't ignore me, Jake," Darla said. "We have some things to settle, and I didn't come all this way over here to have you pretend nothing's wrong."

"Oh, something's wrong all right, you showing up here with Kelly."

"Oh, this is rich," Darla said. "This isn't the time to get jealous."

"You think I'm jealous?" Jake looked at the ceiling, and Tim had no idea what he thought he'd find up there. "You oughta get your head examined."

Darla was about to protest, and Tim didn't have time for this. They fought like cats and dogs, and their argument could go on all day.

"Hey, Wheeler, you want to step into my office for a minute? I gotta talk to you about something," Tim said.

Darla snapped her mouth shut and rolled her eyes, turning her attention to the motel room, looking for evidence of another woman.

Jake looked over at him, then cocked his head down the balcony walkway, and Tim followed him.

"Heard you cracked Roth a good one last night." Jake lit Lucky Strike. Tim didn't miss Jake's glance at his bruised knuckles, and he resisted the urge to hide them away.

"He deserved it."

"Way I heard it was you were playing the knight in shining armour and rescued some broad."

"You heard it wrong," Tim said. "Besides, I don't think she needed rescuing. Roth's face just needed a little punching."

"Ain't that the truth." Jake sucked on his cigarette and blew a thin stream of smoke out the side of his mouth. "So what's up?"

"I need a truck," Tim said, deciding not to beat around the bush. "A rig, at least a forty-eight foot trailer. I thought you might know someone."

Jake narrowed his eyes. "This ain't about Darla?"

Tim shook his head in frustration. "I ran into her looking for you. You oughta see someone about your paranoia."

24

"Fuck off." Jake took a drag of his cigarette again. "What do you need a truck like that for?"

"Business opportunity," Tim said. "You find me a truck, and I'll cut you in ten percent of the first run."

"If I find a truck you're cutting me in twenty percent," he said.

Sometimes he hated dealing with Jake. He never knew when to stop.

"Fine," Tim said.

"I'll keep my eyes open. But I'm training for Helldorado, I may not have the time."

"You only get the money if you can get the truck," Tim said.

"What's the truck for?"

"I told you. Business opportunity."

"You know I'll find out anyway."

Tim didn't bother with a reply.

He watched as Jake's gaze drifted back to the motel room. Darla was standing in the doorway watching them, her curves filling out her dress just right. Jake was staring at her, a look that bordered on longing. Jake was getting soft.

"If you're not interested, I can find someone who is."

"Never said I wasn't interested."

"Didn't have to," Tim said, nodding toward the room with a knowing grin. "I can see you'd rather play The Bickersons with your girl than make some dough."

"So I guess knockin' Roth out had nothing to do with the chick with the nice ass behind the bar, huh?" Jake asked, his voice laced with practiced innocence.

Tim laughed. Jake always could match him point for point.

"Just keep your eyes open for a truck." Tim slapped Jake on the back good-naturedly. "Don't breathe a word to no one either."

Jake nodded, and they shook hands.

Tim moved toward the stairs, then turned back.

"Jake."

Jake looked at him, and in that moment he decided it was better if Jake saw the mark on Darla himself. Telling would do him no good; Jake was paranoid enough without worrying about the men who watched Darla in the shows.

"Never mind."

Tim watched him go back into the motel room with her and shut the door behind them. He didn't envy Jake the fireworks that would follow, not one bit.

25

Monday, April 18, 1966

Ruby settled into a routine of exercising the horses in the morning and spending most afternoons in the third floor apartment, since it was the only one with an air-conditioning unit. Everett's argument against putting one downstairs was that hot people were thirsty, and thirsty people bought his beer, and she couldn't argue with logic.

Everett was still in a world of pain from his broken nose. He hadn't opened the bar since, and she was glad about it.

She hunted for the keys to Everett's El Camino that morning, but they were nowhere to be found. Usually they were hung up on a nail in the bar kitchen. It didn't matter much, because the car wasn't there either.

She had no choice but to walk to the stable. Everett had told her not to walk there by herself, but she didn't have a choice, and no one paid her any mind. She was hot and dusty and had wasted a good forty-five minutes of her morning by the time she got to the ranch though.

Wick was nowhere to be found, so she supervised the unloading of the hay off the truck and had tried to put empty pallets onto a flatbed with the forklift, but couldn't get it in gear. The transmission grinded, and she cringed. A gear shift was a mystery to her, and no matter how hard she tried she never got the hang of it. Better to leave it for Wick than to bust Everett's machinery.

She saddled Bella and took her out for some exercise. She rode around the riding ring, accidentally catching her lip with her tooth. Her lip had swollen, but was nothing she wasn't used to. She'd been tossed off enough horses to be familiar with ice and bruises, and her lip looked close to normal now.

She couldn't help but wonder about Tim Kelly. There was something sinister about his face, but beneath it was a quiet stillness she couldn't figure out. He commanded a lot of respect at Everett's place, and if he could smarten up a guy like Ray Roth, then he was alright to her.

She dismounted and unsaddled her horse, then let her loose in the paddock. She shut the gate behind her and went to stow the saddle in a small office Everett kept. She stopped in her tracks when she spotted a man inside the stable.

He was alone, leaning against a post by one of the stalls, his back to her. She took in the broad shoulders and the low cut jeans, admiring his silhouette, outlined by the sun. She moved to the side, accidentally kicking a metal bucket, and he turned around to see what the noise was. It was the guy from Everett's, with the aviator jacket—Jake something.

"What in the world are you doing?" she exploded. She set the saddle on a sawhorse and marched toward him. He was startled at her outburst.

"What the hell?"

"Put that out!" She grabbed his cigarette and doused it in a bucket of water.

"What's your problem?" He grabbed her wrist and pushed her back against the post, her head hitting the worn boards. "Nobody ever teach you any manners?"

"What's *my* problem?!" she asked, incredulous. "You just came into a stable full of bedding and feed with a lit cigarette!"

He looked around for a second, his russet brown eyes narrowing. His breathing was returning to normal, and she was conscious of how close he was to her. His hand was still closed roughly around her wrist, and he was so close she could feel the heat radiating from his body. Her face flushed at how short the distance was that separated them, and he must've noticed too, because he backed away from her.

"Saw you in Rett's," he said, letting her wrist go. She held it to her. "You're his sister, huh?"

"What? Yeah." She was distracted by his thick southern accent. "But that has nothing to do with you smoking in here."

"You owe me a cigarette," he said. His eyes relaxed, but it didn't soften his hard face. "That's you gettin' off easy seeing as you're his sister."

She stared. "Me getting off easy? You're something else. You don't bring a lit cigarette into the stable or the barn."

He shrugged. "Coulda asked me to put it out."

He wandered through the stable taking stock of the horses, and she huffed out a breath.

"You're from Alabama," she stated.

He gave her an appraising look. "Not many folks get the state right. Miss Texas."

She smiled. "Born in Mobile. Moved to Abilene when I was a kid. You're Jake?"

He nodded. "Jake Wheeler."

"Ruby Gordon. But apparently you knew that," she said. "What are you doing out here?"

"I train here for the rodeos."

She looked at him in surprise. "Rodeos? Rett said you break his horses, and I thought he was joking."

"Let's not go getting me angry all over again," he said, a look of contempt on his face. "I know plenty about horses and rodeos."

"Well, not enough to not smoke in here. You should know better."

"I ain't never killed a horse yet, so don't go gettin' your panties in twist."

She bristled at his words. She'd been around tough talkers all her life, but this guy didn't care whether she was used to it or not. She wasn't sure of his age—maybe mid-twenties.

Jake walked toward the last stall.

"Any of them yours?" she asked.

"Nah, can't afford to keep one. Rett pays me to get them rodeo ready, he sells them to stock contractors. I'm gonna break Midnight Bandit," Jake said. "He's as ornery as they come. I do that and Rett's gonna let me put him in the Helldorado Days rodeo for saddle bronc."

"You really ride saddle bronc?" she asked, not believing her ears.

"And bareback." He tucked an unlit cigarette behind his ear, as if he had to have one with him at every moment. "I guess you ride?"

She nodded. "Bella's mine . . . the palomino mare in the paddock."

He turned and walked toward the tack room without acknowledging she'd spoken.

She studied him as he walked away. He had blue jeans on, cowboy boots, and a dark t-shirt, which made him look half the part. But the leather aviator jacket hanging on the post, the crew cut hair, and scowl were decidedly not cowboy. He was the strangest rodeo rider she'd ever met, and that was saying something.

"So when is this rodeo?" She followed him to the tack room. He came out with a saddle and went back toward Zephyr, a bright bay stallion.

"May," he said. "You wouldn't be interested."

"You don't know me to know what I'm interested in."

She watched as Zephyr puffed out his chest, and Jake brought his knee up to the horse's ribs, causing the horse to exhale long enough for Jake to cinch the girth tight. He knew what he was doing.

"You plan on buzzing off and lettin' me work at any point in the day?"

"Depends, you planning on burning the place down if I go?" She stepped inside the stall and handed him a bridle.

"You're a mouthy little broad." He walked over to her, his pace slow, and she backed up against the stall rail as he approached.

"You can't boss me around, I work here just like you."

"Oh yeah?" he asked, leaning in to her, his breath hot on her neck. He smelled like cologne. "I bet I can."

She moved away from him and out of the stall, listening to his throaty laughter, and she cursed herself for not standing her ground.

"You know I'm going to have to check out this little rodeo," she said with as much levity as she could, afraid she was blushing.

"It's not little," he said. "Sometimes I bull ride, too."

She turned around and caught his gaze. "I can believe it. You look like you're comfortable with a lot of bull."

She turned around and walked away, smiling to herself. As she walked out of the stable she wanted more than anything to look back and see his expression, but she was sure he was watching her and waiting for her to do it.

Her good mood evaporated when she got outside and saw that he'd shown up in Everett's El Camino.

"He has got to be one of the most aggravating people I've ever met!" Ruby fumed as she made a late lunch. She planned to go back to the stable later in the day, and if she had any luck, Jake would be gone. "Did you know he took your car?"

"Jake's okay." Everett looked sheepish. "You're lucky he didn't pound you into the ground for snatching his cigarette like you did. He's belted people over less."

"Girls?"

"Well, I've never seen him hit a girl," Everett admitted. "But I wouldn't put it past him."

"A lit cigarette in the stable!" she said again. "Can you imagine if he'd had it in the barn with all the hay? His engine's runnin' but there sure ain't nobody drivin'."

"You get all West Texas when you're mad," Everett said with a tiny grin. "Sit down and eat for a minute."

Ruby sat at the table and looked out the window, not touching her soup.

"That girl that was with him, she's his girlfriend?"

"Who, Darla?" Everett asked. He nodded. "Been going together awhile. Nobody can figure that one out."

"He's one of the strangest people I ever met."

"He was in the Air Force at Nellis, rumour has it he got tossed out of pilot training or something," Everett said. "And he's good with horses, despite how he looks. He won't interfere with yours."

"Well, he better not pull anything like that again. I'll douse *him* next time, not just the cigarette."

Everett chuckled. "You wanna work this weekend? You can waitress again if you want to. Might be a big enough crowd to make tips."

Ruby resisted the urge to groan. But he'd pay her at least, she could make sure of that.

"Jed'll be here, you don't gotta do much if you don't want," Everett said, looking uncomfortable that she was taking so long to reply.

"It's not that," Ruby said. "It's been a big change coming here, is all."

Everett chuckled. "I forget how Las Vegas must look to someone new in town. Guess it's a bit of a change for you, huh?"

"It all is," she said. "Abilene's a dry town, don't forget. I'll work. As long as that Ray guy doesn't show up."

"If he does he'll be on his best behaviour," Everett said, eating his soup. "Kelly'll make sure of that."

4

Two weeks after his meeting with the Californians, Tim showed up at Everett's before noon, hoping to get a beer and talk with Bill somewhere private. Even though it wasn't the weekend, Tim knew Everett would let him in to use the place—if the money was right.

He was tired of not having a car. If he could get this truck and do this first run for the Californians, he was going to get a car first thing with the proceeds. It looked bad being ferried around by Bill or walking everywhere, and he wasn't about to take the bus.

He noticed Everett's car was missing from the side of the building, but he opened the screen and banged on the door anyway. He peered inside the window, and the place looked quiet. A few minutes later he saw Everett making his way into the bar from the stairs.

"What do you want?" His eyes were shadowed yellow.

"I need to meet with Bill," he said. "Thought this place would be most private."

"Don't you got some kinda hideout for that?"

"It's a warehouse, not a hideout," Tim said, his patience wearing thin. "Ray and Carl are hanging around there, and I don't need them part of this meeting. But if you don't want the money, that's fine."

Tim turned around and was down two concrete steps when Everett called him back.

"I never said no," Everett said. He held his hand out, and Tim gave him a couple dollars. Everett held the door open. "If Roth shows up this weekend, he better be on his best behaviour."

"I told you before Roth won't bother anyone," Tim said.

Everett nodded, then left without another word, shuffling upstairs and leaving him with an empty room. It was eerie being in Rett's without the loud jukebox music, the crowds, the clinking of glasses, and the smell of smoke thick in the air. There was something unnatural about it.

Tim cracked his neck. Two weeks, and not a clue about where to get a truck. Jake was no help at all, more interested in holing up and making nice with Darla.

It looked like they would have to steal one, and that was going to be a tall order. His only relief was the phone call from the Californians had brought good news instead of bad.

Five minutes after they'd scheduled to meet, the familiar sound of Bill's car was in the lot. Bill came inside muttering an apology and sat with Tim in the centre of the room.

"You haven't heard from the Californians I hope?" Bill lit a Chesterfield.

"I got a call from Wayne last night." Tim refused to refer to him as Insane Wayne like the fool did every time he was on the phone. "He said they're running late getting things set up. It buys us some time."

"Thank God for small favours," Bill said. He rolled the tip of his cigarette around the edge of the cut glass ashtray. "We're still at square one, though."

"I know it," Tim said.

He was glad he hadn't said a word to the boys about any of this. It was why he didn't want to meet at the warehouse. Carl was staying there since he got kicked out, and Ray crashed there when he couldn't afford a motel, which was most of the time. The minute those two yahoos knew Tim was having trouble getting a truck the rest of the gang would know.

After this first run, he'd see about getting some of his stuff on the trucks. His fence in Vegas was getting lazy when it came to getting rid of what Tim brought him from the Raceway, due to fear of what the Chicago Outfit might think since the Stardust owned the Raceway. If Tim could get things out of town they could make good money.

Tim was about to tell Bill they were going to have to resort to stealing a truck when footsteps rushed up the stairs. The dark-haired girl hurried inside, the door slamming shut behind her. She wore blue jeans and a western shirt, and she picked a straw cowboy hat off her head and plunked it on a hook inside the door. He could smell the scent of hay, earth and something sweet, maybe perfume of some kind.

She turned around, surprised to see them sitting there, then, undeterred, she made her way behind the bar to a small refrigerator under the counter and pulled out a Dr Pepper, puncturing the can with a church key.

"You boys want anything?" she asked.

Tim looked over and shrugged. She pulled something out of the fridge, opened two cans, and came over to the table with two beers. She put a Lone Star in front of him and a Pearl in front of Bill. It didn't escape his attention they were both Texas brews.

"Everett telling you to give out the good stuff now?" Bill asked her. "I'm Bill, by the way. Bill Pearce."

Tim resisted rolling his eyes at the syrupy tone Bill's voice had taken on. He felt no need to introduce himself; it wasn't often he had to. But he wondered all the same if she knew who he was.

The girl shook hands with Bill.

"Ruby Gordon. And the beers are on me," she said. Tim looked up, and she met his gaze head on, looked him right in the eye, and it pleased him. People tended to avoid eye contact with him, especially if they didn't know him. The guys would avoid it for fear of pissing him off, while the girls probably couldn't stand to anymore, what with his face as messed up as it was.

His face had scared her that night a few weeks ago, but now she looked at him without a hint of that fear.

"For the other weekend," she said. "I never said thank you."

Tim nodded, and she smiled. He watched as she walked back toward the bar, her jeans hugging her curves, and he licked his lips. She wasn't bad looking at all.

She sat on a bar stool and opened a magazine, reading it with no concern to them. Anyone else would've beat it out of the room by now.

She glanced back at the table and saw he was still watching her, and he resisted the urge to look away, embarrassed to have been caught at it.

"Do you need me to leave?" she asked, now aware she'd walked in on something.

He was quiet for a second. "Not if you know how to keep your mouth shut."

She didn't look offended at his comment and smiled.

"I've only got tongue enough for one row of teeth," she said.

Bill raised his eyebrows. "You talking English?"

"Texas," Tim said. Her accent had a bit of a West Texas twang to it.

She nodded, a smile playing on her lips. "Is it that obvious?"

He shrugged.

"What part of Texas are you from?" Bill asked.

"Abilene."

She looked at Tim again, and he held her gaze for a moment. He felt triumphant as she blushed and looked away. She went behind the bar, picked up a cloth and wiped the shiny surface of the bar, then sat back on the stool and stared at the magazine. He didn't think she was reading it.

Bill looked at Tim and jerked his head toward her, a questioning look on his face. Tim shrugged.

"Is a forty-eight foot trailer the biggest?" Bill asked in a low voice. "I don't know."

"Don't think so," Tim answered. "But he said that was the minimum, so I'm aiming for it or better. I hate to say it, but I think we may have to swipe the truck."

"We may have to swipe a trailer too," Bill said. "Lord, how are we gonna do that? You know none of the boys have a license to drive a rig."

"Figure I'd do it myself," Tim said. "Can't be much harder than a stick shift."

"You're wrong about that," Ruby said.

He looked over in surprise, and she spun around on the stool to face them. "I don't mean to butt in, but I was eavesdropping."

Tim's mouth twitched as he tried not to smile. At least she was honest.

"You're talking about rigs, right?" She wandered over. "You've only got four or five speeds in a manual transmission. Most trucks out there are five and four transmissions with two sticks. That means two-handed double shifting, and that takes awhile to learn. Tractors have unsynchronized transmissions, and if you can't float the gears you have to double clutch, and that takes time to learn, too."

Tim leaned back in his chair, a smile on his lips. Damned if he wasn't getting hard listening to her talk about transmissions.

"Now how does a pretty thing like you know all that?" he asked, regretting the words the instant they left his lips. He used to be able to flirt without sounding like a total dipshit.

"My daddy's a truck driver," she said, her cheeks pink.

"You ever drive one?" Bill asked.

She shook her head. "He let me on flat stretches, but not to shift. If you've never driven a rig before you ain't gonna learn in a couple days, especially with a trailer, loaded or not. Then you gotta learn to drive it with one, and that's a whole 'nother thing."

"Well, that'd be all well and good if we had a truck," Bill said. Tim wanted to kick him under the table.

He looked at the girl. They might be able to use her.

"You mind taking a walk?" Tim asked Bill. Bill looked at him in confusion, then gave him a knowing grin and winked as he left the table and headed outside.

"Have a seat," Tim said, kicking the chair on his left out toward her.

"This has something to do with your business a couple weeks back?" she asked. She sat next to him.

"I need a rig." He didn't bother to answer her. "Needs to have a forty-eight foot trailer."

"I can talk to my daddy when he calls tonight, he might know of one around here. If you'll be here tomorrow I can let you know what I hear." She hesitated for a second. "I take it you don't have a commercial license?"

His smile was wry. "Is it that obvious?"

"Just in that you have no idea what you're talkin' about," she said with a smile.

He grinned back.

"You plan on paying for this rig?"

"Not if I can avoid it." He took a long drink of the beer.

"So that's a no," she said. He grinned—she was pretty sharp. They sat in comfortable silence for a second, and she sipped her Dr Pepper as he drank his beer.

"If you do find a truck, I can explain double clutching and how to shift a five and four. I can write it all down if you want." She fiddled with the pen in her hand. "Or I could show you."

"You'd be willing to help us out?" he asked.

"As long as you don't say anything to Rett," she said, looking over her shoulder like he might be standing right behind her. "He'd likely hit the roof."

Tim resisted the urge to laugh. "If I remember right, your brother's got a couple slot machines in the back that don't pay a dime of tax to the state or Sam Wyatt. He sure as hell shouldn't judge."

"Well don't that beat all, he told me they don't work," she said. She glanced at him again. "I guess I could help you out. Whatever you need to know."

"Everything," Tim said. "Only don't tell no one that."

She looked at him in a way he couldn't read and tilted her head. "Tim Kelly knows everything, huh? And no one can know he doesn't?"

He inhaled and did his best not to smile.

So she did know who he was.

"Something like that," he replied.

Saturday, April 23, 1966

Ruby met Everett's bartender Jed about an hour before people arrived on Saturday night. The man nodded and hung up his cowboy hat inside the door. He looked to be in his late twenties and like he was used to hard living. Everett had told her he thought Jed was an ex-con.

As soon as he opened his mouth Ruby knew she was in the company of a fellow Texan.

"Spent the last ten years in Huntsville," he said.

Ruby wondered if he meant he lived in the town of Huntsville or the prison there.

Jed had her cut some lemons and limes for drinks, then she served drinks to some of the tables once the crowds showed up.

She sighed and weaved through the crowds back to the bar. This wasn't what she had in mind when she moved from Abilene. She thought she'd spend her days riding, training for a rodeo, and practicing all those moves she'd seen the Lucas sisters do.

She hadn't told a soul yet, but she was going to put together her own trick riding show. She'd audition for someone like Montie Montana and go on the road with a rodeo, then put her own show together and tour with her own troupe, and all she'd have to worry about in life was riding her horse.

She slid away from a boy who drunkenly tried to grab her leg and vowed to stomp on his foot next time she walked by. She sighed when she reached the bar.

"It's been forty minutes," Jed said, a wry smile on his face that didn't reach his eyes. "You wanna pack it in?"

She gave him a look. "I worked a couple weeks ago for the whole night. Doesn't mean I have to like it. I like standing behind that bar better, there's no wandering hands back there."

When she got a break from all the orders she slipped into the kitchen to bring more beer from the pantry out to the small icebox under the bar.

She was keeping an eye out for Tim, but was rewarded with Jake in a bad mood. He walked into the place with an expression like a thundercloud. His knuckles were busted open on both hands. He walked right past her into the kitchen and over to the pantry.

"What are you doing?" she asked.

He wrenched the pantry door open, and she cursed herself for forgetting to lock it. By the time she rushed over, he was already headed toward the side door, a couple bottles of beer in his hands.

"You have to pay for that!" she yelled after him.

He didn't turn around, didn't say a word, and stalked off into the night like a highway robber. She sighed, locked the pantry, and headed back into the bar room. The bottles cost more than the cans—he knew that. At least Jake had sense enough to leave the El Camino behind this time.

"I swear I'll use that gun on him," she said.

"Not the first time I've heard someone say that about Jake," a cheerful voice said. She turned around and saw a man with a fifties style pompadour leaning against the bar, a grin on his face, despite the bruises he sported. "You got any Coors back there?"

"Depends, you gonna pay for it?" she asked. Everett had already docked her pay for giving free beers to Tim and his friend Bill yesterday. She was out a few more cents now thanks to Jake.

He grinned. "I'll do my best not to tick you off and pay full price."

She couldn't resist smiling back. "I'm Ruby."

"Hollis Warner." He shook her hand.

"Haven't seen you around before."

"I'm around here plenty, we just haven't been introduced. Word has it you're Everett's sister. He was telling us during the poker game last week. We didn't know he had any."

"Word's right." She handed him a bottle of Coors. She could see a line of stitches whenever he turned his head, and his lip and eye were both healing from bruises. "You know Jake?"

"Yep, and don't worry, it's not you, he's like that to everyone," he said. He took a long drink. "He courts fights."

"With you?"

He looked surprised, then smiled. "No, these came courtesy of someone who didn't like my sleight of hand at a poker game over at the Brown Cow last week."

"You were cheating at cards?"

"How else am I gonna win when I get dealt a bad hand? Jake jumped to my defence." He took another drink of his beer and winked. Despite his flirtatious behaviour, she liked him.

"Really?" she asked.

Hollis nodded. "He could do with a personality transplant, but he's good in a pinch. But I wouldn't go telling him that if I were you. Jake knows it already."

She laughed. This guy was okay.

"Slandering my poor boyfriend's name again, Hollis?"

Ruby looked over and saw the blonde, the one Jake was dating, at Hollis's elbow.

She was more beautiful close up. She looked like an actress, with perfectly curled blonde hair, a clear complexion, and bright blue eyes. She wasn't dressed in costume, but her makeup was exaggerated. On anyone else it might look overdone, but on her it just looked beautiful.

Ruby looked at her own dusty jeans and calloused hands, then at the girl's figure-hugging dress and perfect nails and felt like something the cat dragged in.

"Jake doesn't need my help to slander his name, Darla," Hollis said. "Shouldn't you be dancing tonight?"

"I'm not on until ten," she said.

37

"You two met? This is Everett's sister Ruby, and Jake's girl Darla."

"Hi," Ruby said. "I've seen you around."

Darla had a polite smile, but there was a shred of distrust in her eyes as she looked at Ruby.

"I heard Ray Roth busted your brother's nose," Hollis said. "I don't much like Roth, and anything that gets his face pounded in is alright with me."

Ruby was about to ask what he knew about Tim Kelly, but as soon as she had the thought, the door opened, and he walked in. He shook hands with people as he made his way through the crowd to the bar. He glanced over and headed straight toward her. Whatever Hollis was saying went in one ear and out the other.

She crouched and got a beer out of the small fridge.

"Saved one for you," she said to Tim, punching two holes in the top of the can with the church key and setting the beer in front of him. He nodded his thanks to her and slid some change across the table.

"Warner." Tim sat with his right side facing her and greeted her entertainment. "Darla."

"Hey Tim," Hollis said. He turned his attention back to her with a wink. "Don't let this ol' hood give you any trouble now."

"Do you want anything?" Ruby asked Darla. She hoped Darla would take off so she could talk to Tim without anyone around.

"I'm looking for Jake," she said. "Anyone seen him around? He was supposed to meet me."

"He took off with some of my beer awhile ago," Ruby said. "Stalked out the side door like the devil was after him."

Darla glanced at Tim.

"Don't look at me," Tim said.

"I shouldn't, but I'll have a beer," she sighed. Ruby got a can out of the ice box. She punctured two holes in the top and poured the can into a glass. None of the girls liked to drink them out of the can.

"You hear from your old man?" Tim asked Ruby. She nodded. "Good. I'll be back in a minute."

He weaved into the crowd and approached some of the boys she recognized as ones he ran with. Everett called them a gang.

She studied the way Tim moved, noticing how everyone got out of the way for him. Some of the girls gave him looks, a few giggling behind their hands, and a blonde Ruby hadn't seen before sidled up to him and kissed his cheek before he shooed her away. She gave him a sour look and disappeared into the crowd.

"Can I give you some advice?"

Ruby looked over at Darla.

"Might be a good idea to try and hide that admiring smile," Darla said. Ruby couldn't tell whether the girl was sympathizing or mocking her, but either way her face was hot. "If I can see it, so can he. Men like a little mystery."

Darla took the glass of beer and wandered into the crowd. Ruby let out a nervous breath. Jesus, the whole world was gonna know.

Tim wandered back to the bar a few minutes later, and Ruby tried not to stare at him. He said nothing, drank his beer, and watched the people around him. After a few more minutes, she couldn't stand it.

"You said you wanted to talk?" she asked, her voice as low as it could be over the din.

He nodded, and she came out from behind the bar and headed to the stairs, checking over her shoulder to see if Tim was following. A few doors were shut on the second floor—Everett had given out a few keys and was hinting he'd have her take over that duty too—and she scooted past them quickly, not wanting to hear what was going on behind them.

She went up the stairs to the third floor, Tim on her heels, and wondered if he'd ever been up here before. She opened the door to the apartment, glad that Everett was downstairs making the rounds. She had a feeling he wouldn't be too happy about Tim Kelly being in his apartment.

"I figured you'd want to talk in private." She held the door to the apartment open for him. "Someone's using the back room."

He strode over to the couch like he lived there and sat on the near side. He looked up, his green eyes unreadable. She shut the door behind her and watched him pull out a pack of Pall Mall cigarettes.

"You mind if I have one?" she asked.

He looked at the pack, shrugged, and tossed it to her. She took one out and laid it on the table, then handed the pack to him.

"I talked to my daddy last night." She inched over to the couch and sat on Tim's right. "He has a friend in the state pen for eight more months, and this man usually drives a truck. He has insurance on his tractor until the end of the year, paid up. It's sittin' at his place, not rolling, and his wife might be willing to let it be borrowed."

"How're we gonna move it?"

Something thrilled inside her, and she hoped he meant he was going to have her come along and help him. Her daddy would skin her alive, but her daddy wasn't here.

"I don't think his wife can drive it. We'll have to see how you do with it," she said. "Do you think you can handle it?"

He sat back, his arm stretched across the back of the couch. The smile on his face was hard, but unreadable.

"I can handle anything."

He held her gaze, and a shiver worked its way up her spine. A flush of heat rushed to her head as he looked at her. It was as if she was sitting there naked in front of him. She had the unnerving feeling he knew exactly what she was thinking, and was telling her so.

She took in a shaky breath as she looked at the couch and studied the pattern on the upholstery. She wondered if the urge to kiss him would pass.

"Oh, I almost forgot." She picked out a folded sheet of paper from the front of the apron she wore. "I wrote out all kinds of stuff you'll need to know . . . how to start up, double clutching, when to shift, how to attach a trailer . . . if you get one. All kinds of things about trucks. I dunno if it'll help. Sometimes it's easier to learn by doing."

She held out the piece of paper, willing her hand to stay steady. He took it, gave it a cursory glance, and folded it up, tucking it into a pocket. He studied her for a moment.

"I'll pick you up here tomorrow morning, we'll go take a look at this truck," he said, downing the last of the beer.

"Oh . . . well, I'll be at the stable in the morning, just down Washington a bit. Could you pick me up there?" she asked.

He nodded. "I know the place."

He stood, and she followed suit, walking with him toward the door. He opened the door, then turned to face her and leaned against the door frame.

"You did good, kid," he said.

"I'm nineteen, I'm not a kid," she answered with a small smile.

His gaze travel slowly up her body, and her face grew hot as his gaze hesitated at her chest before he looked her straight in the eye. "I'm aware of that."

She swallowed, looking up into his face, his eyes unreadable again. He nodded, then turned and went down the hall toward the stairs. Ruby shut the door and leaned back against it, her heart hammering in her chest.

5

Ruby forced an eye open and shut it quickly against the bright light streaming through a gap in the curtains. She turned over in bed and saw the clock arm inching toward seven thirty. The noise from the bar had carried on until four in the morning, and it felt like she drifted off to sleep only a few minutes ago.

She gave a bone deep sigh and tossed the covers off, her feet relishing the cool of the worn floorboards as she walked to her dresser. She got her riding clothes out and packed an extra set of clothes in a rucksack to take to the stable.

She hated walking down to the second floor. The doors were shut, and she knew there were couples behind them. She hated the fact Everett had all these people shacked up here like some kind of whorehouse, but he told her it was like a hotel and that was altogether different. She wasn't so sure.

She put cleaning the sheets and rooms on her mental to-do list. Maybe if she thought of it like a hotel like Everett said it'd help. Good Lord, this place was gonna send her to an early grave.

She groaned as she came down the last flight of stairs and got a good look at the bar. There was sawdust and peanut shells on the floor and spilled drinks on the tables making a nice sticky mess. There were empty beer bottles and cans, dirty glasses and more furniture in disarray than she'd ever seen in one place. It was going to take the rest of her life to clean it up.

She looked into the bar kitchen—Irene hadn't bothered to wash a damn thing. Her throat tightened, and her eyes threatened tears for a minute. It wasn't fair she had to lose everything she loved and end up here. She took a deep breath and let it out quickly, the strained feeling in her head loosening.

This would all have to wait until the afternoon. She needed to get over to the stables, get her practice in with Bella, and get ready for Tim Kelly. She was nervous. If this truck didn't pan out, she'd never see him again.

She wasn't sure why she wanted to see him. He was polite to her, but there was an undercurrent of something dangerous that both intrigued and scared her. In some ways, Jake's anger was easier to manage. He was just mad and said it, and she could deal with that. Tim was inscrutable, and instead of scaring her it made her want to know more about him.

She hadn't said a word to Everett about *that*.

Ruby pulled out her set of keys for Everett's car. She walked outside and around the side of the building, but the El Camino was nowhere to be found. She stood in the gravel lot fuming. That boy helped himself to whatever he wanted, and it seemed nobody ever stopped him. She hoped Jake hadn't taken the horse blankets off the things she put in the truck bed.

A forty-five minute walk later, she was dusty, thirsty, and glad she packed extra clothes. Her western blouse stuck to her skin, and she knew she looked like a fright when she walked into the stable.

Dr. Jenkins, a stout man with a round face, was taking a cursory look at Bella's hooves. Ruby watched Jake Wheeler unsaddling a horse after a ride, the El Camino nowhere to be found. She settled up the bill with Dr. Jenkins and turned to Jake once the man had left.

"I thought you took the car. And you owe me for the beer, it ain't free when I'm working." She walked over to the locked office to get her custom saddle and found the door wide open. She and Everett were the only ones with keys.

She looked over at Jake and pointed to the office door.

"It's not a complicated lock," he said, with more than a hint of a smile.

"You are unbelievable," she muttered. She went into the office, but nothing was missing.

"I hear that a lot, only the girls are usually in bed with me when they say it."

His voice was much closer, and she turned around to find him standing in the office doorway with a smug grin. She ignored his comment, and she could tell he was disappointed. He was probably used to shocking girls with all his language.

"What is that thing anyway? Doesn't look like any saddle I've ever seen," he said.

She took the white saddle from the top of the filing cabinet. The saddle was old, the leather cracking and dry in places, and the colour more dingy grey than white in places, but it was the only trick saddle she had. They were expensive, and there was no way she could ever save enough now to get a new one.

"It's a custom saddle," she said. She tried to get past him, but he blocked the doorway. He looked at her with a wolfish grin, then moved out of her way, making sure there was only enough space so that she'd have to touch him as she slid past. He made a lewd groan as she did, and she stalked toward Bella's stall without looking at him. She heaved the saddle onto a stall rail.

"Custom for what?" he asked.

"Trick riding," she said.

"No joke?" he asked. "I saw some of that once. You really do that?"

"Stick around long enough and you'll see." She saddled Bella. "Oh . . . here. I owed you, remember?"

She took the Pall Mall out of her shirt pocket and held it out to him. He looked at it, and her, as if she'd lost her mind. Then he shook his head and smiled.

She adjusted the girth and tightened the cinches. She placed the breast-plate on so the saddle wouldn't slide and slipped Bella out of the halter and into the western bridle. She made sure her drag straps were fastened onto the saddle D-ring and the cinch ring, adjusted the hippodrome strap, and attached two tail drag straps to the crupper hand holds on the back of the saddle. Jake was watching her every move.

She led Bella outside and let her loose in the paddock for a few minutes while she mucked out the stall. She was aware of Jake watching her from outside the stable doors where he was having a smoke, Zephyr running in the paddock nearby, exciting the other horses.

She marched out of the stable and past Jake, trying not to look over at him as she brought Bella out of the paddock and into a large riding ring. She knew he was done with his riding for the moment and was only sticking around to see what she could do. He probably thought he was in for a good laugh.

"Let's show him what we're made of," she whispered to her horse.

Tim pulled the car off the road into the dirt between the stable and a bunch of paddocks, a big riding ring and a pasture gate. He had spotted Ruby's dark hair streaming out behind her like a flag. He parked Everett's car, having helped himself to the keys the night before.

He spotted Jake standing against a fence rail, watching Ruby with an intense look on his face. Tim cracked his knuckles.

He got out of the car and walked to the fence rail Jake was leaning on. Tim watched as Ruby cantered the horse around the ring. It looked as if she was falling, but she had flipped onto her back, hanging sideways and upside down off the horse, only one foot in a strap on the saddle keeping her from hitting the ground.

"Holy shit," he said.

"She's been doing that all morning," Jake said. "Broad's fucking nuts."

Ruby flipped back into the saddle, and he could tell Ruby had spotted him, her posture straighter. He watched her do a few more tricks, including some kind of flips on and off the horse while it was moving.

She got back in the saddle and rode around the ring, then hung off the horse perpendicular to the ground by just her feet. A second later the upper strap holding her leg broke, and she tumbled onto the ground, her horse pulling her along, her other leg still caught in the stirrup.

"Shit!"

He and Jake both vaulted over the fence rails and ran toward her. Her horse had stopped, and she was getting up.

"I'm alright." She unhooked the other leg from the strap. "Damn saddle."

She got up and dusted herself off, but Tim saw she moved gingerly.

"I take it you aren't supposed to do that?" he asked.

Ruby picked up a strap on the right side of the saddle and held it up.

"The keeper broke on the drag strap," she sighed. "I had it taped together, but I guess the tape gave. What I need is to get it fixed, I can't be eatin' dirt like that in a show."

Tim realized the broken piece of leather was a slide to tighten the strap on her foot. When it had come loose, the loop on the strap grew too big and her foot slipped out.

"You could kill yourself doing this," Tim murmured.

"Haven't yet," she said with a smile. "Go on. I'm alright. I won't be able to practice much more, but there's a couple more things I can do. I won't be too long."

Tim looked at Jake, who shrugged, and they both walked over to the rails and climbed back. Ruby remounted the horse, cantered around the ring a few times, then stood on the front part of the saddle, her arms above her head.

"I'm 'sposed to be holding a flag out behind me, so just imagine it," she called out as she rode by.

Tim looked at the ground, hiding his smile. She had to be the weirdest girl he ever met, and the strangest one in Las Vegas by a mile.

"What are you doing here anyway?" Jake asked. Took him long enough to notice.

"Picking her up," Tim said, taking out a pack of Pall Malls.

"I wouldn't if I were you." Jake eyed the cigarettes. "She drowned one of mine after I lit up in the stable."

"I'm not in the stable." Tim lit the cigarette. He grinned to himself and looked over at Jake—that must've been why she'd bummed the smoke off him.

44

"What're you picking her up for?" Jake asked. "You foolin' around with her?"

"Nope."

"What then?"

He was usually glad when he gave out so little information the other person had to do all the asking. He learned early in life that to be in control, you needed to control who knew what and when they knew it. It was going to be fun telling Jake a chick had come up with a truck before he had.

"Business, Jake. She found me a truck."

"She what?"

"You heard me."

"You've gotta be kiddin' me," Jake said, staring at Tim like he half expected him to grin with the fun of a lie.

Tim looked up as Ruby trotted over on her horse, then slid off as she neared the fence rail. Her jeans were covered in dust and frayed at the cuffs, and her fitted western shirt had a rip in one sleeve. She had a smear of dirt down the side of her face and a burr in her hair.

"I just have to cool her down, clean the tack, and water the stall . . . it'll take about a half hour?"

Tim nodded and watched her walk away, leading her horse.

"You're staring," Jake commented.

"At what?"

"I'd guess her ass, since I'd be worried if it was the horse you was starin' at," Jake said. "You must be real hard up to be lookin' at her. She's real bossy. Look at her. Looks like she fell in a trough. You won't see Darla caught dead with dirt all over her like that."

Jake could be a serious pain in the ass when he wanted to. Tim pushed his back off the fence rail and walked toward the stable doors, mindful to finish his cigarette first since he'd already unwittingly lost one to her and wasn't aiming to lose another. He had no doubt she'd snatch a lit cigarette out of his fingers if she was bold enough to do it to Jake, and he damn well liked that she was gutsy enough. Weak girls never held his attention long.

"Maybe you oughta make a good impression, since she's already seen your face," Jake taunted.

"You have a nice walk back, Jake," he said as he reached Everett's car. He knew Jake had probably gone looking for it before heading here, and he was pleased to see the irritated expression on Jake's face when he saw the car.

"You really like this chick, huh?" he asked.

Tim paused. "It's business, that's it. But it don't matter what I say, you'll think what you want."

"You could always trap her in the barn over there, have a real roll in the hay," Jake laughed. "Or, you know, I could take her off your hands, saddle break her for you. Show her what a real man's made of."

Tim turned away and walked toward the stable doors and didn't turn around until he was inside. He turned slowly on his heel until he was facing Jake.

"Yeah, how would you do that?" he asked, walking backwards. "Word has it you think Darla's been bucking underneath some other cowboy. Guess that'd mean she's not satisfied with her *real man.*"

Jake's face clouded over, and Tim couldn't resist smiling as the bullet hit the target. Jake's face looked like a thundercloud, and Tim's hands were itching for a fight.

He willed Jake to step up and say he wanted to go, but Jake turned abruptly and stalked down the road, his hands jammed into his pockets, and a scowl on his face.

"Pansy," Tim murmured under his breath, disappointed.

He tossed the cigarette into the dirt and ground it out with his heel.

Tim stayed outside to make sure Jake didn't circle around and come back to slash Everett's tires or something. After satisfying himself that Wheeler was a guy who could dish it but not take it, Tim walked inside the stable. Ruby was brushing her horse, and she wore a fresh pair of jeans, a sleeveless shirt, and a checked short-sleeved blouse she'd tied at her waist. Her face was clean, but he noticed a bandage wrapped around her elbow, blood soaking through it already. She wasn't concerned about it.

She fed her horse a carrot and glanced over at him.

"Do you ride?" she asked.

"Never learned."

"Never too late to try."

He shook his head. "Let's get this done."

She nodded, a frown line on her forehead, and followed him out of the stable. She slowed as she approached Everett's El Camino.

"How did you—"

"Keys were on the coffee table," he said.

"I moved them out of the bar kitchen, thinking it would keep them away from Jake, I didn't think I had to worry about you," she said, irritation in her voice. Tim smiled to himself.

"I was gonna bring it back." He slid into the driver's seat. Ruby tossed her bag in the car's truck bed, then got into the passenger seat.

"You always take other people's things like that?" she asked.

He put the keys in the ignition and grinned wickedly. "Only if it's something I really want."

She blushed and looked away. He cranked the engine. He wasn't fond of Everett's car—it was an automatic.

"Where to?" he asked.

"Oh," she said. She pulled a crumpled piece of paper out of her pocket and handed it to him. Their fingers touched for a second, and he was surprised at how soft her hands were for someone who used them in such rough work.

He looked away, then at the paper and nodded. "I know the area, out of town some, 'bout a twenty minute drive."

"Okay by me," she said.

Ruby grasped the side of the seat with what was left of her short nails, unsure if she was going to make it to see the truck. Tim bombed the car around another corner, going at least fifty, dirt flying out from behind the back wheels.

"Who taught you to drive, the devil himself?" she asked, bracing herself against the dash as they hit a pothole.

He slowed the car as he took both hands off the wheel to light a cigarette, and Ruby held her breath, both terrified at him driving with his knees bracing the wheel, and glad for the break from the speed.

"You know, you won't be able to drive that truck like this, unless you're aimin' to roll over and die on the highway," she said.

"I'll take it easy on the truck," he said. "Relax. You worry too much."

He eased off the gas a little, and they sped at reckless speed rather than breakneck. She relaxed enough to undo the lap belt that was cutting into her. It was jerked tight by Tim's driving.

She looked over at his profile again, the unmarred side of his face facing her. His hair was darkened by all the hair grease he used and barely moved in the wind. His skin was smooth, and his nose had a slight bump she assumed was from breaking it. It was hard to remember the other side of his face didn't look as untouched as the right side, and there were still times it startled her.

She realized Tim was careful with the way he positioned himself. More times than not he sat or stood with his right side closest to her, as if blocking her view of the lopsided left half of his face. Everett said the Chicago mob did it to him but she had no idea why.

"You ever hurt yourself riding like that?" he asked. She blushed, afraid he heard her thoughts. He seemed to be able to do everything else in the world, reading her mind wasn't out of the question.

"Bunch of times," she said. "Broke my wrist last summer when I fell on that same move I did today. That was the first time the keeper broke. I've had more scrapes and bruises than most girls, I guess. The girls at school thought I was a tomboy."

"What do you do it for?"

"It's fun. Always a big draw at rodeos and things like that," she said. "Bella was born to it anyway, best trick riding horse I've ever seen, she's steady as the day is long, and pays no mind to someone moving around so much. I don't even have to use blinders on her. Before I had to move here I was giving lessons to make some money, but it wasn't enough to keep the ranch. My daddy went on the road full time, and I came here."

She snapped her mouth shut, feeling like an idiot for rambling about herself when he hadn't asked.

"Your mom not around?"

"No," Ruby said.

She sensed Tim looking at her and turned her head to meet his gaze.

"She died in a sanatorium when I was twelve. Tuberculosis."

He said nothing for a few minutes and they drove in silence, the wind whipping by the car as he sped toward the address.

"It's right up there, I can see the tractor." She pointed to a small clapboard house off the road. Tim pulled in with a shower of dirt and dust.

They parked next to an old Buick, and Ruby got out and climbed the stairs to a small porch and knocked on the door. Tim prowled around the dark blue and silver truck, shining in the midday sun.

A moment later a worn looking woman answered the door, drying her hands on a towel.

"I'm Ruby Gordon, Ed's daughter," she said.

"He called last night, told me you want that pile of junk over there." She waved a hand toward the truck, which Ruby would've called anything but a pile of junk.

"For awhile," she said. "Tim here's gonna drive it."

"I don't care if he wants to fly it to the moon. Anything to get it outta here," she said. "Ed told me you had some bit of payment for me."

Ruby nodded and walked toward the car. Tim looked with a questioning expression.

She tossed a horse blanket off the boxes in back and unloaded a few cases of Budweiser and Coors Banquet she'd loaded in there late last night. The El Camino truck bed was packed full.

"Lord have mercy." She rushed down the stairs to look at the cases. "Honey, you can take that bucket of bolts 'til Walt gets out of the pen."

Ruby could see Tim watching her, his expression unreadable. Ruby moved cases up the front porch and into the woman's house.

"I'll unload the rest," he said when she came back outside. "You can start the truck."

Ruby nodded at him, took the keys from the woman. She unlocked the driver's door and climbed up into the tractor, marvelling at how new it was. It was a Peterbilt 351 and couldn't have been any more than a year old from the look of it. It had a five and four transmission and a double size sleeper. She couldn't have found a more perfect truck, and she had to admit it was nicer than her daddy's 280.

She started the engine up, hearing it rumble to life, and a pang of nostalgia hit her right in the chest. That sound encompassed everything for her.

She ran her hand around the steering wheel and stared at all the gauges. Now they only had one problem.

Getting it out of here.

The truck's idling engine left the smell of diesel in the air. Ruby sat in the driver's seat, staring off at the horizon like she was at a funeral. She moved over when he climbed up the stair to the cab.

He sat in the driver's seat and glanced into the sleeper cab of the truck. His breathing slowed as he watched her, bending over to pick up a few papers off the floor. She wore a fitted pair of blue jeans, and he realized he'd never seen her in anything else.

She didn't look like the girls he usually went for, like Carolyn, who always wore skirts and was stacked up top. Ruby was a straight up-and-down kind of girl. The only thing accentuating her waist was the way she tied up that western shirt. But she looked just fine bent over in front of him, he had to admit. He looked up at the ceiling and took in a deep breath before shutting the door.

"You're gonna have to learn real quick." Ruby shoved papers onto the dash. "Otherwise we'll have to leave it here and come back for it. If you can get the hang of it today I can drive the El Camino back since it's an automatic."

"I'll get the hang of it," he said. He'd read over the little note she'd given him the night before, but hadn't paid it much attention. He'd pick it up better inside the truck than reading about it.

He turned his head and watched her bend again, then turned his gaze back to the dashboard. It was going to be a long afternoon.

"Where'd you get the beer?" he asked, as if he didn't already know.

"Rett's pantry," she said.

"He's gonna be mad," Tim chuckled.

"He ain't gonna know," she said. "Don't you breathe a word of this, but Rett never keeps track of his beer. I told him I'd keep track. He won't notice they're missing, he'll just think people drank them."

He had to admire stealing from her own brother to pay for a truck with beer. Kid had guts. And, if he was reading her right, ulterior motives. She wasn't good at hiding her feelings, and he could see a mile away that she liked him, the way she blushed every time he looked at her, and the way she was willing to risk Everett chewing her out for giving away all his good beer.

It bothered him. He had one rule, and that was not to mix business with pleasure, and this was business. All the more reason to get her dealings in his business over with as fast as possible and get on to other things.

He wasn't sure whether those other things were pleasure with her or not.

"Okay." She kept her head ducked to avoid hitting it on the roof of the cab. She leaned over his shoulder from behind, and he inhaled sharply as her hair spilled onto his neck.

"These knobs are your air controls . . . truck air and trailer air for the brakes, push them to fill, pull them to release. This lever is the parking break," she demonstrated. "Get in the habit of setting them whenever you stop to get out, all three, no matter if you have a trailer or not."

"Got it." He smelled fresh hay in her hair.

"Transmission is a five and four," she said.

He looked at the two shifters next to the truck. He'd never in his life seen two in one vehicle.

She put a piece of paper on the steering wheel. She'd drawn the shifting pattern for both sticks. The left stick had reverse, neutral and five gears, while the right had neutral and four gears. The shifting pattern on the main was similar to a four-on-the-floor he'd driven once or twice, but the right was a U pattern.

"Left is your main, the right's the auxiliary. Start in first gear main and first gear aux, then release clutch. Next three shifts are up on the aux to forth."

He nodded his understanding.

"Trouble comes when you shift the main to the next gear, because the aux will still be in fourth. So you gotta bring the main to the next gear while you shift the aux back to one, so they gotta shift at the same time. Some drivers go through the wheel like this."

Tim swallowed as she bent over his shoulder and took his left arm, threading it through the lower part of the steering wheel so it could grab the main while his right hand shifted the aux.

"You gotta watch though," she said. "You crash this thing, you'll snap your arm off in there."

He turned that over in his mind as she showed him all the switches on the dash, for lights, wipers and all the pressure gauges. He paid attention to nothing, watching the other things she was showing, her shirt loosely tied at her waist, the top underneath falling away from her body slightly. She was unaware of the view she gave every time she leaned over him from the side.

"Let's get this thing moving," he said impatiently, wishing she'd sit and quit distracting him. He remembered now why there was not a single girl working with him, why they did their damndest to avoid involving girls in anything they did. They'd never get a damn lick of work done with a chick around.

"Let me tell you what you're going to do first," she said. "You'll want to push the air knobs, let the parking brake go, and brake. Then you can shift into first gear on the main like you would in a car, give it some fuel. It's shifting when you're moving that's the hard part. Do you float gears in your car?"

"No," Tim said. "Clutch."

"Alright, then, we'll double clutch to start."

Ruby moved to the passenger seat and sat down and before she could say another word, he pushed the clutch in and jammed the truck into first gear, moving forward with a lurch. He was surprised at the weight of the truck and how sensitive the steering was.

He went to shift into second and a terrible grinding noise filled the cab.

"You've gotta double clutch!" she urged. "And you can't shift the main, you gotta shift the aux now."

Tim stopped the truck before it stalled. He looked at the twin shifters. He hated this truck. Getting a girl to teach him was a bad idea, especially one that couldn't do it herself.

He got the truck moving again and managed to get it into gear and on the road. He stalled out more than once, swearing at the damn truck. He headed back to the car about half an hour later.

"You did real good," she said when they returned. "Much better than when my daddy tried to teach me. He said I was a hopeless case, I just about dropped his transmission out on the highway and gave him a few more grey hairs. Said the sound of me drivin' was like the apocalypse."

He said nothing.

"You thirsty? I'll be right back."

She left the truck, and he let out a breath.

She was driving him crazy with all her chatter. He could tell it was nervous energy making her talk, but he needed to sit with the truck and figure it all out himself. It'd be a hell of a lot easier if he didn't need her. She kept looking over at him, staring at his face, and he wondered if she was scared of it.

She came back a few seconds later and jumped back up in the cab with a Dr Pepper and a Coke and handed the Coke to him. He took a church key out of his pocket and popped the bottle caps off and they drank in silence for a few minutes.

He swirled the Coke around in the bottle, tapping it with his fingers.

"Some guys from the Chicago Outfit jumped me awhile back," he said.

"Excuse me?" She turned around in her seat and was facing him. That frown line back on her forehead.

"My face. You can't tell me you weren't wondering." He rubbed the broken side of his face. "Town like this, you're always stepping on someone's toes. Chicago boys didn't like I was placing bets for guys in the black book."

"Black book?"

"Banned gamblers."

"What'd those Chicago boys do?"

"Came to talk to me with a Louisville Slugger," he said. "Broke almost every bone on the left side of my face. Got more metal in there than this damn truck."

She was quiet, studying his face.

"Happened about eight months ago," he said. "I looked pretty good before that."

He glanced over and paused, seeing her reaction. She flushed pink under his gaze and turned toward her window.

"Still do," she said.

She drained the rest of her drink and took his empty bottle, getting out of the truck to toss them in the back of Everett's car. By the time she'd climbed back in the pink blush in her cheeks had faded.

She looked over and nodded at him to start the truck. She was about to speak when he held his hand up.

"Lemme try it on my own," he said, trying not to sound harsh. "I think I can get it."

That furrow in her brow was there again, but she pasted on a smile a second later and nodded. Her shoulders were slumped despite her best efforts at not looking bothered. He hesitated before cranking the key in the ignition.

"Ruby. You don't have to try so hard."

She looked stunned for a second, then blushed to the roots again. He saw her sneak a look over at him, and he couldn't tell if she was happy or nervous.

He turned back to the road and started the engine.

6

Saturday, April 30, 1966

For the next week, Ruby got used to hearing the truck engine start up most mornings. Tim never knocked on the door to ask her to come along, and she was left staring at the wall feeling sad and useless.

He took to it like a duck to water, and her only thought now was why he was avoiding her. She was stupid to think someone like him would want to ask her out. Lewis back home only asked her out on a dare, and Lewis rolled off a turnip truck compared to Tim Kelly.

She had that familiar feeling in the pit of her stomach, that rock that always formed when she thought about Lewis and Abilene and all the horrible things people said. She hadn't wanted to leave the ranch, but leaving Abilene was a welcome relief. She told everyone she left school to help keep the ranch up, and that was true with her daddy away all the time, but she knew the bigger reason she left was the fall-out from her relationship with Lewis.

Tim Kelly was nothing like him, but Tim Kelly didn't appear to give one lick about her. She tried her hardest, and here she was listening to him drive off without her every morning. Everyone drove off without her.

Saturday morning she was surprised to be awakened at six, loud grinding gears startling her out of a deep sleep. A few choice curse words drifted on the wind. She hopped out of bed and threw the curtains open.

Bill Pearce sat in the driver's seat, and Tim was in the passenger seat gesturing wildly. She didn't know why Bill was driving, but from the sound, he aimed to kill the truck.

They chugged off down the road a few minutes later, and a thick plume of black smoke huffed out of the smokestacks as the truck stalled in the middle of the street. It started up again a minute later and lumbered off like a lame elephant.

She listened for Everett, but her brother was one of the soundest sleepers she knew, especially after he knocked a few back. She got under the covers and fell back asleep, but she was awakened an hour later by the same noise.

She squeezed her eyes shut against the horrible grinding, then got out of bed and looked out the window. Bill climbed out of the driver's seat. He gave the front tires a good kick when he was on the ground.

"Dammit, I told you to watch the clutch!" came Tim's angry voice as he circled around from the passenger side. "You wanna pay to get it fixed?"

"This thing's a bucket of trouble." Bill gave the tires another kick.

Ruby covered her mouth with her hand.

"I think the problem's more that you're an idiot." Jake Wheeler was leaning against Rett's car. She hoped he wasn't there to drive off in it.

"You think it's so easy, you try it!" Bill walked around the side of the building towards the front door.

The front door creaked as it opened downstairs. Ruby dashed to her dresser and rifled through it for a pair of blue jeans and a button down shirt. She slipped into a pair of sneakers and tied her hair up in a ponytail with a red ribbon. Dabbing on a bit of pink lip gloss, she bolted for the door and walked down the stairs to the bar.

Bill sat at the bar with his head on the table.

"Long morning?" she asked.

"I hate that thing," he sighed. "You got any coffee?"

She went into the small kitchen and put on a pot. Bill excused himself to the bathroom, and Ruby glanced at the door as Tim walked inside.

"Coffee?" she asked.

He looked over, his expression weary and pained.

"Something stronger?" she asked with a smile.

"There's not enough alcohol in the county." His voice was serious. He sat at the bar.

"He's that bad?"

"I thought I was gonna have to shoot him like a lame horse," Tim said.

"Oh, come on," Bill said, his shirt tails loose as he came back in the room. "I wasn't that bad, was I?"

Ruby stifled a laugh at the look Tim gave him, then excused herself to the kitchen, returning with coffee.

"Looks like you're sentenced to the jump seat, like me." She poured him a cup.

Bill poured a generous amount of cream in. Tim drank his black.

Jake walked in and sat at the bar. He took the cup of coffee Ruby poured for herself.

She got another mug and poured herself another cup, slamming the sugar in front of Jake when he asked for it.

"You ain't a morning person, huh, darlin'?" he asked.

She ignored him.

"What are you learning to drive for?" Ruby asked Bill.

Bill and Tim shared a look, and Jake smiled at his coffee, like he knew she wouldn't get an answer. Jake drained his cup of coffee in record time, then stood.

"I'm outta here," he said. "Kelly, you'll have to swallow your pride and call me if you need a driver since ol' Billy here ain't gonna be any help."

"Fuck you." Bill glanced over. "Sorry, Ruby."

"I wouldn't apologize, she's probably got a mouth on her." Jake raised his eyebrows suggestively.

He left without another word.

"You got anything to eat?" Bill asked.

Ruby pasted a smile on and went into the kitchen, finding some bread and jam in the refrigerator. They talked amongst themselves in the other room, and she burned with embarrassment that Tim didn't want her knowing anything.

"We need to get on finding a trailer." Bill's voice carried into the kitchen.

"All I need is the plate number for now," Tim replied. "That's all Wayne asked for, that's all he's getting until he finds me a run."

Ruby excused herself a short time later, grabbed her things, and took the El Camino to the stable, deep in thought.

Monday, May 2, 1966

Monday afternoon Tim was refuelling the truck when he and Jake spotted each other at the gas station. Jake ambled over to the truck.

"If you think you can drive this thing I may need you to back me up," Tim said.

"With what?"

"The job I mentioned," Tim said. "I'll cut you in. It'd only be if I can't make the run."

Jake hopped up into the driver's seat.

"What'll you be busy doing? Everett's sister?" Jake laughed.

"You wanna can it and learn how to drive this truck?" Tim asked, his patience wearing thin.

"I already know how," Jake said smugly.

"Right." Tim rolled his eyes.

Jake was one of few people who pushed his buttons enough to make him lose it. The two of them prided themselves on pissing the other off; it was fun, a game, but he was wasn't in the mood for it. He still had a trailer to find and learn how to drive, and Wayne needed a plate number, or else learning to drive this truck was a waste of time.

Wayne had called and Tim gave him the plate number from the cab and told him he'd have the trailer in a few days. There wasn't much time.

Bill was his first choice as a back up driver, until he saw his skill. He'd bet a hundred dollars Diana could've done a better job behind the wheel, and she couldn't reach the clutch.

Tim got in the passenger seat.

"Let's do this," Jake said, starting the truck. He pulled into the road, double shifting like he'd been born to it. Tim watched in silence. Jake didn't notice—too busy trying to needle him about Ruby.

"You sure you ain't asked her out?" Jake asked. "Cuz I think you like her."

"What the hell does it matter, Jake?" He tapped his fingers on the arm rest. "I told you, I got my mind on more important things."

What Jake had his mind on was making Tim lose his, he had no doubt about that.

"So what's the deal with this run?"

"Don't know," Tim said. "They'll tell me where and when."

"And if you can't go for some reason, then I go."

"Yeah," Tim said. "You think you can handle that without screwing up?"

Jake flipped him the bird while double shifting. "As long as it's not a rodeo weekend."

They pulled into the lot in front of Everett's as Ruby got out of Rett's car. Tim cursed. That was the last thing he needed. She asked a lot of questions, and he didn't want to tell her to buzz off, because he did want to ask her out.

He didn't know why. She talked a lot, she was weird, and she wanted to be in his business.

She got out of the car and spotted Tim in the jump seat. He didn't miss the smile that lit up her face.

"Your girlfriend's home." Jake pulled the air brakes and set the parking brake. He knew where every switch was, and didn't ask Tim one thing about how to drive.

"She's not my girlfriend."

Jake laughed. "Yeah? I guess it wouldn't bother you if some other guy came sniffing around her, then? Maybe it wouldn't bother you if I asked her out."

"In case you forgot, you got Darla."

Jake grunted and shut down the engine, a scowl on his face. That only meant one thing—those two were fighting again.

"If you ain't gonna ask her out, no use in her going to waste." Jake opened the truck door.

Ruby shielded her eyes against the sun and looked their way.

"She ain't desperate enough to go out with you," Tim said, getting out the truck.

"Yeah?" Jake asked. "You sure about that?"

Jake slammed the door shut and Tim quickly circled around the front of the truck. Jake was walking toward Ruby.

"Shit," Tim muttered.

"You're teaching Jake to drive?" Ruby asked, looking over at the truck as Tim approached.

"Yeah, and I didn't do too bad," Jake said. "You out ridin'?"

"For awhile." She dusted off the front of her jeans, then the back.

Tim took out a pack of Pall Malls and lit one, cupping it against the breeze. He watched Ruby hitch her thumbs into the belt loops near her front pockets, then take her hands away, smooth her shirt, and run a hand through her hair. He wondered why she was so nervous.

"You look real nice today," Jake said. "You do something different with your hair?"

Ruby's cheeks flushed a pale pink, and she stared at the ground for a second. "No. It's the same as always."

"You know, it's kinda good we got some Texas blood around Everett's," Jake said. "I gotta say a lot of the girls around here are kinda dull."

Ruby laughed.

Tim paused a second before taking a drag. Jake was doing it to annoy him, but Ruby was falling for his put-on charm for some stupid reason.

"Doesn't seem all that dull to me when Rett opens the bar," she said. "The girls around here are pretty flashy."

"Something to be said for not flashy, right?"

Ruby shrugged, a half-smile on her face. "Your girlfriend's pretty flashy."

Tim bit down on a smile. At least she hadn't forgotten that.

"You know about the rodeo happening on the twenty-first? You oughta enter yourself for trick riding. Nobody around here does it."

Jake walked over to Ruby and put his hand on her back, directing her to the front of the building.

"Really?" she asked. "You think I could? They'd let me?"

"Sure, why not?" Jake asked. "We should go talk about it. I been around rodeos forever, an' I know some folks at this one. I could put in a good word."

Jake looked back at Tim and grinned wolfishly. Tim resisted the urge to slit his throat from behind.

"Well, okay," Ruby said, her tone wary. "We got some pop inside, nice and cold if you want one."

"Actually . . . you busy right now? I could take you over to the Silver Slipper."

"I can't," Ruby said. "I'm not twenty-one yet."

A conniving smile lit Jake's face. "Only need to be twenty-one to gamble. We can go to the restaurant and take Everett's car."

Tim paused as he brought the cigarette to his lips. Jake aimed to get his ass beat later, he could tell. He took a quick drag, watching Ruby to see her response.

"Where's the Silver Slipper?" she asked.

"It's on the Strip. Western themed," Jake said. "It's real popular, everybody goes there."

"Really?" she asked, her voice hopeful.

Tim studied her, wondering if she realized the Slipper was where Darla danced. He wanted to say something, but that's exactly what the bastard was waiting for. Tim watched Ruby's expression, but he glanced away when she looked toward him. Jake sure had balls to do this right in front of him.

"Well, I'd sure like to get out and meet some people," she said. "I haven't seen much around here yet."

"You're not going anywhere," Everett's voice interrupted. The screen door slammed. "Where the hell is all my Coors gone?"

Tim never thought he'd be relieved to see Everett Gordon, but there it was.

"What Coors?"

"Don't 'what Coors' me," Everett said. "Half the cases are gone from the cellar."

"It's not gone," Ruby said. "You just aren't looking in the right place, I swear it's in the corner, past those rolls of old newspaper stacked up like cord wood."

Everett turned around and marched inside and Ruby turned toward Jake.

"If we're going, we're going now," she said. "Come on."

She yanked Jake toward the El Camino, and Jake pulled out a set of keys. It didn't go unnoticed by Ruby either.

"Jesus, does everyone around here have a set?"

Ruby looked over at Tim, and he kept his expression blank. She looked at her hands for a moment, then back at him, that line creasing her forehead again. Jake babbled on about something to do with horses, and she stared at Tim for a second before getting in the car. Jake cranked the engine and pulled out of the lot, spraying rocks and dust.

Tim stood there, seething. That asshole needed his face pounded into the ground.

"There ain't no Coors in that cellar and half my Bud is gone!"

Everett looked around at the settling dust.

"Where the hell did she go? And where's my car?"

Tim turned toward Everett. "Jake took her out. To the Silver Slipper."

Everett groaned, and Tim secretly agreed. Tim turned away and walked down the street toward the warehouse.

Wheeler was asking for it.

Ruby looked over at Jake as they drove toward the Silver Slipper. He hadn't asked to drive, he zipped right over to the driver's seat and got in like he owned the car.

She was too busy being glad to escape Everett to get too annoyed over it. It figured her brother would notice the missing beer after paying attention to nothing the last few weeks.

Jake drove the car hard, but he wasn't a frightening driver like Tim. He went on about the rodeo—how he would ride in some of the events and what else would go on.

"They ain't had trick riding in it for a long time. I remember a couple years back they had a guy doing bareback tricks and stuff, but not like you were doing. The horse moved in a circle and someone had a lunge line."

"Sounds like vaulting," Ruby said. "It's sort of like gymnastics on a horse."

"And what you do isn't?" Jake laughed.

She laughed too. Sometimes she forgot how trick riding looked to people who never saw it before. She was comfortable flipping around on Bella, and it wasn't acrobatic to her while she did it.

She studied Jake's profile. She wasn't sure why he asked her to the Silver Slipper—one minute he was derisive and making lewd comments, the next he was nice and taking her out to eat.

She hoped she could meet some friends. She liked going to the stable every day, but it'd be nice to have a girlfriend or two to go out with some time. She glanced at Jake again. It might be nice to go out on a date on a Saturday night, even if it was with just a friend. Jake was handsome, but she was no beauty queen, not like his girlfriend.

That bothered her enough to say something.

"Look, it's real nice you wanted to talk about the rodeo an' all," Ruby said. "But I know you got a girlfriend, and I'm not like that."

"Who said anything about a girlfriend?" Jake asked. "We broke up."

"Oh," Ruby said. She wondered if he asked her to the Silver Slipper just to talk about the rodeo. There wasn't anything against them being friends, and maybe she ought to stop looking a gift horse in the mouth.

They cruised Fremont Street and onto South Main before ending up on the Strip, Las Vegas Boulevard. He told her stories about all the casinos before pulling into the lot of one with a giant slipper rotating on top of the sign advertising Minsky's Follies '66 and a World Famous Buffet. She bet it looked amazing at night.

Jake stopped the car and pulled the emergency brake. Ruby got out and rubbed her damp palms against her jeans.

They walked to the main doors and inside, Jake nodding at a few people at the doors. No one stopped her to ask for ID. He knew where he was headed, so she followed him toward the restaurant.

All kinds of people were inside, from tourists to locals. It was a decent place, but she had no idea why he couldn't take her to a soda fountain or a diner or something.

"Here, lemme get us a place to sit."

They sat in a booth, and the waitress took their order. She got a Dr Pepper and the Village Burger. He talked about the rodeo until the food came, then he excused himself a few minutes later.

She wiped her hands on her jeans after Jake left the booth and studied the pattern on the table. Glancing to her left she saw a table of girls eyeing her coolly. She looked around helplessly, feeling like she ought to slide under the table.

"Well now, look who's here." Hollis Warner slid into the booth.

Ruby smiled. "Hi."

"What brings you here all by your lonesome?" he asked.

"She ain't by her lonesome."

Hollis looked up at Jake, then slid out of the booth, his gaze still on him. "That right?"

Jake nodded before he slid into the booth, tucking a ticket of some kind away in his wallet.

"Just got out of a poker game. I'm surprised to see you two here." Hollis raised an eyebrow at Jake.

A tense look passed between them, and Ruby took a sip of her drink, feeling self-conscious at the weird tension.

"Me an' Ruby are talking about the rodeo," Jake said. "I'm gonna convince her to enter."

"Doing what? Barrel racing?"

She shook her head, relaxing again as the tension dispersed. "No, trick riding. I've been doing it for years, but I only performed in a rodeo once."

"Hollis." A familiar girl with ringlets and blood-red lipstick approached.

"Hey, Bren. Ruby, this is my girl, Brenda Pearce, you know her brother Bill from around Rett's."

"Hi," Ruby said. She was surprised this girl was related to Bill. They didn't look alike, but there was something familiar all the same.

"Hi." Brenda's voice was cool. A group of girls, the ones that were sitting at the table nearby, came over to the table.

"Hollis, you wanna go get me a Coke?" Brenda asked.

Hollis gave Jake a pointed look, then sauntered off to find a waitress.

"Jake," Brenda said. "What brings you here?"

"I needed a drink. People need drinks. It's hot out."

The other girls looked her over, and Ruby stared at the table.

"Well, aren't you going to introduce us?" Brenda asked. Her voice dripped with sweetness, but it was as fake as the day was long.

Jake's eyes darted from Ruby to the girls.

"This is Ruby, she's Everett's sister," Jake said. "She's gonna enter the rodeo. This is Brenda, Jacqueline and Susie."

Jake slid lower in the seat a little, playing with his ring finger. Ruby saw a faint tan line around his finger.

"Hi." Ruby smiled at the girls. "I don't think I've seen y'all around Rett's before."

"We go sometimes," said Jacqueline, who had short, dark hair. "With Darla."

"Why don't you girls get lost?" Jake asked. "Ain't you supposed to be in rehearsal, Suze?"

Ruby was convinced they'd shoot daggers at Jake if they could. They wandered back toward their table.

"Don't pay them any mind," Jake said. "They're mad I dumped Darla."

"Oh." Ruby tried to put the weird feeling in the pit of her stomach out of her mind. It was like being back at high school, sitting in the bleachers watching the football games, gaggles of girls pointing and laughing. It was unbearable, it was happening all over again, and none of them knew her.

"I gotta hit the men's room, I'll be back," Jake said. "Don't go nowhere."

She wouldn't know where to go if she wanted to leave. She couldn't finish the rest of her burger since her stomach was in knots. She bent the straw from her drink around her finger.

A shadow fell across the table. "It's pretty low what you're doing," Jacqueline said. "Jake may have asked you out, but you ought to know better."

"Know better about what?" Ruby asked. "It's not a date or nothing, I swear it. He just wanted to tell me about the rodeo."

"Uh huh," Brenda said. "That's why he came here? Look, I'm no stranger to people cozying up to my boyfriend, but if you know what's good for you, you'll stop hanging around Jake before Darla decides to rip you a new one."

Brenda leaned over; her nails were as red as her mouth. "And trust me, if you think I'm scary you don't want to see Darla all riled up when someone's trying to get their claws into her boyfriend."

The blood rushed from her head as she took in the girl's words. "I-I thought they broke up?"

"Did Jake tell you that?" the blonde girl—Susie—asked.

Ruby could only manage a nod.

"Well," Brenda huffed. "You'll learn not to believe a word he says. He's got some nerve bringing you around here."

"Why here?"

"We work here, sugar," Jacqueline said. "We dance in the show. So does Darla. If you think Jake asked you out for any reason other than to terrorize her, you're dumber than you look."

"I didn't mean anything by it, I swear!" Ruby said, scooting to the end of the booth and standing up. "I had no idea!"

The girls already were moving through the crowd to the entrance, and Ruby sat down in a panic.

"Oh Jesus," she breathed.

"Hey, you wanna go drive by the rodeo grounds when we're done? You can check the place out and see what it's like?" Jake asked, returning.

"I better get back," Ruby said. "Rett's on a tear about the beer, and he'll lose it if I don't get back in time to make him dinner."

He slipped an arm around her shoulders and walked out into the casino with her, staring down the girls as they passed. Ruby tried to shrug out of his grasp, to no avail.

They got in the El Camino without a word. Those girls were mad, and what they said about Jake made too much sense. All she wanted was to meet some people, and now those girls thought she was a boyfriend-stealer.

"What's got you so quiet?" Jake asked. "I didn't think it was possible."

"Just thinking, that's all."

They arrived back at Everett's in no time, and Ruby turned to ask Jake what was going on. Before she said a word, he placed a hand on her shoulder and slid it up the side of her neck, pulling her to him.

She had no time to think before his lips met hers. His lips were soft and insistent, and a second later she came to her senses and pushed him away.

"Look, I'm not like that." Her face was hot. "Those girls said you and Darla weren't broke up, is that the truth?"

"What does it matter?" Jake asked, a smile on his face.

"It matters plenty! They said she worked there and you brought me on purpose."

He grinned wolfishly. "We're having some fun, right? Ain't my fault if Darla hears about it."

"Fun?" Ruby shoved him again. "You got a real wise idea about fun!" She got out of the car and slammed the door, then turned around.

"Wait a minute! That's our car! You get out!"

Jake grinned as he cut the engine.

"And gimme those keys!"

He tossed his set to her.

"You can't blame a guy for trying, right?" Jake asked. He got out of the car.

"It's not funny!" Ruby said. "Those girls said all sorts of things, they're gonna put it around I'm some kind of boyfriend snatcher. Which I'm not."

"We're still friends, aren't we?" Jake asked, his tone amused

Ruby turned around, looked at him for a second, and rolled her eyes. "You are so aggravating."

He flashed her a smile. "But you can't resist, right?"

She went inside and slammed the door. He laughed as he walked away.

"Why the hell did you go to a casino, and why did you go there with Jake Wheeler?"

Everett didn't say hello as she walked into the apartment.

"Keep your shirt on, Rett, he took me to make his girlfriend jealous," she said. "He's lousy, you know."

"I still can't find that beer," Everett said. "You can't be giving it out to every hood you think looks good in a pair of tight jeans."

"Rett! I didn't do anything of the sort," she said, thinking that it was technically true.

"Yeah, well, I'm keeping an eye on it, so don't get any wise ideas."

"I bet someone broke in and made off with it," she said.

Everett grunted, then headed for the door. "I'll be back in a half hour. Gonna check the horses. Oh . . . and I'm opening tonight."

He shut the door behind him, and she sighed. He was probably doing it to punish her. She flopped on the couch.

She got the feeling she was the butt of Jake's joke the whole time, but she still wondered why he kissed her. It wasn't like anyone was around to see it.

Tim would probably hear all about it and think she was fast. Jesus, he would never ask her out now that everyone thought she went on a date with Jake.

She hugged a couch pillow. She might have to settle for not having a friend in the world here, outside of her horse.

7

"Why so tense?"

Carolyn's hands plied across his shoulder blades, digging into the muscle.

He shrugged away and stood, pulled his underwear and jeans back on, then lay on his back on the thin mattress. He could've stayed at the house, but it was easier when he wasn't around his father. Diana didn't understand that.

It was tense at Rett's the night before—he'd opened on a Monday, and Tim bet Sam Wyatt would hear about that in no time—and Jake was waiting for him to do something about his trip to the Slipper with Ruby.

But Darla showed up with the girls, and Ruby had disappeared with her for awhile. Jake took off before they came back, and Tim stuck around just in case, but Ruby had returned no worse for wear and the girls had left her alone.

Carolyn straddled his hips and lay down on top of him, her lips brushing his collarbone.

"I heard Ray and your sister are seeing each other," Carolyn said.

"Fat chance of that," Tim replied.

"Not what I heard." Carolyn crawled off him and got up to find her clothes. "Diana was bragging about Ray at the Round-Up the other day. Couldn't stop talking about him."

He hoped Diana was lying to impress her friends. If not, he'd have to have a chat with Ray.

"You're sure in a lousy mood," Carolyn said. "Cops hassling you again?"

"Nope. Wheeler this time."

"Jake's trouble." She was so close, her perfume made him nauseous. She ran a hand up his thigh, like they hadn't just been going at it like rabbits.

"Jake's a bastard," he agreed. "You wanna quit that?"

"I don't know why Darla Redmond goes with him," Carolyn said. "He's too rough."

She was trying to get a rise out of him—that was her game. She got a rise out of him one way, now it was time for the other since she wasn't getting her way.

"Jake Wheeler's real good looking." Carolyn's voice was syrupy. "All the girls say so."

He took another drag, resisting the bait she threw out.

"He's one of the handsomest guys in these parts." She pulled on her skirt with a shimmy and did up the little buttons on her blouse.

"Yeah, and I bet you took it well when he turned you down," Tim said.

"You're a real bastard, you know that," Carolyn said, dropping the soft, teasing voice. "See if I ever come back here and spend time with you again!"

"You'll be back, Carrie." He used the nickname to tick her off.

"Why would I? Plenty of guys around here that fight as good as you, run people as good as you and they aren't in prison every five seconds. Bobby Tafani comes to mind."

"Bobby Tafani's got shit for brains," he answered.

"At least he's not all cut up like Frankenstein!" she hollered, pitching the empty beer bottle at him. It sailed by his face as he dodged out of the way.

Carolyn slammed the door on her way out, and Tim lowered his head onto the pillow and rubbed the scar on his chin. That one was courtesy of the pavement outside of State Line after flipping his motorcycle rather than the Chicago Outfit, but it mangled him all the same.

If Jake wanted to mess things up with him and Ruby, he'd return the favor. Ruby was a half decent kid—a naïve kid, if he read her right. There wasn't a broad around here that couldn't see Jake's tricks a mile away, and she fell right into them. A little payback was in order.

Tim leaned back against the thin feather pillow and smiled. He knew one way to get Jake back that wouldn't fail.

Tim sat in Bill's car with the engine idling and watched a group of girls outside of the Silver Slipper. They'd been standing outside smoking and gabbing their heads off for nearly a half hour. He lit another cigarette and blew a stream of smoke out into the night air.

He breathed a sigh of relief when they crushed their cigarettes and walked up the street. He was gearing up to gun the engine and separate her from the herd when they split up and Darla walked up the street alone.

Darla never drove her car to work—her boarding house wasn't far away, but he suspected it was more not wanting to show it off at her job. Girls were catty, and someone like Darla in a cherry red Corvette got attention.

But it was a stupid move for a girl to walk alone after dark. He gunned the engine, catching up with her a minute later on a cross street. He pulled the car into the oncoming lane and stopped against the left curb.

She glanced over her shoulder, then rolled her eyes.

"Tim."

"What're you doing out here all by your lonesome?" he called out the window.

"Walking home. You know that since you've been watching the casino for the last half hour."

His struggled to keep the surprise from his face, but she laughed.

"You boys always think you're so slick, but us girls notice more than you think. Lila's gonna owe me a quarter tomorrow. I bet her you'd stop me."

"Well, if you don't wanna ride that's fine with me."

She crossed her arms and studied him, a slight smile on her face and her blonde curls blowing gently in the breeze. She made a pretty picture.

"I'm never one to turn down a ride. Even if it is with you. Mind your lead foot though, will you?"

She crossed in front of the car, the headlights highlighting her bare legs and the skirt that skimmed the top of her knees. She opened the door and climbed in. He gunned the engine a few times, she gave him a look, and he pulled away from the curb without leaving too much rubber on the asphalt.

He drove toward her boarding house, taking a turn fast and bracing his right palm on Darla's knee. She patiently picked it up and moved it back.

"Don't think I don't know what you're up to," she said.

"Yeah? What's that?"

"I heard all about Jake's trip to the restaurant at the Slipper with that girl," Darla said. "Now, from what I saw at Everett's, that little thing is so distracted by you she can't think straight, so I have to assume Jake asked her there to get under my skin and yours. That boy isn't right."

Tim watched the road, not looking over at Darla. He could tell her gaze was on him though, she was practically burning holes in the side of his head.

"You think fair's fair, and you're going to make sure Jake hears about this. Only Jake has nothing to hear about because nothing's happening."

"You sure about that?"

Darla sighed. "You boys have lost your minds. Why don't you concentrate on getting Miss Bartender in your bed instead of Jake's fist upside your head? It'd make everyone happier, me included."

Tim pulled up in front of her boarding house and saw a shadow pass around the side of the porch. His blood was fired up, adrenaline kicking through his system. This was better than him hearing it through the grapevine.

"Come on now, Darla, be nice," Tim said, stretching an arm across the back of her seat. She raised an eyebrow and looked at the arm.

"Smooth, Kelly. I didn't notice a thing."

"I owe you a favour for when you gave me an alibi over that stolen Mustang last year."

"And your idea of a favour is trying to make it with me in the car so Jake finds out? Boy, you got a real funny idea about favours. Let me do you one. Get lost, Tim."

He grinned. If there was something there—some kind of spark, some sort of thrill in his stomach when he flirted with her, then he could see fireworks with her for a long time. But for some reason, there wasn't. It was a shame.

He leaned forward, took her chin in his hand, and kissed her right on the lips. It took a split second, but her purse was upside his head in record time.

She shoved his chest and got out of the car.

He opened the door and followed her up the walk, closing the gap with his long strides. He took her by the arm and she tried to slap him, but he grabbed her wrist just in time.

"You think Jake was a perfect gentleman with Ruby the other day? Not what I heard," he said.

"He'll get his, don't you worry. Now get off me!"

"Yeah Kelly, get off her."

Tim stepped back, the blood pounding in his ears. Jake emerged from the darkness at the side of the porch and chucked his lit cigarette onto the sidewalk. He saw Darla roll her eyes.

"Great," she muttered.

"You wanna get inside?" Jake asked her. "Me an' Tim are gonna have a discussion."

"You aren't having anything. Tim, get lost. Jake, we gotta talk. I heard all about your little date at the Slipper."

"Wasn't nothing."

"That's what you say. The girls said something different."

Jake hadn't taken his eyes off Tim. Jake could be unpredictable, and it made fighting him fun. Tim was watching for that first punch.

Jake pushed Darla out of the way.

"You got a real problem putting your hands on what's mine," Jake snarled.

"Same goes for you."

Jake barked out disbelieving laughter. "You gotta stake your claim before it's yours."

SIN CITY

"I'm not anyone's property." Darla crossed her arms, shooting daggers at the back of Jake's head. Jake wasn't listening to a word she said. "And you both better take off because Miss Clayton'll call the cops."

"You gotta learn some manners, Kelly."

Jake took a swing and clipped the side of Tim's head, but he sidestepped it quickly enough so it didn't do much damage. He nailed Jake in the eye, happy he'd send him away with at least a swollen eye and his pride hurt.

Before he could swing again, Jake clocked him in the nose. Pain bloomed behind his eyes as his nose crunched as it broke.

"You asshole!" Tim swore.

"Keep your hands off what's mine and we ain't got no problem!"

"Keep it down!" Darla hissed.

Jake came at Tim again and he stepped to the side, expecting a swing from Jake, but instead, Jake's hand shot out, arcing toward Tim's stomach. Tim saw the glint of the knife at the last second and didn't make it back far enough. The t-shirt ripped, and cold steel touched his midsection. He lunged at Jake when his hand swung past. Tim shoved Jake back, bending his wrist, and he heard the knife clatter to the ground a second later.

Darla was trying to get between them, hissing at them to quit it before her landlady came outside. The front porch light flicked on, and Jake swore. Tim stumbled back. His t-shirt was warm and wet, clinging to his skin, and he felt sick.

Jake swore again, snatched up the knife, and disappeared into the darkness. Darla looked from Jake's disappearing form to Tim, her eyes wide.

"Get going!" she hissed. "Dammit, go!"

Tim stumbled toward the car as Darla went to the front door and fumbled with her keys, aiming to head off her landlady. He pulled away from the curb, blood soaking his clothes. All he wanted was a fight to set some boundaries with Jake. Now he had the St. Valentine's Day Massacre all over Bill's car.

He had to make it downtown where Bill was crashing tonight or he wasn't going to make it anywhere ever again.

Everett's place was dead quiet that night and she was glad for it. She was sure he'd opened the night before to punish her, but she saw he had second thoughts when Jake showed up along with Darla and her friends. Between them and Tim sitting at the bar, Ruby felt like she was in town square wearing a great big A.

Darla surprised her. Ruby met with her outside and had reservations about getting in Darla's car, but she'd driven her along the Strip—that was a trip with all those lights—and understood it wasn't her fault Jake had taken her to the Silver Slipper.

She also said Tim was looking at her and Jake was trying to make him mad, too. That was something. She didn't know what exactly, but something.

She was glad for the quiet—Everett was asleep upstairs and since they were closed the second floor was empty.

She sighed. She didn't want Tim to think she liked Jake, but God knew what people were saying about her now. Jake probably blabbed all over town about it.

She went with Lewis for awhile before Christmas, and he was alright at first, but it wasn't like she'd fall out of her saddle looking at him or anything. All the girls at school had teased her about not kissing a boy and being behind them in everything even though she was a year older thanks to being held back a grade when her momma was sick. So when Lewis wanted to go further, she hadn't stopped him.

She knew after making it with him she must be missing something. All the girls at school talked about boyfriends like they were the greatest thing ever. Lewis turned out to be anything but alright in the end. She hadn't liked it much, and she chalked it up to being different than the other girls, yet again.

She pulled her robe on and took the license plates from her rucksack, then padded downstairs in bare feet. She unlocked the beer pantry and tucked the plates in the back. They'd been sitting on an old flatbed in the barn, and she aimed to present them to Tim. If she could make herself useful, maybe he'd pay her some mind.

Just as she came around the corner into the main room, a loud commotion on the front steps made her jump. The knocking at the door sounded like rifle fire, and she rushed over and looked out the window, surprised to see Bill standing there with blood on his clothes. He was supporting Tim's weight.

She flung the door open. "What happened?"

Bill half-dragged Tim inside.

"He got into it with Jake Wheeler," Bill said, straining from supporting Tim's weight. "There some place I can put him down?"

"Upstairs," Ruby said, rushing over near the cash box and grabbing the set of keys Everett had for the rooms upstairs.

She dashed upstairs in front of Bill and circled around to the room closest, facing front. It was furnished sparsely, only a metal framed double bed against one wall, a rocking chair in a corner, and a single dresser against another wall. Bill crashed into the room, and Ruby ran over to help him.

"Shit, this is some bumpy ride," Tim mumbled.

"What's wrong with him?" Ruby asked as Bill placed him on the bed.

She could see Tim's nose was broken, blood covered his face, and his eyes were shaded dark. He was trying to smile as he reached for her, his knuckles raw and bleeding.

"Is he drunk?" she asked, leaning closer.

"Had to be," Bill said, nodding toward Tim's midsection. Blood had soaked through and dried on his ripped green t-shirt, and Ruby hesitated a second before lifting it.

"Oh my God," she said.

He'd been slashed from below his ribs on the left side, and the gash moved across and down his midsection to his right hip. But the gaping wound was sewn shut crudely, with thick black thread.

"Who did this?" she asked, horrified at what she was seeing.

"I stitched him up best I could, he said no hospital," Bill told her. "He means it too, don't go calling an ambulance."

She looked back at the wound in shock, and Bill walked over to her and grabbed her shoulders.

"No ambulance, no hospital, you got that?" Bill said, shaking her roughly. "You promise?"

"I promise." She was afraid of Bill just then—the anger in his eyes was plain. He released her, and she caught her balance. "When I asked who did this, I meant who hurt him."

"And I told you, Jake and him went at it."

"Jake did this?" Ruby felt sick. "But he's his friend ..."

"Tim messed around with Jake's girl or something, and Jake got wind of it, best I can tell," Bill said. "Jake's not looking too hot either, don't worry."

Tim was with Darla? Ruby felt a surge of disappointment. Tim moaned when he tried to sit up, and Bill pushed him back onto the bed. Tim opened his eyes a little, and they lazily focused on her.

"Hi kid," Tim said. He swallowed and his eyes rolled back in his head as Bill put a pillow behind it. Her hurt ebbed away as she saw the pain etched on his face.

"Drank a half bottle of straight bourbon before I sewed him up," Bill said. "You alright to look after him 'til the morning?"

"Me?"

"I gotta go take care of the boys, let them know Tim's okay. A couple of them saw Tim come into the warehouse and all hell's gonna break loose if they hear who did it. This isn't what we need right now, I gotta smooth it all over before some knucklehead of ours grabs a shotgun and goes looking for Jake."

"Okay," Ruby said, looking at Bill with trepidation.

"Give him these when he wakes up." Bill handed her a vial with some pills in it. "Penicillin. So he won't get infection."

Ruby watched Bill go, her mouth hanging open, Tim humming in his drunken stupor.

The door closed downstairs when Bill left. The faint sound of a car engine started up, and she looked out the window and saw tail lights disappear down the street.

She sighed and walked back over to the bed. Tim's eyes fluttered shut, and he was silent. The sound of his even breathing was the only thing letting her know he was still alive.

She stared for a moment, unsure what to do.

She lifted the edge of his tattered shirt up, and her stomach heaved as she saw the crude black thread holding the wound together. She was no ace at sewing, but Bill had mangled it badly.

She glanced toward the stairs, confident Everett didn't hear a thing, or else he'd be there asking what the heck was going on.

She wanted to load him in the car and cart him off to a hospital, but Bill looked at her like it would be a crime against nature. The last thing she wanted was to get Tim in trouble, and a gash like that . . . well, it meant trouble.

She padded out of the room and down the stairs, avoiding the creakiest ones. She picked up the telephone behind the bar and made the call with trepidation. She wasn't technically disobeying, and anyway, Tim might croak if those stitches got infected.

She went back to the second floor with a shallow basin and filled it with cool water. She brought the basin and a cloth into Tim's room and set them on the nightstand. She pulled the rocking chair near the bed, sat down, and wiped Tim's brow.

He was out of it, barely able to open his own eyes, but was aware someone was there. He kept trying to look around at where he was.

His hand groped the air, and Ruby took it gently, setting it on the bed.

"Shh," she said. "Don't move so much. You're liable to tear those awful stitches."

He relaxed at the sound of her voice and laid still as she wiped his face. His nose, which looked broken, was crusted with blood. When his face was clean, she gently bathed his raw knuckles, the water in the bowl turning the colour of rust. She looked at the ugly wound on his midsection, wondering how on earth Jake Wheeler could gut his own friend.

She lowered his tattered shirt over the wound again and was startled when his hand grabbed her wrist.

"Tim?" She leaned over him.

"Ruby?" he asked, his voice raw. "Shit . . . I hate being this drunk. Don't have ... control."

At least he knew he was drunk. She dipped the cloth in the water and wiped his forehead, eliciting a chuckle from him.

"Don't have a fever," he said, his eyes remaining closed.

"I know," she answered. "My momma used to do this, no matter what ailed me. Made me feel better."

"You're . . . a good kid," Tim said. He opened his eyes. They looked glazed over and it took a minute for him to focus on her. "Pretty, too."

She huffed out a puff of air. "That's the whiskey talking."

She smiled, then froze when he brought a hand up and cupped her face.

"Nah," he whispered, pulling her head toward his. She turned her face away—his breath was 150 proof at least—and gently manoeuvred out of his way. She didn't like him this way. It scared her.

"Tim, what the hell happened?"

"Jake," he said simply. He wasn't bothered that she'd turned him away.

"Why'd he do this?" She stroked his forehead.

"Jake got the message . . . knows now . . . he knows," Tim said, a wry smile on his face.

"Knows what?"

"He doesn't mess with mine, and I don't mess with his."

"With your what?" she asked. He wasn't making a lick of sense.

A staccato knock at the door downstairs interrupted them. Ruby placed the cloth on Tim's forehead. His chest rose and fell with each breath. He had passed out cold.

She rushed down the stairs and opened the door for Doctor Jenkins.

"Ruby, you said you had a sick horse, and I don't see a single horse anywhere around these parts," he said.

"Well, that's because I lied," she said. "He's upstairs, and it's bad."

He climbed the stairs after her, his stout frame causing him to puff the whole way. He paused in the doorway.

"I don't usually work on two legged patients." He wiped his brow with a handkerchief and walked into the room, then bent over the bed.

Ruby raised up the shirt, and the doctor recoiled.

"What in the..."

"You can't say anything to anyone," she begged. "Can you fix it?"

His moon face hovered over Tim's midsection. "What'd he do that he's not in a hospital?"

She shrugged. "I dunno. That's the God's honest truth. He got in a fight. Please."

"You're gonna have to help me," the doctor said.

He laid out some catgut from his big medical bag, and pulled on some gloves, handing her a pair. He rifled through his bag again and handed her a pair of big scissors and told her to cut the shirt off. It was ruined anyway, and she clipped the material from hem to neck then down each sleeve, exposing Tim's pale skin, his chest rising with each breath.

"I don't have anything but horse tranquilizers in here," he said.

"He's out anyway." She shook Tim's arm, but he didn't stir. "Bourbon."

Doctor Jenkins looked up at the heavens for a second. He took a pair of small silver scissors and cut through all the stitches Bill had badly placed, picking out the threads and swearing under his breath, which was always followed by a quick apology toward Ruby. She looked away when he cut the last one, the skin gaping and bloody.

He took a bottle of iodine out of his bag, wet a cloth, and wiped the area of the wound. Tim made a feeble protest from the bed, and the doctor looked up at Ruby.

"Get him some more drink," he said. "I'm gonna need more light."

She moved a floor lamp from another room into Tim's room and refilled the bowl with clean water, then brought a bottle of Jim Beam upstairs with her. When the doctor was ready she knelt beside the bed and took Tim's cool hand in her own, watching the doctor get Tim to drink more. She held his hand as he drifted off again. They were large, strong, and rough, as if they held the memories of a hundred fights. She hoped Jake's face was the size of a balloon.

She watched with a queasy stomach as Jenkins sewed up a layer of tissue below the skin, closing the wound. It took a good amount of time, and a half hour later he told her he was going to close the skin wound with silk stitches.

"They'll come out in a month or so," he said, working carefully. "The catgut ones underneath, they'll disappear on their own. Judging by the scars this young man has, he'll take these silk ones out by himself. It's not going to be the prettiest job, but if he didn't want a hospital, he's gonna have to settle for this."

It took another half hour for him to finish closing the wound, and once it was cleaned, Ruby relaxed. He looked much better. Jenkins dressed the wound, then packed his bag, leaving her with plenty of gauze.

"Change the bandages in the morning, get him to take it easy," he said. "It gets infected, he'll need a hospital, right away."

She nodded and followed the doctor downstairs and to the door. She locked up after he left, then climbed the stairs to the second floor. She stopped in the bathroom to fill a pitcher of water and took a glass with her back to his room.

She spied the bottle of bourbon on the night stand and grabbed it, taking a sip. The liquid burned as it went down and she coughed, then relaxed as the warm feeling spread through her body. She took a deep breath to settle her nerves more, then pulled the rocking chair back toward the bed again, but sat gingerly on the narrow piece of mattress available to her instead.

His skin was so pale he looked like a cut marble statue. He had a lean build, skin tight over sinuous muscle. He was breathing slowly, his face still pale, and his brow furrowed as if he was disturbed about all of this, even in sleep. His midsection was wrapped in gauze, his t-shirt in tatters on the floor. She pulled the blankets up to his waist, his skin surprisingly warm for someone who looked so ghostly.

She stared at his damaged face for a second, his eyes fluttering open and closing again slowly, and he looked young to her. Even with the deep scars on his face and a few shallow ones that disturbed the skin on his chest, he looked much younger than she had thought him. She brushed a few damp hairs off his forehead, re-wet the cloth, and placed it back on his head, shushing him back to sleep when he tried to talk.

"You're a pile of trouble, Tim Kelly," she sighed, putting a bucket beside the bed in case he was sick in the night. She looked at him for a moment, reassured he was asleep, then leaned over, and kissed the scar beneath his eye.

8

Tim opened his eyes and was sure he was being stabbed in them.

"Oh, fuck."

His voice sounded like sandpaper. He shut his eyes, waiting for the pounding to lessen. He didn't know where he was.

He opened his eyes again, and the light hurt them less this time. He didn't want to think about what had happened to him. He lifted his head off the pillow and waited a moment for the dizziness to pass. His mouth felt like it was filled with cotton, and his head felt two sizes too big.

He spied the bottle of bourbon beside the bed and remembered the night before. He closed his eyes and dropped back onto the pillow.

Jake always said Darla was two-timing him. He knew Jake thought it was him, but figured Jake thought it was just about every guy in Las Vegas at some point. Tim touched the raised lump on the side of his head where her purse had caught him. If Darla was two-timing Jake, he'd eat his hat. That girl had it bad.

He expected a fight for kissing her—he expected a knock down drag out fight, one for the books that they'd talk about years later. A fight where Jake would get the message that Ruby was off limits, whether Tim wanted her or not. He figured Jake and him would have it out, grab a beer a few days later, and he wouldn't have to endure any more of Wheeler's stupid tricks.

Only Jake lost his damn mind and whipped out a knife. It wasn't a fair fight when the other guy used a weapon with no warning. Tim hadn't had time to go for the switch in his boot.

He remembered the slash across his midsection and the blood pouring through his hands. Darla had barely blinked, hissed at them both to get lost, and he stumbled to Bill's car in disbelief.

Things got fuzzy once he arrived at the warehouse. He remembered bourbon.

There was a memory of pain snapping across his mid section at even intervals, Bill swearing, and the sense that he was going to be lucky if he ever woke up. The sensation of being in a car, and . . . it went blank.

He travelled through the holes in his mind and remembered Ruby's voice, stinging pain, and a cool hand on his forehead. He remembered her lips and didn't know why. He must be at Everett's.

He forced his eyes open again, and he saw the ugly curtains stretched across the window. Everett's place. Ruby *was* there.

He looked to his left and saw Ruby asleep in a rocking chair, her head resting on a small pillow wedged between her shoulder and head. She wore an old fashioned robe over a virginal white nightgown.

He moved off the pillow and winced at the pain, then lay down again.

He lifted up the blanket and saw gauze taped to his midsection. He lifted the corner of the bandages and peeled them back. They were stained with blood, and he marvelled at the stitch job, wondering if Ruby had done it.

His head spun, and he lay back against the pillow. His nose felt too big for his face, and when he inhaled it felt like getting air through a straw. He touched his nose gingerly. Broken. He was going to nail Jake's balls to the wall for that.

The room swirled, and he closed his eyes. He was not going to throw up. He was going to get up and get the hell out of here.

When he could move.

"You're awake."

Tim opened his eyes again and saw Ruby moving toward him. She knelt beside the bed, and he noticed what must be his own blood, the deep colour of rust, on her sleeve.

"You look terrible," she said honestly.

He managed to crack a small grin. He tried to speak and couldn't. She poured water into a glass and held it for him, cradling his head in her hand, and helping him raise up enough to drink.

The nausea made the room tilt, and he forced himself to think of something else. He was not going to throw up.

"This is nothing," he said. He pulled on the blanket. "Who the hell did that?"

She looked nervously from the hack job to his eyes.

"Bill said no hospital and no ambulance . . . so I called the vet."

"The what?"

"Doctor Jenkins, he looks after Rett's horses. He stitched you up. Bill really did a number on you, I'd never seen anything so awful. The doc cleaned it out best he could and stitched you back up, it looks real good," she said earnestly.

"Sewn up by a damn vet," he murmured, thinking about how it would be if that ever got out. "Jesus Christ."

"You're supposed to take it easy, and I can change the bandages."

Tim nodded. "Just leave me be."

"But—"

"Ruby," he cut in, his voice harsher than he meant it. "Go on. Leave me alone a bit."

She frowned at him, then tightly wrapped her robe around her and headed out of the room, closing the door behind her.

Tim waited to hear her steps on the stairs; then, satisfied she was gone, promptly vomited into the bucket beside the bed.

Tim stared at his reflection in the bathroom mirror. Both his eyes were shaded black and blue from the broken nose, but his face was free of blood. He grabbed a face cloth and rolled it up, then bit on it. He turned the shower on full blast to mask any noise, then felt alongside his nose. He was lucky it hadn't shattered along the thin plates in his face.

He sucked in a breath and pushed on his nose, biting down on the pain and trying to breathe through his mouth. He felt some of the small plates alongside his nose and found the small ridge where the bone was broken. He forced himself to keep going. There was a pop, and his nose cleared. He could breathe again.

He sat on the edge of the tub and turned off the water. His head spun, and he sunk onto the floor and sat there a minute waiting until the dizziness passed. He dry heaved twice, then took two controlled breaths.

A few minutes later he stood and made his way to the sink. He splashed cold water on his face and rung out the wash cloth, draping it on his neck. He had a sudden memory of Ruby, and he wasn't sure why.

He stared at the bandages. He didn't doubt the stitches were better than what was there before, and she found a way around Bill's instructions. He wanted nothing more than to get out of Everett's and away from Ruby. God only knew what she thought of him.

He made his way down the stairs awhile later, feeling worse than he had in all his days. He didn't get drunk like that often . . . come to think of it, only when he'd been cut up bad. He'd have beers with the guys and all, but never enough so he was out of control of his own body or mind. Too much could go down when you weren't paying attention.

Ruby was drinking a cup of coffee and flipping through the morning paper, but Tim didn't think she was reading it. She had the look of someone who was listening for him.

"You shouldn't be up." She watched him move slowly over to the bar and sit down. He had found his t-shirt was ripped to shreds, and he had nothing on but his jeans, crusted with dried blood.

"Got things to do," he said simply. He wondered what he had said to her last night. Bill told him once he was a talkative drunk and he hoped he hadn't said anything stupid. He didn't want to ask how much she knew about how he got like this.

"I can call Bill to come and get you, you aren't driving with those stitches," she said.

"I'll call him myself."

He inhaled as her face fell, then she disappeared into the kitchen as he used the phone. She returned a minute later with a cup of coffee, and the smell almost made him lose his lunch again.

"Drink up," she said. "My daddy always said it was the best cure."

He warily took a sip and closed his eyes at the taste. It stayed down at least. He took the vial of penicillin he'd found on the night table and took two.

"Where'd Bill get those?" she asked. "He came in with them."

"Drug store," Tim said simply.

Ruby's brow wrinkled. "Drug stores were all closed when he brought you here."

"Yeah, well we go in the back door instead of the front," Tim answered. His headache was threatening to squeeze his eyeballs right out of his head.

"What'd Jake do this for?" she asked quietly.

He looked up. Obviously he'd said that much to her about what had happened. Christ, why couldn't he remember much of it?

"That's between him and me."

"Oh." She looked at her fingers. Her nails were short and boyish, and she wore no nail polish or rings. He looked at his own hands, his raw knuckles, and remembered getting a few good, hard punches in at Jake before he'd gone down at the end of Jake's knife. The blood was gone, the knuckles raw and red. There hadn't been a drop of blood on his face, either. She must've cleaned him up.

He put his hand over hers, and she looked at him in surprise.

"You did good last night."

She smiled, and he watched her intently, waiting for her to blush and look away. Only this time she held his gaze, and he broke it first.

Cursing himself inwardly, he moved his hand off of hers.

"You got a shirt around here I can borrow?"

"Rett's got one," she said. She disappeared around the corner and came back with a work shirt a size too big, but at least it covered the stitch job.

He nodded his thanks, trying to keep the pain off his face as he shrugged into the shirt.

"That reminds me, I have something else for you," she said, grabbing the keys and disappearing in the back again. She came out and placed a license plate on the bar in front of him.

"From a flat bed trailer at Rett's." She presented it like a bird dog with its prey. "Figured you could use it for that trailer plate you need."

He rubbed his chin, rough with stubble since there'd been no razor in the second floor bathroom. Even if there was, he wouldn't have trusted his hand with it.

"You shouldn't have done that," he said, looking at the license plate.

"But you said you need a plate number to give that man—"

"You can go put that back." Anger rose in his chest. "I'll handle it."

"You handle everything by yourself, don't you?" she said. Her voice was tinged with anger.

He was relieved to hear Bill's foot falls on the stairs. The door opened a second later.

"Christ, you look ten times better than last night." His voice boomed, and if Tim could've reached the gun he knew Everett kept behind the counter, he would've shot Bill's ass off for talking so loud. Bill looked at the two of them, his gaze resting on the license plate, then Ruby's crossed arms.

"Am I interrupting something?" Bill asked.

"Let's go." Tim got up and bit his lip to keep from wincing at the pain. It was going to be a long, uncomfortable day.

"Thanks Ruby," Bill said, with a grin and wave.

Tim said nothing, the door slamming shut behind him.

It took Tim a minute to get into Bill's car.

"I told her no doctors," Bill said, nodding towards his wound.

"You told her no hospital or ambulance. She had a doc come sew me up," Tim said.

There was no way he was telling Bill, or anyone else, it was a vet she called.

"It's alright," Tim said, noticing Bill's look. "Police didn't show up knocking on the door."

Bill started up the car and drove toward downtown and the warehouse. Tim closed his eyes and wished the foggy headache would go away.

"Things almost went to hell in a handbasket last night," Bill said with a sigh. "Don't suppose you remember much?"

"I remember up 'til the bourbon started." He lit a cigarette. The sulphur of the match relaxed him.

"Most of the boys were at the warehouse hiding all the car parts from the Raceway. Jesse was the only one that saw me bring you in, but he ran his mouth, and it's not like they didn't see the blood on me. Boys were hell-bent on finding Jake, but I got 'em focused on trying to stop you from bleeding all over the office. I think Dale's gonna be scarce awhile, he looked worse than you did after. Anyhow, no one's murdered Jake yet."

Thank God for small favours. The last thing they needed was a war when all this stuff with the Californians was going on.

Bill hesitated a second before speaking again. "We need to give Insane Wayne a trailer plate number. He's expecting one, gonna call later today. I don't know where we're gonna snag a trailer today. Ruby have any ideas?"

"I didn't ask her, seeing as I was unconscious most of the night," he said irritably. The last thing he wanted to talk about was Ruby.

She looked so pleased with herself getting the plate, and dammit if it wasn't what he needed. But he wanted her out of his business, and she kept sticking her nose farther in. Business and pleasure never mixed, and he was aiming more for pleasure, if all the indications she were giving were right.

But they still needed a plate.

"You could call over there and ask," Bill said. Tim glanced over at him. He knew full well Bill had seen that license plate on Everett's bar. Sometimes his quiet disapproval was worse than having it out.

"I'm not calling over there."

Bill looked over, and Tim turned his head away. Bill had that look on his face.

"We still need her, Tim," Bill said evenly. "For a trailer, for teaching you to drive with one. I wouldn't do anything to mess that up. Fix things, get what we need, then go from there."

Bill Pearce knew the score. It was one of the things Tim liked best about him. He could always depend on his level head, only now he didn't much like what it was saying. He hated when Bill was right.

"Write this down," Tim said. He gave Bill the plate number he memorized. Ruby didn't have to know it came in handy.

Saturday, May 7, 1966

Ruby was setting up glasses behind the bar when people arrived, and every time the door opened she hoped to see Tim, but he hadn't shown up.

She didn't know why she was so eager to see him again after the way he'd acted. She practically saved his life, and he pretended like it was nothing. She wiped the bar and sighed. She had it bad.

As the night wore on, Ruby realized she was getting the hang of things. She knew who tried to pinch a free beer, who deserved one, which girl was going with which guy—the most useful information of all, since Everett's was the place people showed up at if they wanted to step out on their girl-friend or boyfriend.

She was thinking about how lucky she was she hadn't run into Jake Wheeler when he showed up. She had no idea what to say to someone who'd cut Tim open like a can of sardines.

"Got any Hamm's back there?" he asked.

"Only if you have money." She couldn't keep the anger out of her voice.

Jake searched his pocket for some change and plunked it on the counter. She popped the top off a bottle and put it in front of him. He grabbed it, but she wouldn't release it.

"Why'd you do it?"

"Do what?" Jake asked.

"Cut Tim up."

"Saw that, huh?" Jake said, the hint of a grim smile on his face. "You play nursemaid, too?"

"I thought you two were friends."

Jake turned and leaned against the bar, watching a couple drunkenly dance in a corner.

"We are. He has to learn to keep his hands off what's mine." Jake took a drink of his beer.

Ruby frowned. "What do you mean what's yours?"

Jake turned around, a grin on his face. "I guess you ain't heard. He tried to pick up my girlfriend, tried to make it with her the other night. I took exception."

"B-but ... you kissed me. How's that any different?"

Jake shrugged. "Just is."

"Does he always hit on your girlfriends?" She scrubbed at a white ring on the bar.

His smile was a wicked grin.

"Why?" he asked. "You jealous he ain't hittin' on you?"

She didn't dignify his question with an answer.

"Tim Kelly ain't no choir boy, darlin'," he said, his voice rough. He turned and lifted his shirt up. She looked around to see if anyone else was watching this show.

She glanced over and saw his bruised ribs, tape around his midsection.

"Tim did that?" She looked at it in morbid fascination. Jake slid his shirt back down, his gaze challenging. He raised his eyebrows, a smirk on his face.

"You deserve it for trying to kill him."

Jake shrugged, a look of irritation on his face.

"That ain't all he done," Jake said. He showed off a jagged cut down his arm. "Pulled a knife on me there. And you see this?"

Jake titled his head up and Ruby saw a faint, jagged scar across his neck. "Yeah."

"Tried to slit my throat once."

Ruby's stomach soured. "What for?"

Jake shrugged. "Didn't like the way I was beating him in a fight."

Ruby stared.

"I don't gotta tell you about the time he snapped my wrist, broke it in three places. Or the time he gave me a concussion."

"Why'd he do all that to you?"

Jake clamped his mouth around his cigarette and took a long drag, blowing the smoke out toward her.

"He's just that kinda guy."

Jake picked up the beer and headed into the crowd. Ruby stared after him, then looked out the window, unsure about Tim Kelly after all.

Tuesday, May 10, 1966

Tim pulled into the gravel lot at Everett's, the drizzle turning part of the lot into a mud puddle. The El Camino was nowhere to be found, but that didn't mean much.

He wasn't sure what kind of reception he was going to get. He skipped out on Everett's over the weekend and hadn't been there since the night he was hurt. He remembered Ruby's expression as he left, her closed face.

He eased out of the driver's seat and shut the truck door, walking toward the front steps. His mid-section was still hurting, but it wasn't anything he couldn't handle.

The front door was unlocked and Tim found the downstairs empty, save for Everett, who had finished putting new records in the jukebox.

"She's at the stable," Everett said.

Tim nodded, grabbed a beer for himself, and put the change in the cashbox under the bar. He sat at a table and nursed the beer. Everett left him alone in the empty bar room, the light from the windows barely lighting the place. Footsteps sounded on the stairs, but he was surprised to see Bill instead Ruby.

"Glad I found you here," Bill said. "Insane Wayne called my place, he said he wants you in Los Angeles on the fourteenth with the truck and trailer ready to roll. Wouldn't gimme any more than an address."

Tim took the paper Bill held out, and Bill helped himself to a beer and sat across from Tim.

"We need that trailer," Bill said.

Tim said nothing, rankled that Bill was right.

"Where is she anyway?" Bill asked. "Maybe we oughta go over to the stable."

Tim glanced at Bill, who raised both eyebrows. Now he was being a bastard.

The door creaked behind him, and he could tell by the soft tread it was Ruby.

She walked in, looked over at them, and then counted beers as if they weren't there.

"We paid for them, if that's what you're thinking," Tim said. She slammed a cupboard shut somewhere back there. She didn't say a word.

Bill looked over with a raised eyebrow, and Tim shrugged. He couldn't help it if she was hacked off. He didn't miss the eye roll and shake of the head Bill offered in return, and he knew he wasn't shaking his head at Ruby.

He knew Bill was staring, and Tim sipped his beer and looked straight ahead, ignoring Ruby as she sorted through the glasses and alcohol behind the bar.

Bill sighed, shook his head, and then gulped some of his beer.

"So Ruby," Bill said, a smile in his voice. "Saw you out riding the other day, you about scared the devil outta me the way you were flipping on that horse. You do it professional?"

Her body language relaxed. She turned around and talked to Bill about her horse and trick riding, and pretty soon she was sitting at the table with them, drinking a Dr Pepper, and pointedly ignoring him. It would've been funny if he didn't have so much to worry about.

"I gotta run." Bill gave Tim a meaningful look.

A split second after the door shut, Ruby stood.

"I have some things to do, too," she said. He grabbed her wrist before she could walk away, saw her eyes widen in fear and was taken aback. She was never afraid of him before.

"You up for helping me out with a trailer?" he asked.

She looked around the empty room, at everything but him.

"Ruby?"

"I guess."

She pulled her wrist out of his grip and went behind the bar, and Tim watched her curiously. She was rearranging things that didn't need to be rearranged, cleaning things that were already clean. He stood and walked over to the bar.

"What's got into you?"

"Me?" she asked with a laugh. "I should be asking you the same thing. First you beat it out of here like the devil himself was after you last week, without so much as a thank you."

"Thank you," he said with as straight a face as he could muster. She was cute when she was mad.

"Very funny." She tossed a dish towel on the counter. "It was bad enough Jake had to go and cut you up like he did, but as ornery as he is I guess I should've expected something like that from him. But for the life of me, I don't understand you trying to pick up his girl. You and Jake are beyond me."

She took the dish towel up and scrubbed at the shiny wood.

"I mean, I guess I can see a little retaliation, but Jesus, you guys are supposed to be friends from what I hear, and there you go trying to cut his throat out and snapping his wrist in two."

Tim frowned. "Ruby, what the hell are you talking about?"

He was looking at her like she had three heads. Ever since the weekend she'd been driving herself crazy thinking about what Tim and Jake did to each other. She didn't want to step into the middle of some strange war between them. There was no way after all the trouble in Abilene that she was going to be Tim Kelly's pawn.

Still, she was disappointed if that's all she was. She hoped he liked her a bit and maybe that was what the fight was about, but if they did this all the time then she was hoping for nothing.

"Ruby?" he asked.

"Bill said you tried to pick up Jake's girlfriend that night." She tried to sound like it didn't bother her. She saw Tim smother a grin.

"Yeah. That bother you?" He picked his cigarettes out of his pocket and lit a match with his thumb. He lit his cigarette then put the match out between his fingers, and she shivered.

"I don't get it, is all."

What she didn't get was how she was going to compete with a blonde beauty like Darla if Tim was interested in girls like her. Maybe she shouldn't try.

"It was a little payback."

"Oh yeah? Then what about that hack job on his neck? Or the broken wrist? Was that payback too?" She paused as she realized he'd said payback. She took in a sharp breathing, wondering if that meant he knew Jake kissed her. And if he did, and he'd gone after Jake's girlfriend to get back at him ...

Tim was frowning again.

84

"What hack job? What are you talking about?" Tim asked.

"All those things you did to Jake, the cut on his arm, cutting his neck, the broken wrist. Y'all aimin' to kill each other or what?"

She hoped he had some kind of explanation and saw his mouth twitch. A second later he laughed, a low and throaty sound that made her catch her breath. She loved how the honest laughter changed his expression.

"Hey, let me in on it," she said. Maybe he was off his rocker and thought cutting people up was a fun pastime.

"He told you I tried to cut his throat, did he?" Tim's eyes twinkled in amusement.

"Well," she said carefully. "He told me you weren't a choir boy and showed me the scar ...."

Tim took a drag of his cigarette, stifling his laughter again as he shook his head. "That lousy motherf- . . . jerk."

"You didn't do it?" She was too relieved to be bothered over his language.

"You should know better than to believe anything Jake Wheeler says." Tim ground out his cigarette. "He caught some razor wire in the neck at a rodeo in New Mexico in awhile back, the horse tossed him, and he broke his wrist. I was nowhere near him."

"Oh," Ruby said, feeling like a moron. "Well, what about the scar on his arm?"

"That I did do." Tim blew a smoke ring. "First and only—well, until the other day—knife fight we had."

"Oh."

Heat crept into her face as Tim stared, an amused glint in his green eyes. She realized he was handsome when he didn't have his guard up, his eyes both laughing and dangerous.

"You were mad because you thought I'd cut him up?" he asked. "Or because I was trying to pick up his girl?"

Ruby turned away from him.

"Jake's got rocks in his head," Tim said. "Doesn't like it when people try and play his own game and get under his skin. He has to learn not to get in other peoples' business."

She looked at him, wondering if she was other peoples' business.

"He plays a lot of games." Tim said. "You'd do well to remember that."

Darla had told her the same thing. He may not have cut up Jake, but they were dangerous either way. Tim's eyes glinted with laughter.

"Ruby, I've never been anything but polite to you," he said patiently, appraising her with his gaze.

"Except for beating it outta here after I helped you like I did."

"'Cept for. You wanna help me with a trailer?" he asked.

She stared for a second. "So you only need my help when it's convenient for you? Ruby get me a beer, Ruby get me a truck, Ruby get me a trailer, Ruby—"

"Ruby, shut up." His voice was teasing.

"I was trying to help before," she said quietly. "With the trailer plate, I mean."

"I know. But now I'm asking."

So maybe that was it . . . maybe it was pride and he didn't like accepting things if he hadn't asked for them.

"You're going to need to learn how to hitch a trailer up and how to drive with one on. I can teach you the hitching part at the stable. There's another flat bed there," she said. "You could drive with it on too, but a flat bed is nothing like a trailer, so it won't be much use, except for learning turns. I've asked around, haven't been able to find you a trailer."

"I've got a handle on that."

She looked at the wood grain, disappointed. He glanced up with an amused expression.

"Still need you to help me."

She smiled back.

"Everett's not gonna like it," he said laconically.

"Rett hates everything," Ruby said, half-seriously. "And he doesn't need to know."

"I'll meet you at the stable tomorrow morning," Tim said. He got up and put some more change on the counter. "I lied before. Bill didn't pay."

She grinned at his back as he headed out the door.

9

Wednesday, May 11, 1966

Ruby held a tissue to her forehead and struggled to get the heavy saddle off her horse. She got to the stable early and was finishing up a practice session with Bella when she wiped out in spectacular fashion. She was glad no one was around to see it.

The keeper on the Cossack strap had broken, and she almost killed herself since she'd been hanging upside down off her horse when it snapped. Her forehead was bleeding from where she'd hit the ground, her neck was sore, and she was ready to call it a day.

She dabbed more blood off her forehead and tucked the bloody tissue into her pocket. She lifted the saddle off Bella and set it on a sawhorse. The keeper was shredded, but the strap itself was torn and useless. She'd never get in that rodeo show if she didn't have the right equipment. She had to find a cheap replacement soon.

She went inside the office and found a small mirror and cleaned off her forehead, her eyes watering from the sharp sting of the antiseptic from the first aid kit. She had no idea how Tim coped with being cut up like he was. The cut oozed blood, but it was close enough to her hairline she hoped no one would notice.

"Boy, do I look like a fright," she said to her reflection. She was covered in dust and could see she had half the dirt from the riding ring up her nose. Her normally pale skin looked tanned because of the yellow-brown dust. Her clothes were filthy and reeked of hay and horses.

She pulled open a filing cabinet and pulled out a pair of clean denim Capri pants and a striped shirt. She kept a change of clothes around after Everett had complained about how she dirtied his precious car after being at the stable. She got changed, wiped off her skin, then searched her bag for a comb. Finding none, she used the closest substitute.

"I'm doing my hair with a mane comb," she sighed. "Some girl I am."

Her preening was interrupted by the horn of the truck, and she smiled at her reflection before tucking the mirror and the mane comb in a filing cabinet drawer.

Tim stopped the truck in the dirt yard and slowly climbed down from the seat, his stitches pulling. Driving Bill's car was one thing, but the truck was ten times harder, and it wasn't doing this gash across his midsection any favours.

"I should've told you to back in, you'll have to turn around in a minute," Ruby said apologetically. "How's your stomach?"

"I'll survive," he said. "What'd you do to your head?"

"Introduced it to the ground suddenly," she answered. "I was hoping no one would notice."

He grinned wryly, and they walked slowly toward the flat bed that was parked near the barn.

"How big's the barn?"

"About eighty feet or so," she said. "Why?"

"C'mon," he said, ignoring the question. "Let's do this."

He was itching to get started ever since the plan for getting a trailer had come into his head. Bill maintained he was crazy, but then, whenever Bill said that things usually turned out okay. He followed Ruby as she walked toward the flat bed trailer, his gaze trained on the exposed skin at the small of her back, the sleeveless shirt tied tightly at her waist.

"Coupling a trailer is pretty basic." Her voice reminded him of a substitute teacher. "That greased plate looking thing on the back of the tractor is the fifth wheel. Under the trailer is the king pin. What you want to do is make the king pin slide into the fifth wheel."

Tim couldn't resist smiling. "Sounds like something I'm familiar with."

Her cheeks turned pink as she averted her eyes and looked back at the flatbed.

"After they're coupled," she began, her cheeks still pink and his mind still elsewhere, "you need to attach three cables—electric, air, and emergency air. Then you raise the landing gear on the trailer, inspect everything, and go."

"Sounds easy enough," he said.

She walked toward the truck, and he enjoyed the view from behind before getting in. He started the truck up, then turned it around in the yard. He tried not to suck in his breath too much at the pain he felt every time he had to crank the wheel. It better heal up fast or he was in for a world of hurt driving this truck.

"You wanna line the truck up so it's even. It'll be easier with a trailer, the flatbed's so low it's hard to see, watch your mirrors," she said.

One thing he'd learned pretty quick was to rely on the mirrors. There was no rear view mirror in the truck, since there was no back window, but he still caught himself looking for one. She gave him tips on lining the truck up with the flat bed until they were at the back of the flat bed, and he got out to check they were lined up.

"Now, when you back under it, do it slow . . . you'll have to feel for when the king pin's in place," she said.

"Slow . . . and really feel it, huh?" he said suggestively. She didn't look away this time.

"Let's see if you can handle it," she challenged.

She was impressed.

Tim hadn't missed the fifth wheel once as he practiced coupling the tractor and flatbed a few times. Tim had a good feel for it from the get-go.

She got out of the cab and climbed up on the back of the tractor and waited for Tim to join her. She noticed he winced when he had to move or stretch too much. Her own head was aching and stinging from her little episode earlier, and she couldn't imagine how much he must be hurting.

"Maybe this was a bad idea for today." She looked at his midsection.

"I don't have time to wait," he said. "I have to be in Los Angeles on Saturday morning with a trailer."

"Saturday? That's only three days away," she said. She had no idea if she could teach him to drive with a trailer on in three days—if he had a trailer. Practicing with a flatbed wasn't going to do him much good. He was evasive when she asked what he'd be hauling too. She wondered if he knew.

"Well, let's quit wasting time. Show me what we're up to," he said.

"The fifth wheel locks the kingpin in here. Now you attach your air hoses." She picked up a red and a blue hose. "You attach them to the gladhands on the back of the trailer, like this."

"Gladhands, huh?" he asked, with a chuckle. "Truck driving . . . pretty dirty business."

"There's gloves in the jockey box, sometimes this is dirty." She ignored his true meaning. She took a green cable. "Last one is your pigtail for power. After that, you've got to raise the landing gear."

Tim jumped off the back of the tractor, and Ruby was surprised to see him turn and bring his hands up toward her. She inhaled sharply as he placed his hands on her hips. She put her hands on his shoulders, and he lifted her to the ground slowly. She could tell despite his best effort it hurt him.

"I see what they mean by glad hands," he said with a smirk, his hands still settled on her hips.

"Oh for goodness sake." She couldn't hide her smile. She turned and walked purposefully over to the landing gear crank and tried to move it herself, but it wouldn't budge. Tim stepped in behind her and gave the crank a solid push, and it moved.

She wordlessly cranked the landing gear up under Tim's watchful eye. They got back in the truck, and Ruby held her breath as they moved forward.

Tim was surprised at how much one short little flat bed made a difference. He could feel the weight behind him, and turning was ten times harder.

Once they were on the road it wasn't too bad, although taking curves and turns was harder with the extra weight. Ruby gave corrections as they drove, making him go through a few empty intersections to practice left and right turns.

"You're good at this," Ruby said. "Ever thought of doing it professional?"

"Driving a truck?" he asked, surprised. "Hell, it's not any fun when it's legal."

She looked over and laughed. "You're a real piece of work, you know that?"

They drove back toward the stable, and he spent awhile trying to back the trailer up, going crazy over the fact that everything was in reverse, including how you turned when reversing. Soon he caught on and backed the flat bed up right where it was before. He pulled the air and set the brakes, then Ruby followed him as he set the landing gear down, disconnected the hoses, unlocked the kingpin, then returned to the truck and drove out from under the flat bed.

"Don't get too comfortable," Ruby said after she climbed back in the cab, and he headed for Everett's place. "A forty-eight foot trailer is a whole 'nother thing. I hope you really have a trailer sittin' somewhere, because you're going to need all the practice you can get."

"You'll come with me and Bill tonight, we're gonna get it then," he said.

He stopped the truck in the gravel parking lot at Everett's and cut the engine. Ruby opened her door to get out, and he followed suit, walking around to her side of the truck and moving so he was in front of her. Her back was against the truck, and he noticed the shirt she was wearing had come unbuttoned a little further.

"Where are we gettin' it?"

He leaned in to her, his lips close to her ear. "It's a surprise."

He pulled away, noticing her flushed cheeks and the thud of her pulse in her neck. He felt his own heartbeat in his chest and wondered what her lips tasted like.

He stopped himself from kissing her just in time.

"Wear dark clothes." His lips were inches from hers.

She looked up in confusion, and he broke his gaze and walked back to the truck, eager to get the hell out of Dodge before he did something stupid.

Ruby smoothed the front of her jeans and pulled the t-shirt over her head. Most of her clothes were light colours, but she had a few old shirts she used in the stables.

She'd tied her hair up with a ribbon, put on a pair of tennis shoes, and walked out to the small living room to look at herself in front of the only full length mirror in the place.

"Where're you headed?" Everett asked, watching her preen in front of the mirror.

"Tim and Bill are picking me up," she said.

She saw Everett sigh and put the records down that he was sorting through. "Ruby, how many times do I gotta to tell you to stay away from those boys?"

"You don't stay away from them," she said.

"That's different."

"How?"

"They bring in a lot of business," he said. "Lotta money I can't do without."

"Tim's been nothing but nice to me," she said, shoving the memory of his surliness toward her out of her head. "Bill, too."

"Don't mistake that for nothing," Everett said. "Tim Kelly gets in a heck of a lot of trouble, of his own making, and Bill Pearce is on his heels for every bit of it, and most of it sanctioned by guys like Sam Wyatt. You're gonna get yourself in a mess of trouble with them."

"You rather I spent my time with Jake Wheeler?" she asked.

"I'd rather you stay home and read a book or watch some television," he said seriously. "Got a brand new colour television, and you haven't looked at it once."

"Well, I'm not staying in and watching some stupid program." Ruby studied her reflection in the mirror. People were right, she was too pale.

"What would our daddy think?" he asked. "Me letting you run wild like this?"

"I'm hardly running wild," Ruby said. "You know as well as I do that daddy was in jail once or twice. I know you've been tossed in there, too, for that matter. So that don't mean anything."

"Kelly and his boys are different."

"I'm a big girl, Everett," she said.

"You're nineteen, and that's not so old," Everett said. "Ruby, I know what I'm talking about, I've seen a lot of stuff around here that'd curl your hair."

"Ain't I seen the same things, being around here?"

"Ruby." Everett walked over and stood in front of her. "Ruby, look at me. These boys are bad news. I don't want you getting tangled up with them."

"I'm tangled already." She looked her brother in the eye. Everett's shoulders sagged.

A car engine rumbled as it pulled into the gravel lot. Two doors slammed outside.

"Be careful," Everett said with a sigh.

Ruby didn't ask questions as they got in the truck and started it up. She noticed how he looked at his mirrors and how fast he'd gotten at double clutching—so much that she barely noticed he was doing it anymore. Bill followed behind in his car.

"So where are we going?" she asked, cursing herself for not being able to think of any other topic of conversation.

"You'll see," was all he said.

They drove through downtown Las Vegas, awash in neon, and she gawked at the signs as much as she had when Darla had driven her down the Strip.

"You ever seen this before?" Tim asked, noticing her gaze. He slowed his speed.

She nodded. "Darla took me. It's wild."

"Darla?"

"She took me the night Jake took me out," she said. "She wanted to talk."

"And she didn't scratch your eyes out?" Tim asked.

Ruby smiled. "She's nice."

Tim nodded. "She knows the score."

The signs danced and shifted in the night. Thunderbird, Riviera, Stardust, Silver Slipper, Desert Inn, Sands, Flamingo. Each one looked different than the last. She had no idea why anyone came to Rett's when this was out here.

"Is this what people do when they're not at Rett's?" she asked.

"Yeah, the casinos are always busy. They got shows on almost every night, good food," Tim said.

Tim turned off the Strip and took a road out into the desert, the bright lights giving way to darkness and a million stars overhead.

They were in the middle of nowhere with industrial buildings and warehouses nearby. She was used to places like this; these were only parts of cities she ever saw when she was on the road with her daddy.

Tim pulled onto a narrow road and slowed as they approached a large stand of buildings. He pulled the tractor off onto a dirt side road and parked it on the shoulder, facing the street they'd come in on. She looked over and saw the entrance to a large truck yard.

"Your trailer's in there?" she asked, her stomach flipping over. "Why don't we just go get it?"

Tim gave her a quick look, and she knew.

"You don't have a trailer at all. We're stealing one."

"You okay with that?" Tim asked, appraising her. She felt it again, that feeling as if he was reading her mind, looking at parts of her she didn't know she had. She was queasy looking at him, his eyes intense and dark. She swallowed a hard lump in her throat.

"Yeah, I'm okay with it," she said nervously. "How? This place is crawling with trucks."

It was true. Since pulling up she'd already seen three rigs pull in, drop their trailers, and bobtail out.

"Place shuts down around ten," Tim said. "This place doesn't have any connections, so I won't have to worry about the Chicago Outfit or anyone else. They chain up the gates at the front, no patrols around the place, doors on the main building are chained, and trailer doors are chained. Trailers are all white, no markings, it'll make it easier to stash."

He'd done some research.

"What am I here for?" she asked.

"I need you to tell me which ones are coming in empty," he said. "We can't waste time opening them all up to check, and I can't afford to get a full trailer and have to deal with what's inside."

He looked over again, as if he was sizing her up.

"Gonna need some help getting it out of here too," he said, looking off toward the truck yard. "We'll have to do this fast so we don't get caught."

"This truck's dark enough it could pass for black or blue and there's no logo on the doors. These Petes are pretty common, so it wouldn't be too easy to identify us," she said. "Trailer's gonna have numbers, but if you stash it somewhere it'll give you time to paint them over. Shut down your running lights when we go in."

Tim had a hint of a smile.

"You sure you haven't done this before, kid?"

She blushed and looked at her lap.

"We got awhile to wait before they lock up," Tim said. "Come on."

They sat in Bill's car with the radio on, since there was more room in his car than the truck cab. No one spoke much, save for Ruby pointing out which trucks were likely empty as they drove in, writing the trailer numbers on a scrap of paper. Tim had chain smoked his last four cigarettes. His knuckles were itching and his body ready to move, keyed up as usual before a job like this.

"There's the last of 'em," Bill said, watching as a lone man in a truck got out and chained up the fence before driving off.

"We'll wait five or ten minutes," Tim said. He looked over at Ruby, who was sitting forward, eyes bright, looking intently at all the trailers.

"Where are you going to keep it?" she asked.

He was startled by the stark paleness of her skin in the moonlight, framed by her black hair.

"I thought you'd have figured it out by now." He watched her lips and wished he had another cigarette—anything to keep his own mouth busy.

Her brow wrinkled.

"The barn," she said. "You're going to stash it in the barn?"

Tim grinned wickedly.

"Rett's gonna kill you if he finds out," she said.

"Everett's gonna do nothing of the sort," Tim said. "Come on."

Bill grabbed a pair of bolt cutters and headed for the front gate, while Tim got in the truck and started it up. Ruby hopped in the passenger seat. It took Bill seconds to cut through the chain lock and swing the gates open. He jumped on the truck runners and held the grab bar as Tim drove into the yard.

Tim swung up the left hand side of the truck yard, passing rows and rows of trailers, all backed in to the docks.

"There!" Ruby pointed to a trailer at the left and read off the number. "That was one of the empties."

Tim lined the tractor up and, under Ruby's instruction, backed it up and hooked up the fifth wheel. Tim got out and hooked up the hoses, while Ruby cranked up the landing gear on one side and Bill did the other.

"Check the trailer anyway." Bill went to check. Tim turned to Ruby. "Make sure we're good to go."

He saw her nod and smile slightly before heading around the front of the truck, looking for all the world like she was having the time of her life.

"It's empty, just a few wooden palettes inside," Bill said. "I locked the doors up without the chain lock."

"Good," Tim said. "Let's make this quick."

"I'll keep an eye out from my car," Bill said.

Ruby was coming around the front of the truck.

"Everything's clear, we're ready to go," she said. Tim nodded and Ruby climbed in the truck through the driver's side, sliding over to her own seat.

Tim hadn't shut the truck down and he shifted into gear the moment he shut the door.

"Swing a bit to your right before you turn left. Remember, you're over sixty feet long now," Ruby said.

Tim swore as he pulled the truck out, the weight of the trailer surprising and the bulk of it difficult to direct. He had to back up twice to avoid hitting things before moving forwards to the gate. He had to shift so many times thanks to the weight, and it frustrated him.

He looked into the left mirror. "Shit."

"What?" Ruby asked. A man, waving his arms and yelling at them, was coming out of the warehouse.

"Hold on."

Ruby gripped the side of the seat as Tim floored it toward the gates.

"Slow down!" she exclaimed. "You could flip this whole rig over, you've gotta make it around this turn!"

He slowed, swinging over wide to the left and back to the right again, the truck slowly lumbering into the correct lane. She could see Tim's hands tense on the wheel as he shifted gears a handful of times then sped up along the straightaway.

"Keep your eyes out for the cops," he said grimly.

Ruby's heart hammered like she was running a hundred yard dash. She was both terrified and excited; at any moment they could be caught. She turned to Tim and noticed how relaxed he looked, controlled as ever behind the wheel, and she tried to calm down.

"Liked that, huh?" he asked, glancing over.

"Yeah," she confessed. "It was kind of exciting. Jesus, that's awful."

She saw Tim grin, then check his mirrors. She looked out her own, but could only see the side of the trailer in the darkness.

"It's about to get more exciting," Tim said grimly. "Sheriff car on our tail."

"What?"

"Stay cool," he said. They came to an intersection, and she watched Tim concentrate on manoeuvring the truck around the turn without screwing it up. He succeeded, and she let out a long breath.

"If they stop us, we're done." She twisted the piece of paper in her hands. "We've got no papers, you don't have a license, and there's no way we can out run him . . . "

"They're not gonna stop us," he said.

"You can't be sure, that man at the warehouse could've given the police the trailer number and a description of the truck, any second now he might turn on those lights and—"

"Ruby, you trust me?" Tim asked her.

"What? Well . . . yeah."

"Nothing's gonna happen," he said. "Take a look."

She moved over to look out Tim's side mirror and saw Bill's car weaving back and forth between lanes, alternately speeding up and slowing down behind them.

"What's he doing?" she asked.

Tim didn't have to answer her, as the lights and sirens of the sheriff's car went on behind them. She held her breath, watching as Bill sped past the truck in the oncoming lane, the police car behind him. The police car stopped moving, and as they approached, she saw the police officer getting out of his car to talk to Bill Pearce, who was now pulled over at the side of the road.

10

Tim took back roads the rest of the way to the ranch. It took him a few minutes to get the trailer into the barn and uncoupled. He parked the truck with the headlights pointed toward the barn so they could see what they were doing. She was about to shut the barn doors when Bill drove up and parked in the dirt next to the truck.

"They didn't arrest you?" she asked.

"A fine upstanding citizen like me?" he asked innocently. Tim snorted with laughter.

"I thought for sure they would," she confessed. They walked inside the barn, lit only by the lights from the truck outside, and Tim closed one of the doors. Ruby sat in a pile of fresh hay in a darkened corner.

"Told 'em I had a wife about to have a baby at the hospital, played like I was nervous as hell, they escorted me all the way there, lights and everything," Bill said proudly. "Went inside the hospital and waited 'til they left, then ducked out and drove over here."

"Anyone ever come in here?" Tim asked her.

"Wick does. He won't say nothing though," Ruby said. "Rett and Jake might come in. That's about it."

Tim walked around the trailer.

"You got any paint?" he asked.

"Don't think so," she said.

"I'll come by with some tomorrow," Bill said. "Paint over the numbers. Should get new plates too."

Ruby got up and walked over to the other side of the barn, feeling around under a small hay bale. She pulled out the flat bed trailer plates and held them out.

"I thought I told you to put those back?" Tim asked, his forehead creased.

"The flat bed was gone when I came to put 'em back, another one here with plates of its own," Ruby said. "Good thing too. Now you've got these."

Bill flashed her a grin. She watched Tim nervously. He looked at the plates she was holding and rubbed his chin.

"Guess they'll do," he said. He reached out and took them. Ruby bit her lip to stop from smiling.

She walked back to the pile of loose hay and crashed into it, starting to come down from the high of stealing a trailer.

"That was wild," she said, more to herself than anyone.

Tim and Bill were sharply outlined in front of her. Ruby studied Tim's face, his right side positioned toward her. His features were sharply chiseled, and she felt the queasiness return as she admired his face. She had the unnerving feeling he was watching her watch him.

He and Bill wandered over to her, and Tim put the plates on a stack of hay. He held out his hand to Ruby. She took it tentatively, surprised at the strength in his fingers as they closed around her own. He pulled her out of the hay, and they stood looking at each other for a moment, his hand still closed around hers.

"I think it's time I got to sleep," Bill said. "You need a ride, Tim?"

"I'm taking the truck." His gaze was still on Ruby. The barn was hot and close.

"See ya later." Bill slipped outside, pulling the other barn door shut on his way out. They were blanketed in darkness, save for the slivers of light filing through the wood slats. They stood together without speaking, listening to the engine of Bill's Chevy start up and roar down the street. The idling of the truck's diesel engine was the only sound left.

"It's blacker than midnight under a skillet in here," Ruby said, breaking the tense silence. Tim still had hold of her hand.

She looked up, and a beam of light hit Tim's face, highlighting one pale green eye looking into her own. He was so close she could smell his aftershave. He pulled her into the darkness and backed her up against the trailer. Tim's hand slid tentatively up her arm and into her hair, then cupped her cheek.

His mouth was anything but tentative when it met hers.

He kissed her deeply, his hand woven into her hair. Every cell in her body felt like it was stampeding as she kissed him back, and she wondered how on earth she'd lived nineteen years and never felt like this before now. His other arm slipped around her waist, and he ran both hands down her back, pulling her hips toward him as he backed her up more firmly against the trailer. She slipped her hands around the back of his neck, her breath catching as he kissed her, his mouth hot on her skin.

She brought a hand to his face, and he stilled beneath her touch as she ran her finger slowly across one of the scars, then let her fingers slip over his lips, tracing the scar on his chin. She trailed her lips along the scar under his eye.

"You've done that before," he said, his voice husky in her ear.

"Yes." Her breath was coming in sharp gasps.

"At Everett's. The night I got slashed. I remember now."

His hand was on her face again, brushing her hair back. His lips hovered above hers before crashing down on them, leaving her breathless. She kissed him back, relishing the slow way he explored her mouth. She wondered when she was going to catch fire.

She was drawn out of the moment by loud crashes from the stable. She broke their kiss, Tim's forehead pressed against her own.

"That horse ... Midnight Bandit," she said, finding it difficult to talk. "I think the engine's getting to him. I'd best let him loose in the paddock, or he'll break down the stall door."

Tim slowly released his hold on her, and she hesitated in leaving his arms.

"Go on," he said. "I'll turn the truck off."

Ruby wasn't sure her legs would make it across the small dirt yard to the stable, but they did. She felt like she'd been thrown out of an airplane.

Bandit was kicking up his heels in the stall, bobbing his head and dancing around impatiently. She had to talk to him for a few minutes to calm him enough to slip the halter on. He balked as she opened the stall door, and she held the lead firmly so he wouldn't run.

Tim had shut the truck down, and it was silent now. The stable was in near darkness, just two bare light bulbs glowed in the cavernous room. She led the horse outside and let him loose in the paddock, where he ran and danced around as if he'd been set on fire.

"You ready?"

She turned quickly, surprised by his voice so near her. She hadn't heard him walk up behind her. The moon was out, highlighting his face, and she felt like blushing as she looked at him and remembered the way his mouth felt on hers.

"Ruby?"

"Yeah, I'm ready," she said, looking him in the eye. He turned slowly and walked away. She cut through the stable, following behind him and stopping to pet Bella on the nose. She shut the two dim lights off, locked up the doors, and followed Tim toward the truck.

They drove back to Everett's in silence. She smoothed a few threads on her jeans, picked at a hang nail and stared out the window, her mind unable to come up with anything worth saying.

"You don't gotta be so nervous around me, kid," Tim said, his voice startling her.

"I'm not. And I thought I told you I wasn't a kid," she said.

His eyes were twinkling. "I could tell."

She blushed again, glad he couldn't see in the darkened truck. He pulled in the lot at Everett's a few minutes later and cut the truck engine. He opened his door, and she followed suit, climbing out of the truck cab. Tim walked her up to the front stairs.

"You working tomorrow night?" he asked.

"On Friday," she said.

"That's tomorrow," he said with a grin.

"Oh," she said dumbly, realizing it was far past midnight. "Yeah."

She stood perfectly still, her gaze trained on the leather jacket he was wearing. A moment later he put his finger under her chin and tilted her head up.

"Gonna invite me in?" A wicked smile played on his mouth.

She looked away and smiled. "Maybe another time."

He stood there for a second, then laughed. "See ya later, kid."

She only let him get about three steps before she rushed down the stairs, took his hand, and pulled him toward her. He must have been waiting for her to do it; his mouth was on hers before she had a chance to say anything.

"Bye," she said a moment later. She watched him get in the truck and drive away, the tail lights disappearing down the road.

Thursday, May 12, 1966

Ruby woke up early, her sleep punctuated with dreams of Tim. She hardly believed he'd kissed her last night; all this time she'd wondered if he even liked her a little bit.

She got out of bed and hummed as she put breakfast on. Everett roused himself awhile later and showered, then sat at the table and watched her with a suspicious gaze.

"What the heck's got you so cheerful?" Everett asked, as Ruby slid freshly cooked bacon onto his plate alongside over-easy eggs, slices of wheat toast, and freshly squeezed orange juice.

She hadn't showered yet. The smell of Tim's cologne still clung to her skin.

"Can't I just be in a good mood?"

"On four hours sleep? Don't think I didn't hear you sneaking up here at one thirty in the morning." Everett shovelled a forkful of eggs in his mouth.

"I was not sneaking, I came in just regular." Her face felt hot.

"What were you out doing until that hour?" Everett asked. He squeezed the bridge of his nose. "Did he get you in the casinos? Maybe I don't wanna know."

"Nothing like that," she said. "You don't see me asking about your sex life, why are you quizzing me about mine?"

Everett choked on his orange juice, and Ruby slapped him hard on the back.

"What? Don't tell me you're sleeping with Tim Kelly," Everett said. "I don't wanna hear it. Unless you aren't, then I wanna hear that. Tell me that, even if it's a lie."

"I'm not sleeping with him," she said. "But if I *was*, I wouldn't go telling you."

"Dammit, Ruby," Everett said, rubbing his fingers against his temples. He pushed his chair back from the table. "You remember visiting me in El Paso when you was a kid? You were about eight I'd guess, I was seventeen or so, right before I left home. Our daddy dropped you at my folks' place for two weeks without a word? Your mama was in Mobile with her parents."

Ruby shifted uncomfortably in her chair. "I don't know."

She didn't like thinking about that time, everyone scattered to the wind. They'd been tight on money all her life, but that time was different with her mother starting to get sick.

"You followed me all over the damn place, wouldn't leave me alone for five minutes," he said. "Kept asking if he was coming back for you. I started feeling sorry for you, and when my stepfather was getting agitated with you for fussing so much, I took you with me near the creek, you remember?"

"You played house with me," she said with a smile. "In a stand of trees, like a fort. You snuck one of your mom's aprons for me to wear, you brought all this broken china and let me make you pretend tea all afternoon."

She forgot all about that. She'd polished up that broken china like it was brand new. Everett's gaze was sad.

"Ruby, I've seen trouble all my life. I took you outta there because my stepdad would've beat your head in like he did mine. He may have been a war hero big shot on the outside, but inside was something different. All that broken china . . . my mother's broken china. He'd dash it all over the damn place. I picked up every piece, thinking I could put it all back together again, but I never could."

"Everett, what's this got to do with me?" she said gently.

"Nothing . . . everything," he said. "Look—to me, you're still that eight-year-old kid following me around that I gotta make sure don't get clobbered.

101

Every time you visited after that, I felt like I had to watch out for you, and that hasn't changed."

Ruby sighed. He wasn't so bad sometimes.

"I'm not gonna get clobbered," Ruby said. "Tim's been nothing but nice to me. A real gentleman."

She ignored Everett's snort of laughter.

"And anyway, it's not like I came here pure as the driven snow," she said pointedly, noticing the distasteful look on Everett's face. "I like him, and I'm gonna spend time with him. You can't go tellin' me what to do."

"No, I can't," he said seriously. "Just be careful, Ruby. I don't wanna be trying to put broken china back together again."

Ruby walked to the stable after her odd breakfast with Everett and rode Bella for awhile, trying to get her mind off Tim and the conversation with her brother. She was interrupted by Bill showing up before noon.

"Brought some paint," he said cheerfully as he walked into the stable. "You wanna show me what I'm supposed to cover up on this thing?"

"Sure." She lead him out to the gambrel-roofed barn.

Bill quickly changed the trailer plates, and Ruby hid the ones he took off. She pointed out which numbers on the trailer were company ones that might identify the trailer and Bill painted over them.

"You've known Tim a long time, huh?" Ruby asked as she dipped a small paintbrush in the can of white paint and sloshed it over the trailer number.

"Since we were kids," Bill answered.

"Has he always been like that?"

"Like what?"

"I dunno," Ruby said. "Controlled, I guess. Like he's never wasted a moment in his whole life."

"Best person to ask about Tim Kelly is Tim Kelly," Bill said matter-of-factly. "I'm not promising he'll answer though."

"He reminds me of the Cheshire cat," she said. "Always lookin' like he knows things you don't."

"He usually does."

Ruby finished painting over the numbers and crouched to set the paintbrush on the lip of the can.

"Ain't this cozy," a voice said, interrupting her thoughts. Jake Wheeler stood in the doorway, a cigarette hanging out of his mouth.

"You step in here with that cigarette and I swear I'll make you eat it," she said.

"Ain't lit, don't get your panties in a twist," he said irritably.

"I think I'm all done here," Bill said. "See you tonight?"

"Yeah, I'll be working," Ruby said. Bill slipped out the barn doors.

"This the trailer he snagged?" Jake asked.

"No, it's another stolen trailer," Ruby said sarcastically. "We keep hundreds hidden around here in case we need them."

"You've got an attitude problem." Jake stepped closer to her. "I might have to adjust it."

"Yeah, you've got a lying like a bastard problem." Ruby stepped past him and lifted few sections of hay into a wheelbarrow. "I know Tim didn't try and slit your throat."

Jake chuckled as he walked over to her.

"You think it's funny?" she asked.

"What, that you're all put out I blamed Tim for this?" He gestured toward his neck. "Yeah, it's kinda funny."

"You're lower than a snake's belly." Ruby turned away from him.

"You're real hard up for Kelly, huh?" Jake said. He pressed up behind her. She picked up the handles of the wheelbarrow, then Jake leaned close to her ear. "You oughta let someone better equipped show you a thing or two. You'd forget about Kelly in a real hurry."

She shrugged away from him, dismayed her heart was racing and her legs trembling.

"I figure your girl would take exception to it," Ruby said.

Jake laughed again as she moved toward the door. "Funny . . . you didn't say you would."

Ruby hurriedly left Jake in the barn, his low laughter following her out.

Friday, May 13, 1966

Everett's place was packed with people.

Ruby had never seen it so busy, but luckily Jed was behind the bar picking up her slack and she had some time to enjoy herself.

She had fussed over her clothes so long before coming downstairs Everett had about skinned her. He'd taken one look at her short skirt and rolled his eyes before heading into a poker game.

She kept her eyes open for Tim, but it was late when he arrived.

Bill entered first, followed by Tim and a group of boys she was starting to recognize. Ray Roth was still there, for unfathomable reasons to her. Jimmy Lewis rivalled him in the looks department, but he was a big flirt from what she could see. Carl Hamilton was a hulking man who didn't talk much. He and Pete Hamilton, a pale, nervous type, hung out with Ray most, and so she avoided them. Adam Barnes was good-natured and strong, always arm wrestling at the tables. Jesse Lennox was the youngest, and despite his propensity for getting in fights, she liked his guileless nature.

She noticed Tim's knuckles were raw and bleeding. He sat at the bar and noticed her gaze.

"Someone's face needed punching."

She hoped it was Jake Wheeler's.

"You got any good stuff back there?" Jesse asked. "Tim says you keep some for him."

Ruby tried not to blush, wondering how much people were talking about her and Tim. She went into the back and found a bottle of Pearl and placed the beer in front of Jesse.

"Your knuckles are startin' to bleed," she said quietly to Tim. He nodded.

"Think I busted a stitch or two," he said, taking a drink of Jesse's beer. He stood, walked behind the bar, and took her hand. "C'mon."

Tim led her up the stairs, and Ruby stole a glance at Everett. His face was reminiscent of a storm cloud. She followed Tim up to the third floor and was shocked to see him take out a key and open the door to the apartment.

"Where did you get that?" she asked.

He shut the door behind them and backed her up against it, pressing his body against hers. Her pulse quickened, and her stomach stirred.

"Had it for awhile now," he murmured, his hands on her hips.

"Oh." She was vaguely aware she should be angry about it. His lips hovered above hers, and she was weak with the need to taste them.

"What's with the skirt?" he asked, his fingers brushing against the skin at her waist.

"Thought I'd try something different," she said. "I feel like I'm in a Halloween costume."

"So you gonna patch me up or what?" His eyes were full of mirth.

"In a minute." She pulled on the lapel of his jacket. He lowered his mouth to hers and brushed her lips lightly with his own. Ruby slipped her hands behind his neck and pulled him closer. He didn't need more encouragement than that and kissed her deeply, pressing her firmly against the door. She put her hands over his shoulders and helped him as he shrugged his jacket off.

She ran her hands down his arms, and he pulled her away from the wall. She reached for his t-shirt, and he broke their kiss for a second, looking at her seductively.

"If I'm gonna patch you up ..." she said innocently.

He pulled the shirt off himself. Her hands fluttered nervously across his chest and she circled her arms around his neck, kissing him again. He pulled her toward the couch.

She opened her eyes as her leg hit the armrest, and Tim winced as he tried to lower them both to the couch. She glanced at his mid-section.

"Lordy, you really did bust a few stitches," she said, running a hand down his chest, her fingers caressing the skin above the sutures. Tim inhaled sharply as her fingers lightly ran across his rib cage.

"I'll get a first aid kit," she said.

She walked toward the bathroom on shaky legs, her skin flushed and heart pounding.

Tim leaned back on the couch before she returned. She hadn't seen his back yet, and he wasn't in the mood for questions about the myriad of scars. He looked at the slash—it was healing, but he'd busted at least two stitches where the cut was deepest, and it was weeping blood. Eddie Demarco had made a smart comment about Ruby in the parking lot, and Tim made short work of his face.

Ruby returned a minute later with antiseptic, some tissues, and tweezers. He could see how hard she was breathing, her cheeks still flushed pink, and he decided it would be nice to see her that way more often. She sat on the floor beside the couch.

"This is gonna hurt." She wet a tissue with some antiseptic. She dabbed at the wound, and he bit his lip to keep from wincing.

She straightened up and looked at his jagged stitch job.

"I think you just broke two," she said. "I can try and tie the ends if I can grab them with the tweezers."

"Do what you have to," he said. He inhaled sharply as she bent her head over his wound, her hair sweeping his stomach and her breath warm on his skin. He was so distracted he could barely feel her pull on the broken stitches.

"What time do you have to get to Los Angeles?" she asked. He watched her loop the tiny threads around into a knot at each end with a pair of tweezers.

"Before noon," he said. "I'll be leaving early."

"When should I be ready?"

"Ready for what? I'm going by myself," he said.

"You can't," she told him, raising her head up and looking at him.

He raised an eyebrow. "I'm willing to bet I can."

"You need someone with you who knows what they're doing," she said.

Tim felt the back of his neck prickle.

"Ruby, you're not coming." He swung his legs over and sat up.

"You still need me," she said. "There's so much stuff you still don't know—"

"I said you're not coming. I'm not gonna say it again."

"I get it, you think you can do it all yourself, huh? Well, you can't, and that's a fact."

"Ruby, why are you doing this?" He could feel a headache coming on. "It's taken me three damn weeks to get you out of my business so we could have a little fun, and here you are sticking your nose right back in it."

"A little fun?" she said, her voice trapped between hurt and confusion. "That's all? Well ... you can't do this yourself, you don't have a commercial license."

He reached into his back pocket, pulled out his wallet, and took the card out to show her.

"Where'd you get this?" she asked. She handed the Class A commercial license, with his name and picture on it, back to him. He didn't bother answering her.

"I'm not going anywhere," he said. "You don't need to be involved in this for me to spend time with you."

"I'm not doin' this to spend time with you," she said. Her cheeks turned pink. "Although it was a nice consequence of helping you."

She got up and walked into a bedroom, and a few seconds later she came out holding an armful of booklets.

"Log book." She slammed it on the table. She picked up another from the stack in her arms. "Vehicle inspection report. Shipment record. Mileage record. Bill of lading."

He looked at the booklets and papers impassively.

"When you blow on past the scales and they send the cops after you, what'll you tell them?" she asked. "When you pull into the scales and your load is overweight on one axle, how do you correct it? They won't let you roll until you do, and seeing a driver who doesn't know what he's doin' is gonna send up red flags. If they ask to see the log books you don't know how to fill out, ticket you, and discover your license ain't real, then what'll you do? If you're in California you can't distribute weight by moving the tandems. Tell me what tandems are, Tim!"

Anger bubbled up in his chest and he took a few breaths to control himself. He should've gotten the trailer a lot sooner. She should have shown him all this damn stuff before, for Christ's sake. He flipped through the log book and reports, all of it looking like Chinese to him.

"Tim, you need me." She sat down on the coffee table and faced him. "Trucking's a lot of paperwork, and you could get in a lot of trouble if you don't have it done up right. Let me come, at least for this one trip, to show you the ropes."

"Ruby ..." he said, rubbing his hands over his face. He had no idea what kind of game she was running, keeping all of this stuff from him. He sat back against the couch. "You sure you're not doing this on purpose?"

She looked up. "I'm not the one that got a trailer with only days to spare. It's not on purpose."

She was looking at him with those doe eyes, and he saw the flicker of want in her eyes. She was hungry to come on this trip, and it likely had nothing to do with paperwork. He took a breath, trying to control the sudden need he felt. His gaze flicked toward her bedroom door.

"There's only one bed in the back of that truck, Ruby," he said. He looked her in the eye, making sure she understood what coming along on this trip meant.

"I know."

He thought through the various scenarios.

If he didn't take her, he'd to risk messing up the truck or being tossed in jail if they caught him running without all that stuff she'd said. He'd lose everything right from the get-go if that happened, and there was no way the Californians would ever work with him again.

If he did bring her he knew he wouldn't be able to stay away from her. They'd end up in bed before the weekend was out, and he couldn't guarantee he'd be keeping his mind on business if she was underneath him every night.

"Shit," he said with feeling. He grabbed his t-shirt off the couch and pulled it on before he stood. "I'll pick you up after seven."

11

"Are you out of your ever-lovin' mind?"

Ruby cringed at Everett's voice. It was after seven in the morning, and he surprised her by waking up early, despite his late night of partying. She was sure he'd be so hungover he wouldn't get out of bed for hours and she could slip out, leave a note and avoid the lecture altogether.

Instead, she came out of her room with a bag packed and he asked her where she thought she was going. She told him straight up she had to go with Tim to help him with the truck.

"You're kidding yourself if you think all he wants you along for is to help with a truck," Everett said derisively.

"I ain't kidding myself about any of this," Ruby said. "I know what I'm doing."

"Ruby, he's dangerous, he's gonna get you in trouble," Everett said.

"The police can't arrest me for anything," she said. "I'm just a passenger."

"That's not the kinda trouble I mean," Everett said.

"Oh, for cryin' out loud!" Ruby exclaimed. She put a few bottles of Coke in the bag with the sandwiches she made the night before.

"Ruby, you think you're the only girl Tim Kelly has?" Everett asked her seriously.

She thought for a moment. Tim was handsome in his own way, if you ignored the strange, scarred half of his face. She saw how the girls looked at him, a mixture of fear and longing. There were a few that looked at him with more familiarity than she liked. She didn't doubt he had his share of girls.

"No, I'm probably not." She wondered how she could ensure she would be after the trip was done.

"You don't want a guy who ain't gonna respect you," Everett said.

"What, like my boyfriend in Abilene? He wasn't real interested in me until we went all the way. Tim's treated me with more respect than Lewis ever did. All he cared about was makin' sure everyone knew he was doing it."

"Why'd you go with someone like that?"

"I dunno, maybe I wanted to see what all the fuss was about. Why am I having this conversation with you?" She looked up at the ceiling and sighed. She picked the bag up. "I'll be back soon, it's only to Los Angeles, I think."

"You think? Ruby, don't do this," Everett said.

"Make sure someone exercises Bella, and tell Wick to watch Rigel, he looked a bit colicky the other day." She headed to the door. She shut the door behind her and went down the stairs, Everett's voice echoing in her ears.

Tim pulled into the lot with the tractor and spotted Ruby standing outside, a bag at her feet. She walked over to the truck, opened the passenger door, and climbed in.

"Hi," she said brightly. Tim looked over and nodded.

"You're still mad," she said.

"I'm not mad," he told her evenly.

Tim drove the tractor toward Everett's ranch. She went into the back and stowed food she brought. At least she thought of food. The only thing he thought to bring were blankets and pillows for the bed, and that showed him where his mind was at. This was going to be a long trip.

They didn't speak as he pulled in near the barn. Ruby got out of the truck wordlessly and opened the barn doors. He backed the tractor up and expertly aligned it with the trailer.

"It's a lot easier pulling out of here than backing in." Her voice was subdued.

Ruby followed him when he went to attach the hoses and crank up the landing gear. He had to say something to get that look off her face.

"This is a business trip, Ruby. I can't blow this."

"You won't." She tilted her head up towards him. He moved to avoid her lips. Five minutes; that was all it took for business to be shoved right out of his head and be replaced with thoughts of doing her up against the truck. He ignored her crestfallen expression.

"You really are mad," she said.

"Dammit Ruby, I'm not mad," he said. "This is business. It's not time for fun."

He watched her for a second and felt like kicking the shit out of someone as he saw her jaw line harden.

"Business it is, then," she said, her voice steady. "I'll show you how to mark the log books."

Coming on this trip was a huge mistake.

Tim almost took out a carload of people as he merged onto the highway. She screeched at him to use his mirrors, and he laid on the horn like nobody's business. She'd never seen a car move out of the way so fast.

Things were okay since then. There were no weigh scales to worry about since they were empty. The highway was a pretty easy drive, and she relaxed as Tim got more and more comfortable with the size of the truck.

The scenery flew by on the highway; dead trees, sand, and desert the only things out there. They maintained an uneasy silence.

"Look, I'm sorry," she said. She looked over toward Tim and saw him glance her way. "I should've shown you all the paperwork and what to do. I should've taken you out on the highway before. Then I wouldn't have had to come."

"Why didn't you?" he asked.

She shrugged and looked at the windshield, studying the bugs splattered on it.

"I guess I liked being needed," she said.

She saw Tim glance over out of the corner of her eye.

"It was the only time I felt like I was ever doing any good," she said. "My daddy was gone so much, he'd give me over to relatives after my mom died and go on the road. One summer I couldn't take it; I begged him to take me. I took care of everything on the road, and for the first time I felt like I was close to him. It was nice until we got the ranch. I ran that place, since he was gone so much, but it wasn't the same."

"You run stuff around Everett's," Tim said. "You do for him."

"Rett gives me things to do to keep me busy; whole place runs without me," Ruby said. "It was nice having *you* need me is what I meant. I get the feeling you don't need people very much. It made me feel special."

He was quiet for a minute.

"We get down to Los Angeles and you'll have to stay out of the way." Tim lit a cigarette. "Don't go telling them I don't know what I'm doing. I said otherwise."

"You know what you're doing for the most part," Ruby acknowledged. "What are you hauling?"

"Could be anything," Tim said. "Don't go asking. You're to stay outta the way."

"I got it," she said. She yawned and looked out at the vast expanse before them.

"Go lie down in back if you're tired," he said.

"Nope," she told him. "My first rule of driving is that I'm up when the driver's up. Ain't no fair if I get to rest and he doesn't. I've still got a lot to tell you about the paperwork anyway."

She settled into her seat and took out the inspection report booklet, ready to school Tim Kelly.

They arrived at the address, northwest of Los Angeles in Calabasas, right before noon. Tim pulled the truck off the main road and onto a dusty secondary road until coming to the ranch and driving through imposing gates with a brand on them.

Tim stopped the truck short of some outbuildings, and Ruby jumped down from the passenger seat in awe before he cut the engine.

"Oh wow," she said.

The grass was brilliantly green despite the sandy landscape of the hills around them. The white post and rail fences spoke of money, but the only thing that held her interest was the giant stable, brand new and fit for a king. There was even a tall green silo nearby. She saw cowboys out in the corral with purebred Quarter horses, their hind legs working hard as they practiced cutting.

There were Arabians in a paddock close by and Thoroughbreds being exercised in a riding ring. There were two gambrel-roofed barns, painted red with white trim, and in the distance was a gorgeous mansion of a farmhouse complete with a wrap-around porch. She hurried over to the fence and stepped up on the lowest of the four rails. She looked around the ranch in awe—it was as if it had stepped straight out of her dreams.

"Ruby!" Tim hissed her name.

A curious dapple grey Arabian trotted over to her and sniffed her head, playfully nipping at her hair as it blew in a light breeze.

"You're a beauty." She nuzzled the horse.

"Ruby!"

Tim grabbed her roughly by the upper arm, and she looked at him in annoyance as he pulled her off the fence and half-dragged her back toward the truck. She could see two men coming out of the large barn closest to them.

"I told you to mind me," Tim said.

"You're hurting my arm!" she said. He didn't apologize, but he did loosen his grip. As the men approached, he slid his hand down and took hers in his own.

He let her hand go to shake with the younger man first—the one who called himself Insane Wayne. Stupid nickname if she ever heard one. He was likely Everett's age and wore jeans and a western shirt, shiny Tony Lama cowboy boots, and a big Texas belt buckle. He had a weather-beaten look about him, but she doubted he could ride a horse.

The other man may have been older, but it was hard to tell with the moustache. He was wearing a western jacket, open enough that she could see the two guns he wore—one on his hip, the other in a shoulder holster. They looked as big as the one Everett kept under the bar.

"Wayne, Roy," Tim said, nodding at them.

"Who's the broad?" Wayne asked. She resisted the urge to shudder.

"My girl, Ruby," Tim said. "She ain't gonna be a problem."

Ruby stopped herself from smiling. Even if he had said it to explain away her presence . . . well, he still said it. She resisted the urge to turn a cartwheel.

Wayne nodded, then turned and looked at the truck, walking the length of the trailer.

"We'll have you leave this one here," he said. "You'll be hauling a new refrigerated unit."

Ruby looked over at Tim, but he didn't get this was a big deal. Refrigerator units were pretty new on the market, and they were expensive. She was pretty sure these guys weren't into hauling grocery items for that kind of money.

"We need to speak about a few things," Wayne said, glancing her way. Roy, a hand resting near the gun at his hip, still hadn't spoken a word. "Reefer truck isn't scheduled to show up for another few hours, then we'll load the merchandise."

Tim nodded. Ruby saw a young Mexican woman walking toward them. The woman said something in Spanish to the men, and Roy nodded.

"We can talk over lunch," Wayne said, looking again at Ruby.

Tim took some money out of his pocket and handed a few bills to Ruby.

"She's tired," he said. "Gonna hole up in that motel we saw down the road. I suspect this'll take some time?"

"You'll be out of here sometime tonight," Insane Wayne said.

Ruby took the money wordlessly, angry that she was being shoved off while Tim got to eat a nice lunch. She watched the Mexican girl out of the corner of her eye. The girl was watching Tim with curious intensity. Tim walked with Ruby toward the cab of the truck, got her bag out, and handed it to her.

"Tim," she began, trying to think of a good argument against her leaving. He studied her with steely eyes.

"Go on," he said.

She let her shoulders droop. She was not looking forward to spending the day in a dirty motel room. She tried to think of something to say that would make him change his mind.

Tim sighed. "Let me put it in words you'll understand: Time to paint your butt white and run with the antelope."

Ruby bit her lip to keep from laughing. Her grandmother in Mobile used to say that to her when she wanted her to stop whining and do what she was told. "How long have you been saving that Southern gem for?"

"Since I met you." The hint of a smile was on his lips. "Go on. I'll come and get you when I can. Tell the manager to hold a key for me."

She hesitated a second. "These guys are no more cowboys than you are."

"Ruby . . . go on," he said again.

He leaned over, kissed her on the cheek, and walked off without a look back. The Mexican woman smiled broadly at Ruby then turned and followed the men.

Ruby sighed, picked her bag up, and began the long walk down the road to the motel.

Tim was surprised Ruby went as quietly as she did. The Mexican girl sidled up to him the minute Ruby was out of view and walked with an arm linked in his own as they approached the sprawling white house in the distance. They reached the wraparound porch and sat at a circular table.

The woman snaked her arms around Insane Wayne's neck before he sent her to fetch the food.

Tim glanced at the prison tattoo on Wayne's forearm, mostly hidden under the rolled-up sleeves of his shirt. He could tell it was a prison tat from the ink.

"How long were you in?" Tim struck a match on the table and lit his cigarette.

"Two years," Wayne said. "You?"

"Long enough," Tim said. He spent more time in Clark County lockup and the Las Vegas City jail than the state prison, but a cell was a cell.

They stopped talking as the Mexican girl brought out food and set plates on the table. Tim felt her brush close to him. She took cloth napkins from a basket she was holding and draped one over his lap, her hand running up his thigh. She set out the utensils then served the food. Before she left she slipped an arm around Wayne's shoulder and kissed him on the earlobe.

"Rosa's a hellcat in the sack," Wayne said. "It'll be a bit of a wait 'til the reefer trailer's here, you can have at 'er if you want."

Tim tried to mask the disgust he felt at Insane Wayne trying to pawn off his whore on him. Girls like that were something he didn't want to look at thanks to his old man. He remembered those trips along the US 95 into the desert, the long arguments at home that followed, sometimes the broken china and the fists and crying. Anyone who had to go to a whore for a good time had a problem. Wayne was looking at him expectantly.

"I'd be dealing with a hellcat of my own if I did that," Tim said, glad he could use Ruby as an excuse.

"She looked like a bit of a firecracker," Wayne said. "Me, I like girls that know when to shut it and do what they're told."

"This place yours?" Tim was eager to change the subject so he wouldn't feel so much like punching Wayne in the face.

"My old man's," Wayne said shortly. "Laid up with a stroke. Place'll be mine now."

Tim didn't miss the low noise Roy made at that. He didn't think Roy had said a word, even when they met in Las Vegas. But if there was one thing Tim learned, it was that sometimes the quiet ones knew the most.

He studied Wayne carefully as they ate. Ruby was likely right, Wayne dressed the part, but he didn't fit in with this ranch. Neither did Roy. He could picture Wayne in a pool hall, a prison cell, a dingy bar, or a whore house, but not on horseback around this place. But then, Jake had never looked like the horse type, either, and the bastard rode like a son of bitch.

"You'll be hauling something over to Phoenix tonight." Wayne wiped his mouth with the napkin and dropped it on the porch deck. "Got a few clients in town, so you'll have to deliver to three different places. Got it all outlined in the paperwork. Roy'll take you down, you can move your trailer in the empty barn 'til you're back next week. Need you on the twentieth."

Tim nodded and watched as Rosa came out to clear the table. She bent over seductively to pick up the napkin Wayne had dropped, a grin on his face as he watched. Tim blew the smoke out of the corner of his mouth and got up from the table wordlessly, following Roy back toward the barn and stable.

They walked in silence until they were far enough from the house.

"His old man's dying, and Wayne is ignorant thinking he's getting this spread, so don't go thinking you'll be making the big bucks with us for long," Roy said, lighting a thin cigar as they walked. He had a Midwestern accent, and it surprised him. "Got an older brother who's in tight with the old man. He won't give this place up to his ex-con son. This operation could fold up pretty fast if that happens and it'd take awhile to get it running again. It's a small piece of a big pie."

"How long's the old man got?" he asked.

Roy shrugged, puffing on his cigar. "Doc doesn't give him more than a couple months."

"Well, let's make me some money in the meantime, then," Tim said grimly.

Tim walked toward the door of the motel, hearing noise from the television inside. It was after midnight and things took longer than he expected.

It took him forever to get the truck backed into the barn Roy showed him to. Lucky for him Roy had walked back to the house and there hadn't been anyone around to witness the escapade. He was sure going to have to improve his skills in backing up with a trailer.

Tim received all the paperwork detailing which customer in Phoenix got what and stashed it in the truck. The refrigerated trailer hadn't shown up until seven at night. They had a quick dinner back at the house, Rosa eyeing him the whole time and making blatant sexual movements while she served their dinner. She was annoyed Tim showed no interest in her. If anything, it emboldened her.

He finished two beers before he noticed Wayne looking at him weird, like he thought something was up since he'd shown no interest in the chick. He didn't want Wayne thinking he was some queer. The girl rubbed against him as she lit a cigarette for him. So he backed her up against the porch railing and whispered the most insulting thing he could remember in Spanish. The Californians had a good laugh when she hauled off and slapped him before stalking into the house like she wasn't a goddamn whore.

They capped off the night with a shot of bourbon and the taste of it turned Tim's stomach.

It took nearly four hours for them to load all of the beer into the refrigerated truck, since the forklift was broken, and they had to do it by hand. Tim crawled in his skin, itching to get onto the road. They paid him half for the run upfront, promising the rest when he returned the next Friday. He walked to the motel in a hurry to get the hell out of Calabasas.

He turned the key he got from the manager and the motel door opened with a creak. The room was dark, lit only by the black and white flickers from the television screen. He shut the door and walked toward the bed, turning on a small lamp. He turned the television off, then walked back to the bed. Ruby was curled under the covers like a caterpillar in its cocoon.

"Ruby," he whispered, sitting on the edge of the bed.

She didn't stir. He brushed a few stray hairs off her cheek and leaned close to her ear.

"Ruby," he said.

She flinched and grabbed his hand, which was still on her face. Her skin was cool and pale. He could never figure out how someone who spent so much time outside could be so pale.

"Tim?" Her eyes sleepily focused on him.

"Time to get going," he said.

"What time is it?"

"Past midnight," he said. "We gotta be in Phoenix in the morning, we'll be driving all night."

He made it sound like they were in a hurry, but he still hadn't moved.

"Come on, get up," he said. Then, as an afterthought, he added, "Kid."

She smiled knowingly. "Now you're tryin' to get a rise outta me."

"Only fair," he answered. "You're getting one outta me."

She smiled softly and surprised him by leaning up and kissing him. She was wearing one of her sleeveless western shirts again, only this time there was nothing underneath but her bra. He deepened the kiss, exploring her mouth with slow deliberateness and sliding a hand around her back, the feel of her bare skin making him reckless.

She slid a hand behind his neck and pulled him onto the bed with her. His fingers slipped under the edge of her shirt, pushing it up her ribcage. He felt himself sinking onto the bed with her.

Keep your feet on the damn floor Tim, he thought to himself. If he didn't, the only thing that would be on the floor would be their clothes. He still had to get to Phoenix.

He braced his arm against the bed and broke their kiss.

"We gotta roll, Ruby." He was surprised at how much regret was in his voice. He took her hand, then stood, pulling her gently out of the bed.

"You're frustrating," she said, in a mock-petulant voice. Her cheeks were flushed pink as she inched her shirt back down.

A maddening ache strained against his jeans, and he tried to push all thoughts of her out of his head.

"You have no idea," he said quietly.

12

They walked in silence down the dusty road back to the ranch. The stars were out in full force, and the air was cool. She liked being out in the country like this; it reminded her of home.

She frowned. She supposed Las Vegas was her home now, not Abilene. She wasn't sure she'd get used to thinking that.

As they reached the ranch, Ruby took a minute to go and feed the little grey Arabian the two carrots she bought at the roadside stand on the way to the motel earlier. The horse nuzzled her neck and bobbed its head, trying to poke through the fence to check her pockets.

"That's all, you cleaned me out," Ruby laughed.

She turned to walk back to the truck. Tim was leaning against it, finishing a cigarette, and watching her with a thoughtful expression.

"Don't take this wrong," he said, turning around and opening the passenger door to the truck for her, "but you kind of remind me of a horse."

"In what way?" She was secretly flattered he compared her to one. "It's not long legs and a tendency for colic."

"Steady," he said. "Like a work horse. I saw you watching those boys with their guns when we got here—you didn't flinch one bit."

"I'm from Texas. We all have guns."

He hid a grin. "Even so. And when we stole that trailer, you were on the ball. Takes a lot to spook you, I think."

Ruby climbed into the truck and looked at Tim. "Same could be said for you."

He shut the door and walked around the front of the truck to the driver's side and climbed in.

"I still can't believe they have a refrigerated trailer," Ruby said, watching him start up the diesel engine. "They're expensive."

"Yeah, well, there's a whole lot of beer in there," he said.

They were silent for the next little while as they navigated out of Calabasas and filled up at a diesel station on the way out of town. Ruby held on to the maps and directed Tim to the part of the highway that would take them toward Arizona. The highways were practically deserted, just other rigs on the road for the most part.

"We gotta worry about the cops," Tim murmured. "Just my luck they'd bust me with this cargo."

"Let me see the paperwork they gave you," Ruby said. He handed her a mess of papers and waited for her verdict. "It looks like a real shipment. Bill of Lading looks legal enough, alcohol purchased by a restaurant or bar from a brewery."

"That look like a brewery to you back there?" he asked with a smirk.

"No." She looked over at his strong profile, a street lamp illuminating his face every few seconds. "But they won't know that. Says here we came from a brewery in Azusa. I'll have to cook the books a little to adjust the mileage, but no one will be the wiser."

"Just don't wanna get pulled over," he said. She watched him run a hand through his greased hair.

"Well, one way to prevent that," Ruby said. She picked up the handheld CB microphone and tuned it to channel nineteen. There were a few male voices talking. She depressed the mic button. "Can I get a break, one-nine?"

"Go 'head break," came the reply.

"Can I get a bear report on the one-oh at Rosemead heading eastbound?" she asked. She saw Tim look over and grin.

"You're clear 'til Ontario, then we gotta full grown bear in the grass in Fontana," a reply came.

Ruby turned toward Tim. "There's a state trooper near Fontana, but that's a ways off," she told him.

"Got a clean shot on the ten on out of Shake Town," another voice said.

"Lady Driver, you're five on my back door, I'm hittin' the ten at El Monte. Dial to double Harley and I'll keep you in the know," another said. Ruby switched the station to eleven.

"Thank you driver, 'preciate it," she said. "But I'm the co-pilot, ridin' the jump seat. I'm on standby on one-one with ears on."

"Ten-four sweet thing," came the reply.

"What'd you just say?" Tim raised an eyebrow.

"A driver about five miles ahead of us is gonna let us know if there's any cops or things to look out for. He thought I was the driver; I told him I'm the passenger and that I'd be listening but not talking," Ruby said. "You'll catch on. It's kinda fun—you can talk to all kinds of people when you drive."

"Sweet thing?" Tim asked, his voice mocking.

"Just means a girl." She blushed. "Lady drivers and CBers are pretty popular out here."

"I'll bet," Tim grinned.

As night crept into dawn and they crossed into Arizona, Ruby got quiet. Tim saw she struggled to keep her eyes open, her head bobbing every so often and jerking back up again.

"Ruby, go lie down before you collapse on the dashboard."

"I'm awake," she said sleepily. "Talk to me. Keep me from nodding off."

"Isn't that supposed to be your job?" he asked. He was wide awake, his eyes on the road as the sun peeked up ahead of them.

"Usually I'm pretty good at staying awake." She rolled her window down. The cool air poured into the truck, and he watched Ruby stick her face out the window. A moment later she was rolling the window up and coughing.

"Oh yuck, I think I ate a fly," she said.

Tim shook his head. "You're the strangest chick I ever met."

"I guess that's a good thing, huh?" Ruby asked. "Seein' as you aren't taking any of the other girls from Rett's along with you."

"Yeah, and I only brought you because you bribed me," he said.

"You brought me because you wanted to," she said, her voice serious. "I know that much about you."

Tim stopped himself from grinning.

She was quiet for a few minutes, then got up and climbed into the bunk.

"Keep your eyes forward," she said.

"Why's that?"

She was quiet, and he quickly looked over his shoulder into the bunk, where she was unzipping the bag she'd brought.

"Because." She put a hand on his cheek and pushed until he was facing the road again. "I'm changing clothes, that's why."

"Shouldn't have told me that." He looked back again.

She tossed a pair of socks at his head, and he turned back to the road. He cursed under his breath when he remembered there was no rear view mirror.

"I saw that," she said.

"Saw what?"

"You lookin' for the mirror," she said.

When he heard her undo the zipper on her jeans, he almost drove the truck off the road. It was quiet a moment later and he could tell she was looking at him.

"You aren't seein' anyone, are you?" she asked, trying to sound casual and failing miserably. "Not anyone from around Rett's anyway."

"Nope," he answered. It was the truth. He wasn't seeing Carolyn, like dating her or anything. If she asked about anything more than that ... well, he'd have to tell her.

"Probably a lot of girls that would want you to be seein' them, huh?" She moved back up to the passenger seat wearing a t-shirt and long pants. She picked up one of her sneakers and undid the laces, fiddling with them for no apparent reason.

"You fidget when you're nervous," he said.

"For future reference, it's a bit disarming when you point stuff out I'm doing my best to hide," she said. She paused for a moment. "You change the subject when you don't want to answer a question."

Tim was quiet for a second. She called him on that one.

"Not too many girls look past the face." He rubbed a hand over the section of his cheek where he could feel one of the thin metal plates underneath. "The ones that do aren't exactly choosy if you get my drift."

"I know you ain't throwin' yourself a pity party," she teased. "I've seen the way the girls look at you. Maybe you don't."

"And how's that?"

"Like they're afraid of you. But at the same time, it makes them want you," she said frankly. "You know a whole lot, but I don't think you realize your effect on people."

"You weren't afraid," Tim said, stuck on the fact Ruby had said girls were scared of him. He always wondered if that's what it was.

"No . . . not exactly," Ruby said. "I wasn't afraid of you. I was afraid of how you made me feel."

Tim shifted in his seat. She was looking out the window at the sunrise, her face lit by the sun.

"You always look like you're separate from everyone else," she continued, still not looking at him. "Like no one in a room can be what you need them to be. I can say from experience it's pretty tempting to want to be the exception to the rule."

"What rule is that?"

"The one that says Tim Kelly doesn't trust anyone."

He shifted uncomfortably in the seat again. His ass was numb from driving for so long. They had a couple of hours to go before they reached Phoenix, and he didn't know how many more of her questions he could take.

Tim put the visors down, hoping to block the sun that was shining in his face.

"You have a boyfriend back where you're from?"

"Abilene," she said.

120

JENNIFER SAMSON

"Abilene, then," he said impatiently. He'd give anything to get in a good fight right now. His hands felt itchy. Christ, he should've just did her back at the motel in Calabasas and got it out of his system. Bringing her was a bad idea. "You have a boyfriend back there?"

"Had. His name was Lewis," she said.

"You sleep with him?"

"That's an awful personal question." She crossed her arms.

"You're the one getting personal," he said. "Fair's fair."

She was quiet again, studying her nails.

"You gonna answer or stare into space all day?" he asked.

"Depends, is this gonna change how you look at me?" she asked.

He held her gaze for a moment, making sure she knew he thought she was stupid for asking.

"Yeah, I did." She looked like she was bracing herself for the worst. "Probably think I'm a tramp like those girls you said weren't choosy."

"Ruby," he said, his voice overly patient. "You'd be hard pressed to throw a rock and hit a virgin in Rett's place. It's not a big deal."

He told the whole truth that time. All the girls he knew were doing it with someone who wasn't him.

Hell, even Jake had managed to talk Darla into bed, and he'd sure like to know how. They were a strange couple, and it annoyed him Jake was doing it on the regular. He blamed his face, but it wasn't like he had flocks of women knocking down his door before the Outfit messed it up. Jake had the personality of an ornery horse, and if it was him, he'd choose the messed up face over that.

"People at school treated me awful when they found out," Ruby said. "I was a year older than everyone, I got held back when my momma was sickest. Even so, I always felt like the youngest one there. Lewis went and told everybody a lot of stuff that wasn't true. 'Course, the part about us doing it was true enough, and that's all that mattered to anyone. Lord, the names they called me. It's strange being around Rett's where no one cares."

"Where'd you two do it?" He let his mind wander, imagining her naked and willing in the backseat of a car. He shifted into a higher gear and sped the truck up a little.

"I'm only answering if you will," she challenged.

"Alright," he said roguishly. "First time I did it was in the front seat of a Nash Ambassador I'd boosted when I was fifteen."

"Front seat?" she asked.

"Seats fold down into a bed," he said. "The car's ugly as sin, but it has its good points."

121

He tried to remember the name of the girl. Betty. Barbara. Something with a B.

"I believe I answered." Ruby was now visibly uncomfortable. Her cheeks were bright pink, and she was fiddling with that shoelace again, one leg tucked under her. She was pretty when she blushed.

"You're gonna make fun," Ruby said with a sigh.

"You ever hear me make fun of anyone since you met me?" he asked.

"No, I guess not," she said. "You don't say much about other people when I think of it. I wouldn't peg you for a gossip, neither."

"Quit stalling." He was amused at her feeble attempt to throw him off the topic.

"A haystack," she said.

He looked over. "Serious?"

"Serious," she smiled. "But only once. You do it in a haystack once and you'll never do it again."

He leaned back in the seat and stretched his back, his foot still heavy on the accelerator.

"In a barn?" he asked.

"No," she said. Her face was still pink. "Outside."

She was turning out to be more fun than he thought. Tim wished he was close enough to whisper in her ear and make her blush a little bit more.

"So how was ol' Lewis?" he asked. "You like it?"

Ruby shrugged nonchalantly. "It was nothin' to write home about."

Tim popped the clutch in and pushed the transmission into the highest gear, bombing down the road with abandon.

"Then, Ruby," he said seductively. "He wasn't doing it right."

Sunday, May 15 1966

They arrived in Phoenix early in the morning and unloaded the first order by one in the afternoon.

"We gonna push on to Las Vegas after this?" She handed him a sandwich from the small cooler in the bunk.

"Don't think so," he said. "I'm starting to fade. We'll see how long this takes."

They said nothing more to each other, settling into a comfortable silence. When they pulled up at the last location, Ruby was happy to see six guys pour out of the bar to help unload the truck.

"Why don't you go lie down," she suggested to Tim, who was leaning against the side of the trailer drinking a Coke.

"I'm alright," he said.

"You were up all night driving, I know it takes a lot out of a person," she said. "And your stitches are hurting, I can tell. Go lie down. You don't gotta be Superman all the time."

Tim shook his head, then lit up another cigarette. "I'm alright. We'll be outta here soon enough."

"Where to?" she asked.

He held her gaze for a moment. "Where do you wanna go?"

"I meant . . . well, I was wondering where . . . "

"We were spending the night?" he finished, eyeing her with a smouldering gaze.

She nodded, trying to remember to breathe.

"May as well get a room." He took a long drag from his smoke. "Couple places on the way outta town. Better than cramming in that bed, don't you think?"

Her heart was hammering. She hoped she wasn't having a heart attack or something.

She was about to ask him another question when one of the men called to Tim. The truck was empty, and they could go on their way.

Tim sighed as he went over the paperwork again. They were parked in a dirt lot next to a small motel in Surprise, Arizona. He'd chosen the place because it was out of town.

He hadn't been in to get a room yet—the office was closed when they wandered over a half hour earlier, but there was a 'vacancy' sign swinging in the wind outside. It was a shabby place, but Ruby wasn't bothered when he pulled the truck into the parking lot.

"I showed you the inspection report and the shipment records," she said. "You think you'll remember everything?"

"I better or else you'll make me drag you along next weekend too," he said, sliding a lock of her hair through his fingers.

"Can't next weekend," she said. "Rett got them to ask me to perform at the Helldorado rodeo."

"So I'm on my own," he murmured into her ear. She still smelled like fresh hay.

"Not yet," she said.

He wasn't entirely surprised this time when she turned and kissed him. He kissed her back, enjoying the fact that she was eager to keep it going. He broke the kiss and felt like smiling when he saw the disappointed look on her face.

"We should get some dinner," he said.

Tim stopped to get a room at the motel before they walked to the bar down the street. He ordered a couple hamburgers for himself and had already downed one lousy beer. Ruby'd been spoiling him with the good stuff, that was for sure.

She brought her small bag with her into the bar; why, he didn't know. He watched her nibble on French fries, lick salt off her fingers, and he relaxed for the first time since he'd met her.

He had finished the first run, he had half the money in his pocket, and was on his way back home. He was comfortable with the truck and driving now. He had another job lined up with these Californians. The only thing left was getting to enjoy himself.

"I'm gonna get changed," she said. She stood up with her bag. Tim got up too.

"I have to call home," he said. "What're you changing for?"

"Just wanna get out of these dusty clothes," she said.

He followed her to the hallway in the back of the bar.

"I'll be back in a few minutes." Ruby nodded toward the ladies' room.

Tim picked up the phone, plunked some change in, and dialled his home phone number. He was surprised when Bill picked up.

"Do I wanna know why you're there?" he asked.

"Ran into your sister. At the Calypso."

Tim closed his eyes. The Calypso was a downtown casino, and his baby sister wasn't eighteen, never mind twenty-one.

"You brought her home?"

"Yeah, after I chased off her date."

"Her what?"

"Now Tim, I wanna say I wish I was there to see your face right this second, but she was out with Ray Roth."

Tim looked up at the ceiling. He'd meant to talk to Ray about the rumours he'd heard and hadn't gotten around to it.

"Ray Roth took out my sister?" His blood boiled. "He's five years older than her!"

"I hate to be the one to tell you how much older than Ruby you are."

"That's different." He wasn't sure how, but it was. "So my own mother let her out of the house with a twenty-one-year-old with a car?" His mother must have lost her damn mind.

"Don't think she knew. Thought Diana was at a friend's house. For a slumber party. An overnight slumber party."

Tim's pulse was in his ears. He was going to flatten Roth into next week. There was yelling in the background, and Di was on the phone.

"You tell Bill to keep his nose out of my business!" Di yelled into the phone. Tim held it away from his ear. Ruby came out of the bathroom and raised her eyebrows at the ruckus.

Tim was momentarily distracted by the sleeveless shirt she had tied up high on her waist, the buttons undone at the top more than he'd ever seen them. She had changed into a tight pair of jeans and didn't notice the way he stared. He noticed the bruise on her upper left arm and frowned at it. Had he done that?

Ruby looked at him quizzically.

"Are you listening to me, Tim?" Di said. "He's damn near impossible. He followed me on a date! He's crazy!"

He covered the receiver.

"My sister," he said. "Why don't you go sit down, and I'll be there in a minute."

Ruby nodded, looking for all the world like she wanted to laugh.

"Di, Bill did the right thing, the one out of their mind is you," Tim said. "What the hell are you thinking going out with Ray Roth? I thought I told you to stay away from him?"

"He's not as bad as you say," she said. "He's real cute, too."

"Di, for Christ's sake," he said. "He screws everything in a skirt. Stay away from him."

"You can't tell me what to do!" Di yelled. "You aren't here, so it's not like you care, and Bill's doing this to look good to you."

"Di," Tim said.

"You're starting to sound like Mom, who's got a bruised arm now," Di said venomously. "Dad started in on her when Mr. Hero here brought me home!"

"Di," he said again, rolling his eyes. She was like a locomotive when she got started.

"Bill said you took some girl with you anyway, so you're one to tell me not to date people," she said. "What tramp have you got with you this time? I know it's not Carolyn, she showed up here madder than a hornet."

"Di," he said.

"You and Bill make Ray sound so bad with all this love 'em and leave 'em garbage, the two of you are just as bad," she said. "No, you're worse, you know that?"

"Di, for Christ's sake, shut your mouth for one second," Tim said. "Roth isn't going to be up to walking when I get back to Las Vegas, you got that?"

"I can date whoever I want," she said icily. "And you better not lay a hand on him!"

"He's going with you to bother me, Di. There's only one thing he'd want out of you. I hear you're seeing him, and I'll break his legs, you got it?"

"You are such a jerk!"

Tim winced as Di slammed the phone down, severing the connection.

"Chicks," he sighed.

"You're a girl," Tim stated as he sat at the table.

"As far as I know," Ruby said wryly.

"And that boy you went with, he was a sack of shit, right?"

Ruby nodded.

"So what possessed you to date him, then? You don't seem that stupid."

Ruby studied her nails and shrugged before looking over at Tim.

"The other girls . . . I wouldn't call 'em my friends, but girls I knew in school . . . they raved on and on about their boyfriends. Didn't matter they broke up with 'em every week, and half the boys were seeing other girls behind their backs. They'd tease me cuz I hadn't kissed a boy before and there I was, eighteen years old," Ruby said, a flush of pink forming on her cheeks. "Lewis lived up the road on a small farm. One of the girls passed on I liked him and pretty soon he was at my door asking me out."

"And?"

"He was alright," Ruby shrugged. "We went out and I let him kiss me— didn't get why the girls were all gaga over making out, didn't seem like much to me. So when he pushed things further, I didn't bother stopping him. I thought that was what everybody did, and I better catch up."

She stared at the amber coloured beer bottle, a frown on her face.

"He was nice to me, told me I was pretty, paid all kinds of attention to me when people were around. When it was just us he didn't care much for flattering me. Told the whole school we'd done it the next day. I could never figure if the other girls were jealous or they thought I was a tramp, since it turned out most of 'em lied about how far they'd gone." Ruby paused to take a drink. "I broke it off with Lewis after Christmas, when it looked like we were gonna lose the ranch, and I left school. He told everyone all kinds of awful things about me and started dating another girl a week later. He was suddenly popular, God knows why."

Tim looked thoughtful. He could've told her right from the get go that Lewis was up to no good. Funny she never saw it.

"Sometimes I think if my daddy was around more, or my momma was alive to tell me things about boys, I wouldn't have gotten mixed up with a boy like that," she said quietly. "You know what's funny?"

"Hmm?"

"I didn't like him that much," she said sadly. "He was just the only one that had paid me any mind."

Tim sat back in the hard wooden chair and took hold of his beer bottle. Maybe Di was going with whoever paid her any mind.

He thought about Diana, really thought about her, for the first time in awhile. She'd be seventeen in a few months. He knew Diana was pretty, enough guys said it. He knew she drank and smoked, none of that unusual in town like Las Vegas, but with a reckless streak like Di had, it could get her in some trouble.

With their mother pulling casino shifts into the night, he worried for Diana being alone with the old man. She usually went out far later than any of her friends would be allowed, and he didn't like thinking about where she went. She'd get home late and get in hell-raising fights with their mother until the old man would stir from his bourbon induced sleep and threaten to kick everyone's teeth in. On the bad nights he'd try.

It'd all be different if he could get enough money together to get her out of that house.

He looked over at Ruby, her skin golden in the light. She was pretty in a different way—not tarted up like most of the girls he dealt with, but not stuck up and looking like she was headed for a nunnery either. He liked the contrast of her dark hair and pale skin, as far away from Carolyn's wild blonde tresses as you could get. Not to mention she was looking pretty damn good in that outfit, too. He had spotted a couple guys eyeing her and he didn't blame them, seeing what they were sitting with.

He made sure she saw him looking her up and down.

"You said you didn't think making out seemed like much. Still think that?" he asked.

He watched Ruby look up, her eyes dark in the low light of the bar.

"Not when it's you," she said, looking him in the eye. "I feel more sitting across from you at this table than I ever did sleeping with Lewis."

He downed the last of the beer, stood and held his hand out.

"Come on," he said. "It's been a long day."

13

Ruby stood outside the bar, the cool breeze doing nothing to calm her nerves. Tim was paying the bill, and she told him she'd wait outside. The sky was threatening rain, and she was nervous and keyed up.

She rubbed her bare arms. She knew what she was getting herself into going back to a motel room with Tim. Hell, she knew it the minute she asked to come on the trip, but it didn't mean she was any less nervous.

She didn't know why she was so jittery. It wasn't like she hadn't done it before. Maybe it was that Tim was something different than Lewis altogether. Lewis was on the outskirts of the popular crowd, unsure of himself when he was alone and more unsure when he was with her. Doing it with him in a haystack, the barn or in the backseat of his car parked on a field somewhere outside of town was boring after awhile, like a chore she figured she had to get done. She didn't miss him when he was gone.

Tim made her nervous in a way Lewis never had. He was self-assured and showed it. She had the feeling he could handle anything and had. He said Lewis hadn't been doing it right. She blushed when she tried to imagine what that meant.

She swallowed a lump in her throat, wanting Tim to come out the door and take her back to the motel, but scared to death he would.

"Hey, you lost there, honey?" a voice said.

She looked over at two boys, a little older than her, in the parking lot. One of them was a lanky blond; the other had close-cropped hair the color of chocolate. The chocolate-haired one threw his cigarette butt down and ground it out before he walked toward her.

"You know, it's awful dangerous to be out here alone," he said. "You never know who's going to come along."

His blond friend had a cackling laugh that was like nails on a chalkboard. Ruby looked over at them coolly, but said nothing.

"Too good to talk to me?" He leaned closer to her. "Or too scared?"

"Neither," she said. "I ain't that desperate."

The blond one laughed until his friend glared at him. Ruby went to pick her bag up, but the chocolate-haired one was standing so close he got there first.

"Don't be in such a hurry," he said, shaking her bag. "What do we have here?"

"Give that back." She steadied her voice. She remembered the girls in the bathroom at school playing keep away with her purse once. She stopped carrying one after that.

The boy went to unzip it and Ruby grabbed the bag away from him. He didn't let go, but stared her in the eye.

"Let go." She remembered how Tim always commanded attention, and she tried to copy his self-assured demeanour.

"You're feisty, I like that." He let go of her bag. "You from Texas?"

"That ain't none of your business." She moved closer to the door of the bar.

He stepped in front of her. "I'm willing to make it my business."

"Get lost," she said, looking him in the eye.

"I thought we established you were the one who was lost." He leaned in close to her. She tried to move away, but he followed. "I'm finding you."

"You couldn't find your ass with a map," she said. "Get lost."

"What are the chances you'll come have a drink with us, huh?" He tried to put a hand on her shoulder, but she shrugged away from him,

"Slim to none, and slim done got up and left," she said. "I said get lost."

He closed his hand around her right arm, so tight she couldn't move. She winced as he closed it harder.

"What about you and me taking a ride?" he asked. "I got a '62 Falcon, back seat has your name on it."

"Let her go."

Ruby turned to see Tim standing at the entrance to the bar, a lit cigarette between his fingers. He took a drag and blew the smoke out slowly as he walked toward them. Ruby had never felt so glad to see anyone in her life.

Ruby wrenched her arm out of the chocolate-haired boy's grip and moved over near Tim. The blond walked up to his friend, both of them looking at Tim like this was some kind of a joke, and boy were they gonna have some fun.

"You boys found yourselves a mess of trouble," Tim said, his voice casual.

"Two against one, pal," the blond said. "I don't like your odds."

"I don't like yours," Ruby murmured, remembering Roth's face hitting Everett's bar.

Tim put the cigarette between his lips, looking like he was taking an evening stroll. The two boys must've thought the same thing, because the chocolate-haired one was unprepared for Tim's gut punch. The boy doubled over and his friend tried to jump in.

Tim cracked him across the face, and the boy fell like a ton of bricks. Ruby saw the light glint off Tim's hand and realized he was wearing brass knuckles. He gut punched the blond, then held his head back and slammed a fist into his nose. Ruby gaped as the blood flew.

The chocolate-haired one got up and came charging at Tim's midsection, slamming him into the side of the building. Ruby cringed, hoping to God that Tim hadn't busted any more stitches. Tim pushed on the man's shoulders, then brought his knee up into his face, causing blood to pour from his nose. The man reeled back, and Tim punched him twice before the guy fell onto the pavement next to his friend.

Ruby walked toward Tim, who took the cigarette from between his lips. He took one more drag, then ground it out on the chocolate-haired boy's head, near his temple. The boy moaned in a low, pathetic voice.

"You ever see her walking around here, you keep going," Tim said, his voice low and dangerous. Ruby shivered.

Tim stood, watching the blond try to get to his feet.

"I'd stay down if I was you, buddy," Tim said. He tucked the brass knuckles into a pocket. He turned to Ruby and took her hand, leading her out of the parking lot. His thumb massaged between her thumb and forefinger.

They walked in silence along the dusty road leading to the motel, leaving the noise of the bar behind them. Ruby stopped short, and Tim turned toward her.

"What's wrong?" he asked.

"Nothing," she said. "Thank you."

He shrugged his shoulders like he hadn't done anything. She remembered that first night she saw him in Everett's, how he pulled Ray Roth off her and punched him and how he held the handkerchief against her bleeding lip. She was mesmerized by him in that moment. No one had ever stood up to someone for her before.

Now he had done it again.

She took hold of the lapels of his jacket and looked up. He was gazing at her left arm, and she followed his gaze, noticing the bruise on her upper arm.

"From when I grabbed you in Calabasas?" he asked.

"I'll have a matching one tomorrow from that yahoo," she joked. She saw Tim frown. "It's alright, I know you didn't mean it."

He ran his fingers lightly over her bruised skin. "Not alright."

"Tim," she said. He was still looking at her arm, a frown on his face. She touched his face and made him look at her. He brought his lips down on hers lightly, and she stood on her tip toes, urging him to kiss her harder.

She slid her arms around his neck, and he pulled her closer to him, his fingers entwined in the belt loops on her jeans. She was lost in his arms.

A car honked as it drove past, and they broke their kiss. She rested her head against his chest. Wordlessly, he took her hand again. As they got closer to the motel, his arm slipped around her waist, his hand resting against the back pocket of her jeans. She felt like running toward the room.

He took the key out of his pocket, then struggled to get the stiff lock open. The door relented, and he grabbed her wrist gently, pulled her into the room and kicked the door shut behind him.

The room was dark and he wanted the full goddamn view. He had waited this long, and he needed to see her. All of her.

Ruby's lips were hot on his neck as he struggled out of his jacket. He told her to wait for a second, then made his way over to the night stand and flicked the small lamp on, bathing the room in a deep gold glow.

She stood near the foot of the bed, her chest rising and falling hard with each breath she took. He closed the distance between them in half a second, pulling her to him, his hands on either side of her face. She kissed him back as deeply, her hands curling into the fabric of his t-shirt at his neck. He undid the knot in her shirt at her waist, felt the fabric loosen and for one split second, lost his mind. He pulled her shirt open roughly, hearing a button pop off and land somewhere on the floor. She didn't notice and let the shirt fall to the ground.

She wore jeans and a white bra, and he smiled, unable to keeping himself from laughing at the faint lines near her shoulders.

"What?" she asked, stepping back from him, her arms crossed in front of her. Her bra was white lace, and she wasn't doing the best job of hiding it with her hands. In fact, it made the picture that much more alluring.

"I'm not laughing at you." He took hold of her elbow, trying to pull her back toward him. Her face looked troubled, her grey eyes big and untrusting.

"Sounds like you are," she said warily. She looked at her shirt lying at her feet. He put a hand behind her head, pulled her closer and bent his head to kiss her. She resisted weakly.

"You've got tan lines," he murmured against her lips, an amused tone in his voice.

"Yeah." Her arms were still across her chest. "So what?"

He circled his hands around her waist, ran them slowly up her back again and felt triumphant as she dropped her hands, letting them rest on his forearms.

"Didn't think you could get any paler." He couldn't drag his gaze from her chest.

She smiled, her face relaxing as she realized his laughter wasn't meant cruelly. He kissed her again, her lips full and willing. He explored her mouth, tasting her, and held her to him as he ran his hands up the bare skin of her back. Ruby pulled his t-shirt up, and he let her go for a second, helping her pull his shirt off and dropping it somewhere on the floor.

The pain in his midsection was forgotten when she ran her hands up his biceps and across his chest. She circled her hands around his neck, her lips dancing along his jaw line. He braced for it.

Her hands slid down his back. He tried to stop himself, but he flinched.

He focused on a bad painting on the wall, above her head.

"What's wrong?"

He shook his head and pulled her to him again, kissing her, willing her to kiss him back. She deepened the kiss a moment later, and he tried not to shudder when her hands moved down his back again.

He broke the kiss. She frowned, her hands on the thin scars criss-crossing his back. He could see plainly she was wondering what they were.

She brought her hands around to his waist and ran them up his chest, and he relaxed. He couldn't hide it from her. She frowned again, the line between her eyes making her look like a tiny deer.

He prepared himself for the questions, for the feel of her hands on his back again. He stood as still as possible.

Instead, her hands fluttered down his chest and pulled at his belt. His gaze flew to hers—her eyes held no questions, and he brought his hands up her back, relishing the feel of the smooth, unmarred skin. He undid her bra clasp with one hand, and she laughed.

"Lewis couldn't do it with two hands," she said, her voice barely above a whisper as he dropped her bra on the floor.

"Then he's as dumb as a bag of hammers," he murmured. He looked at her, half-naked in the dim light, and smiled.

He ran his hands up her ribcage, watching her inhale sharply.

"There's no turning back after this, Ruby," he said.

"Who said anything about turnin' back?" she replied.

Ruby gasped as he trailed his thumbs across her nipples.

His hands slid down her sides, and a second later he picked her up. She circled her legs around his waist, and he carried her toward the bed.

She lay back, pulling him with her. He leaned over her, undoing the button on her jeans and she wriggled out of them, watching as he took his off too. She could see the evidence of his attraction to her, and it emboldened her.

He crashed down on top of her and covered her mouth with his. Her pulse thudded in her chest. Maybe he sensed her reserve, because he undressed them both himself.

She watched him study her, the lust in his eyes making her pulse quicken. She couldn't bear to keep eye contact, feeling like he was seeing her entire soul.

He covered her body with his, kissed her deeply, and she arched into him. He touched her skin and made her feel like she was on fire. She let her hands drift down his arms, along his sides, careful to avoid his back. She slipped her hands lower, around his ass, along his thighs. His breathing changed, and it made her smile.

She touched him slowly, working her fingers up the length of him, hearing his breath hitch as she stroked him. Knowing she could make him do that gave her a thrill. His fingers slipped between her legs, and she gasped as he touched her.

A flush of heat made her feel like she would explode. She was lost in the feel of his lips, his fingers, his skin. She ached to touch his back, run her fingers across his skin, marred or not, but it would break this moment, and she couldn't.

He kissed her again, and she wrapped her legs around him. A moan escaped from the back of her throat when he entered her. She opened her eyes and found him staring into hers as he thrust. She tightened her legs around his waist, holding him to her. His hand wrapped around her hair, and she grasped his shoulders, trying to say his name, say anything, but she couldn't.

The crash of pleasure hit her like a ton of bricks, and she forgot about the world. There was only Tim.

Ruby didn't want to move.

Tim's breathing was even and slow now, and she wondered if he was asleep. She was lying on his chest, his right arm cradling her, his hand resting on her hip. She raised her head up slowly and saw his eyes were open and staring at the ceiling.

She lowered her head again, slowly.

He had flinched when she touched his back. The second time she did, she realized why. She felt the lines of scars, and the discomfort radiated off him like heat. He reminded her of a skittish colt, and so she treated him like one. She kept her hands away from his back, asked no questions and threw herself into the moment with him, trying to make him forget whatever terribleness her touch had stirred in him.

She moved closer, and his arm tightened around her. She shuddered at that simple touch, her body tired and happy.

She ran her hand down his chest, through the sparse hair, and hesitated at the stitches in his mid-section.

"Does it still hurt?" she whispered.

"Not too bad." His voice echoed in her head as she listened through his chest. His breathing changed as her fingers followed lightly along the healing scar, settling against his hip. She slinked her hand across his abdomen, feeling him jump under her touch when she rested her hand lower.

She shivered and moved her hand to pull the blanket up higher. This was nothing like being with Lewis. Lewis had never made her toes curl, never made her lose her breath, or gasp in pleasured surprise. She never realized that who you were with could make such a difference.

"You were right," she said quietly. Her fingers skimmed along the hair trailing below his belly button.

"'Bout what?"

"He wasn't doin' it right."

Tim chuckled, and she took in a deep, contented breath and arched her back, stretching her body alongside his.

Tim inhaled slowly, taking a long a drag from his cigarette. Ruby was splayed across his chest, her breath warm against his skin.

He grimaced as he tried to move, the abdominal muscles aching along the line of stitches. Ruby shifted, her hair sliding onto his arm.

He stroked her back distractedly. Carolyn and most of the other girls he'd gone with weren't exactly the kind that stuck around much after. Hell, he usually didn't stick around.

He was starting to wonder if he was out of his mind getting involved with Ruby like this. Maybe he should've waited until they were back in Las Vegas and not in such close quarters.

He ground his cigarette out in the ashtray on the nightstand, then put a hand on Ruby's shoulder.

"We should get some sleep," he said. "I wanna be out of here early."

He waited for her reaction, remembering how Carolyn would bitch at him for wanting his space the nights she'd stay over.

But Ruby sleepily leaned up and kissed him softly on the mouth, then lay back against the pillow and rolled onto her right side, away from him. She curled up slightly, a hand under the pillow supporting her head. He frowned, then snapped the light off.

He waited as his eyes adjusted to the sudden darkness, heard her slow, regular breathing and cursed inwardly. He rolled toward her and rested an arm around her waist.

14

Monday, May 16, 1966

Ruby turned over slowly, a stream of light shining in her face. For a moment she didn't know where she was, not a wholly unfamiliar sensation. She couldn't count how many times she woke up in a different town, in a truck, in another city or with another relative.

Tim's side of the bed was empty and Ruby's throat tightened with momentary panic before she heard the running water in the bathroom. She relaxed, letting the tension fade out of her limbs and the sick feeling drain from her stomach. For a split second, she thought he'd left.

She blushed as she remembered last night. She closed her eyes and remembered the feeling of Tim's lips on her skin, the way he made her feel. Lord in Heaven, she was in for it with him.

When the water stopped, she stilled under the covers, feeling slight apprehension seeing Tim for the first time that morning. She and Lewis had never stayed a night together. She was always home in her own bed before her curfew.

She watched out of the corner of her eye as Tim came out of the bathroom, clad only in a pair of low slung jeans, with his hair wet and slicked back off his face. He casually tossed a towel onto the foot of the bed.

He turned his back to her, rifling in his bag for something. She frowned. His back was covered in angry looking scars. They were thin, white and healed long ago. She felt them last night, but in the low light of the room she couldn't see them—she hadn't wanted to. She only wanted to focus on him and how she could make him feel half the thrill she did.

But now in the light she saw how many there were. She wanted to ask him what they were and where they came from, but she knew he wouldn't give her any answers. He may have no choice but to wear them on the outside, but this was some kind of inside horror, and he wasn't going to share, she knew that much.

She watched him pull on a dark t-shirt and roll up the sleeves. He collected his things and shoved them into his bag. She closed her eyes as he moved around the room.

The bed dipped as he sat next to her.

"I saw your eyes open," he said. "Come on, we got a big drive ahead."

She opened her eyes slowly and looked at him. Her stomach did a slow flip flop as she took in his brown hair, the drops of water clinging to his neck, and the intoxicating smell of his aftershave.

"Could you pass me my clothes?" she asked.

He raised an eyebrow.

"Ruby, I think I've seen all there is to see," he said, his gaze practically burning holes in the sheets. "Quit being silly and get dressed."

She let the covers fall and got out of bed, picking up her underwear from beside the bed. Tim sat where she'd been lying and leaned back against the pillows. She grabbed his towel from the foot of the bed and wrapped it around her.

"Weren't this shy last night."

"That was different," Ruby mumbled.

Tim laughed, and Ruby looked at him with a frown. "What?"

"You sound like Everett, mumbling like that," Tim said. "First time I've ever seen any kind of resemblance between the two of you."

Tim watched with an amused expression as Ruby got dressed and combed her hair. She couldn't explain why she was so self conscious.

She turned around, presentable, and stared at him sitting on the bed for a moment. She walked over, climbed onto the bed and leaned up to kiss him. He tangled a hand into her hair, kissing her back, then pulled her onto his lap, and rolled over on top of her.

He broke the kiss a moment later.

"This is why I don't mix business and pleasure," he said. "We gotta go."

She tried to see what was behind those turbulent green eyes. She had the strange feeling that Tim had seen and learned everything about her last night and she still knew nothing of him.

Even in bed he had barriers up, like he couldn't let go of himself for one second.

He got up off the bed, offered her a hand and pulled her up next to him. She looked back at the bed as they left the room and sighed.

Ruby had been quiet since they left the motel and got on the road, and it was creeping him out.

It usually wasn't a good thing when a chick got that way—it usually meant she was mad. Tim stifled a sigh and tried to weigh the pros and cons of asking her what was up.

She saved him the trouble.

"Do you sleep with other girls?" she asked.

"I have," he said. He hoped she'd take that at face value and drop it. He remembered now why girls like Carolyn were easy to deal with on one level—they always knew the score and there wasn't much need to have a conversation about what it all meant.

"I mean, since you met me."

He glanced over.

"Never mind," she said swiftly. "I get the picture."

"Are we getting married or something?" he asked.

To her credit, she laughed. "No."

"Well, then," he said.

"I know I can't hold anything against you that happened before now," she said. "Are you still going to is what I mean."

At least she had some sense. Tim thought about what she was asking and felt the truck close in around him. Maybe jumping into bed with her was a huge mistake. She may as well handcuff him to her and call it a day.

He cursed himself when the mental thought of her and handcuffs turned him on.

He decided to play it forthright.

"I'm not one for hiding things, Ruby," he said. "I hate playing games. You're different and I like that."

"Different how?" She looked worried at the idea.

He shrugged. "Just are."

He saw her hesitate, like she was choosing her words carefully. "I guess what I really mean is, are we ever gonna do that again or was that it for you?"

He looked toward her, the sun shining directly on her cheek. Maybe she wasn't asking him what it all meant after all.

"Ruby," he said, his voice husky, "just one time with you isn't gonna do it for me."

"Me neither."

He dragged his gaze from her self-satisfied smile and focused on the highway.

"I wanna keep seeing you," he said. "Just don't box me in. I'm not aiming to tie you down."

He inhaled sharply, images again jumping into his head the moment he said "tie you down," only these ones were pretty good compared to how he meant it. No, he wouldn't mind these ones at all.

She looked at him, a smile on her face. He returned the smile, and they settled into a comfortable silence, punctuated by a bit of conversation here and there. Las Vegas drew closer, and Tim was left feeling like he both dodged a bullet and took a hit, all at the same time.

They arrived back in Las Vegas Monday afternoon, and Ruby was disheartened to find Everett's was busy with people. She had no idea why he was open for business on a Monday night, and she suspected he did it to get under her skin.

Tim came inside and found Bill at a table in the back. She went upstairs to stow her things and came back to the thin crowd, noticing Tim had a thunderous expression on his face. Bill held court with a bunch of people around them.

Hollis Warner was at the bar, taking great delight in telling the crowd about his adventures at a weekend poker game that involved a showgirl, three Air Force pilots, five hundred dollars, and a fist fight he made sound like the Invasion of Normandy.

The girl from the Silver Slipper, Brenda, was with him. She looked halfway between angry and sad, and when she went to powder her nose, Hollis came over to Ruby.

"Are you sure she's Bill's sister?" Ruby asked him. "They don't look related."

"Not only sister, but his twin."

"I never would've guessed," Ruby said. "They don't look a thing alike."

"Thank God, or I'd never have slept with her," Hollis said, the seriousness in his voice gone, replaced by his usual comic tone.

"She okay?" Ruby asked.

"She's not gonna scratch your eyes out for talking to me, if that's what you're wondering," he said. Ruby rolled her eyes.

"She looked upset, I mean."

"Right. That," Hollis said. "Bill got his draft notice. Gonna be a long night."

"That's awful."

Ruby looked over towards Bill in surprise. Tim wasn't at the table any longer, and Bill was in the middle of a story. She couldn't believe he got drafted. He didn't look a bit upset about it.

"Rumour has it you've been spending a lot of time with Mr. Kelly," Hollis said, taking a sip of his beer.

Ruby looked over. "What of it?"

Hollis shrugged. "Just thought Jake was trying to get Darla all riled up, but maybe it wasn't Darla he was aiming for."

Ruby's face got hot, but she was saved from replying as Tim arrived at the bar. She smiled, but he sat without a word and nodded towards the beer keg. Ruby filled up a glass and put it in front of him.

"I'll see you later," Hollis said.

Bill showed up a minute later.

"I never would've guessed that's your sister," Ruby said, nodding toward Brenda who was headed to a table with Hollis.

"That's what most people say," he agreed. Bill had dark hair, while Brenda was all blonde ringlets. She didn't have his easy smile, either. "Brenda's about gone to hell the past few days, what with me getting my good ol' government orders."

"I heard, that's just awful. I'm real sorry."

"Sorry?" Bill laughed. "That's what Brenda said. You girls are all the same. I think it's a hoot the government wants me. Just think, I'll be walking around with one of those rifles all legal-like. I bet the cops around here'd quake in their boots if they heard. Anyway, I got a seat at a poker game at McLaney's in an hour. I'll catch you later."

He clapped Tim on the back, and Tim didn't look up.

"Is he serious?" Ruby asked. Everett's place was nearly empty now, save for a couple guys Everett liked to play cards with. "He's going into the Army?"

"He's out of his mind," Tim said morosely. "Thinks it's a real good laugh they drafted him."

"Why him? I don't get it."

"It's the order of things," Tim said. "First men they call are, and I'm quoting here 'delinquents, oldest first.' After that volunteers, then single and married men, oldest first. That means we're always the first to go."

"That ain't fair."

Tim nodded. "Bill got his letter Friday. He has to go for a physical in a week. Stupid bastard's excited about it."

Ruby was quiet for a minute. If Bill could get drafted, Tim could too. He was in his twenties after all. The thought didn't sit well with her, not at all.

Ruby took a sip of her Dr Pepper to try and douse the nausea swirling in her stomach. "He'll be sent to Vietnam."

"Don't worry. Bill's not going anywhere," Tim said.

"How do you know that?

"I'm gonna make sure he doesn't."

Tuesday, May 17, 1966

Tim woke as the sun came up and stared at the ceiling in his bedroom at home. Bill was the only guy that could run things aside from him. Dammit, he trusted Bill more than anyone and that was saying a lot since Tim didn't trust people as a general rule.

Tim had some idea of how he was going to keep Bill from seeing the world. It would have to be handled the right way or else everything could go sour in a hurry. He hated to do it, but Bill wasn't giving him much choice. Tim sighed.

There was a knock at his door—soft, so it had to be Di. She stumbled sleepily into his room.

"You better get ready for school," he said. He scratched his stomach. The stitches were itching like crazy now and he could see the formation of a tight, red scar.

She sat on the edge of Tim's bed and picked at the corner of her pink bathrobe.

"You minding what I said about Ray Roth?" he asked.

Di gave him a look. The kid was good at facial expressions, probably why she got in so many fights. She could hack someone off without even opening her mouth.

"For now," she said cryptically. "How come you gotta treat me like a kid? I'll be seventeen in August and a senior next year."

"Which still isn't old enough to be running around with Ray," Tim said irritably.

"I heard you took some bartender girl with you. Heard she's my age," Di said, bouncing her leg up and down, making Tim's bed shake.

"She's older than you," he said. His alarm clock rang, and he turned over and smacked it off.

"Sometimes I forget," she said quietly, which was unusual for Di.

He looked over his shoulder at his sister, who was staring at his back, her forehead creased. He was quiet for a second.

"Sometimes, I do, too," he said.

"So who is this girl you took with you?" Di asked. She picked up a package of Tim's cigarettes.

"Leave 'em," Tim said. He grabbed for them, but she held them away from his reach. "Go buy your own."

"I wouldn't smoke Pall Malls if you paid me, they're disgusting," she said, tossing the pack onto his dresser. "So, who is she?"

Tim sighed. Di always quizzed him about the girls that hung around. She didn't ask him about Carolyn anymore, but if anyone new ever came around, Di was right up in his business. But the minute he was in hers, she was a raving lunatic.

"I remember you cussing me out and telling me to stay out of your business," Tim said. "Same could go for you."

"Bill already told me she works at Everett's," Di said. "I know Carolyn would love to drop by and check out the competition."

He was going to wring Di's neck one day.

"You're not gonna open your big mouth," Tim said, his voice firm. Di rolled her eyes. "She's Everett's sister, name's Ruby."

"Everett Gordon has a sister?"

"Yep."

"She pretty?"

"Shut up, Di," he said. "Go get ready for school."

She hesitated at the door. "Mom wasn't so happy about Ray. We got into a fight. Old man wasn't too happy about *that*. Mom said she wasn't feeling well this morning, but we both know what that means."

He'd probably worked her over. Not enough it'd stand out at her work since it was a mob owned place, but enough she'd feel it. His old man never would've tried it if he'd been there.

He looked up at Diana. "You want a ride?"

"Sure," Di said. "You know this girl isn't gonna last, like all the rest."

"How many times do I have to tell you, the only folks that'll ever take me away from you are the cops," Tim said. "You don't need to worry about anyone I date."

He looked at his baby sister, her light brown hair highlighted around her face, and probably not by the sun. She looked perfectly put together, even so early in the morning. To everyone else, she was as tough as nails and twice as hard. Only he could see past the firm set mouth that would spew venom in a heartbeat. Only he knew Di's secret fears, the ones she kept hidden behind the hard, pale eyes. Only him around to keep the world from swallowing Diana Kelly whole.

He aimed to keep it that way.

Ruby got to the stable early and saddled up Bella to practice for the rodeo.

Part of her was wishing it was the next weekend. She had a feeling Tim wouldn't mind if she tagged along this time too, but maybe she shouldn't press her luck.

She cantered around the riding ring and tried to organize her thoughts and plan out how she was going to open and close her show. Everett told her

Helldorado Days were a big deal, and she wanted to make a good impression.

She went through all her moves: the shoulder stand, the fender drag, the lazy back and about ten others. She spent the entire morning hopping off of Bella to write an order of moves on a piece of paper she kept anchored on the ground with a rock. She was hoping no one here was much of an authority on trick riding. She didn't have a costume like some of the professionals she saw. Some of them even had matching socks and blinders for their horses. Las Vegas was going to have to settle for jeans and a western shirt.

She used the horn on the saddle to spin off onto the ground and heard a snort of laughter from the gate.

"I'd start practicing more if I was you," Jake said, blowing smoke from his cigarette out the side of his mouth. He had a horse on a lead and tied it to the fence.

"Same goes for you," she said.

"Don't you worry about me, darlin'."

"Rett said there's a big parade before the rodeo," Ruby said. "You ride in that?"

"Do I look like a parade kind of guy to you? Where'd those come from?" he asked, nodding toward her bruises. "Kelly do that? Wouldn't be the first time."

"Handsy guy in a parking lot, mostly," she said. She wondered what Jake meant.

"That's right," Jake said, his voice overly dramatic, like he was trying to piss her off. "Word has it you went with Kelly on his run."

Ruby didn't reply.

"She ain't got a smart come back," Jake said. He moved closer to Ruby and backed her up against one of the gates in the riding ring. "What did you and Tim get up to on your little trip, hmm?"

Ruby looked impatient. "I've got work to do, you know."

Jake ran a finger down her arm, his touch light over her bruises. Her face grew hot. Jake was not supposed to be able to do that.

"Those ain't bruises from some stranger in a parking lot. He did it, hmm?" Jake's voice was voice low and dangerous. His eyes were hard, and she was both scared and oddly fascinated.

"No," she said.

"He didn't pin your arms against the bed?" Jake held her arms back against the fence. "He get what he wanted from you?"

"Let me go," Ruby said, trying to get out of his grip. Jake held her tightly and used his lower body to pin her tighter against the post. She gasped as he moved her legs apart with his thigh and moved in closer. "Let me go, or I'll tell Tim."

"That's right, Tim's your big rescuer now," Jake said with a grim smile.

He still hadn't moved an inch, and Ruby could feel his body move with every breath he took.

"So, you two goin' steady now? He gonna take you out in public around here? Like hell that'll happen." Jake's voice was a sneer.

Ruby felt close to tears, Jake's derisive laughter in her ears. She longed to tell Jake that Tim was her boyfriend, but she didn't think he'd buy it. *She* didn't buy it.

"Yeah, that's what I thought," Jake said, releasing her as if she was of no interest to him now that he knew the score between her and Tim. "Kelly ain't that stupid."

Jake walked out of the ring, and Ruby didn't move until she heard hoofs on the hard ground; Jake riding into the sun.

Everett's place was open again when Tim went by, and he was starting to wonder if Rett had struck a deal to keep the place open heading into Helldorado Days. The rodeo was this weekend, and everyone was jazzed up. Everett was taking bets on everything from bull riding to bronc busting, and if the Outfit got word he was taking bets, Everett'd be part of the new Caesars Palace.

Tim glanced at Ruby, getting beer for every hoodlum that walked in. Bill nodded his goodbyes, leaving the bar with Jimmy Lewis's girl Marilyn on his arm.

Tim stared sourly at the wall. Jimmy sauntered over a second later and sat down.

"He couldn't have left this one alone? I really liked Marilyn."

Jimmy really liked every decent looking girl in a skirt, and Bill prided himself on snatching each one out from under Jimmy's nose, more to get under his skin than he was interested.

Tim looked behind the bar. Both Jed and Ruby were busy, and Irene was out serving drinks like the whole bar was dying of thirst. It was too busy to get behind the bar now. He'd have to hang around until morning, a prospect that wasn't bad at all considering how tight Ruby's jeans were.

He caught her hand as she walked by, carrying two bottles by the necks.

"How late you think this is gonna go?" he asked, his mouth close to her ear.

"Later than I want," she admitted. "Rett's out of his mind, every night this week he's planning to open. I ain't gonna be awake enough to practice riding in the morning."

Tim grinned wickedly. "You can practice tonight."

She stared with her mouth open, then stifled a laugh, shoved his shoulder lightly, and headed into the thick crowd.

It was two in the morning when the crowd thinned, and Ruby was glad to see it.

The bar looked like some kind of Old West movie, everyone in cowboy garb and talking about Helldorado Days like it was the greatest thing ever. She hadn't had much time to talk with Tim, but he sat at a table near the big window and had a couple beers as the night dragged on.

Everett was in the back room in the middle of a high-stakes poker game. Tim walked over to the bar and sat on a bar stool, staring with unabashed hunger.

"I think it's your break time." He ground out a cigarette in an overflowing ashtray.

"There's still a mess of people here," she said.

"Go," Jed told her. "Irene wants tips, and she don't get many when you're working."

"Big surprise," Tim said. Ruby smiled and took off the small waist apron she was wearing and tossed it under the bar on top of Everett's gun.

She walked out from behind the bar, and Tim took her hand in his and pulled her toward the stairs. She hurried up behind him, past couples making out in the stairway and the hallway. Tim headed up with her to the third floor, and she watched him unlock the door to the third floor with his mysterious key.

"Rett's gonna kill you if he finds you here in the morning," Ruby said. She shut the door behind her and turned to Tim, kissing him hard and leaning them both back against a wall.

"No, he won't," Tim murmured. "He won't risk it. No one will."

Ruby sighed contentedly as Tim kissed her, his hands running down her body. It was nice having someone want her. Lewis was never that interested in her, and for some reason it had made her want to prove him wrong, make him find her attractive. Only he likely never had.

Tim kissed her hard and she broke the kiss and looked up into his green eyes. She could see the lust in them and felt a thrill wash over her. Tim didn't need to brag to a room full of high school kids about getting her into bed. If all he wanted was that, he could've found any girl to do it with tonight.

"You gonna stare at me all night?" he asked.

"No," she said. She slid his jacket off his shoulders, and he tossed it on the couch, then wrapped her arms around his neck and pulled him toward her bedroom.

Her heart was pounding in her chest. Rett would skin her alive if he found Tim—or any boy—up here. But Everett wasn't her daddy, and she was nineteen years old and could do as she pleased.

Right now, feeling Tim's hands work their way up her back was pleasure enough.

She shut the bedroom door behind them.

Tim looked around the room, and she tried to see what he was so intrigued with, but she was distracted. He pulled his gaze back to her, snaked his arms around her waist and cupped her bottom.

"You gonna let me stay the night?"

She leaned up and kissed him, then let her lips trail along his jaw.

"You can stay," she whispered. "But you gotta be outta here early, before Rett gets up. He'll sleep late after this shindig."

He covered his mouth with hers and kissed her deeply, and she felt that stirring in the pit of her stomach. Nothing on earth had made her feel like this before.

They stumbled to the bed and crashed onto it, the iron headboard knocking against the wall. Tim undid the buttons on her shirt swiftly, throwing it across the room. She raised an eyebrow, but he didn't notice.

She pulled his t-shirt off, careful to avoid his back. Maybe one day he'd tell her, but to be honest, she wasn't so interested right now, not when his lips were hovering below her collarbone. He kissed below it and made his way between her breasts. She arched her back, stretching the lace of her bra. His hand slipped under her back, and he undid the clasp with one hand.

"Show off," she muttered.

His laughter rumbled deep in his chest, and she dragged her fingers across the muscles of his arms. He discarded her bra somewhere on the floor near her shirt. She moved her hands across his chest tentatively.

"Don't gotta be so shy," he teased, his lips hovering dangerously close to her left nipple. Her back arched without much thought.

"I'm a shy kinda girl," she said. His thumb brushed over her nipple, and she inhaled sharply.

"Weren't the other night."

"Was too."

She looked into his eyes, and his lips met hers forcefully. He made short work of the rest of her clothes. Her fingers fumbled with his belt buckle and zipper, but he didn't make her feel like a dumb kid that didn't know what she was doing.

He discarded his clothes and kissed her, cupping her face. His fingers tangled into her hair as he entered her. He rolled them over so she was on top of him, and she looked into his eyes, her breaths short as they moved together, a breeze blowing into the room and music drifting from downstairs.

15

Tim stirred early in the morning.

He was unsure what woke him, but a few minutes later he heard noises in the kitchen and figured it must be Everett. He glanced over at Ruby, still asleep next to him.

She was more self assured the longer they were together, and he realized his attraction to her was getting worse. It didn't feel like the usual thing that would fizzle out.

There were a few girls, names he couldn't remember. No one that stood out to him. A few close calls with girls who might've held his interest if things were different, but they weren't.

He had to admit he didn't feel the same attraction to them as he did to Ruby. He wondered if it was a passing thing—maybe the attraction always fizzled out. He should enjoy it while it lasted.

Ruby stirred, and he watched as she opened her eyes, staring up into his own.

"Hi."

"Hey, kid," he said. Her back was like cool, pale marble, and he wondered what his own back would look like if it hadn't been destroyed by someone else's anger. She looked like a sculpture lying there, and he thought with some minor alarm in the back of his mind that he wouldn't mind seeing that on a regular basis.

"Oh my God!" She rolled over and sat up in the bed and looked at the clock. "I didn't think he'd be up this early!"

Tim grinned at the panic in her voice.

He watched her get up quietly and hunt up her clothes, pulling them on hurriedly. He stayed in her bed, white sheets tangled around his waist.

"You stay here." She looked over, her eyes big and nervous. "I'll try and get Rett out of here and you can go."

Tim swallowed a laugh and watched her open the door and slip out, shutting it behind her. He tossed the covers off and got dressed, pulled his boots on, and couldn't find his jacket. It was probably in the living room. He opened her bedroom door and strode out like he owned the place.

"Morning, Everett," he said. He grabbed his leather jacket off the couch and shrugged it on. Everett stared with a thunderous expression, and Ruby had her mouth hanging open, like she couldn't believe he hadn't listened. Well, she was going to have to learn sometime that Tim Kelly didn't take orders from anyone.

He approached the kitchen table where Everett sat and grabbed an apple. He headed toward the door, stopping to kiss Ruby, who'd managed to pick her jaw up off the floor.

"I'm gonna kill you," she whispered. He winked, then took a bite of the apple.

"Nice seeing you, Everett," he said. He opened the door, shutting it behind him and heading toward the stairs.

He could hear Everett's explosive "What the hell's gotten into you?" all the way down on the second floor. Tim had an answer for that, but he didn't think Everett would like it much.

He visited the can downstairs, then went into the bar and walked behind it. He shifted the thin apron Ruby always wore to the side and picked up the Smith and Wesson. He gave it a good look. It had a six inch barrel, and the engraving on it indicated it was chambered for .357 Magnum. He swung out the cylinder and found it empty. Great job an empty gun would do at stopping a robbery.

He swung the cylinder closed, tucked the gun into the back of his jeans, and headed out into the rising sun.

The boys were at the warehouse, sorting through car parts picked up at the Raceway that weekend. The score had been Ray's idea, and Tim knew they were pushing their luck. The Stardust Raceway was owned by the hotel, and the hotel was an Outfit joint, so he told them that was the end of it. Ray wasn't too happy, but Tim didn't much care what Ray thought.

He told the boys in no uncertain terms to stick to pulling parts from cars in residential neighbourhoods and to stay away from the Raceway.

Tim pulled Pete Malcolm aside for a chat in his office. Tim discovered a long time ago the best way to keep a guy in line was to take out his transgressions on his closest friends.

Pete had pale hair, pale eyes, and a pale personality. He wasn't someone he would've sought out for his gang, but he could fight, even though it took a lot to get him to do it. Pete's old man owned a gun store, though, and things like that counted in his favour.

"Heard Ray was out with Diana," Tim said, lighting a cigarette.

Pete paled.

"Look, Tim, I-I don't know anything about that," Pete stuttered.

Tim turned and gut punched him. Pete keeled over, choking and groaning.

"What'd you do that for?" Pete coughed. His face was redder than Tim had ever seen it.

Tim hauled off and punched him in the eye, and Pete fell over, then looked up at Tim like he'd lost his mind.

"Maybe in the future, when Ray's making shit decisions, like taking my sister out, people around him'll talk a little sense into him, and we don't need to have these kinds of conversations." Tim hauled Pete up. "And maybe those people looking like they fell into a meat grinder will make guys like Ray think twice."

"Come on, Tim," Pete said, his voice dangerously close to begging. "Ray, it was all Ray! And Carl was there too! We can settle this without messing my face up, right?"

Tim pretended he was mulling over the idea.

"You know, we might be able to." He nodded thoughtfully. "Your old man have any silencers?"

"You mean suppressors?" Pete was startled at the question. "Well, yeah, all kinds, what do you need?"

"Something to fit a Model 28," Tim said.

"Smith and Wesson?" he asked. "It's a revolver. Cylinder gap means you're getting noise no matter what."

"Ammo, then," Tim said impatiently. "Can you get me some?"

"What do you want, .357 or .38 Special? It can fire both," Pete said, scrambling away from Tim when he released his grip on Pete's shirt.

"Get me both," he said. When this all came down, Pete would keep his mouth shut. He'd be too terrified not to.

"And you'll talk to Carl or Ray instead of me?" Pete asked. "I mean, I told Ray it was a bad idea."

"Which part?"

"All of it, all parts."

"I may have already had a talk with Carl," Tim said.

Tim nodded at him to get out, and Pete rushed out of the room and into the warehouse. Tim locked the office and walked out into the warehouse a moment later, and all eyes were on him.

Pete was true to his word and delivered two boxes of ammunition to Tim before the sun set. Tim went with the .38 Special. A guy he was in the joint with had gotten shot with a .357 and said it felt like being hit by lightning.

Bill was drinking a beer, leaning back in a rickety wooden chair, his boots propped up on a few milk crates in Tim's makeshift office. Tim was hoping the chair legs would break. Maybe it'd knock some sense into Bill's head and none of this would be necessary.

"I think I'll look pretty good in one of those uniforms," Bill said, using his switchblade to pick the dirt out from under his nails.

"You really think you're Army material?" Tim asked.

"Shoot, if they think so," Bill grinned. "You know how it goes, Tim. We're not gonna get a break with this draft."

"Any way you can get out of it?" Tim asked.

Bill looked over. "Come on, you know this is my chance to get out of Las Vegas, see the world. Maybe sooner than I thought, but hell, it's something different."

"On the back of a transport Jeep? In the jungle in some country you've never been to?" Tim asked. "You even know where the hell Vietnam is, Billy boy?"

"You don't have to be so sore over it, Tim," Bill said with a sly grin. "I bet I won't even get over there before they settle the whole thing up. I heard stories about the women over there that'd curl your hair."

Bill was already tipsy by the sound of it.

"Marilyn'd go ape over me in uniform, I think," Bill mused.

"Heard she was Jimmy's girl."

Bill snorted a laugh. "That's what he thinks."

"When do you have to see the Army folks?" Tim asked. He wanted to avoid the subject of Marilyn—Jimmy hadn't been too happy about Bill snagging this one. Jimmy still thought he had a shot getting her back, and Tim didn't have the heart to tell him he was kidding himself. When Bill put his mind to something, he did it. That's why this damn draft was so damn irritating.

"The twenty-third," he said. "Dunno what I'm supposed to wear."

"You ready for this job?" Tim asked. Bill drained his beer.

"I don't get why we're knocking this liquor store over," Bill grumbled. "We pretty much drink for free at Everett's now, thanks to you."

"I told you we can sell it, the Californians know someone. I'm sure the Outfit's noticed all the car parts missing from Raceway," Tim said. "Need to get it in the truck, and I leave on Friday."

"As long as we can head over to Everett's after," Bill said. "Aren't you mad you're missing Helldorado Days?"

Tim didn't much care. Ruby took it alright that he wouldn't be around to watch her perform this weekend. She asked Bill to come and round up an audience, and Tim hadn't had the heart to tell her Bill wouldn't be doing much after tonight.

"We'll head over to Everett's later," Tim said vaguely. "You got every-thing?"

"I've got gloves in my car, and the trunk's cleaned out so we can put what-ever we can grab in it. I'll park near the back of this place."

"We'll have to pry the door," Tim said, getting into the spirit of the game. "We'll have to be fast."

"I'm always fast," Bill said. He paused to light a Chesterfield and gave a wry laugh. "I wouldn't go telling any broads that, though."

Tim grinned back at Bill, glad his right-hand man wouldn't be leaving town.

It was far after midnight, and the liquor store was quiet.

They sat in the car on a cross street, watching the neighbourhood and looking for signs of the cops. The store had closed at two, and it was away from the Strip enough that there wasn't much foot traffic.

"Bobby Tafani hears we've been working his neighbourhood, we're in for it," Bill said.

Tim snorted laughing. "I doubt it. He's a punk."

"He's associated."

"Yeah, and how long would that last if he tells the Outfit he can't keep a couple hoods from Fremont out of his neighbourhood?"

"You're playing with fire, bud," Bill said, shaking his head.

Bill had no idea how much.

"I'll pull the car around back so it'll be right at the door for our getaway," Bill said. "You looking for anything in particular in there?"

"Hard liquor," Tim said. May as well go for the best.

Bill nodded and started up the engine.

They pulled around to the back of the liquor store. Tim felt his stomach churning, and the headache that was threatening him all afternoon was now pounding in his temples.

They got out of the car and pulled on gloves on the walk to the back door of the liquor store. Bill wielded a crow bar, and with a few hard jabs at the Yale lock, it broke open and fell on the ground. Bill turned and gave Tim a grin.

Tim allowed Bill to open the door and step inside first. They were inside a stock room at the back of the store and quickly moved onto the sales floor.

Bill grabbed an empty box from the stock room and took bottles of Wild Turkey and Jim Beam. Trust Bill to grab the bourbon.

Tim wandered near the front of the store, looking out the front door. It was best to get things done as quickly as possible.

Tim walked over to the shelf and picked up a bottle of Maker's Mark. He cracked it open and took a long drink. The regret was immediate. He hated bourbon. It reminded him of his father.

"Not like you to celebrate before the job's done," Bill said with a grin.

"I'm feeling lucky," Tim said.

He handed Bill the bottle, and Bill took a drink.

"Don't get that good stuff at Everett's, I'll say that," Bill said, wiping his mouth with his sleeve and studying the bottle.

Tim walked over to the cash register and pried it open with his switchblade, sticking the money in his pocket.

He watched Bill load up one box and take it out to the car. Tim looked out the window again. No sign of anyone.

"We could have a good party with this stuff," Bill said when he returned, taking another long drink from the bottle of bourbon. Tim raised his eyebrows—it looked like Bill had already downed close to a quarter of the bottle. Good thing—it would help dull the pain.

"You really wanna go into the Army?" Tim asked again.

"Why not?" Bill asked. He took a few more bottles of bourbon off the shelf. Why he had to keep taking the damn bourbon, Tim didn't know. He was fighting nausea at the taste. "You get paid to carry a gun around and shoot at things. I still can't believe it. Anyhow, it's not like I have a choice. It's a draft notice, not an invitation."

"I need you here," Tim said.

Bill chuckled. "You try telling the Army that. I'm sure they'll let me out right away if you ask nice."

Tim bit on a reply.

"Come on, I got drafted, may as well make the best of it." Bill's voice was still amiable, but there was some regret underneath, Tim thought. "Won't do any good to moan over it."

Tim closed his eyes. He had to get to that blank place, shut out everything else that was going on.

Tim opened his eyes and aimed the gun at Bill across the room. He cocked the hammer to steady the shot. The click echoed through the empty store, and Tim saw Bill straighten at the sound.

Bill turned around, the smile on his face dying when he saw Tim holding the gun on him. Before he could get out a word, Tim lowered the gun and squeezed the trigger.

The roar was loud and quick. The smell of gunpowder was heavy in the air and smoke escaped from the barrel of the gun. Tim stared at Bill, who was on the ground, his hand around his upper leg and blood quickly pooling beneath him.

"Tie your belt around like a tourniquet," Tim instructed calmly, walking toward Bill. He didn't have much time to get out and make the phone call if Bill was going to bleed like this. Dammit, if he hit an artery they were both dead.

"What the fuck's the matter with you!" Bill exclaimed through gritted teeth. "Shit!"

"You're not going to Vietnam, Bill," Tim said. "There isn't an induction board in the country that's gonna let a guy in that was wounded during the commission of a crime."

"What?!" Bill asked. He was getting pale awfully fast.

Tim stepped over and grabbed Bill's belt out of his hand, seeing as Bill had one hand clamped over his leg, and there was no way he could stop the bleeding on his own.

"Christ," Bill said, struggling to speak. Tim tightened the belt around Bill's leg with a hard pull and Bill gasped for air. "I can't believe you."

"You won't listen to reason, then we do things the hard way," Tim said.

"Listen to reason?!" Bill exclaimed. "Jesus, it's the government. I couldn't talk my way outta this."

Tim smiled tightly. "You still wanted to go."

"I can't fucking believe this," Bill said, his eyes rolling back in his head for a second. "You fuckin' *shot* me, Tim!"

"Well, it was for a good cause," Tim said. He felt the adrenaline kicking through his body. He had to get out of the store.

"I can't believe this. You've lost your mind."

"I'll call the cops as soon as I'm outta here," he said.

"You're leaving me here?" Bill asked. If Tim hadn't heard it, he never would've believed Bill Pearce could sound scared. But he did.

Tim crouched.

"I'll call the cops from across the street. You tell him Bobby Tafani did this." He ignored Bill's sudden laughter. "Sheriff'll be here in no time, get you to the hospital. I'll hang around, make sure of it."

He clapped a hand on Bill's shoulder, and they locked gazes. Bill nodded slightly and held out his hand, his car keys clutched in them. Tim took them without a word, got up and grabbed the gun and the bottle of rum.

"Tim," Bill said, his breathing laboured. The pool of blood had grown, and Tim itched to get out and call the cops. "I'm gonna owe you one. I don't mean no favour, either. I'm gonna pay you back in kind."

154

Tim grinned. "Fair enough."

Tim stepped back through the store and left through the back door. He got into Bill's car and drove it a few streets over then hurried back to the pay phone.

Tim hung around in the darkness, watching the sheriff cars roll up, an ambulance screaming in minutes later. He hated to admit how relieved he was when he saw them bring Bill out on a stretcher and load him inside before racing to the hospital

Tim made his way back to Bill's car, then made a detour near the airport before heading up the Strip. He shouldn't have been too surprised when he found himself in Everett's parking lot shortly after, the place quiet even though it was only one in the morning. He took another long drink of the bourbon, before staggering out of the car and up the stairs.

It took a good five minutes of banging on the door before a light switched on inside and Ruby opened the door wearing nothing more than a nightgown.

"Hey," she said. Her smile faded quickly as she looked him over. "What's wrong?"

"Nothing," he said. "You always answer the door dressed like that? I might make showing up like this a habit, if that's the case."

"What's wrong?" she asked again. She shut and locked the door, watching him warily. He sat at the bar.

"Bourbon?" She took the bottle from his hand. He'd forgotten he was holding it. "What's got you drinking this straight outta the bottle? I figured you'd never wanna see it again."

He stilled as her hand caressed his cheek, tracing the scars. Her forehead was creased, her eyes wide and concerned, and he swallowed hard. He had to play this right, and his head was swimming.

"Bill got hurt tonight," he said shortly.

"What do you mean 'hurt,' what happened?"

"He got shot," Tim said.

Ruby's hand flew up to her mouth, and her grey eyes got wider.

"Is he okay?"

Tim shrugged. "I dunno. He's in the hospital now, I guess."

"What happened?"

Tim shrugged. He wasn't going to say anything until he knew what story Bill was giving out. He looked over at Ruby, took one of her hands, and pulled her closer to him.

"Mind if I crash here tonight?" he said into her hair. "I can take a room, pay Everett for it and everything."

Ruby nodded, grabbed the keys and went upstairs. He leaned over the bar, took the gun from the small of his back, and tucked it under the bar, pulling the apron over it. He slowly made his way upstairs, noting she gave him the room directly beneath her own bedroom.

He studied the bruises on Ruby's upper arms as she unlocked and opened the door and felt sick looking at the one on her left arm. He was nothing like his father. That was a mistake.

He walked into the room and over to the bed, pulled the sheets down and crashed onto the mattress. Ruby came over and pulled his boots off. He felt a sudden tightness in his chest at her gesture and absently wondered if he was having a heart attack.

He shrugged his jacket off and turned over, burying his head under a pillow. The sheets smelled fresh, like they'd been cleaned, and he realized they'd never smelled that nice until Ruby had come to Everett's.

He felt the bed dip as she sat down.

"You should get back upstairs," he said. He was going to have a hell of a hangover in the morning. At least he'd remember the night. He didn't think he'd ever forget it.

"I think I'll stay, if you don't mind the company," she said.

"I'm not gonna be much fun," he said.

"That's okay," she said. "You need to sleep anyway."

She turned out the lights, and the covers rustled as she covered them both with the sheets. He rolled over and pulled her to him, smelling her hair, and hearing the echo of the gunshot. When he closed his eyes, all he could see was blood pooling onto the floor.

16

Thursday, May 19, 1966

Tim woke up in bed alone.

He didn't know what time it was, but the sun was streaming through the curtains, and Ruby's side of the bed was empty. His head was pounding, but he didn't feel as awful as he had the morning after Jake slashed him. At least he remembered last night.

He kind of wished he couldn't.

He tossed the covers off and stood slowly. He was still dressed, so he slipped his boots on and made his way downstairs, running into Ruby on her way up.

"I made coffee," she said kindly. "Thought you might need it."

He nodded, and they walked down the stairs together.

He sat at the bar, and she set the mug in front of him.

"Can Bill have visitors?" she asked.

Tim shrugged. "Dunno. It all happened last night. I don't even know what hospital he's at."

"Southern Nevada Memorial. I called around." She tapped her fingers on the bar. "What happened?"

Tim looked over. "It's best if you stay out of it."

She nodded, and Tim watched her cross her arms and rub them as if she was cold. Or scared. He felt like going back to sleep and pretending the world didn't exist.

"You need a ride? I can drop you somewhere before I hit the stables," she said. "Rett's letting me have the El Camino."

He shook his head. "I've got Bill's car right now."

She nodded and glanced toward the window. He got up and put his jacket on.

"Will I see you before you go back to Los Angeles?" She came around the side of the bar and followed him to the door.

He nodded. "I'll be in tonight."

She said nothing else, and he made his way to the door and outside, feeling his headache grow as he got inside Bill's car.

Ruby was disturbed after Tim left. Maybe it was the hangover, but he was oddly quiet, and not in his usual way. She swept up the floor of the bar and decided she'd visit Bill in the hospital if she could in a day or two. She hated hospitals, but it was the least she could do.

"Thought you were going to practice?" Everett asked as he ambled into the room. "I told the rodeo boys you give a good show. Don't wanna look bad out there."

"I am," she said. "Just tidying up."

She hesitated a second as Everett opened up the jukebox.

"Tim stayed the night, paid for a room," she said. "The money's in the register."

Everett nodded, looking slightly pleased. She didn't know why she had the awful urge to poke at him, but she did.

"I stayed with him," she said, her voice light.

"You don't gotta tell me that," Everett said. "I ain't gonna stop you."

She watched Everett change out the records.

"Then why were you getting on my case so bad about him?"

"Ruby, I've said all I can to you about Tim Kelly," Everett said evenly. "You're not gonna listen, so I'm not gonna talk."

She went back behind the bar and collected the dirty tea towels and cloths. She picked her apron up and almost knocked the gun on the floor.

Everett came over to count the money in the register.

"I bought some .38 Special cartridges for that thing," he said. "I can take you out on the weekend, teach you to shoot it. You should learn."

"Okay." She felt a little better that Everett was talking to her like a normal person. She shouldn't be so awful to him.

Everett returned a moment later with a box of bullets and swung the chamber open.

"That's strange," he said.

"What?"

"There's already five .38s loaded in here, and an empty shell," he said. "You let anyone touch this gun?"

"No." A chill worked its way up her spine. "But anyone could, I guess, it gets busy in here. A few people take liberties and get their own drinks, they come behind the bar. Are you sure you didn't put them in?"

"Guess I could've," he said doubtfully. "But this package isn't opened so I dunno where I would've got 'em."

She felt her stomach flip over as she stared at the gun, the single empty space in the cylinder speaking volumes.

Tim hated hospitals.

He spent close to a month in one after the Outfit worked him over, and now he felt trapped every time he was in one.

Bill was on the third floor. The elevator opened, and Tim stepped out, wrinkling his nose at the antiseptic smell. Bill's sister Brenda saw him and surged toward him.

"Where were you?" she yelled, catching the attention of some of the nurses on the floor. He willed Brenda to shut her mouth, but she didn't. Instead she came at him, flailing fists against his chest. "My brother gets shot and where the hell were you?"

Brenda was a pretty tough chick, and Tim had never seen her like this. She was attracting the attention of a cop at the end of the hall, likely stationed in front of Bill's room.

Tim grabbed Brenda's wrists and pulled her down another hall, backing her up into the wall. He stared for a minute until Brenda calmed down, her eyes spilling over with tears.

"He's gonna be alright?" Tim asked. He hated it when girls cried. Diana didn't cry much unless she wanted something—then it was full-on water-works and whining. He was pretty much immune to tears now.

Brenda nodded, mascara running down her cheeks. "They took the bullet out of his leg, it was in the bone. He's gonna be on crutches awhile. He had to have blood transfusions and everything."

No wonder, all the blood he lost.

"What's he saying?" Tim asked.

"That he saw Bobby Tafani and some others breaking into the liquor store and went to stop them and they shot him," she said. "Which you and me both know is bull. Where were you?"

Tim looked intently. "Cops on him?"

"They aren't sure what to believe, they've got a cop on his door so he don't leave," Brenda said, her face screwing up like she was trying not to cry. "They might charge him with breaking and entering, the back door was forced open."

Tim didn't enjoy gossipy girls much, but in this case, he was glad Brenda was such a gossip. She was obviously paying close attention to the police.

"They went to Bobby Tafani's place and found a bunch of alcohol in his car, so he's in jail," she sniffed. "Where were you, why was Bill alone?"

"Guess he's not going to Vietnam now," Tim said.

"I don't know," she admitted. "He's gotta fill out some form to get re-classified, and—"

She stopped talking as she realized what Tim said. Brenda's eyes were like heat-seeking missiles. Whether she believed Tim set it up for Bill to get shot by Bobby Tafani, or she believed he'd done it himself, he knew Brenda knew the shooting was no accident.

"He can have visitors 'til noon." She took a tissue out of her purse and dabbed her runny mascara. Tim headed down the hall.

Bill was propped up in the hospital bed, an IV in his arm and a bored expression on his face.

"Do me a favour, shut the door," he said. Tim and the cop were staring each other down. "Can't stand the smell of bacon."

The cop rolled his eyes as Tim kicked the door shut on him.

"How you doing?" Tim asked.

"Well," Bill said thoughtfully, "better than I was on the floor of the liquor store, but not so good that I forgot what happened."

Tim nodded.

"You out soon?" Tim asked. He felt awkward looking at Bill laid up like this and knowing it was his fault.

"Dunno," he answered. "Doc had to open me up and dig the bullet outta my thigh bone."

He lifted the sheet up to give Tim a view of a bloody bandage.

"Won't be able to walk for awhile," he said. Tim got the feeling Bill was rubbing it in on purpose. "Lost a lot of blood too, had two transfusions. Pain medicine is nice, though."

"Here." Tim put a form in front of him. "I picked it up for you."

It was a form for reclassification. Bill stared at it for a moment and filled it out.

Tim took a bottle of beer out from an inner pocket in his jacket and set it on the table. Bill grinned wryly.

"What's the score?" Tim asked, looking at Bill.

"Bobby Tafani shot me, it was the damndest thing," he said. "I was being a good Samaritan and everything. Cops aren't so sure. Funny thing how those cops found a box full of alcohol from the store in Bobby's car."

"Funny," Tim agreed.

"You still heading out to California?" Bill said, his voice low in case the cop had his ear to the door.

Tim nodded. "Tomorrow morning."

Tim stood awkwardly at the side of Bill's hospital bed and stared at his friend. He looked like he'd been through the wringer. He was pale, almost as pale as Ruby.

"Cops wanna charge me for robbery, but seeing as I was bleeding on the floor, they can't run with that," he said. "Might get me for breaking and entering. I might plead out, depends on the judge."

Tim nodded. He held out his hand tentatively. Bill took it and shook it.

"Still owe you," he reminded Tim.

"I know you'll collect one day, too," Tim said.

"You wanna do me a favour?" Bill asked. "Seeing as you owe me a hell of a lot."

Tim nodded.

"Get word to Marilyn that I sure am lonely for some company up here," he said, the grin back on his face.

Tim left the hospital feeling better.

Ruby had a headache.

Everett's place was buzzing, and she was getting sick and tired of slinging drinks to a bunch of hoods. Everyone was on edge tonight with word of Bill getting shot making the rounds. A few boys from Tim's gang were hanging around the bar and contemplating going after the guy that did it, someone named Bobby Tafani.

Ruby felt better hearing that someone else was responsible, but that nagging doubt was still there. She didn't know whether to say anything to Tim or not.

"We should stomp 'em out," Jimmy Lewis said. Only the other night Bill walked out of Everett's with his girl and here was Jimmy itching to go and kick Bobby Tafani's behind. Ruby had to admire his loyalty.

"Who is this guy?" Ruby asked, hoping to God it was true he'd shot Bill.

"Bobby Tafani and a few of his boys run an area down near the airport." Jesse smashed his cigarette into the cut glass ashtray. "They're associated."

"With what?"

"The Chicago mob," Jesse said. "First you're associated, do business with or for them. If they want you, and you're Italian, you become a made man, usually by killing someone. Hey, you think that's what this was?"

"If it was, then Tafani blew it since Bill's still breathing," Jimmy said.

Ray rolled his eyes. "Tafani's only associated because he's lucky. His old man was associated in Chicago. Never made though."

"We need to go down there and kick his ass," Carl said. "It's about time the Outfit saw what we can do."

"Yeah, well, your hand is all busted up, and Pete looks like a tractor hit him," Jimmy said. "The Outfit may have sanctioned this, you wanna mess with them?"

Ruby was fascinated by all the talk. These boys were bigger gossips than any girl she ever met.

"I say we go back to Pete's and get ourselves some help and take out those assholes," Adam Barnes said, the muscles in his jaw flexing. "Sorry, Ruby."

"Hold up," Jesse said. "We're not doing anything until Tim gives the okay, you guys hear me?"

Ruby didn't miss the look that passed between Ray and Carl.

Jesse didn't have to worry about keeping order though, as she spotted Tim walking in. Ruby noted the crowd quiet slightly. He wandered over to the bar and nodded at her.

"How's Bill?" she asked. She glanced at the door and saw Jake come in and he was heading straight for them.

"He's okay," Tim said. "Won't be out for awhile though."

"Maybe he can get Ruby to play nurse," Jake said. He sat on the bar stool next to Tim with a knowing grin.

Tim looked over at him impassively, and Ruby said nothing, although she would've had a few choice words for him if Tim wasn't sitting right there. Jake had a lot of nerve coming in and talking to her like he hadn't scared her half to death the other day.

"I thought I might go see him tomorrow," Ruby said. Tim nodded.

"Ain't gonna say hi?" Jake asked with a challenging grin. Ruby looked at him stonily.

"What are you drinking?"

"Whatever's in the keg," he said. She filled a glass and set it in front of him, then wiped the bar, conscious of Tim's gaze.

"What, we ain't friends now, darlin'?" Jake's voice was low and teasing. Ruby didn't miss Tim's whitened knuckles as he grasped his beer bottle, and she felt a surge of pleasure that Jake was getting to him.

"That depends on if you're gonna act like a jerk or not," she said. She was hoping Tim wouldn't bother to ask her why she and Jake were mad at each other. She didn't want to explain what Jake had done. She had a feeling Tim wouldn't appreciate how close he'd been to her, how he grabbed her, how he'd—

"You awake in there?" Jake snapped a finger in front of her face. She took a cloth and wiped up some spilled beer on the bar.

"When are we going after these guys, Tim?" Carl asked.

"When the time's right." Tim lit a cigarette and watched Pete nervously chew a hang nail. "I'm sure Bill wants to be in on it. You're not gonna take that pleasure away from him now, are you?"

Ruby left the bar to deliver a few drinks to a rowdy group in the back room. She returned to find Tim sitting alone at the bar and saw Jake was chatting up Darla, who was half in costume again.

She watched Jesse and the other boys fade into the crowd, searching for their girls, or a fight or a poker game.

Tim looked over, his gaze flicking up her body.

"What's with you and Jake?" he asked.

She shrugged. "He's wolverine mean. Never know what kinda mood he's gonna be in when I go down to the stables."

"Want me to beat him up?" Tim asked with a teasing grin.

"Well, I don't need him dead, so let's hold off for now," she grinned back.

"Let's get outta here," he said.

She watched him as he moved behind the bar and stood close to her. His hands circled around to her back and he undid the knot in the apron. He tossed it under the bar, took her hand and pulled her outside.

"I can't leave, Rett'll have my head." She protested in words only. She was walking alongside him toward the truck.

He opened the passenger door and she got in without another word.

Tim parked the truck near an auto body shop a few blocks from his house.

"So this is where you keep it," she said. "I'd been wondering. Why not park it at your house?"

"The cops see that in front of my place, they start asking questions." He took her hand and crossed the street, heading toward a small lane.

The air was overly warm and held the oppressive feeling that a storm was brewing. She shivered despite the heat. She hated storms.

They approached a house with gravel and scrub in the front. The yard was unkempt, and there was an old car parked on dead grass at the side of the house. The house was dark, and she wondered where his family was, then realized she didn't know if he had one aside from the sister he mentioned.

Tim opened the front door and turned an overhead light on. She was surprised to see the house was fairly clean and tidy, save for the half-empty bottle of bourbon on a coffee table and ashtrays crowded with half-smoked cigarettes.

Tim didn't pause, taking her through the kitchen to a hallway and into the first room on the right. He shut the door and they were plunged into darkness.

"Where is everyone?" she asked, blinking when he switched a small lamp on.

He shrugged. "Old man's out drinking. Mom works the casino cages at the Stardust, third shift. She won't be home for a few hours."

"Your sister?"

"Probably out aiming to turn my hair grey before its time," he said.

Ruby saw a room as devoid of personality as it could be. There was a metal framed bed with a wooden night table, a small dresser against one wall, and a wooden rail back chair in a corner. The walls were plain white, nothing decorating them. There was nothing on the dresser, no clothing, no evidence Tim lived there except for an alarm clock.

"This is your room?" she asked.

He shrugged, then sat on the bed and lit a cigarette. "I stay somewhere downtown most nights."

"So is Bill gonna be okay?" she asked.

He nodded slowly. "His leg's messed up, but it'll heal."

"And you'll go after the guys that did it?"

"That's up to Bill."

"You're worried about him," she said. You feel guilty, she thought. But whether it was guilt over not being there or guilt because he was, she couldn't tell. Maybe she didn't want to know.

She jumped as a flash of lightning lit up the room, then a low rumble rolled overhead. Her breath caught in her throat at the noise.

Tim shook his head. "Bill can take care of himself."

She smiled and sat on the corner of the bed. "Why can't you admit you're upset your best friend is shot and in the hospital?"

Tim got up, ground his half-smoked cigarette on the window sill and threw the butt out the window. She could feel cool air circulating, the storm on the move.

"Don't have a best friend," Tim said shortly.

"Bull," Ruby said. "Anyone with half a brain can see you and Bill are thick as thieves."

Tim looked over with maybe the tiniest hint of a smile and she relaxed.

"I guess now you won't have to worry about him joining the Army, going off to war." She picked at a loose thread on one of the blankets covering the bed.

He looked over, his eyes cold, and shook his head. "Don't, Ruby."

She felt a wave of nausea wash over her and closed her eyes. For the first time since she met Tim Kelly, she was scared. She opened her eyes when Tim sat on the bed. He sat against the headboard and smoked again. She got up, rubbing her arms to warm herself up and walked toward the window. She jumped as the white flash lit the room, then flinched when the crack of thunder came, closer this time.

She was startled when Tim grabbed her hand and pulled her into his lap.

"You look like you're ready to jump outta your skin," he said, his hands massaging her back. Her breath quickened and another flash of lightning lit Tim's face a stark white-blue. She stood and moved away from the bed and the window, pressing herself closer to the dresser.

"Ruby, what's got into you?" he asked. He stubbed his cigarette out and walked over to her, and she felt sick, wanting both to run and to throw herself into his arms.

The crack of thunder was louder this time, and her eyes burned with tears.

"We have to get out of here." Bile rose in her throat and she moved for the door. Tim grabbed her wrists in one fluid motion and pulled her to him.

"What the hell's got into you?" he asked, his voice thick in her ear. She jumped again, the thunder and lightning less than a second apart. Rain drummed on the roof, hard and unrelenting.

"I don't like storms," she said shortly. She squeezed her eyes closed, saw the prairie lighting up, the road washed away, knowing they would never make it in time. "I was scared to death of storms as a kid, I used to have nightmares about lightning chasing me in the house."

She tried to break out of his arms as the wind kicked up, howling around the house and making the old wood creak. She didn't think Las Vegas had storms like this.

Tim held her firmly. Her throat was dry, and she buried her head against his chest.

"Damn it, Ruby, it's just a little thunder and lightning," he said. His hands worked up her back, pressing against her spine. She tried to imagine him holding Everett's gun, and the image came all too easily.

She yelped as another flash of lightning lit up the room, and thunder crashed directly overhead. She shivered, and the tears flowed freely. Tim held onto her tightly.

"It's not gonna hurt you."

"I know," she said. "It's not that, it's ... it makes me think horrible things."

He said nothing. She tried to drown out the sound of the pounding rain by talking.

"When my momma was dying, we didn't get word 'til the last minute. We jumped in the truck and drove through this God-awful storm." The words rushed out faster than she could keep up with them. She had to say something, or she was going to ask him a question she didn't want to know the answer to. "I was fit to be tied, roads were washin' out and there was hail and rain, a real toad choker. There was tornado warnings all over the place. I didn't think we'd make it. I thought . . . I thought God was punishing me for not bein' there, and I can't stand storms like this."

He kissed her neck as she listened to the howling rain and wind and she tried to enjoy the feel of his lips on her skin.

"Did you make it in time?" His lips trailed her jaw line.

"What?"

"Did you get to your mother in time?"

She looked up, knowing her eyes were showing things he always kept hidden. "No. She was dead when we got there."

She was near hysterics as another clap of thunder made the windows vibrate. She couldn't keep the hot tears from overflowing.

The storm passed quickly.

Tim was at his wit's end with her the last twenty minutes, but as soon as the thunder calmed, so did she. She was currently curled up against his chest, her breathing still fast, and her heartbeat still running wild.

When the storm was at full strength she cried hysterically. He kissed her softly, the only thing he could think of to distract her. She was skittish as a colt and looked like she'd bolt at any moment, and he set out to change it.

He moved her to the bed, covered her with his body and pressed her to the sheets. His hands were gentle, his lips insistent. As the rain let up and the time between the lightning flash and the thunder clap became longer, she relaxed against him, her hands gripping his shoulders and her own mouth insistent.

Tim thought the storm they created was a lot better than Mother Nature's.

17

Ruby was startled awake the next morning, but by what, she didn't know.

She listened carefully, hearing Tim's even breathing. The noises came again; a crash, a voice yelling, and doors slamming.

"Just Di and my mom," Tim murmured. "Go back to sleep."

"Your *mom*?" Ruby asked. She pulled the covers up to her chest and sat up in a panic. "Tim!"

Tim rolled over onto his back and looked up, a smile on his face.

"Jesus!" Ruby said. She looked around for her clothes, scattered around his room. "She's not going to come in here, is she?"

Tim chuckled. "Relax. It's not a big deal."

"Ain't a big deal!" She tried to keep her voice to a whisper. "She can't find me in here like this! What would people say?"

"You didn't care what Everett thought."

"I care plenty," Ruby said, leaning over and finding her underwear on the floor. She pulled them on under the covers, the bed creaking. "I didn't think she'd be here. Oh my God. Who else is here?"

"Relax." Tim slipped a hand up her back and around her neck, pulling her to him. She tried to relax, the noise of the house making her more nervous. A door slammed somewhere, and the raised voices were quiet.

It was different at Everett's. Her brother wasn't much older than her, he understood the times. He wasn't her father. There was no way in hell she wanted Tim's family seeing her crawl out of his bedroom first thing in the morning like a harlot.

A moment later Tim's door crashed open.

"You've gotta get her off my back!" the girl screamed.

Tim rolled over in the bed, and Ruby pulled the covers up to her neck and felt her face getting hot. If his mother walked in after the girl, she'd roll over and die right there in the bed.

Ruby peeked out from the covers. His sister looked a little like him, but with lighter hair and piercing blue eyes.

His sister noticed her in the bed, and her expression hardened.

"Who's the flavour of the month?" his sister asked. She walked toward the bed, staring hard at Ruby.

"Di, shut up," Tim said. "Didn't I tell you to knock first?"

"You're Everett's sister," Di said, looking at Ruby with a sharp gaze. "The little fling Tim took to California."

"Diana, I said shut it and get out." Tim pulled a pillow out from under him and tossed it at his sister.

"She's not as pretty as Carolyn," Di said sweetly.

She shut the door behind her, and Ruby was left with her mouth open.

"Don't pay any attention to her," Tim said. "She's got a stick up her behind cuz I told her not to date Ray. She's smart as hell, but stubborn as a mule."

"Who's Carolyn?"

Tim cringed at the question. "A girl."

Ruby stared.

"A girl I used to go with," he said.

He shifted in the bed again.

"A girl I used to sleep with," he muttered.

She was reassured he said 'used to' and kissed his shoulder.

"She's pretty," Ruby said.

"Who? Carolyn?"

"No, your sister," Ruby said. "She's so pretty she'd make a hound dog smile."

"Di's a good kid, don't take anything she says personally," Tim said, turning over and looking at Ruby. "She'll say whatever comes into her mind to get under your skin."

He pulled the covers off him and swung his legs onto the floor.

"Get dressed and I'll drop you at the stables," he said. "I gotta be in Los Angeles by one o'clock."

She wasn't surprised to find Jake at the stable, but she wasn't eager to spend her afternoon in his company, either.

She saddled Bella, who was itching to get out of the barn.

"You still gonna ride in the rodeo?" Jake asked from a few stalls over.

"Of course," she said. "Gotta give those cowboys something to look at."

She heard his low laugh and was startled when she turned and found him standing nearby, his arms resting on the top stall rail.

"You always sneak up on people and scare 'em half to death?" she asked.

Bella nickered and moved toward Jake, bumping her nose against his arm. Ruby watched him scratch her muzzle and comb his fingers through Bella's short forelock. If he could be as nice to her as he was to animals her life would improve.

"Which horse do you hope you pull tomorrow?" she asked.

He shrugged. "Don't matter to me. I can whip anyone on any horse."

She rolled her eyes. His ego was the size of Alabama and then some.

"I was gonna saddle Zephyr and ride him out a bit," Jake said. He looked at her, a dangerous look in his eye. "You wanna race?"

"Bella ain't a racer," she said.

"Come on, one race." He unlatched the stall door. "Field down that way is wide open, no holes, I ride down there all the time."

Ruby attached reins to the bridle.

"I told you she ain't a racer," Ruby said, her voice frosty.

"Scared I'll beat you? I can understand that," Jake said.

Ruby gave him a look.

A strange look passed over Jake's face. "You know, you remind me of my mother sometimes. Tiny, all pale skin and dark hair. Scared of your own shadow, too, just like her."

"I am not," Ruby said.

"You're scared all the way down. You get to town, and the first thing you do is suss out the meanest, baddest son of a bitch on Fremont and cling to him like a barnacle. Why do that if you ain't scared?" He laughed, and Ruby had seen funeral processions with more humour in them. "You can tell Kelly I said that. He'll never believe it."

Ruby shook her head. "It isn't like that."

It wasn't, but Jake didn't deserve an explanation, even if she could explain.

He crossed his arms. "Don't give me that. You're scared of me, too, admit it."

Ruby balled up her fists, but kept them down by her legs. "I've never been less scared of anything in my life."

He laughed again, and there was genuine amusement in it this time. "Sometimes, you toughen up and surprise me." His smile faded. "It ain't always a good thing."

"What do you mean?" Ruby hid her curiosity. Jake would torment her even more if he thought she was the slightest bit interested in anything about him.

Jake opened the stall door, and Ruby led Bella out. "My momma surprised me once. Don't know where she got the courage to run off, but she did.

Probably tired of living with a mean drunk. People said that the old man could coax the birds out of the trees if he didn't have any liquor in him."

"Where did she go?" Ruby asked. She shut Bella in the paddock.

"Nashville." Jake bared his teeth in what might have meant to be a smile. "Thing I remember best was her singing all the time—Ernest Tubb, Texas Playboys, Cumberland Valley Boys, the Tennessee Plowboy and Moon Mullican—no matter what she was doing, cooking, cleaning, the wash." He pronounced wash with an "r," so it sounded like "warsh" and dropped his "gs" like a bad habit. "She listened to the Grand Ole Opry religiously and sang 'Cherokee Boogie' until I thought the old man would lose his damn mind. The older I got, the less she sang. Guess she didn't feel much like singing with the old man clouting her upside the head every time she opened her mouth."

"Did she take you with her?" Ruby asked softly. In her heart, she knew before he answered.

He shook his head. "I was a pain-in-the-ass kid, mouthy and only in elementary school. I couldn't even tie my damn shoelaces. Who the hell wants a snot-nosed kid tagging along while they're auditioning?"

Ruby bit her lip, but didn't comfort him; he wouldn't take it kindly. "Did she ... did she ever come back?"

He lit a cigarette, then took off his cowboy hat and ran a hand through his hair. "She wrote every week at first. She was singing on a radio show or back up on somebody's record. Her big break was just around the corner, and everything would be okay once it happened. I had my ear glued to the radio that whole summer, hoping to hear her voice." He screwed his mouth up into an ugly sneer. "The letters tapered off until they didn't come no more. By the time I joined the service an' got the hell out of there, I hadn't heard from her in years. When I got me some money and some leave saved up, I went to Nashville to look for her." He beat an angry rhythm against his thigh with his hat. "Took me a long time to find her. She was living with some asshole who didn't know she had a husband or a kid. He wasn't pleased with the surprise. She was all used up and working at a laundry. Closest she got to the Opry stars was washing their dirty duds."

"She never told anyone?" Ruby said.

"Her letters were all horseshit. There was no big break around the corner. She ran off on her family to chase a dream that never came true. She said it was easier to just let it all go, act like it never happened, like we never existed. She left everything and everyone behind and had nothing to show for it but a bent back and a broken heart." He ground his cigarette out on his heel. "Dreams are traps for fools. You remember that when you go getting brave and tryin' to surprise me."

170

He turned and walked away, the challenge to race forgotten.

Tim rolled into Calabasas in the afternoon and parked the rig in the dirt near the barns. He spotted Insane Wayne, Roy, and the Mexican girl walking his way from the house. He climbed out of the truck and shook hands with Wayne and Roy.

"We gotta car to load in the trailer," Wayne said, walking toward the nearest barn. "We've got some car parts too, going to Denver. You'll deliver the car parts then swap the trailer with another driver, he's taking the car on to Topeka."

"Car parts?" Tim asked.

"Just shut up a chop operation here, feds busted it. My man in Denver's getting rid of what's left."

This was exactly what he needed. A contact outside of Vegas to take car parts would help him out. He and Bill could ship all the stuff themselves. Tim frowned; he forgot Bill was in the hospital.

Tim looked sidelong at the Mexican girl—Rosa. She was watching him, her brows drawn together in an angry scowl. Tim lit a cigarette as they walked inside the barn, thinking that Ruby would've stamped it out in a second.

The barn was cavernous and held no hay or anything to do with the farm. His trailer was parked inside, and at the end was a mint Buick Riviera.

Tim walked over and took a look at the car.

"Nice wheels, huh?" Wayne ran his hand over the car. "Our guy in Topeka, Kansas, customizes these out for the Kansas City and St. Louis syndicates."

"Where'd it come from?" Tim asked.

"Transport truck. Swiped a whole bunch of cars, most were moved out the week before you came down here. We don't got a lotta space to store them, they have to be in and out quick," Wayne said.

He could see himself driving a car like that. Hell, he could see himself driving anything right now. He was sick and tired of driving around town in the tractor and using up all the diesel fuel, not to mention looking stupid doing it. He couldn't cruise around in Bill's car forever, either.

"I'm in the market for some wheels," Tim said.

"Maybe we can work something out," Wayne said. "I'll ask around. Me and Roy gotta hunt up some ramps so we can get that car in the trailer. Start it up if you want." Wayne tossed the keys to Tim.

Tim opened the door, got in and started it. He rolled the driver's side window down to get some air and imagined himself driving down the streets of Las Vegas in the car. The only way he'd get a car like this is if he stole it.

He turned off the engine, and the cavernous barn was silent again. He sat in the car for a few minutes, leaning back against the headrest and closing his eyes. Driving that truck made him tired. He wondered if Ruby had figured out he shot Bill. He wasn't looking forward to getting back to Las Vegas and facing the questions.

But maybe she already knew. She was so jumpy the night before, he couldn't believe it was all because of a stupid thunderstorm. Maybe she was scared of him after all. He hoped not; she was the only chick that had held his interest in a long time.

A soft noise made him look to his left, out the driver's window. Rosa had stayed behind. She watched him with curious dark eyes, then walked over to the car and leaned into the driver's side, giving Tim a nice view down her shirt.

"You like?" she asked.

"Car's not bad." He knew it wasn't what she was asking about.

She stepped back as he opened the door and got out of the car. The moment he shut the door she was pressed up against him.

"That is not what I meant." She tried to work a hand up his shirt. He caught her wrist in his hand, resisting the urge to shove her away. It'd be a cold day in hell before Tim would pay for a cheap thrill like Rosa. He wasn't anything like his old man.

Rosa made a tsk-ing sound and ran her other hand up his leg to his crotch. Tim shifted back and grabbed her wrist.

"You are turned on, yes?" she said. It was more of a statement than a question and Tim was irritated that his body was betraying his mind. Hell, she had nice tits, he'd have to be blind and dumb not to notice them pressed up against his chest. It wasn't his fault.

He stared her down, and she smiled, twisting her wrists out of his hands and attempting to unbutton his jeans. He grabbed both her hands again.

"¡No me jodas, puta," he said. Don't fuck with me, whore. Prison had at least taught him some Spanish, more than high school ever had.

She tried to pull her wrists away, and he gripped them tighter, then spun her around so her back was against the car. Her eyes narrowed as she looked at him, her chin raised high.

"Pendejo!" she spat, wrenching one arm free and slapping him across the face. "¡Manájate!"

"You sure got a way with the ladies," Insane Wayne said with a grin. Rosa stalked out of the barn, and Wayne set down one end of the split ramps he and Roy were carrying. "Don't know why you're not interested."

"How long until it's loaded?" Tim wanted to be on the road. For all the boredom driving that truck was, at least there weren't any damn whores chasing him around.

"We'll get this car loaded in and you can be on your way," Wayne said.

Saturday, May 21, 1966

Ruby was nervous. She spent a restless night in bed, thinking about her routine. She was going to be performing in front of people for the first time in ages.

She and Wick worked from the moment the sun came up, getting the horses into the horse trailers and ready for the drive to the rodeo grounds.

The rodeo arena was as good as any she'd ever seen. She was the opening event, then they'd do the bareback bronc. She was pretty sure they'd have a big crowd from the looks of all the makeshift stands they'd set up.

Ruby looked around, impressed with how put together the rodeo was. The parade the day before had colourful floats, marching bands, and cowboys on horseback and went on for so long she didn't think it would ever end.

She wished Tim was here. Hell, she wished Bill was here. She had no idea who was coming, and Everett would likely be busy all afternoon. It would be nice to have one friendly face in the crowd.

"You better get moving," Jake said, disturbing her thoughts. "Half your equipment's cluttering up the trailer, and you don't have long until your practice time."

"You're sure bossy today," she said.

"Unlike you, I'm getting paid to ride in this thing," he said. "After this, I got rodeos coming up in Amarillo, Cheyenne and Denver."

"Wait, you get paid?" she asked. She followed him toward a paddock, but he didn't reply.

"Hollis and some of the guys are comin' down to watch this thing." He lit a cigarette as they walked. "Go by and sit with 'em when you're done."

"Why?"

"Hollis could use the distraction," Jake said shortly. A cowboy across the lot hollered at him, and Jake raised his hand and flipped him off. "I'll catch you later."

Ruby watched him walk away and felt very alone.

The stands were starting to fill with people and Ruby spotted Hollis come in with a big group of people, including Darla. They were all sitting up in the stands and Ruby was dismayed to find she was nervous they were there.

She knew if she messed up, she'd never hear the end of it with Hollis sitting in the stands.

Ruby took a deep breath, trying to settle in her saddle. The announcer was preparing to introduce her. She was nervous, and Bella sensed it. She was bobbing her head, eager to get out and move.

She didn't have time to think after her name was announced. She rode into the ring quickly, circling around and preparing for her first move, a fender drag. Hearing the oohs and aahs from the crowd calmed her, and she was more comfortable as she worked her way through her routine.

She managed to fly the flag out behind her easily enough, a move that bothered her during practice. Her taped keeper held, and the dog collar she used as a replacement for her Cossack strap worked well. She completed her last move, a tail drag, to lots of cheering.

The crowd roared as she finished, and she let out a relieved breath. She had Bella take a bow in the centre of the ring, a trick she worked three months to teach her.

The hands were preparing to set everything up for the bareback bronc. She walked Bella into the paddock near the ring and let her run. Ruby climbed up on the rails and sat on the top most one to get a look at the ring.

They made the announcements of the riders' names, and Ruby watched as they all drew for the horse they'd ride. Jake drew a horse she didn't know for bareback bronc and drew Midnight Bandit for saddle bronc.

She took Bella back to the pen. She hung up the tack and stored everything in the horse trailer, then shut the back of the horse trailer up. She'd need Wick's help to get Bella in, and she didn't want to do it until the last minute since Bella hated it so much.

A short time later she wandered over to the concession stands and got herself a hot dog and a Dr Pepper, then went over to find Hollis. She was surprised by the number of people that stopped her to say they liked her show.

"Well, look, it's Miss Rodeo Star," Hollis said as she approached. "This is Ruby, everybody."

Hollis already looked on his way to black out drunk from what Ruby could see. Ruby smiled tentatively.

"For Pete's sake, Hollis, learn some manners." Darla stood to make introductions. "This is Rusty Sawyer and Charlie Gray. They're going with Jacqueline Molino and Susie Blackman. The girls are at the concessions right now. And, of course, you have the misfortune of knowing Hollis already."

"The girls are here?" Ruby said.

"Don't worry," Darla said. "I told them the episode with Jake wasn't your fault. They won't be trying to scratch your eyes out."

"That's a relief."

Ruby sat next to Darla and felt more underdressed than she ever had at a rodeo. Darla wore a skirt cut higher than anything Ruby owned and a low cut blouse that looked like something you'd wear to a nightclub. She had cowboy boots on though, like she was trying to look the part. She caught Ruby looking.

"Not rodeo enough?" she asked, an artful eyebrow arched high.

"It's something, alright."

"You haven't come to the show yet," she said.

"Oh, I will," Ruby said. As soon as she was sure the other girls wouldn't run her out first. Susie and Jacqueline returned with popcorn and drinks, looking at Ruby for a moment, then sitting down next to Darla.

"Heard Bill's doing okay," Hollis said, taking a long drink from his beer. "No one can figure out what Bill was doing in that store alone. Tim and Bill are usually joined at the hip for something like that."

"I guess Tim was busy," Ruby said stiffly.

"Uh huh," Hollis answered. He took another drink of his beer.

Ruby felt uncomfortable at Hollis's comments and turned toward Darla.

"I heard this rumour you were gone for two days with him. Guess it's true, huh?" Hollis asked her.

Ruby felt her face getting hot and turned back toward Hollis. "I had to make sure he could drive the truck."

"That blue one, always parked at Everett's?" Hollis asked. "Shoot, it's got a bed in the back and everything."

"Hollis, really!" Susie said, shocked.

Hollis looked shamed for a split second before he elbowed Ruby lightly.

"You and Tim seeing each other?" Hollis asked, an eyebrow raised. She could tell everyone else was listening, although they were trying to look like they weren't.

"I guess you could say that," she answered.

"I can't imagine anyone wanting to date Tim Kelly," Jacqueline said. "He's about as talkative as a brick wall."

Ruby raised an eyebrow.

"Leave Snow White alone, girls," Darla said. "You could say the same about Jake, and all the words he knows aren't fit to print."

Ruby noticed a heavy ring on a chain around Darla's neck, silver with a blue stone on top. She was surprised Jake was the type to give a girl something to wear like that, because he sure didn't look it.

"Jake's Air Force ring," Darla said.

"I figured," Ruby said, remembering the tan line from when she went to the Silver Slipper with him. They hadn't been broken up since he wasn't wearing it then. Even though Darla had told her they weren't broken up, she was angry all over again.

"Jake's up last. I hear it's a tough field this time, he may not win," Hollis said.

"He'll win," Darla answered. "He's angry enough at me, he'll win."

Maybe that was why he looked so irritated earlier.

Hollis left to make a bet, and Ruby spotted Jesse and some of Tim's boys in the stands, drinking and hollering at the passing girls. Some well-suited men were at the side of the riding ring, talking to a man tricked out in cowboy gear, his horse with a silver bridle.

"That's Moe Dalitz," Darla said, noticing her gaze. "He owns the Desert Inn, some of the Stardust and who knows how many other casinos. He's associated with the Cleveland mob and friends with just about everyone who's associated. He's one of the most powerful men in Las Vegas. I'd give anything to dance in Lido de Paris at the DI."

"Are all the shows very different?" Ruby asked.

Darla nodded. "Oh, there's a real hierarchy among us dancers. There's two shows every dancer wants to get cast in—Lido de Paris at the Desert Inn or being a Copa girl at the Sands."

"I dunno," Jacqueline said. "I've always wanted to dance in Folies Bergère."

"Ugh, their cowgirl costumes are worse than ours," Darla said.

"Well, I like our show just fine," Susie said.

"Jake better win tonight," Hollis said, swaying as he sat next to Ruby again. "I got all my money on him, and I'm aiming to get pretty crocked tonight."

"You look like you already are," Ruby said. Hollis always drank a lot, but he was in a mood, which wasn't like him. His usually jovial comments sounded mean tonight, his voice a bit sarcastic. She couldn't remember him being anything but a lot of fun. Jake had said something about Hollis needing a distraction, and she wished she'd asked him what he meant.

Ruby looked around the stands and spotted Bill's sister winding her way through the crowd toward them.

"Great," Hollis muttered.

"Hollis," she said. Hollis didn't move over or ask her to sit.

"Brenda," he said. "I think you know everyone here. Maybe not Ruby too well."

"We see each other around," Ruby said.

Brenda leaned close to Hollis, but her whisper was loud enough for everyone to hear.

"I hear we have some talking to do."

Hollis stiffened beside her.

"You aren't avoiding me," Brenda said. "I heard about the girl at the casino."

"It wasn't anything."

Ruby sat awkwardly. It was impossible not to listen. She noticed the other girls were busy studying their fingernails too.

"Oh, I think I trust in what my friend saw rather than your denials."

She stared him down for a second, then stalked off. He got up and followed her, and Ruby lost track of them in the crowd. He returned ten minutes later looking morose.

"Women," Hollis sighed.

The crowd was reaching a fever pitch of excitement as the bareback bronc got under way.

Ruby hadn't placed any bets since she was saving up her money for a new saddle, but it was going to take some time to get there. It was tempting to go and bet, but she didn't want to risk it. Jake would lose just to send her into the poorhouse.

The crowd cheered and jumped and yelled for each go-round. Jake was the last rider in the chute, everyone was on their feet, and the excitement was palpable.

The horse shot out of the chute, bucking hard. Jake held on to the rein with one hand, and his other arm shot through the air with each buck. Ruby watched the clock, and Jake managed to stay on the whole eight seconds. It took him a second to get off the horse before the riders went to corral the bucking bronc. They waited for the score to come up—seventy-nine of a possible one hundred, putting him number one.

Hollis gave a war whoop and rushed off to collect his winnings before everyone calmed down.

The atmosphere was electric. After the steer wrestling and team roping, it was time for saddle bronc to go.

Jake didn't do as well with saddle bronc, but Ruby thought that had more to do with Midnight Bandit, who was still wild and didn't much like being under saddle. He didn't finish as high—only a sixty-nine—but the group was excited nonetheless.

"Can we go down?" Darla asked.

Ruby nodded. "There's a break before the tie-down roping, barrel racing, and bull riding. He'll put Bandit in the corral awhile before we trailer them and go. Are y'all comin' to Rett's tonight?"

She got affirmative answers from Rusty, Charlie and Hollis.

Ruby took everyone toward the trailers, and they met Jake as he was leading Midnight Bandit toward the corrals.

"You really can ride," Ruby said.

"Yeah, you didn't think so?" Jake asked, a grin on his face. "You may be a Texas girl, but a 'Bama rider'd beat you every time."

"I'm gonna be drinkin' like a king tonight," Hollis said with a grin.

"Jake, you said we'd talk about it after the rodeo," Darla said. "It's after the rodeo."

"It's the middle of it, and we ain't got nothing to talk about," Jake said.

Darla crossed her arms. They both looked poised for a fight.

"We're gonna talk about it sometime, you can't just pretend it away," Darla said. "I'm going no matter what, and I'd rather it be on good terms. I don't have a lot of time before I leave."

Jake turned away, shaking hands with a few cowboys that came to congratulate him.

"What's going on?" Ruby whispered to Hollis, who rolled his eyes.

"Jake," Darla said.

"I gotta get the horse trailered." Jake took off without another word.

"Jake, don't walk away from me, we are having this conversation!" Darla said, trying to follow Jake. He was moving quickly away from her.

"What's up with them?" Ruby asked.

Hollis shrugged. "Darla's leaving in awhile. Going out to Hollywood or something. Jake ain't too happy about it."

Ruby stood in silence for a minute. Jake sure was a strange one. She figured he'd up and find another girl, but maybe it bothered him. It was strange to think of him as the boyfriend type when Tim wasn't.

"I gotta get Bella taken care of," Ruby said.

"I'll catch up with you after the other events," Hollis said. "Ain't got a car, and it was a tight squeeze in Rusty's before, I'll catch a ride back with you, Ruby?"

"Sure."

Ruby took care of Bella and managed to catch the tail end of the barrel racing. She left part way through the bull riding to get Bella trailered. Hollis met her awhile later, and she noted it was pretty hard for him to walk a straight line. They spotted Jake near their trailer.

"Where did Darla go?" Ruby asked him.

"Who knows, who cares," Jake said shortly. He looked over at Ruby. "You know, I don't know why you're running around playing girlfriend with Kelly. You know full well he don't give a shit about you."

Ruby's throat constricted. One second he was nice, the next he was bringing her to the knife's edge of crying.

"Come on, Jake," Hollis said, his voice edgy and sounding unlike him.

"Tell me I ain't right," Jake said to Hollis. "Anyone know them two were seeing each other? Nope. Why not? Cuz Tim don't give a shit, that's why."

"It's not any of your business anyway," Ruby said uncomfortably.

"You keep foolin' yourself, darlin'." Jake blew a plume of smoke toward her. "Tim ain't stupid enough to get himself attached to a broad."

Ruby felt the anger bubble up in her chest. "And maybe you're mad because you are!"

She watched as Jake's face hardened, and his eyes got the cool, empty look she'd seen in Tim's so many times.

"I ain't attached to nothin'," he said. "Never was, never will be, so you can keep your opinions to yourself, bitch."

He stalked off toward the parking lot, shoving past Everett who was asking him why he wasn't taking care of the horse. Ruby tried to take in a deep breath, shaking.

"He is such a damn liar," she said.

"Don't be too hard on him, Ruby," Hollis said, his voice sad. "You need some help with the horses?"

Ruby looked at him apprehensively, the fear leaving her body. "As long as you don't kill any of 'em."

He slung an arm around her shoulder and walked toward the pen with her.

18

It took awhile for her and Hollis to get Bella in the horse trailer. Everett left with Whiskey Jack right after the rodeo ended so he'd be at the bar before people showed up. He left Wick, Ruby, and Hollis to get Midnight Bandit and Bella back since Jake had blown off the duty.

"I can't believe him." Ruby angrily packed his equipment into the truck.

"Jake's got a temper," Hollis said. "Are you gonna give me a few freebies for helping you out?"

Ruby grinned. "You won a boatload of money, you can pay."

Her grin faded as she watched Hollis sit up on a fence rail and crack a can of beer open.

"You're drinking a lot tonight," she said.

"Celebrating," he said. "It's not every day I win big at the track."

"You gamble a lot?" she asked, although it was more of a statement.

He shrugged. "More than Brenda would like. It's why she dumped me."

"Dumped you?"

"Long story."

They had two old pickup trucks to pull the horse trailers. One was Everett's, used only on the ranch, and the other was borrowed.

Ruby watched with a creased brow as Hollis stumbled on the way to the truck and got inside. She got in the driver's side and struggled to shut the rusty door.

She started up the engine and grinded the truck into gear, lurching forward. Manual transmissions weren't her strong suit.

"Sure you don't want me to drive?" Hollis cringed at the grinding.

"I can do it." She forced the clutch in and shifted into gear, the truck lurching.

She pulled onto the road slowly, watching the horse trailer behind her in her mirrors. As soon as she was on an open stretch and didn't have to shift, she relaxed behind the wheel.

"So where is Tim at, anyway?" Hollis asked.

"Away," Ruby said.

Hollis chuckled. "You're getting to sound more like him every day."

"Well, I don't think he'd appreciate it if I was talkin' his business all over town," she said practically.

"What about Bill?" Hollis asked. "That whole thing smells fishy to me."

She looked over at Hollis, then back to the road. "Why's that?"

"Bill shot, Bobby Tafani in jail, Tim nowhere to be found," Hollis said. "Brenda was madder than a hornet and suddenly fine with it. And it isn't like Kelly to leave a guy to work alone like that. Unless something else was going on."

Ruby sighed. "Hollis, what are you gettin' at? Just say it, and don't beat around the bush."

"I don't think things went down the way they say it did."

"What does that have to do with you?" she asked.

Hollis shrugged. "They don't run things around here, the Outfit does."

"I don't follow."

"The Chicago Outfit, the Syndicate, guys out of New England, Cleveland, St. Louis, Detroit, and some downtown boys like Binion and Wyatt, they run this town. They don't stand for gangs running the street without their say. Tim's playing with fire if he's doing things like that. If there's one thing those guys don't like, it's people cutting into their profits. If Tim starts up something, they could come down on him. People in the crossfire could get hurt. I figure he would've learned after the Outfit tried to turn his face into hamburger."

"Well, then you better talk to Tim, because I ain't havin' any part of it," Ruby said.

"If you're his girl you do," Hollis said seriously.

Ruby sighed again. "I don't even know if I am."

The only sound in the truck was the engine and wind whistling past the windows.

"I think you are," Hollis said quietly. "Otherwise you wouldn't know jack about what's going on with him. But you do, even if you won't tell me. And the fact you're not tells me he's your guy."

"People around Rett's are always telling me you only got one oar in the water," Ruby said. "I think they got no clue how smart you really are."

"Shoot, kid," he grinned. "Wouldn't win a damn poker game otherwise."

When they reached the ranch, she had a time of it getting the horse trailer backed up. Wick ended up in the driver's seat and did it for her. He said he'd take care of the horses, so she took the pickup and spent another few minutes ruining the transmission on the way to Rett's.

"Jesus, remind me never to lend you my car," Hollis said.

"I can drive automatics just fine. I hate these manual transmissions!"

"I can tell by the way you're trying to murder it."

She rolled her eyes. Things were fine until it was time to downshift as she got to Everett's. It took forever to find a place to park.

"Good Lord," Ruby muttered, turning off the truck. "I'm gonna be up 'til the cows come home."

Hollis was already out of the truck and shaking hands with some friends in the parking lot. Ruby made her way up the stairs and into the packed bar. She'd never seen the place so full.

"Let's get moving," Jed said. "I'm about to die, and Irene looks like the whole world's workin' her last nerve."

Ruby tied the apron on and served drinks to the rowdy group. She watched as Jake came down the stairs, alone, and threaded his way toward the bar.

"Get me a bourbon, will ya?" he asked.

She poured a shot of bourbon. One of Tim's boys, Jesse, came up to the bar for a beer.

"You looked good out there, Ruby," Jesse said. "Tim'll be mad he missed it."

Ruby smiled gratefully and handed him a beer.

"You mean if he remembers he was nailin' her when he gets back from California," Jake said, downing the shot.

"Lay off, Jake," Jesse said.

Ruby turned away from Jake, burning with anger, and watched his reflection in the mirror. He was scowling at everyone around him. She wondered where Darla was.

She walked into the back kitchen, hoping Jake would be gone when she came out. Instead, he followed her.

"I've about had it with you, Jake." She turned around and found him lighting a cigarette and watching her with dead eyes.

"I don't give a shit what you've had," he said. He grabbed a bottle of whiskey off a shelf and opened it.

"Give it back," she said.

"Go fuck yourself." He took a swig right out of the bottle.

She marched over and took the bottle from him, putting it on a counter. He paid no attention to her and looked through Everett's inventory in the pantry, coming out with a bottle of Wild Turkey.

"Jake, come on," Ruby pleaded. She tried to take the bottle, but he held onto it with an iron grip.

"Everett said I could have it," he said.

"Fine," Ruby answered. She let go of the bottle, not caring about anything but getting Jake out of her hair. "Just take it, and get the hell outta here."

"You sure would like that, huh, darlin'?" His voice had taken on a dangerous tone. Ruby backed up and realized with some alarm her back was against the wall inside the pantry. "Getting rid of me must sound mighty good to you, huh?"

Jake was less than half a foot from her, and he stood looming over her with a strange expression in his face.

"Where's Darla? I figured you'd be spending time with her," she asked.

"Ain't no point," Jake said, talking around his cigarette. "I guess everybody knows she's goin'?"

Ruby wanted to close her eyes to shut out the look in Jake's eyes. He was so close to her, she could feel the warmth of his skin. He looked like he was on the edge of losing it, and she had no idea why.

"Look," she said, her voice pleading. "I'm sorry for what I said before, okay? It's not like I know anything."

"Little girl falls apart so damn easy." His voice taunted her. He plucked the cigarette from his lips. "You think Tim'd want you apologizing . . . making nice so I'll go away?"

He pushed her shoulder back against the wall with one hand, the cigarette dangerously close to her hair, his other hand holding the bottle of bourbon.

"Jake, let me go," she said desperately, her voice wavering. She would give anything to be out in the other room.

"Let you go?" He snorted with laughter. "Just like that? Like it's so damn easy, just let you walk on out like it's nothing?"

"What are you talkin' about?" she asked, watching his cold eyes, which weren't even seeing her.

"It ain't that easy to walk away," he said. "You want out, you'll go when I say."

She swallowed hard and noticed his hand was gripped around the bottle of Wild Turkey so tight she thought the glass would shatter. His knuckles were white with rage and she prayed he wouldn't lose it and hit her with the bottle.

"Leaving shouldn't be that fuckin' easy." Jake's voice rose. Ruby swallowed hard.

Jake let her go, whirled around and threw the bottle of bourbon at the wall. Glass and liquid flew everywhere, and she shielded her face.

She lowered her hands and stood there, motionless, watching the liquid run down the wall and pool on the floor. No one came running; the noise from the bar was so loud the crash was ignored. She watched Jake with bated breath as he ran a hand through his hair a few times. He looked over, his expression unreadable, then swore, grabbed another bottle off the shelf and stormed out the side door, letting the screen slam behind him.

Ruby moved away from the wall, her legs shaky. She took in a deep breath, then picked up a mop.

Hours later, Ruby moved behind the bar and looked at the mess. Broken glass littered the floor, which was sticky with spilled beer. Everywhere she looked there were overflowing ashtrays and empty beer bottles. The pile in the corner was so large it looked like a mountain.

Everett was passed out upstairs, and the last of the partiers were collected around the room in haphazard fashion.

Jed had left around three in the morning, and Irene had given up, tossed her apron on the counter and left shortly after, tired of breaking up fights and dealing with drunks.

Now the bar was quiet, and Ruby was about ready to fall over. She looked over at Hollis, who paid for another jukebox song and was singing along to Smokey Robinson.

He crashed onto the bar stool and clumsily lit a cigarette, his voice scratchy.

"Hey, Hollis," she said. "You about ready to go?"

His big brown eyes lifted up and looked through long lashes. He was half slumped over his drink, and she noticed with concern that he was nursing an awfully big glass of rye whisky.

"Hey," she said softly. "You okay?"

"I dunno," he sighed. "Sometimes I wonder."

His eyes were bloodshot and sad. The only sound in the bar was Smokey, asking them to take a good look at the tracks of his tears.

"What's up?" She placed a hand on Hollis's arm. The cigarette he was holding between his fingers was smouldering down, as if he'd forgotten he was holding it.

"I made a big mistake." He took a drink of his rye. "A huge one."

"What's that?" she asked. She carefully plucked the cigarette out from between his fingers and put it in the ashtray.

"Brenda," he said. "It was all my damn fault."

"What was?"

"Girls around here don't look at me," he said morosely. "They all know I pass most of my time in the casinos or poker. I shoulda known something was up. That girl was prettier than anyone I ever saw and all over me at the tables for half the night."

"Who, Brenda?"

"No. Girl I met at the tables."

"So what happened?" Ruby asked.

"I bought her drinks, and she was like a good luck charm, you know?" He tossed back more rye. "I dunno. It all went to hell. Gimme another."

"Hollis, I don't think—"

"Just pour me a goddamn drink," he said bitterly.

She hesitated, feeling like she should say no. He never sounded as mean as he did then, not since she met him. His eyes softened as he looked up again.

"Please." His voice was desperate.

Ruby sighed and took his glass, then added a bit of water when he wasn't looking. She opened the bottle of Crown Royal and poured a small amount in the glass. He looked with a raised eyebrow, and she poured a little more. Everett went all out with his winnings. He'd be angry Hollis drank the good stuff away.

He took the glass without a word and downed half of it in one swallow.

"So you're seeing this other girl? Is that why Brenda's mad?" Ruby knew he needed to talk. The only time these men ever did was when they were drunk and their guard was down.

He laughed. "No. She put on a real good show at the tables. Friend of Brenda's saw it all and told her I was kissing this other girl. I won the game, then invited this girl back to my place. They cleaned me out before I hit the parking lot."

"What do you mean?"

Ruby circled around the bar and sat on the stool next to Hollis, afraid he was going to fall over.

"It was a scam, Ruby," he sighed. "I was winning too much. They thought I was cheating. Don't know if it was set up by the casino or I got grifted by some gang. Either way, they took all my money and knocked me unconscious."

"Unconscious! Are you okay?"

He nodded miserably. "Pride hurts more than my head."

"Brenda didn't believe you?"

He shook his head. "Thought it was a story. Guess I can't blame her, I've told a few before. She's a real good girl. The one time I land someone like that and I mess it all up."

His voice was so quiet Ruby was straining to hear him talk. He took another gulp of his drink, downing the last of it and rubbing his eyes.

She was never much good at cheering people up. She listened to the song play and wondered if Smokey Robinson had someone like Hollis in mind when he wrote it.

"I won't find anybody like that again," he sighed, his head lolling toward her and back down again.

"Do you love her?"

"Brenda?" he asked. He was quiet, toying with his pack of matches. "I could have. I really could have."

Ruby tried to help Hollis outside, but quickly realized he'd come to the bar with her and had no ride and no car to sleep it off in.

"Come on," she said, trying to support his weight. "You can stay up-stairs."

"You're being awful nice, Ruby," he said. "I didn't even tip you."

"Come on, help me out a little, Hollis." She struggled to help him up the stairs.

"A week's time you'll be doing this with Jake." He grabbed onto the rail-ing and swayed. Ruby struggled to keep him upright.

"Fat chance I'd help him," she said.

"Don't be too hard on him," Hollis said, dragging a foot up a stair.

"Hard on him?" she exclaimed. "Hollis, he's awful to me, you have no idea."

"It's not you." He stumbled as they reached the top of the stairs. Ruby turned and headed to the first room, unlocking it, and Hollis almost fell on the floor in the process. She got him to the bed, and he fell onto it like a brick. She went into the bathroom and brought out a bucket, a pitcher of water and a glass.

"What ain't me?" she asked. She was breathing heavily from dragging him up the stairs. She sat on the side of the bed, making sure Hollis was still breathing.

"Jake's not mad at you," Hollis mumbled. "He's mad cuz Darla's leav-ing."

"For Hollywood? She wants to be an actress or something?"

Hollis nodded, then obviously thought better of moving his head. "You're easier to take it out on."

"Well, it ain't fair," Ruby said.

"Nope," Hollis said. "But it's not fair for Jake either. He'd never admit it, but he loves her. He loves her, and she's going anyway."

Ruby turned the thought over in her mind. She knew what it felt like to love someone and have them leave you; to simultaneously love them and hate them and know they would leave no matter what. Her mother had no choice, but her father did. He just hadn't chosen her.

"I was pretty mean to him earlier," she said.

"He's mad because you were right," Hollis said. "Don't be too hard on him. He doesn't know what he's doing. None of us do."

Ruby pulled Hollis's boots off and set them on the floor at the foot of the bed, then helped Hollis, who was halfway to unconscious, out of his jacket.

"There's a bucket here in case you're sick," she said, looking into his sad eyes. "Some water, too. If you need somethin', my room's upstairs, come knock on the door. Rett's passed out, and he sleeps like the dead when he's drunk. I'm a light sleeper, I'll hear you."

"Thanks," he said.

She pulled a blanket over him.

"You'll fix this with Brenda, Hollis," she whispered. "I know it. You lay off the sauce long enough, you might know it, too. And maybe . . . maybe stay outta the casinos or something?"

He tried to grin, but didn't make it. His eyes shut slowly, and Ruby listened quietly for a minute, making sure he was breathing okay. She shut the light off and went upstairs as quietly as she could.

Sunday, May 22, 1966

Ruby slept late, and by eleven o'clock she stumbled bleary-eyed toward Hollis's room. She poked her head in, found him sleeping and was relieved to see he was still breathing. She walked down the stairs and was afraid of what she'd find.

"Oh God," she mumbled, looking at the mess. The downstairs was empty of people, but full of garbage. The floor was a mess, there were empties everywhere, and it was going to take her years to clean it all up.

She went over to the bar and uncapped a bottle of vodka.

"A little early to be drinking."

She turned around and saw Tim standing in the doorway.

"You're back!" she exclaimed, stepping through the garbage and walking toward him. She smiled and slid her arms around his neck.

He bent his head and kissed her, and she realized how much she had missed him. She felt shy, as if it were weeks since she last saw him instead of days. She shivered, thinking about Tim holding a gun on Bill and firing. She wanted to ask him about it.

"How was the trip?" she asked. "You did it all okay?"

"It was all good," he said. "What the hell happened in here?"

"We had a night, I'll tell you that," Ruby said, walking behind the bar. "It wasn't so bad. After Jake left, at least."

Tim looked at her. "What was Jake up to?"

Ruby stared at the floor and cleared beer bottles off the top of the bar.

"He was just mad to be mad," Ruby said. "Hollis said he's all swole up because his girl's leaving."

She saw Tim's forehead crease.

"Darla's leaving?"

Ruby shrugged. "That's what Hollis said."

"Jake leave you alone?"

"Yeah, he stalked outta here madder than a hornet, with a bottle of Wild Turkey," she sighed. "That boy's gonna find himself in a mess of trouble one day."

Commotion on the stairs got her attention, and she turned to see Hollis slowly make his way into the room, looking pretty rough.

"Mornin'," she said.

"Warner," Tim said, nodding at Hollis.

Hollis looked over at Ruby and frowned.

"How the hell'd I get up there?" He pointed toward the ceiling.

"I helped you up, remember? You were pretty gone, passed out cold not too long after you hit the pillow," she said.

She watched out of the corner of her eye as Tim took short drags on his smoke.

"Where's my car?"

"I dunno," she said. "You rode here with me, remember?"

She saw Hollis knit his brows together, as if struggling with some invisible enemy to remember.

"Something about horses?"

"You helped me with the horses after the rodeo," she said. "Good Lord, how much did you drink yesterday?"

"A lot, I guess," he said. "I don't remember anything."

Hollis staggered toward a bar stool and braced himself against it. His eyes were bloodshot, and his hair a mess. She had never seen him with anything but a perfectly coiffed pompadour. Now it looked less pomp and more dour.

"Guess you better get yourself moving and get the hell outta here," Tim said, eyeing Hollis coolly.

Ruby shot Tim an irritated glance, then turned back to Hollis. "You ain't in any condition to go anywhere."

"Shoot, I'm alright," Hollis said. "Still drunk I think, but alright."

"You want me to call someone?" she asked.

"No," he said. "Heck no. I'll walk home. The air, it'll clear my head."

"I'll get the door," Tim said curtly. Ruby shot him a look.

"Are you sure?" She helped Hollis toward the door.

"Yeah," he said, staggering back from the light outside. "See? I feel better already."

He was back to joking, so he must be on the mend, Ruby reasoned. She looked at Tim's blank face, an unreadable mask, and wanted to kick him for being such a jerk. It was all too easy to think of him shooting his best friend when he acted like this. Ruby shivered as she followed Hollis outside.

"I guess you don't remember talkin' to me last night then," she said. Tim watched from the doorway.

Hollis sighed. "Maybe I lied before. Maybe I remember some of it."

She smiled softly. "Don't worry, I won't say nothin'."

Hollis nodded and rubbed the bridge of his noise. "Thanks, kid."

"Be careful, don't fall in a ditch or nothin'."

She watched him walk through the gravel lot, his steps getting a little surer.

"Don't get hit by a car neither!" she yelled after him. She waited until he was on the shoulder of the road before she made her way back inside.

Tim watched her as she walked past him. She didn't like the look in his eyes.

"What was he doin' here?"

"Hangin' out at the bar," she said coolly. "Just like the rest of Las Vegas was doin'. You don't gotta be so mean to him."

"You spent a lot of time with Warner last night," he said.

She turned around and looked at him, with an expression halfway between angry and happy.

"Are you jealous?" she asked, walking over to him. He gave a coarse laugh.

"Of what?"

"Seems like you're jealous." She couldn't stop herself from smiling. He had an unreadable expression, and the apprehensive feeling returned. Tim had never scared her before, why was he doing it now?

Maybe it wasn't him; he hadn't said or done anything he hadn't before, yet now it made her nervous when he got that look. She wanted to ask him about Bill, but had no idea what to say.

"I got some cleaning up to do." She wondered what was running through his head. "I could use some help."

He smirked, then watched her, and she shrugged and headed for the stairs, expecting to hear the screen door shut. She prepared herself for the fact that sound might make her cry. But when she reached the landing, she heard his footsteps following her instead.

Tim climbed the stairs slowly.

Ruby was stripping the old sheets off the bed when he came into the bedroom. A light breeze blew, rustling the old curtains hanging haphazardly across the open window. She stepped past him and tossed the bundle into the hallway.

She shook out a sheet, and it billowed above the bed and settled on the mattress.

He wondered how Bill was; wondered if Ruby knew. She hadn't said a word about it, but she was as nervous as a cat. She was trying to keep her hands busy, cleaning things and bustling about instead of looking him in the eye.

Tim shut and locked the door to the bedroom and walked over to the window. Outside, the day was bright and warm, and the sun was naked in the sky. His head felt full of cobwebs.

"What's wrong?"

He turned around. Ruby stood near the bed.

"I got something to tell you," he said shortly. He took out his last cigarette and lit it, taking a deep puff. She stood and looked toward him. He left his cigarette smouldering in an ashtray and walked toward her slowly. She looked relieved.

"I know," she said.

He looked her in the eye and realized she was talking about Bill.

"I know you shot him." Her voice wavered. Man, he hoped she wouldn't cry.

"How?"

"You left the bullets in the gun."

He closed his eyes and exhaled quickly. That was a damn rookie mistake. He never would've done it if he hadn't been drinking. He opened his eyes again, and she was staring at him with a look he couldn't read.

"What'd you do with them?" he asked.

"They're still in the gun, along with another Rett popped in there," Ruby said. "He didn't see any reason to waste five good bullets by throwin' them away, even if he didn't know where they'd come from."

Tim took his jacket off and tossed it on the chair then walked back to Ruby. He took her hands and pulled her to him. She hesitated, looking up at him questioningly.

"I didn't wanna do it," he said. "I had to."

She nodded, her eyes wide and sad. She stepped toward him, and he almost cursed out loud when he felt the relief flood his body when she put her arms around him. Since when did he give a shit what she, or any broad, thought about his business? Since when did he *tell* them?

He was dismayed to find his arms circling around her tighter, like he was waiting for her to break away and run from him. But she pressed herself to him tighter.

He placed a hand on the side of her head and ran it down her hair. He tangled his hand into her hair at the base of her neck and brought her lips to his. This time it felt different, his skin felt alive. He wondered what that meant.

She struggled with his shirt, and he let her go momentarily to help her out. He pulled her to the bed.

"I just made it up," she whispered against his neck, her breath hot.

He looked at her, feeling like he was burning up. He raised his eyebrows slowly and kissed her lightly, raking her lips with his teeth.

"I can make it again," she gasped.

Ruby lay next to Tim, her face pressed against his arm. She sat up slightly and ran her hand over the stitches under his ribcage.

"Quit it." He batted her hand away. "It itches like hell."

"It's healing good," she said. He'd picked out some of the stitches, and a thin red scar was forming. She could tell Tim had scratched at them. So much for his patented self control. She smiled.

"What?" he asked.

"Nothing." She settled back against the pillow. Tim leaned over and rifled through his jean pockets. He was rewarded with an empty package of Pall Malls and cursed.

Ruby studied the scars on his back. They all looked similar, and probably happened all at once. She wondered how in the world they had gotten there in the first place. She moved her hand toward his back and tried to stop herself from reaching out to touch them. At the last minute, she slid her hand around the top of his shoulder instead.

He shrugged her hand off lightly, and she let her finger tips slide down his right shoulder blade slightly. She was taken aback when he visibly flinched.

"Don't," he said. He lay back onto the bed and looked up at the ceiling, toying with the empty cigarette package. She picked it out of his hands and leaned over him, placing it on the night table.

"You don't like people touchin' your back, I guess?"

He shook his head, not making eye contact. "Nope."

"What happened?"

"Nothing."

She nodded, disappointed that he hadn't told her. She shouldn't feel that way, it was his business after all. She lowered her head to his and grazed his lips with her own. He hadn't shaved and his skin was rough against hers.

"Gonna be here all day?" he asked.

"You saw this place. I'll be here the rest of my life," she said dramatically. "What about you?"

"Gotta find Jake," he said.

"Jake? Why?" she asked, feeling slightly worried. She hoped he wasn't going after him or something. The last thing she needed was to be nursing a cut-up Tim back to health again.

"I need to teach him how to drive the truck with the trailer on it," he said. "I'm gonna need to him take a run or two so I don't run myself into the ground."

They were interrupted by loud yelling.

"Ruby! Where the hell are you?"

"Oh God." She buried her head on Tim's chest. Everett's voice carried easily through the thin walls.

"Why the hell ain't this place cleaned up yet?" he hollered.

"Why the hell ain't you doin' it," she muttered.

"I locked the door," Tim said. His fingertips tumbled the length of her spine like he was playing the piano.

"Thank God," Ruby murmured.

19

An hour later, Ruby came downstairs with Tim on her heels. Everett was sweeping up the floor and glanced over, an irritated expression on his face. He said nothing and continued sweeping, his brows knitted together forcefully.

"Mornin'," she said. She got silence for her trouble and rolled her eyes at Tim. Everett stopped sweeping and put the broom in a corner, then took a cardboard box full of empty beer bottles out the front door toward his El Camino.

"Is Bill getting out soon?" she asked, uncomfortable with the sudden silence.

"I dunno," Tim said. "I might go by tomorrow and see him."

Ruby nodded and played with the belt loop on her jeans. She wished she could take off from here, go with Tim wherever he was off to and Everett be damned. But she not only had to help her brother clean up, she had to head over to the stable and exercise the horses. Maybe she could find a way out of cooking dinner.

"So I heard a bunch of people talkin' about this drive-in restaurant, the Round-Up. You think we could go there some time? Maybe?"

She saw Tim's eyes dart over to her and watched his expression.

"Maybe," he said.

She tried not to let the disappointment show on her face as they walked to the door. Ever since Jake had said those things at the rodeo it made her wonder. She and Tim were alone or at Everett's most of the time, except when they'd been on the road, in places no one knew either of them.

Anytime there was a crowd at Everett's, Tim was careful not to show her too much attention. He never kissed her in public or held her. It hadn't bothered her much until Jake pointed it out, and maybe there was a reason he noticed. She was nauseated thinking Tim might not want anyone to know about them, and there were only two reasons she could think of for that: He was embarrassed to be seen with her or he had a girlfriend he hadn't told her about.

Her throat constricted and she tried to keep the tears at bay. It was ridiculous to think like that. Hadn't he just come and spent time with her when he didn't have to? She tried to let that reassure her, but then she wondered if he used her for sex like Lewis. The thoughts gnawed.

She walked with Tim to Bill's car and leaned against the door.

"Will I see you later?" she asked.

"I got business," Tim said shortly. Tim walked her around to the driver's side, and he opened the door. He hesitated before getting in, and kissed her on the cheek. "Maybe tomorrow I'll take you up to the hospital with me to see Bill."

She smiled and stepped back as he got in the car, shut the door, and roared the engine to life. He took off out of the parking lot like a demon was chasing him, a spray of dust the only thing he left behind.

The hospital wasn't much of a date, but maybe she should shut her mouth and be glad they were going anywhere at all.

Tim drove around for awhile. Jake wasn't at the stables, and he wasn't at the Silver Slipper, so the only place left to look was his shitty motel room. He found Jake sitting on the stairs, Darla with him.

"Kelly," Jake said, looking pretty worse for wear.

Tim glanced over at Darla, who looked like she'd rather have Tim go on his merry way than interrupt them.

"You look like hell," Tim said.

"Everett had a blowout after the rodeo."

"That right? I heard you cut out early," he said. "Rumour has it you got up to some stuff last night."

He was glad Jesse and his boys gossiped worse than high school girls. It paid off sometimes.

Jake's face got that warning look; it was nearly invisible to most people, but Tim had seen it so many times since he met Jake, it was easy for him to see it.

"You want something?" Jake asked.

"The truck," Tim said. "I might need you to take it on a run soon. You'd best learn how to handle it."

"I can handle it fine," Jake said. "I'm busy Kelly, get lost."

Tim shrugged. "Fine."

He walked around the corner toward Bill's car. He leaned against the bumper and lit a cigarette. A few minutes later Darla came sashaying down the street.

"You've got him in a fine mood," she said. She was wearing a dress and heels, her hair done, her lips red.

He shrugged. "Heard some things I don't like."

Darla looked back over her shoulder. No sign of Jake.

"I heard some things too," she sighed. "Jake and Carolyn down at the Thunderbird necking so the whole world could see. Don't think I don't know that's what you were trying to do, getting him in trouble with me."

"Yet here you are."

"Here I am," she agreed. She leaned against Bill's car with no concern for her dress. "He always comes back, Tim. He can't stop himself. Only he thinks he owns me, and he doesn't."

"Heard you were leaving town." He blew a stream of smoke.

She nodded, a smile tugging at the corners of her mouth. "Talent agent came out to the show last week and asked a couple of us girls to come out to Hollywood for screen tests. My aunt lives out there, she said I can stay with her. It's a chance, Tim. Only one I'm ever gonna get."

He wasn't so sure that was the case with a girl like her. She was already dancing three shows a night at the Slipper, and lucky for her she wasn't working nude or Jake would've killed that for her.

"He doesn't want me to go," she said. "He won't say it. I just know."

No, instead Jake would make her last days here hell if he could. He'd cheat on her, dump her and do whatever he could to make her cry. Only he didn't think Darla would break. They were one strange couple.

"Good luck out there, Dar," he said.

"You keep outta trouble," she said. She leaned in and lightly brushed his lips with her own. She smoothed the front of her dress, then smiled.

She walked down the street, purpose in her step, and a little extra hip in her walk. Tim chuckled, wiping her lipstick from his lips.

A few minutes later Jake came strutting down the street.

"You're an asshole." Jake lit a cigarette.

"You wanted Darla to know you can't keep it in your pants."

Jake looked over at him. Tim didn't bother to look at his expression. Jake was pretty proud of himself. Too bad for him he didn't care what Carolyn got up to.

They got in Tim's car and drove to the auto body place where the truck was. Jake settled into a grumpy silence.

"What the hell are we doing?" Jake asked. Tim parked and they walked over to the truck.

"We're gonna take the truck and pick the trailer up at the stables, and you're gonna learn how to drive with the trailer," Tim said, getting in the passenger seat. "I might need you to do a run or two down to Calabasas."

"I know how. And what makes you think I'm gonna want to?" Jake started up the truck engine like he was born to it.

"You're gonna want the money," Tim said. "You do the run, you get ten percent."

"We agreed on twenty for me finding the truck. Only fair."

"Fine."

They pulled into the stables at Everett's, and Tim was relieved to see Ruby wasn't around. She was going to be trapped inside that bar all day from the looks of the place that morning.

Jake jumped up on the back of the truck and hooked up the trailer. Tim watched Jake with suspicious eyes. He knew what the hell he was doing. They got on the road later and even though he took the turns a little short, he had no problem changing lanes and merging, even with the trailer on.

"You've done this before," Tim said.

Jake looked over and smiled bitterly.

"I told you before I knew how. Everyone thinks I was in flight school. No flight school at Nellis. I was motor pool. Drove a truck."

"You're an asshole, you know that?" Tim had suspected something when he'd taken Jake out to learn to drive awhile back, but this wasn't it.

Tim shook his head and looked out at the Las Vegas landscape, burning in the midday sun. He didn't know why, but he felt like levelling Jake. They were quiet all the way back to the stable.

"I'll do the next run, this weekend. You can take the one after," Tim said.

"Sounds like a real drag."

"It is," Tim said. "Watch out for Rosa. Some whore Wayne picked up in Mexico."

"Is she good lookin'?" Jake asked, getting in the passenger seat.

"If you like that sorta thing," Tim said. "Wayne don't mind sharing. I don't gotta pay for it, myself, but it might work out for you."

"What, did the whore turn you down?" Jake asked.

"Fuck off."

"You're getting soft since you started banging Everett's sister," Jake said.

"Speaking of, I heard you were hassling her." Tim stared him down. "I hear you're bothering her, I'm gonna have to murder you a little."

Jake shrugged. They reached the motel and both got out of the car.

"You got it bad for her, huh?" Jake asked.

Tim shrugged. "Nope. Just looking out for what's mine."

"I ain't got a problem with mine," Jake said with a grin.

"Until she leaves town, anyway."

Anger flickered in Jake's eyes.

"Ruby sure is a mess of trouble," Jake said. "The way she's always got her eye on me when I'm around. You sure she's getting what she needs from you?"

"At least my girl isn't leaving me in the dust. Maybe, like you said, she ain't getting what she needs."

Tim ducked Jake's first punch and swung back, connecting with his jaw. Jake switched it up and caught him with a fist that glanced off his temple. He didn't go for his mid-section since he knew the minute he did, Jake would do the same and lay him out. The last thing he needed was to rip it open again.

His fist connected again with Jake's head, then he saw stars as Jake managed to land a glancing blow to his mouth.

A second later they were both apart, staring each other down. He tasted blood.

"I meant what I said, Jake." Tim spat blood in the dirt, glad to see Jake's nose was bleeding. "I hear you're giving her a bad time, you'll be dealing with me."

"You're a shit liar, Kelly," Jake said. "You got it bad."

Jake walked off, and Tim waited a moment before getting in the car and driving toward the warehouse.

Tim fixed his lip up then lay on the mattress in the small room off the hall. He couldn't stop thinking about the jeering tone in Jake's voice.

He turned over on the mattress and spied the bottle of aspirin and dry-swallowed three. His lip was going to look fantastic the next day. Ruby would get on his case about it, and he'd have to think of a reason why he and Jake had gotten into it.

He thought about Ruby's crestfallen expression when he hadn't committed to taking her to the Round-Up. It shouldn't be a big deal. But the minute he took her out, people would know she was his girl. He wasn't sure he wanted it that way.

Jake was right. He couldn't lie worth shit, even to himself. But still—it was a dangerous time to let anyone know he was seeing her.

He heard rumblings that Bobby Tafani was out on bail and wanted face time with him thanks to what happened with Bill. Heads were going to crack over this, he knew that much. That wasn't his only problem—Tafani was making noise, and that meant some of the downtown guys might hear. God forbid the Outfit did. He wouldn't put it past any of those hoods to use Ruby to their advantage.

So there it was—make Ruby happy and take her out or keep everything under wraps. He knew what that meant; lots more crestfallen expressions, and Ruby looking at the ground like a sad kitten.

It's a drive-in restaurant, not a wedding chapel, he thought to himself. Take her for the damn burger.

He relaxed as he came to the decision and thought of the benefits it might bring when he told Ruby. It wasn't a big deal, taking her out. Hell, people did it every day. She couldn't go to the casinos and was probably stir crazy hanging around with Everett all day.

It'd take a lot for him to look like as much of a pansy as Jake the way he and Darla were always breaking up and making up and fighting in public; taking Ruby to the Round-Up was nothing.

But first, they'd see Bill.

Monday, May 23, 1966

Ruby was cleaning glasses when Tim walked in.

"I thought you'd give up and burn the place down." He sat on a bar stool. "I never guessed I'd see the floor again from the way it looked yesterday."

"I thought about it, I'll tell you that," she sighed. "What happened to your lip?"

Tim touched his lip thoughtfully. "Got in a fight."

"With who?" she asked.

"Nobody."

Ruby rolled her eyes. Trust Tim to be back to one word answers. She had a feeling she knew who he was sparring with.

"I'm going over to the hospital to see Bill," he said. "You wanna come?"

Ruby nodded. "I rode this morning, and there's nothing for me to do all week. Will you be here on the weekend?"

Tim shook his head. "Another run, shouldn't be gone more than a night."

She was hoping he'd ask her to come along, but he remained silent, and so did she.

"Should I bring him something?" she asked.

Tim shook his head. "He'll be out soon anyway. Just save him some beer, and he'll be happy."

Ruby walked outside and let the screen door slam behind her. She watched Tim's sure steps as he took her hand and walked her to Bill's car. It would be interesting to see if things were strange between him and Bill since all this happened.

"How did Jake do with the truck yesterday?" she asked. Wick told her Tim and Jake had shown up at the stables in it.

"Drives it like he was born in one," Tim said, with irritation in his voice. "Turns out that's what he did in the Air Force."

"You're kiddin'?" Ruby was genuinely surprised. "He never said anything to me."

A few minutes later they pulled into the hospital parking, and Ruby breathed a sigh of relief when she found herself on solid ground again. She felt like walking into the emergency room and asking for some oxygen.

"Why do you always drive like the devil's chasin' you?" She followed Tim's long strides toward the hospital doors.

"Because usually he is," he answered, holding the door for her. Ruby hid a smile and, as they stepped into the elevator, he took her hand.

They rode upstairs in silence. They exited the elevator, then Tim stopped and turned to Ruby.

"If the cop's outside his room, keep your voice down and don't mention anything about California," he said.

Ruby nodded. "I know."

"I guess you kinda do know these things, huh?" he asked.

"I'm working at a roadhouse underage, I ride in rodeos, and I'm on my way to visit a guy who was shot by his best friend," Ruby whispered. "I think I've caught on."

Tim smiled one of his rare, genuine smiles, and she was surprised at how much it changed him, how different it made him look. He looked less like some too-knowing Cheshire cat.

There was a cop sitting outside Bill's room, reading a paper and looking bored.

"Well, look what the cat dragged in," Bill said. He looked restless and antsy rather than tired. Tim shut the door behind them.

Bill and Tim shook hands, and Ruby shyly said hello.

"Looks like you've been keeping busy since I got laid up in here," Bill said, nodding toward Tim's face. "Who was that courtesy of?"

"No one," Tim said. Bill laughed.

Ruby watched Bill look from Tim to her, then at their clasped hands.

"I guess I don't have to ask how the two of you are doing." He grinned at them both, an eyebrow raised. Ruby blushed and looked at the floor. "You gotta smoke, Tim?"

Tim tossed him a package of Pall Malls and Bill made a face.

"Put word out to the boys I'm in the market for some Chesterfields," Bill said. "I'll expect a pack before the night is out."

Tim nodded.

"Some Army pansy showed up here this morning to interview me," Bill said shortly.

"What for?" Ruby asked, her voice quiet.

"Reclassification," Bill said, blowing the smoke out the side of his mouth and away from her. "Guess they gotta make sure I'm not faking. My leg's healing alright now that they got the infection under control. But I'm gonna have trouble walking for awhile. Doc had to leave a small piece of the bullet in there. Anyhow, it could be a problem in the future. Or so the boys at the draft board'll hear."

Tim nodded.

"Anyone been up?" Tim asked. Ruby looked from Tim to Bill and felt the slightly strained tension in the air.

"Marilyn came up yesterday," he said with a grin. "Brought me chicken soup and fawned over me like I was a dying man. She's a breeze, that's for sure. Lewis came up earlier, giving me some lip about snagging his girl and saying all kinds of things about getting her back."

Ruby smiled. "That's funny. The night he heard you were shot he wanted to go and finish off the guys that did it."

"Did he now?" Bill smiled broadly. "Well, I guess ol' Jimmy ain't that bad after all. Maybe I'll leave his next girl alone."

"He's a good man in a clutch," Tim said.

"Would've been quite the scene if they'd gone out hunting for who did this," Bill said slyly.

Tim looked at him with an unreadable expression.

"Especially since I get my chance first," Bill said.

"Chance for what?" Ruby asked apprehensively.

"Bill wants to even the score one day," Tim said smoothly. "An eye for an eye and all that. She knows."

She didn't miss the look Bill shot Tim.

"Did you save me some beer?" he asked, a twinkle in his eye.

"A whole case of Pearl, straight from Texas," she said.

"That a girl," Bill said. "How'd your rodeo go?"

"It was okay," Ruby said. "I think I did alright."

Tim stepped closer to Bill's bed. "You heard anything about what's going down with any charges?"

"I gotta see the judge Wednesday morning when I get outta here. They're sending O'Lafferty to escort me over. I heard that Judge Lambert pulled my case," Bill said, his voice conspiratorially low.

"Good deal," Tim said. "Lambert's fair."

Bill nodded. "I've been listening to the cops, word is Tafani got bail since they haven't found the gun. Any way you could make that happen?"

Ruby's stomach turned to ice, and Tim's gaze raked over her, as if he was looking at a business proposition rather than her.

"I'll get it done," Tim said, not asking Ruby's opinion. She stared, her mouth open in protest. She didn't make a sound though, thinking about the officer outside the room. She wasn't itching to go to prison for knowing about all this.

Bill took in her expression and whistled low.

"It was that gun from Rett's place, wasn't it?" he asked. "The one he keeps under the bar? Well, damn. That's not where I would've figured it'd come from. That was pretty slick."

"Figured that'd be the last place the cops would check if they came looking my way," Tim said. "I'll see what I can do about it."

Ruby wanted to throw up. He used her. Maybe that's what this was about all along. Tim had made her fall for him, got her into bed, and used her to get the gun. Tears stung her eyes, but she was not going to cry in front of Tim Kelly. Not one tear was going to fall.

"I have to go," Ruby said. "Come by Rett's for that beer when you get out."

She whirled around and opened the door, startling the cop outside as she swept down the hallway, walking in stunned silence toward the elevators. As the bell dinged and the doors opened, she let the tears spill over.

Tim watched Ruby turn and go for the door as if she was running from a stampede. It must be the stupid gun. She was probably ticked he took it. Well, they'd have it out, but either way, he was getting that gun.

Tim hesitated a split second. Bill chuckled. "Go."

Tim walked down the hallway, and the elevator dinged as the doors began to close. He got one hand inside and forced the doors open, startling Ruby, who was wiping her eyes with the back of her hand.

"What's got you so uptight?" he asked. Her arms were crossed, and she was avoiding his gaze.

"Don't talk to me," she said bitterly.

"Ruby," he said patiently. The elevator reached the main floor and opened, and Ruby was out the doors in the blink of an eye. She was pretty fast when she was mad. Tim took longer strides to keep up with her as she charged across the lot.

"Ruby, come on," he said. "I don't got time for this."

"You used me!" She whirled around and made him stop short. "Just to get that stupid gun!"

Tim shut his eyes. Jesus Christ, he'd like to go one day without something going wrong.

"Ruby," he said.

"I can't believe I fell for it, too." She wiped her eyes. "Here I thought you were different, but you were usin' me all along. God, I am so stupid."

"Sure as hell are," Tim said.

"What?" she asked, looking like she was seconds away from slapping him.

"Kid, you think I couldn't get myself a gun if I wanted one? You think I'd have to go through the trouble of working you up for that long, just for a gun?"

She was quiet, watching him with suspicious eyes.

"Pete Malcolm's old man runs a gun store," Tim said. "If all I wanted was a gun, I could've picked it up from him."

"But you didn't," she said, accusations ripe in her voice.

"Nope." He stepped closer, watching her body language. She was distrustful now, but of her own thoughts more than him. He took hold of one of her hands. "What do you think the cops would do first? Question Pete's old man, check out his store. I needed a clean gun."

"So you used me."

He shook his head. "If I hadn't ever met you, I still could've got my hands on that gun. Everybody knows it's under the bar. I could've come in any time, I didn't need you in bed to do it."

He saw Ruby turning that over in her head and coming to the realization it was true. She was looking at the ground now, trying to hide her face from him. Her cheeks were blazing red, and she looked so down in the mouth he wanted to laugh. He remembered her story about the kid she'd slept with back home and stopped himself from smiling.

"Kid, I'm not using you," he said softly. She looked up at him with her liquid grey eyes, her brow full of those worried creases.

"I . . . I'm sorry," she said. "I didn't think, I got so mad when I thought—"

He leaned down and kissed her, snaking his hand around the back of her neck and pulling her closer to him. She feverishly returned his kiss.

He broke the kiss and smoothed her hair against her head, holding her against his chest.

"I need that gun," he said. "Just so Bill doesn't get sent away. I owe him that."

"You owe him a hell of a lot more than that," Ruby said, her voice muffled against his jacket.

He smiled a grim smile. She hadn't said no.

"I'll get Everett another one," he said. "A better one."

She nodded, pressing herself against him, and he had the urge to take her right there in the parking lot, to hear her breath quick in his ear and his name on her lips.

"Come on," he said roughly, taking her hand and pulling her toward Bill's car. "We can go out to the Round-Up."

She smiled winningly, and he felt like a bastard only for a second.

20

Ruby was nervous about going to the Round-Up. Sure, it was just a drive-in restaurant, but now she was going to walk into this place on Tim Kelly's arm, and that was something else altogether.

She wondered if she'd know anyone there. Even if she knew someone from Everett's, they probably never thought of her much beyond being the girl who served them drinks. She was always wearing blue jeans and western shirts or t-shirts, and she didn't wear much makeup. She hoped the girls at the Round-Up wouldn't look at her like Tim was out of his mind for bringing her there.

"Do I look okay?" she asked, turning toward Tim.

"It's a drive-in restaurant," Tim said. "Nobody to impress there."

He was quiet and threw his cigarette butt out the window.

"Can I ask you something?" she asked.

"Sure," he said.

"How come you did it yourself? How come you didn't get someone else to shoot him?" she asked.

They pulled up to a red light. Tim's expression was thoughtful.

"Wouldn't have been fair," he said. "It was my idea, my responsibility. I'm not about to ask my boys to do anything I wouldn't. Sam Wyatt told me you have to be able to do whatever you'd ask of someone else."

"The casino owner?"

Tim nodded. "He's cool."

"Well, he *is* a Texan." Ruby was quiet again before she asked the next question. "Do they know? The boys you run with?"

He shrugged. "Pete Malcolm's got a pretty good idea. I got the bullets from him, after all."

That explained why the boy looked so nervous around Tim lately. She mulled over what Tim said. Despite the fact he did something so awful, she had to admire the fact he hadn't let the task fall to anyone else.

She relaxed and watched the scenery fly by the window. Tim drove down the Strip, telling her stories about each hotel, mostly regarding who owned what. Every casino had mobsters from all over owning a small piece.

Tim pointed at the Desert Inn. "Moe Dalitz out of Cleveland's partnered up with Lansky who's part of the Syndicate to own the DI."

"The Syndicate?"

"New York mafia," he said.

"You sure know a lot about this."

"Have to in my line of work. Gotta know who not to anger. Even if it is the Outfit."

"You haven't liked them since before they attacked you." She stated that, rather than asked it. "Otherwise you wouldn't have been trying to operate under their noses."

He didn't answer for a moment.

"When I was ten years old, a guy named Mel Crucio showed up at the house and tied me, my mom and sister up. He sat around the house waiting on my old man." Tim lit a cigarette, balancing the steering wheel with his knees. "Old man never showed. Someone tipped him off."

"What'd he do to you?"

"Crucio? Nothing. Worked my mom over. But she didn't know where the old man had gone. He'd run straight to his partner. Turns out they'd robbed an Outfit guy who'd been skimming off the skim himself."

"The skim?"

"Mob skims off a percentage of the casino wins before it's counted and sends it back to the head of the mafia family. All the mob families do it, all the casinos. Word has it the Gaming Commission's investigating Moe Dalitz and John Scalish. Scalish heads the Cleveland family."

Ruby was fascinated. She nodded at him to go on.

"Once they get the money, they hand it off to a bag man who gets the money out of town, back to Chicago usually. This particular bag man'd been skimming off the top of the skim. My old man and a friend robbed him. The Outfit had an idea about their bag man and weren't too happy someone else got to him first."

"What happened?"

Tim shrugged. "Old man went to the Outfit, fell on his sword and said he was going to give the money to them and out their bag man as a thief. A pile of bullshit, but he had the money with him when he met with them, and that probably saved him from being buried in a hole in the desert. Now they drag him around by the nose making him think he could be made if he was smart about things. So he kisses their asses, gets nothing in return. They're never gonna make a North side Chicago Irishman, no matter what he thinks."

Ruby was frowning.

"Made . . . means make him a full on member of the mafia," Tim said. "My old man grew up in Chicago, the north side. The Irish side of town. They weren't so friendly with the south side Italian mob. They have long memories, and he won't outlive that. Fool was a hanger-on as a kid with the North Side Gang, until the Outfit took a bunch of them out. My old man was friends with of one John May's kids. May got killed in the St. Valentine's Day massacre. Mafia only make other Italians."

Ruby sat in silence, pouring over all of that in her mind.

She was quiet as he pulled into the Round-Up. People were eating in their cars, on their cars, at a few picnic tables set up outside and inside the restaurant.

Ruby looked around as Tim parked Bill's car. The place was crawling with people. She spotted Jesse Lennox and Carl Hamilton. Rusty and Jacqueline were with Hollis Warner and Brenda Pearce, and those two weren't fighting so maybe things were looking up for him.

Tim opened his door, and Ruby followed suit.

"Hey Ruby!"

She looked over and saw Hollis push himself off of Rusty's car and make his way toward her. She didn't miss the fact Tim had stepped in behind her and snaked an arm around her waist.

"Hey, Hollis," she said. "You're lookin' no worse for wear."

"Not a hangover in the world that can stop me," he said with a grin. "What brings the two of you down here?"

Brenda stepped up beside Hollis and was looking carefully at Ruby and Tim. It took all of Ruby's energy not to smile like an idiot, what with Tim's arm around her in front of the whole world.

"We came from the hospital," she said.

"Bill's getting out on Wednesday," Brenda said. "I guess he told you. He's gotta see the judge first, though."

"He won't be thrown in jail," Tim said shortly, looking at Brenda with an odd intensity. "You'll find him in Everett's before he ever finds his way to lockup."

Brenda smiled, and it made her look pretty. "It'll be a load off my mind when they say he isn't fit to serve."

"Word has it Bobby Tafani's mighty hacked off at you," Hollis said.

"Now why's that?" Tim let her go to light a cigarette, shielding it from the wind.

"I'm guessing it's because he got picked up for robbery and attempted murder. Still, he got bail," Hollis said.

"Is that so?"

Ruby watched Hollis. He suspected, she could tell that much. She didn't know how or why he knew, but she could tell he did. Maybe Brenda had told him. She saw by the way Tim studied Hollis that he had picked up on it too. Maybe that's why Tim was so weird with Hollis around lately.

"Speak of the devil," Hollis said, nodding behind Tim and Ruby. They both turned and saw the '53 Pontiac cruising into the Round-Up.

Ruby clasped her hand around Tim's. The car cruised slowly into the parking lot, like a shark smelling blood. Tim untangled his hand from hers, and she took in a breath as his face became an empty mask.

This was not welcome company.

Bobby Tafani was out of his territory, and Tim knew exactly why he was there. He spotted Joe Micelli in the passenger seat and two others sitting in the backseat.

He saw Jesse raise his chin up and subtly nod toward the car. Tim nodded slowly and walked toward where Bobby had stopped. His boys closed in on the car from the other side, just a casual group, but everyone could feel the tension in the air. People had quieted and were watching to see if a fight was about to unfold.

Tim could feel the tension. Ruby was pressed up against his side, and he wanted to shove her out of the way in case something bad was about to go down. At least it was here and not at one of the casinos. The last thing he needed was getting on the Outfit's radar over this. Unless he already was.

Tafani got out of the car and circled around until he was facing Tim.

"You and me need to have a few words," he said.

Tim stepped away from Ruby, and she looked up in concern.

"Go wait with the girls," he said. Hollis and Rusty had stepped up, ready to jump in if necessary. Ruby frowned, and Tim gave her a meaningful look. "Go on, Ruby."

She turned and walked toward Brenda and Jacqueline. He noticed how Brenda put a hand on Ruby's shoulder, and Jacqueline stood closer to her. He was pleased to see they were taking up for her. Whatever games girls might play, at least they knew how to close ranks.

Tim walked toward the pay phone near the corner with Bobby.

"Cops picked me up, said Bill Pearce says I shot him."

"Why'd you go and do that?" Tim asked. "I might get angry if you're telling me you shot him."

Bobby gave him a look. "Then the cops find stolen alcohol in my car. Imagine that."

"Guess you're not so good at breaking and entering."

"That's a funny thing. Cops didn't find a gun, so I got bail," Bobby said, looking at Tim. "There was no gun at the scene, and I know I sure as hell wasn't there. So who does that leave?"

"You think Bill shot himself in the leg?" Tim asked, raising an eyebrow at Bobby.

"No, I think you did it."

"Now why would I go shooting my right-hand man in the leg?" he asked. Tim looked over and saw Jesse and Joe Micelli exchanging words. He hoped Jesse was keeping his head; if he started a fight with Joe things would go to hell pretty quick.

"Hell if I know, and I don't really care," Bobby said with a smile so full of smugness Tim wanted to slap it off him.

"Come on, I'm too nice a guy for that. Besides, I was at Everett's all night." Bobby looked at him disbelievingly.

"Come on, you think if I shot Bill Pearce he'd look at me again?" Tim said.

"The cops come down on me for this, I'm throwing you straight at them."

Tim nodded, looking as if he had not a care in the world. He had a backup plan if Tafani decided he'd was going to go that route. They walked back toward the car.

People were talking and hanging out again since they could tell no fight was going to occur.

"That your girl?" Tafani nodded toward Ruby.

Tim looked over at Tafani and said nothing.

"She ain't half bad," he offered.

Tim said nothing, and he tried to will Ruby to stay where she was, but she walked toward them. He saw Bobby watching her, and he let Bobby get away with the smirk on his face. Tafani rounded up his boys and headed for his car.

Ruby relaxed as the car drove away from the Round-Up. Tim already had a cut lip, and she didn't think he needed a black eye to go with it.

"What was that all about?" she asked.

He casually slung an arm over her shoulder and walked with her toward Hollis and his crowd.

"Nothing," he said. "You thirsty or something?"

"I guess so. Could you get me a Dr Pepper?"

He left Ruby with Hollis's group.

"He's gonna get himself into trouble if Bobby Tafani decides to get even."

"For what?" Ruby asked.

Hollis grinned. "You're a loyal little thing, I'll give you that. You know full well what I mean."

"I'm sure I don't."

Hollis laughed again. "And what did I tell you? Tim Kelly don't show up with just anybody at a place like this."

"Really?" Ruby asked hopefully.

Hollis's smile was brotherly in its softness. "Really. He doesn't bring girls out with him like this. And seeing as how he's all over you, I guess that means I was right, huh?"

Ruby smiled. "I guess so."

"You look like the cat that swallowed the canary, I'll tell you that," Hollis grinned.

"Brenda's talking to you again?" She nodded over at Bill's sister who was talking with some girls by a Ford Fairlane.

"Once she saw the knot on my head she started to believe me a bit. I think it'll turn out." His expression was thoughtful and a little wary. "You didn't say anything to anyone?"

"Of course not," she said.

She stepped back when she saw Tim coming back, holding two sodas by the necks. He took a church key from his back pocket and popped the top off her Dr Pepper and handed it to her.

"See you later," Ruby said, as Tim grabbed her hand and pulled her away from the group and toward a picnic table settled in the dusty parking lot. Ruby sat on the shaded side, and Tim sat up on the table.

She finished her Dr Pepper, locking gazes with Tim as she did it. He smiled slowly, his eyes darkening. She looked past him for a moment and inhaled sharply as she spotted the person coming toward them. Jake Wheeler.

Tim noticed her expression and turned around, his face blank and disinterested.

"Jake," he said.

Ruby noticed the bruised jaw and busted knuckles on Jake's hand. So she was right about Tim's sparring partner.

Darla was trailing behind Jake, an annoyed look on her face.

"Kelly," Jake said. "Nice fat lip."

Tim flipped him off.

Ruby relaxed. It didn't look like the two of them were about to go at each other. Darla stepped up beside Jake, but didn't say anything.

"What are the two of you doin' here?" Jake asked.

"I guess I remembered who I was sleeping with when I got back from California after all," Tim said.

Ruby looked at Tim in shock. She wondered who told him what Jake had said to her the other night at Everett's. Her stomach stirred as she looked at Tim, who was gripping his Coke bottle as if he was trying to decide whether to drink out of it or pitch it at Jake's head. It couldn't be possible that he'd gotten in a fight with Jake over her. But she could think of no other reason for it, and she wanted to fling herself into his arms.

"So I guess it's official then, the two of you seein' each other?" Jake asked, taking a drag of his cigarette. "Ain't that sweet."

Ruby recognized that tone in Jake's voice. Tim was facing Jake, staring him down with a stony look. The tension was palpable, and she was nervously watching Tim's right hand hovering near his back pocket, where she could see the outline of a switchblade.

"Jake," Darla said. "Can we get something to eat?"

So she had sensed it too. Ruby looked over at Darla, whose gaze was on Jake. But he was looking only at Tim, a challenging smile on his face.

"Maybe you and Darla better move along," Tim said. "You ain't got much time together, ain't that right, Darla?"

She looked at Tim like she couldn't believe he was poking a bear with a stick.

"I leave next Tuesday," she said. "Timothy."

Ruby watched as Jake's eyes narrowed.

"You seen Carolyn around lately, Tim?" Jake asked. "Heard you have."

Ruby looked to Tim, who was staring at Jake with an unreadable expression. That name turned up again and again. Ruby felt sick.

"You sure jumped at the chance to get outta Las Vegas," Tim said to Darla. He looked at Jake, then back at Darla. "No big surprise." Ruby bit her lip.

"Come on, let's go, maybe I can finish the job this time," Jake said, his hand hovering near the back of his pocket.

"You sure like getting your ass kicked," Tim said. He stood, his hands fisted at his sides. They circled each other like piranhas.

"Stop it, just stop!" Darla said. "There's a cop car pulling in to the parking lot, you really want to do this right now?"

Tim and Jake looked at each other, then the LVPD car circling the parking lot. Tim looked at Jake.

"We're not finished."

"Never are," he answered.

Tim took Ruby's hand and led her back towards Bill's car.

Wednesday, May 25, 1966

Ruby turned over slowly, sliding away from the sun that was shining onto her face through a crack in the curtains hanging in the window of one of Everett's upstairs rooms. Tim was sleeping on his back, an arm flung over the top of his head in what looked like an impossible position.

Ruby leaned up on her elbows and studied him. She never noticed how his face always looked as if he was slightly bothered by something, but now that he was asleep and his features were relaxed, she noted how much softer his face was when he wasn't putting up walls for everyone.

He'd spent the last two nights with her at Everett's, but sharing a room downstairs since it irritated Rett less.

She thought about Jake and Darla. She would never have the guts to go out and be an actress like Darla, but maybe it was something like trick riding. People always told her it scared them to death to watch her flip around on her horse, but to her it was like nothing.

She felt bad for Jake, though.

She knew Tim was going on a run this weekend, alone, and she hated the idea. She couldn't imagine the thought if he up and left forever. If Jake felt half as horrible as she imagined she would, then he wasn't in a good place.

She sighed and looked at Tim's face, then his eyes were open, and he was awake. He was still awkwardly splayed in his bed, but his eyes were alive and focused.

"What're you looking at?" he asked, his voice scratchy.

"You," she said simply.

"Couldn't have been too interesting, seeing as I was asleep." He moved his arm from the pillow and curled it around her.

"You look different when you sleep," she said. She stretched into the curve of his body, relishing the feel of his skin against hers. She didn't want to be anywhere else.

They were quiet for a few moments until running water sounded upstairs.

"You tensed up just now," Tim said. "Scared of your big brother?"

"Rett don't rule me," Ruby said. "He's getting paid for letting me live here, after all."

"Your old man sends him money?"

Ruby nodded. "I shoulda had daddy send it to me, and I'd pay Rett room and board. I know he's makin' out like a bandit on this deal."

"He gets a bartender, a maid, someone to cook and clean for him and to look after the horses," Tim said. "And from what I've seen, he barely pays you a dime."

"I know," she said, kissing his neck, feeling his pulse under her lips. "But I don't mind. It's nice to be somewhere I'm wanted. Rett couldn't get along without me now."

She settled herself against Tim's chest, and he tightened an arm around her. Money or not, wild horses would have to drag her from Las Vegas.

Awhile later Everett left for the stable, and Ruby took Tim upstairs and made breakfast.

He didn't miss her blush or the smile she tried to hide behind a lock of hair that escaped from behind her ear whenever she looked at him. She was so damn uncontrolled sometimes, he could tell what she was thinking or feeling by looking at her. He realized with some trepidation he was starting to like that.

"I'm going to pick up Bill down at the courthouse," he said. "His case is right after lunch. I may need that gun."

He watched the uneasy expression form on her face and took her hand.

"No one's gonna trace it back to Everett. You said yourself he doesn't have a permit, and it wasn't bought legal. No one's gonna know," he said.

"Rett will," she said. "What are you gonna do with it?"

"I don't know yet," he admitted. "I'm gonna wait and see what the judge does with Bill and go from there."

Tim headed over to Pete Malcolm's after he left. They lived above the gun store on South Highland, and he found Pete at their outdoor range where he was target shooting.

Pete looked like he was about to attend his own funeral when he spotted Tim walking toward him.

"Hey, Tim," Pete said nervously. He cleared his throat. "What's up?"

"I need a gun," Tim said.

"Oh good Lord," Pete muttered. "Tim, I swear Ray hasn't been around Diana!"

"I know that," Tim snapped.

Pete relaxed a touch. "Well, then what do you need a gun for?"

Tim was glad he thought up such a good reason. "For Ruby. It's not safe working the bar, she needs a gun back there."

"I thought they already had one?" Pete asked. "It was a Smith and Wesson, a .357 Magnum ..."

Pete's voice trailed off, putting two and two together to make four. And four equalled Bill getting shot in the leg by Tim the way Pete did math.

"Shit, Tim," Pete said, running a hand through his hair. "You're not gonna shoot nobody, are you?"

"Relax," Tim said, clapping Pete on the back. Pete almost dropped the rifle he was holding. So much for Malcolm gun safety.

"Like I said, it's for Ruby. That other gun isn't there anymore," Tim said. In fact, it was tucked in the glove compartment of Bill's car at the moment, but Pete didn't need to know that.

"I can get a nice Colt 1911."

Tim shook his head. "She's a small thing, wouldn't be able to rack the slide. Stick with revolvers."

"We got a couple nice four inch Colt Pythons in. They'll fire .38 Special's, and I think she can handle that."

"That'll work. Get it to me by tonight."

Pete paled for a second, then nodded. "Alright Tim, you got it."

Ruby spent most of the afternoon at the stable, practicing with Bella and exercising Rigel. She drove back home, dashed upstairs and had a quick shower, and when she came downstairs she was dismayed to find the bar filling up with people.

"You said you weren't opening again until the weekend!" Ruby exclaimed.

"This ain't me," Everett said, spreading his arms. "Word's got around that Bill Pearce is out. People are stopping by looking for him. This keeps up, I'm gonna have to talk to Sam Wyatt and see if I can be open all the time."

Ruby had no idea how it happened, but gossip travelled faster through these parts than anywhere she'd ever seen. By the early evening, the bar was packed with people, some waiting on Bill, and others there because they'd seen the lights on and wanted a cold drink.

Ruby sat out on the steps with a Miller, taking a short break from the hot bar.

She was about to go back inside when she recognized Bill's car pulling into the lot. Right away they were surrounded by a group of people, and Ruby watched as Bill slowly got out of the passenger seat. He had a pair of crutches with him and was so busy shaking hands and greeting friends that it took a good five minutes for him to reach the front stairs.

"I hope you got that beer you promised," he said with a grin. Ruby nodded and held the door for him.

Tim followed him inside, stopping to kiss Ruby as he walked in. She followed them both in, then went into the kitchen and found the case of Pearl she stashed. She stuck a half dozen in the ice box earlier that day and brought a cold one out for Bill.

"On the house, of course," she smiled.

He struggled his way onto a bar stool, and Tim sat on his left. Ruby pulled a Lone Star out of the ice box for him.

"How's your leg?" she asked Bill.

"Hurts like a sonuvabitch," he said with a grin. "I'm aiming to dull the pain tonight."

"Hey, Pearce!"

Hollis came by and slapped Bill on the back, and a steady stream of guys followed suit.

"Did you see the judge?" Ruby asked.

"Sure did," he said. "Got off on promise to appear. Guess this bum leg is good for something after all. I gotta go back in a few weeks."

"You lookin' at jail time?" Hollis asked.

"Well, no fingerprints anywhere, but I was lying on the floor in there. They might try and get me for felony burglary, but I'll plead 'em down to misdemeanour break and enter. Ain't my first rodeo," Bill said.

Ruby shouldn't have been surprised he was knowledgeable enough about his crimes to sound like a lawyer, but she was.

A minute later she spotted Jake in the crowd, drinking a beer and chatting with Rusty. He walked to the bar a second later.

"Get me another one," he said, shaking his empty beer bottle.

She handed him a beer from the keg.

"Bill," Jake said. "You're out."

"Promise to appear," Bill said, taking a sip of his beer. "See Jake, it pays to show up for court. That way he doesn't put you in jail when you don't need to be. You might wanna learn that."

"If your leg weren't so lame I'd smack the grin right off you," Jake said, good-naturedly shoving Bill. Jake was in a jovial mood and on his way to pretty drunk. She hadn't seen him show up earlier, so he must've been drinking before he got to Everett's.

She wondered where he lived when he wasn't there. He sometimes took a room upstairs for the night, but she didn't know where he lived the other nights. She realized she didn't know much about him at all.

Jed sent her out to deliver some drinks and when she came back, the crowds had left to give Bill room. She was about to ask Tim where he was spending the night when the girl walked in.

She was a tall blonde, but Ruby doubted it was natural. She had wild, teased, shoulder-length hair. Ruby'd seen her around the bar, but never spoke to her. A girl called out "Carolyn!" and Ruby froze.

Tim and Bill looked over to the door at the same time, and Ruby didn't miss the low curse Tim hissed out. Ruby looked at him, sitting at the bar, nursing a beer and finishing off a cigarette. He watched Carolyn carefully, and Ruby felt like scratching her eyes out.

At least Jake disappeared somewhere; she had a feeling he would milk this moment for all it was worth.

Carolyn sashayed her way toward the bar.

"I'll have a beer please," she said sweetly, laying a hand on Jed's as he wiped the counter.

"Ruby," Jed said.

She filled up a glass from the keg and put it on the table with a thunk. Ruby looked away from Tim's gaze.

"Tim, Bill," the girl said. She sat on the bar stool on Tim's left. "I heard you got shot, Bill."

Bill leaned over and looked down the bar. "You heard right."

"I heard some things about you too, Tim," she said. She picked up her glass of beer and sipped it, then set it down again, running a finger along the rim. Ruby stood away from her, pretending to wipe the bar down.

"Can it, Carrie," Tim said.

"Word has it you showed up at the Round-Up the other day with a girl on your arm," she said. Ruby locked gazes with her for a split second. This girl knew exactly who he'd shown up with at the Round-Up.

"Carrie, I'm not gonna tell you again," Tim said.

"I heard she's a barmaid." Carolyn twisted a piece of her hair between her fingers. "I didn't figure you for slumming."

Ruby was about to throw the towel down and show this tramp a thing or two about keeping her trap shut, but Tim beat her to it. He closed a hand around her wrist and yanked her off the bar stool.

"You always remembered I liked it rough." Tim pulled her toward the hallway. Carolyn looked back at Ruby and smirked.

Tim knew it was going to happen eventually and better to get things settled up sooner rather than later. The minute Carolyn crossed the line, he yanked her into the hallway.

Tim turned around, not wanting to get too far into the hallway with her, making sure Ruby had a good sightline on the both of them.

"I told you to quit it, and I'm not playing around," Tim said.

"Well, well," she said. "Tim Kelly, worked up over a girl. I never thought I'd see the day."

"You never will," Tim said, emphasizing "you." Her face darkened for a second, then she looked past him to the bar, where Ruby was standing, her arms crossed and a wary expression on her face.

"I sure miss having you around," she said, giving Tim her best sad gaze. "There ain't nobody around here who treats me as good as you."

Tim waited for her to snap. She always did.

"We always had a lot of fun, didn't we?" she asked. "Are you gonna throw it all away so quick?"

"You found other places to have fun," Tim said.

She pressed herself up against him, and Tim knew she'd decided to change course. She always got desperate if he wandered too far, but when he went away to jail she got along fine. It wasn't not being with him that was the problem, it was anyone else having him.

"Girl like that doesn't look like she knows how to have fun," Carolyn said, toying with his lapel. "I could tell her about all the fun we have, teach her a few things."

"Funny thing about girls like her," Tim said, looking at Carolyn with blank eyes. "I don't gotta worry where she's been."

He braced for the stinging slap she delivered—Carolyn was a decent hitter at least—and a few of the guys hanging around in the hallway hollered. Tim could see Ruby watching it all unfold, her mouth hanging open. He hoped Bill was paying attention to her.

Tim grinned at Carolyn, who looked like she wanted to slay him on the spot. She should never have come and tried to provoke him.

She shoved him as hard as she could, balled her fists up and tried to hit his chest, but he fended her off easily. She stood there, her eyes blazing.

"Go to hell," she spat, her voice quiet and angry. "I don't ever wanna see you again!"

She turned and marched out into the main room. He watched as Ruby circled around the bar quickly, and Bill winced as he moved off his bar stool and grabbed Ruby at the waist, holding her back from chasing after Carolyn. The screen door slammed, but Ruby was still struggling against Bill's grip.

"Let me go!" she said.

"It's my first night out," Bill said. "Let's not ruin it with a blood bath now, alright?"

Tim walked up to them, and Bill let Ruby go as she stopped struggling. Her cheeks were flushed pink, her eyes were dark, and she looked ready to kill. He grew hard as he watched her breathing heavily, her chest rising and falling.

"C'mon." He nodded his thanks to Bill. "Let's go upstairs."

Ruby smiled slowly, and he took her hand and led her upstairs.

A short time later he was breathing as heavily as she was. The bed sheets were tangled around them, and Ruby was propped up on her elbows, watching him carefully.

"You coulda let me hit her just once," she argued.

"You ever been in a fight before?" he asked.

"No," she admitted.

"She would've clobbered you," he said. He smiled at her angry little face.

"I coulda hit her with something from behind," she reasoned, lying back down on his chest.

"That's cheating," Tim said.

He almost cursed aloud at his choice of words. He could tell from the way her breathing changed that she had picked up on it, and she was thinking it all over.

"Have you been with her since we . . . well, since we've been ..."

"Sleeping together?" he asked. "You can't even say it."

"I can too," she said, a smile in her voice. "Well?"

"No."

He didn't know why he felt so damn guilty, it wasn't like that was a lie. He hadn't slept with Carolyn once since he and Ruby had. He concentrated on her even breathing.

"Take me with you," she said.

"Not this time." His fingertips played along the smooth skin of her back. "Next time. The next run is only overnight."

She sat up and looked at him, her face soft from the glow of the neon lights outside.

"Thank you," she said.

"For what?"

"Shuttin' her up," she said.

He nodded. She looked at him again and he saw something in her face ... he didn't know what. But the way she looked made him feel warm. She leaned down to kiss him, and he remembered the way he felt the minute the doors clanked shut in prison; a mixture of abject fear and complete safety.

21

Saturday, May 28, 1966

Ruby arrived at the stable early on Saturday morning. The bar the night before was quiet; just a few hoods playing poker and plunking coins in the slot machines.

She parked the El Camino outside the stable, then went inside and saddled Bella. She spotted Jake walking into the stable as she rode out, but he didn't follow her. She rode into the pasture.

She turned down a worn path and ended up alongside a dry stream bed. She sat down on the dusty scrub and thought about Tim.

Something had changed between them. Lying in bed with him, his hands across her back, the sheets cool and the breeze hot, she realized she loved him. She didn't know how it had happened, or why, but there it was. She couldn't imagine being in Las Vegas and not having Tim around her.

It made her almost *too* happy. Everett looked wary as she hummed to herself while she cooked and served up beers with smiles too wide, considering the job. She couldn't remember feeling so good.

Even when her father forgot to call on Friday night, it hadn't dampened her mood. She kissed Tim goodbye through the window of the truck, standing on the running boards as the engine idled. She waved until the truck had disappeared.

She felt like telling the entire world she loved him.

"Bella, tell me I'm crazy," she said, nuzzling her horse's neck. "Tell me I'm crazy for falling in love with him."

Bella nodded, and Ruby laughed.

She got back on her horse and rode slowly back to the ranch.

Her good mood evaporated when she noticed Jake was gone and the El Camino with him.

She got back to Everett's in a mood. Wick had driven her in the old pick up on his way to get some supplies.

"Where's the car?" Everett asked.

"Hell if I know," Ruby said, her irritation plain to see. "I think Jake took it."

Everett swore, and he deserved it for ever letting Jake walk off with those car keys.

Without Tim around, she didn't have much to do. She had never minded spending time alone before. When she lived in Abilene and had to leave school she spent most days alone on the ranch, not seeing anyone for days sometimes. She got used to the silence, but it was lonely. Whenever someone came by she tried everything she could to get them to stay longer.

But since coming to Las Vegas and meeting Tim, she hadn't felt isolated or alone. Now it crept back into her head, and she wished Tim would hurry back.

She didn't know any of the girls beyond saying hi to them at the bar, and she wasn't sure they liked her that much. She sighed, then thought about the Round-Up. She sure could use a hamburger and a malted right about now.

She went to her closet and looked through the sparse wardrobe. She had a few longer skirts and blouses and a couple shirtwaist dresses from when she went to school, but every other item of clothing was suited for riding. She felt self conscious at the Round-Up before since most of the girls were in skirts.

She picked out a pair of lavender Capri pants and a matching shirt. Her father bought it for her before he had left her here, but she had never worn it. It would look more fitting at the Round-Up than her blue jeans and a western shirt.

She put a hair band in her hair and looked in the mirror. Now she looked more like some of those girls at the Round-Up.

She skipped down the two flights of stairs to the main floor.

"Where are you headed?" Everett asked, his eyes narrowing as he looked at her outfit.

"I thought I might go to the Round-Up," she said. "It ain't that far to walk, is it?"

"About two miles, at least," Everett said doubtfully. "In this heat? You sure?"

"I'm sure." She rifled through the ice box for her bottle of Coppertone.

It was boiling outside, but she walked slowly and tried not to get too sweaty or dusty. She followed North Main until it was South Main, and it took her right there. She was relieved to see the sign in the distance for the Round-Up, as she was about dying of thirst.

She walked through the packed parking lot and tried to hide her dismay. The girls were dressed in jeans, short skirts, and skimpy tops, like at Everett's. It was Saturday—maybe they all dressed different on the weekends.

She would have fit in better with her riding clothes on. Burning with embarrassment, she headed for the inside of the restaurant to get herself a drink.

"Hey Ruby, hold up!"

She turned to see Hollis walking up to her.

"Hey Hollis." She looked around for Brenda, but didn't see her.

"What brings you out all by your lonesome?"

"I'm dyin' of thirst, that's what," she said.

Hollis walked inside with her and paid for her Dr Pepper. She walked back out feeling more alive with a cool drink in her hand.

"You walked all this way?" he asked.

"It wasn't that bad," she said. She looked around at the crowd again. "I guess I kind of overdid it with the outfit, huh?"

Hollis looked around at the other girls.

"You don't look too out of place," he said. "Why play dress up?"

She blushed furiously. "I wanted to fit in."

"You already do, Ruby," he said seriously. "You don't have to try so hard."

She smiled, still looking around the parking lot self-consciously.

"Where's Brenda?"

"Home taking care of Bill. Or driving him crazy, one of the two," he said, walking over to his car. "I'm meeting a few people at the Thunderbird for gambling and a show tonight, you wanna come?"

"Oh, I can't," Ruby said. "I promised Rett I wouldn't be too long. I've gotta few chores at the ranch tonight, Wick's takin' the night off. And anyway, I'm just nineteen, remember? I can't go gambling."

"I keep forgetting about that," he mused. "Anyway . . . you want a ride back?"

"Oh no, that's okay," Ruby said. "I like the walk."

"Watch yourself walking," he said seriously. "This heat can be real dangerous if you're not used to it."

"I'm from Texas, Hollis," Ruby said with a smile. "I can handle it."

Ruby said goodbye and watched him drive away. She waited until the dust settled, then began the walk back.

Ruby walked along the dusty road toward Everett's. Growing up, her father always told her the trip back was never as long as the trip there, but he was wrong about this one. Maybe it was the heat, but Ruby felt as if she'd never reach home.

She left South Main and skirted over to an access road that paralleled the train tracks, thinking it would be cooler without the heat waving off the asphalt.

Her lavender pants were covered in a layer of dust, and she decided she wasn't made to look like a magazine cutout like Darla. She couldn't imagine Darla sweating, and here she was, dripping like a fountain.

A car came up behind her, and she moved onto the left shoulder up against the railway tracks. The car slowed as it passed her. Ruby frowned as she saw the brake lights go on.

Without warning, the car backed up, then the driver yanked the wheel and the back end veered to her left, the front end pointing into the road, blocking her way.

Her throat turn to ice as she recognized the Pontiac.

She debated whether she should turn and run, but the passenger door opened and a guy got out, leaning on the door frame.

Bobby Tafani.

He wore a pair of beat-up jeans and a sleeveless shirt. He looked her over for a second.

"You're Kelly's girl," he said.

She hesitated. "Y-Yeah."

"Where is he?" he asked.

"I dunno," Ruby said. "Busy."

Tafani's eyes narrowed. Another man got out of the back seat—he was tall and rangy, with red hair and slightly bulging eyes, and Ruby wondered how he ever managed to get a date looking like that.

A man with slicked-back black hair got out of the other side of the car and circled around.

Ruby's heart pounded in her ears.

"I wouldn't run," Bobby said, his voice casual. "You know we'd chase you down pretty fast."

"What do you want?" she asked.

"You," he said simply.

She looked at him in confusion. Bobby turned to his friends.

"Get her."

She turned to run, but Bobby was right—his two friends were on her in a second, dragging her back to the car. The bug-eyed one slung her over his shoulder.

"Put me down!" she yelled, trying to kick her legs and force the bug-eyed one to drop her. She twisted around and bent back as far as she could, and he dropped her. She braced her fall with her arms, crashing into the dirt. She scrambled up, screaming, and slipped in the dirt as she tried to gain some footing to get away.

"Get her in the car and shut her up!" Bobby yelled.

The black-haired one grabbed her arm, and the bug-eyed one snatched one of her legs. "Stop it! Let me go!"

She struggled vainly as they hauled her to the car. They tossed her in the backseat, and she kicked the bug-eyed boy as hard as she could. He sprawled backwards, and she tried to get out of the car, but the other one was on her before she got three steps away. Bobby forged into the fray, and he dragged her up by her arm, twisting it painfully behind her and pushing her to the car.

"Tim's gonna kill you," she said. "Let me go, and I won't tell him nothing."

"Tim's gonna learn he can't frame me for a goddamn shooting," Bobby said. "He needs to be taught a lesson."

Ruby kicked hard, slamming her foot into one of Bobby's knees. He cried out in pain and loosened his grip on her, and she tried to run. Bobby grabbed her wrist again and wrenched it so hard she screamed, then he clamped a hand around her mouth.

They were so busy trying to get her in their car that none of them heard the other car pull up.

"I'd let her go if I was you."

Ruby stopped struggling when she recognized the voice.

"You've got no business here, Wheeler," Tafani said. "Get her in the car."

Ruby was never so glad to see Jake Wheeler in her life.

"I don't think you heard me," Jake said. He walked closer to them.

Ruby jerked sideways, elbowing Bobby in the stomach. He broke his grip on her, and she ran toward Jake. He reached out for her, grabbed her arm, and swung her behind him.

"Get in the car," he said, his voice low. Ruby ran toward the El Camino, still idling on the side of the road, but didn't get in. It was three on one, and there was no way Jake could take them all.

Before another word was exchanged, Jake whipped out a switchblade and took a swipe at the black-haired man from the back seat. He caught him in the arm, and Ruby saw the line of red and heard him cry out.

Bobby and the bug-eyed one rushed Jake, but he was prepared for their assault. She watched in fear as he took a few punches, one that knocked the switchblade to the ground. Jake threw a hard punch of his own. The dust was kicked up, obscuring her view, and she rushed closer to make sure he was okay.

He recovered quickly. He fought as well as Tim, but instead of Tim's calm demeanour, Jake was all ferocity and emotion.

Jake threw the bug-eyed one into the side of the car and smashed the man's nose with a knee to the face. While he was busy with him, Bobby dashed over and tried to grab her again.

Jake was faster. He grabbed Bobby by the collar and spun him around, landing two solid punches before Bobby regained his form and pummelled Jake. Jake tripped him, grabbed the blade off the ground, and held it to Bobby's neck.

"You get your boys outta here, or y'all'll be leaking in the dirt," Jake said.

Bobby looked up at Jake as if trying to judge how serious he was. Jake pushed the blade harder into Bobby's neck and blood ran down the hilt.

Ruby swallowed, hardly believing Jake was doing this to save her. She would have expected him to drive right by and have a good laugh over her bad luck as he did it. Instead, he held a knife to another man's throat to protect her. *Where in the world has this come from?*

"You hear me? You get outta here, or you're gonna have more than Tim Kelly breathing down your ugly neck," Jake said. "This is over, you fuckin' hear me?"

Jake looked over at Bobby's two henchmen, one with blood dripping down his face, and the other cradling his badly cut arm.

"I move this knife, and you get the fuck outta here. You don't do it, I'm gonna bury it in your gut," Jake said.

He removed the knife from Bobby's neck and backed up, and Bobby stood slowly, brushing the dust off his clothes.

"Tell Kelly this isn't over," he said.

"Trust me, boys," Jake said. "You just started it."

Ruby took in a shaky breath and sat in the dirt, watching the car drive away. She couldn't swallow, her throat so dry she felt like she swallowed sand. The ground blurred and hot tears spilled onto her face.

She tried to stand up, but her legs were shaking.

"Hey," Jake said. "They hurt you?"

Ruby shook her head and tried to wipe the tears off her face.

"Hey, come on, don't cry," Jake said awkwardly.

Ruby laughed at how uncomfortable he sounded. Tim hadn't warned her about anyone coming after her. She knew Tim would never intentionally let her get hurt, but she wished he was here to prevent it. Instead, she had Jake Wheeler riding to her rescue, of all people.

She kneeled for a minute, trying to get control of herself, then felt Jake's hand close around her arm gently, helping her up.

"Thanks," she whispered.

"What the hell was that?" he asked.

"Nothing."

"Bull," he said. "I jumped into something that's gonna bring shit down. What were they tryin' to do?"

"They wanted to scare me," she said.

Jake shook his head, then stalked off toward the car.

"Don't leave me here!" She was afraid they'd come back.

He stopped, then turned around.

"What the hell were they tryin' to do?" he asked again.

"I think they saw me with Tim," she said. "I guess they thought they could use me."

"For what?" he said. "Wipe your face for Christ's sake, here."

He handed her a dirty bandana, and she wiped her cheeks off.

"This is about what went down with Bill, ain't it?" Jake asked.

Ruby looked up at him in surprise.

"I ain't stupid, Ruby," he said. "I'm hearin' a lot of talk about what went down that night. I know Kelly. He'd never send Bill in for a job alone. And Kelly's boys may be a lot of things, but they don't run when a man's down."

She looked at the ground.

"Let me see if I got it right then," he said, his voice impatient. "He wants Bill outta the Army, and settin' up Bobby Tafani is icing on the cake. Am I close?"

Ruby kicked at the dirt. She couldn't stop the tears from flowing again.

"Christ," Jake muttered. "Look, get in the car, I'll drive you back to Rett's."

Ruby nodded and circled around to the passenger side. She got in the car without a word and sat with her hands folded in her lap. Her clothes were filthy, her wrist was red and swelling, and she had dirt all over her. Everett was going to be angry she was even breathing near the seats.

Jake got in the car, but didn't put the engine in gear.

"Darlin', I'm not saying nothing 'bout what Tim did," Jake explained patiently. "But if Tafani's looking to even the score with you, then Tim's gotta know. Things could go to hell if he don't know. You tell him about this when he gets back, you got that? I'm leaving later for an overnight rodeo gig, but you tell him."

She nodded.

She was startled when Jake touched her cheek, turning her face toward him.

"You tell him. Got it?" he asked again.

"Yeah, I got it," she said.

She took in a sharp breath when he let his fingers slide down her neck and rest at her collarbone for a second.

"You're a mess," he said seriously. "But you did good."

"Huh?" she asked, swallowing a lump in her throat.

"Kickin' and scratchin' at them like you did. You put up a good fight, even though it wasn't doin' you any good," he said.

They were silent as he drove back to Everett's. He cut the engine, and she opened her door slowly. She hoped that Everett was at the stables. He'd be mad if he saw her messed up like this and likely blame Tim for the whole damn thing.

Jake followed her inside, and she went straight to the fridge and pulled out a few Budweisers and set them on the bar in front of Jake.

"Thanks," she said again.

He nodded thoughtfully. She smiled, then walked to the stairs. Later, she wondered if she heard it.

"You're welcome," he said.

22

Tim pulled into Everett's parking lot and tiredly set the brakes. He bob-tailed it up, as Ruby called it, from Los Angeles. The trailer was in Insane Wayne's barn, and Tim wasn't feeling too good about things.

Wayne was worried when he arrived and sent Tim off pretty quickly with another trailer. He made a short run to San Diego, then back to Los Angeles, taking his own sweet time since Wayne blew him off. When he got back, he saw why.

A big Cadillac was in the driveway at the main house, and a businessman was looking over the ranch. Wayne was having some words with the man, and Tim surmised it must be the brother.

Sure enough, Roy found Tim in the barn and told him that Wayne's brother aimed to take control of the farm. The old man didn't have more than a week or two left in him. The operation would likely fold up if he died and relocate somewhere else, and it may be awhile until they got set up again.

It cut into his plans. He made it known to Wayne that he wanted a run to Denver again. Instead, Wayne had given him a run to Topeka for June sixth that would at least take him through Denver. He still wanted Tim to come on Wednesday the first, but Tim aimed to send Jake in his place.

He stretched as he got out of the truck. This job turned out to be a lot more work than he originally thought. Between paying for fuel and food on the road, Tim wasn't clearing much profit.

He walked up the stairs and into Everett's, staring at the same old tired faces around the bar. Ruby looked over and sashayed toward him, slipping her arms around his neck.

"What's got you so happy?" he asked.

"You."

He grinned wryly, then kissed her. She looked at him differently now, and he didn't know how he felt about it.

"Can I talk to you for a second?" she asked, her voice low. He nodded, and she took his hand and pulled him toward the stairs. They climbed up to the third floor and entered the small apartment.

"What's up?" He sat on the couch and put his boots up on the coffee table. Ruby came by and pushed them off, then sat next to him.

"Bobby Tafani tried to grab me yesterday," she said, with no preamble.

"What?" He could feel his blood pressure rise.

"I was walkin' back from the Round-Up, and this car stopped. It was the Pontiac from the other day," she said.

"What were you doin' at the Round-Up?" he asked.

"I wanted to get a drink, get out for a bit," she said. "I walked there and back. Bobby Tafani and two of his clowns grabbed me. A dark-haired one and bug-eyed redhead one."

Joe Micelli would be the dark-haired one, and the other was Marshall Fairfax, the same one who'd bothered Diana when Ray claimed to have rescued her.

"What happened?" He resisted the urge to storm out of Everett's and take every guy Bobby Tafani had ever met down. No one had dared to touch a girl he was seeing.

"They stopped me and tried to get me in the car. He said something about needing to teach you a lesson," she said.

"Did they hurt you?" he asked.

"My wrist and arm is hurt a little," she admitted. "Jake came along, he'd taken Rett's car. He took all three of 'em on and whipped 'em pretty good. I couldn't believe he'd do that for me, but he did."

Tim felt a mixture of relief and intense anger. Jake was no fool; he knew as well as Tim did that guys who would jump Ruby could do the same to Darla. It only did him good to look out after Ruby if he ever wanted the same in return.

He should've been there.

"I'm sorry." The words were out of his mouth before he realized it. He snapped his mouth shut. Since when did he apologize?

"What?" she asked, equally as surprised.

"I'm gonna take care of this," Tim said, regaining his composure. He took her hands, massaging them in his own, then pulled her onto his lap, resting his chin on the top of her head.

"They're not gonna come back. If they do, I'll take care of it," he said. "They're not gonna touch you."

"They did it cuz of Bill, didn't they?"

"Yeah," he said.

He made slow circles on her back with his thumb.

Ruby's sigh felt like it sunk right into his chest cavity.

"Don't go nowhere, okay?" she asked. Her breath was warm on his neck.

"Don't worry. I'm gonna settle this."

"How?" She curled up against his chest. His throat tightened, and he strengthened his hold on her.

"The gun," he said.

She looked up and him, her eyes big and scared.

"Tim, don't do anything like that." She shook her head, making her dark hair dance. "Please."

"Don't worry." He ran his hands through her hair. "It's nothing like that. I need the cops to find it. But before I handle it, I'm gonna go see Sam Wyatt."

"Why?"

"Insurance."

He pulled her mouth to his and kissed her. No one would be touching Ruby again.

Ruby took Tim to her bedroom, and he went over every inch of her skin with attention. Her wrist was swollen and bruised, and he felt blind rage when he saw Bobby Tafani did to her.

He left Everett's early in the morning, before Everett was up. He tucked the new gun Pete had given him under the bar. Everett obviously hadn't noticed the other one was gone. Everett got a pretty good deal since the one Tim left was nicer than the one he swapped it for.

He still had the stupid truck, which wasn't the most inconspicuous vehicle around.

He left the truck near the auto body shop and made his way to the warehouse. Jimmy Lewis was having a card game with Carl Hamilton and Pete Malcolm.

"And that's why I let Bill walk off with Marilyn," Jimmy said. "I'm a nice guy. I can get any girl I want, and ol' Bill's gonna need some help in that department, limping like a cripple."

Pete scoffed. "You're just sore he took her right out from under your nose."

Jimmy looked offended. "Marilyn may be a looker, but if she's interested in Bill, that tells me all I need to know."

"And what's that, Jimmy?" Tim asked, sticking a cigarette in his mouth.

Jimmy glanced over his shoulder at Tim. "Shoot Tim, I need a girl with better taste than that."

"I'm gonna be a gentleman and not share that with Bill," Tim said. "He's liable to beat your ass with his crutches."

Jimmy grinned in a way that reminded him of Hollis Warner.

"I need a car," Tim said. Jimmy hid his face, and Carl looked at his shoes. Both had cars. Both knew how Tim drove.

Pete looked at Tim.

"Sure, Tim," Pete said, kissing ass like a good soldier. Pete was now the most compliant member of the Kelly gang since hitting on the idea that Tim must've shot Bill. He probably woke up nights wondering if Tim was going to plug him full of holes, considering he'd done it to his right-hand man.

He got keys from Pete and drove up to Fremont. It was dinner, and he was pretty sure he knew where to find Sam Wyatt.

He went inside the South Seas and headed towards the Tiki Room, the tropical dining room. Sam Wyatt was in back in front of a giant steak.

Wyatt wasn't the type to hole up in an office and let his underlings run things in his casinos. He went to each casino every day, walked the floor, shook hands with the gamblers, comped the whales, and ate at his restaurants. He was visible and didn't hide behind anything. He wasn't a silent partner and would never be one. Tim liked that about him.

"Timothy." Wyatt gestured to the chair across from him. "Was wondering when you'd show up. I've been hearing things."

Tim nodded. "Came to talk to you about something."

"Everett Gordon's flagrant disregard of my weekends and beer only instructions to him?"

Tim shook his head. "No. But it's related, in some way."

He proceeded to tell Wyatt about Bill's draft card, the shooting, and his idea to set up Bobby Tafani and his boys.

"Why him?" Wyatt asked.

"Don't like him, and I needed a fall guy. One of his boys was hassling my sister, so he got the nomination."

"Tafani is a cocky little S.O.B.," Sam nodded.

"He was obviously not thrilled about the police attention. He crossed the line the other day."

Tim told him about the attempt at grabbing Ruby. Wyatt listened without interruption.

"I don't abide any man treating a woman that way, 'specially a fellow Texan," he said. "I was told by a friend of mine Tafani's the one who robbed some of my casino patrons after the rodeo."

Tim frowned.

Wyatt nodded. "Got confirmation it was him from cameras at the Golden Gate. I suppose you're here because you want to show him he can't hurt a woman like that."

"I don't want any blow back from the Outfit," Tim said.

"You won't have any. I'll talk to who I need to talk to," Wyatt said. Tim presumed he meant Johnny Moro, the Outfit's boss in Vegas, and someone Tim would like to see buried in the desert. "When a line is crossed like that it needs a special touch."

Tim nodded.

Wyatt took the napkin out of his collar. "Word has it you're connected with Wayne Booker out of Los Angeles."

Tim tried not to show the surprise on his face, and Wyatt chuckled.

"It's a small town, Timothy."

"I don't mean anything by it."

"Times are changing, kid." Wyatt sipped his whiskey neat. "Booker thinks he's making a play for the Los Angeles family. DeSimone's been running things into the ground anyway. Booker won't amount to anything, and from what I hear, he's dealing primarily with Kansas City and St. Louis."

Tim said nothing.

"Things are changing. Legislature's pushing for a change to make it easier for public companies to run casinos, and I think it'll happen. Feds are investigation happy around these parts. The Outfit doesn't see the end coming, but I do. I'll take on a majority percentage owner and keep a minority. The landscape here will be different in ten years, twenty years. This city changes every moment."

"What are you saying?"

"The Outfit won't be holding back street gangs forever. They can't. There's already organization among the Negroes, some of the Mexicans. Get in where you can," Wyatt said. "There's opportunities for a kid like you. Just gotta stay the course and stay outta their interests."

"Don't have any plans to be in their interests. Casinos aren't my thing," Tim said.

Wyatt nodded. "Don't rule out a place of your own one day. This girl, you said she was Everett Gordon's sister? Gordon's been opening up that bar all hours despite what I told him."

"Probably net you a few bucks if you let him keep it open for a percentage," Tim suggested.

Wyatt leaned back. "Don't need the money, you know that. He's a Texan, too, isn't that right?"

Tim shrugged. He didn't know.

Wyatt looked at Tim thoughtfully.

"Go deal with this kid, Tafani." Wyatt drained the last of his drink. "I meant what I said, don't rule out a place of your own. You'll have to play ball with Chicago at some point, Tim. You know that. Stay away from pushing drugs and running women. Get into vending machines, something the

Outfit can use. I'd tell you to keep your nose out of the sheriff's blue book, but you're probably already in there."

Tim nodded. "Showed me my entry last time he hauled me in."

Wyatt grinned. "He's riding Moro hard right now. The sheriff's a pain in the ass, but I can't help admiring him." He stood from the table, and Tim stood, too. "You get enough money together in the next year or so, and I'll sell you those slot machines in Gordon's bar at a deal. Net you a little income."

"You own those?"

"I do now that I know they're there."

Wyatt tipped his Stetson at Tim and vanished into the crowd.

It was dark, and the streets were quiet save for the occasional roar of an airplane overhead at McCarran. He and Bill were waiting outside Tafani's house. It was fight night at the Hacienda, and he'd cruise around before heading home. He lived with an uncle, but the man worked nights at Tower of Pizza, so the house was dark and quiet.

Tim figured Tafani got the idea to snatch Ruby at the last minute after seeing her at the Round-Up the other day. Tim had a hard time believing they weren't out looking for her—they were driving in the direction of Everett's when they'd stopped her.

"You alright to do this?" Tim nodded towards Bill's crutches.

"*Now* you're concerned I can't walk," Bill said. "I got it, don't you worry about me."

Awhile later, Tafani pulled up in front of his house and turned the engine off. Bill and Tim got out of the car, and Bill, moving with a limp, beat Tim to Bobby. He got him in a headlock, choking him. Tim pulled a hood over Tafani's head. The chokehold did its job, and Tafani was out cold. They popped the trunk and awkwardly dropped him inside.

"You sure you can drive?" Tim whispered.

Bill nodded and headed back to Pete's car. Tim got in Bobby's, careful not to adjust any of the settings. He followed Bill west into the desert.

They pulled onto an unpaved road, and the jostling must've woken him, because Bobby hammered the trunk with his hands and feet.

Tim pulled ahead of Bill and stopped the car in the middle of the desert. He took the gun from Everett's out of his waistband and tucked it deep under the driver's seat. A little insurance.

He cut the engine, got out, and Bill met him at the trunk. Tim pulled out a Colt .45 and racked the slide, then tapped on the trunk.

"You gonna quit cryin' like a pansy so we can open up this thing?"

Tafani quieted, and Tim popped the lock.

Bobby came flying out, the hood gone, and Tim swung his arm, hitting Bobby in the side of the head with the gun. Bobby got up to fight, but Tim levelled the gun.

"What the hell is this?!" he spat. "You guys are dead, you hear me? Dead!"

Tim stared at him until he shut up. Bobby looked from Bill to Tim, some of the bravado leaving him as he realized where they were, who had the gun, and that he was utterly alone.

"What's going on?" he asked.

"You got the nerve to ask that?" Tim pointed the gun lower and fired.

Bobby grabbed his foot, screaming.

"Jesus Christ, Tim! You really like shooting people's legs off, huh?" Bill asked him. "You know, professional help might curb that tendency."

Tim shot Bill a look. Bill struggled over to Bobby and hauled him up, pinning his arms behind him.

"You're lucky I didn't aim any higher," Tim said, tucking the gun in his waistband and slipping brass knuckles on. "I'd bury you out here, but I want Ruby to see you hobbling around town looking like you were in the ring at the Hacienda rather than outside it. You catch my drift?"

"You're dead, Kelly," Tafani spat. "I got friends, they'll bury you."

"Let 'em try," Tim said gesturing at his face. "They fucked up the first time."

Tim walked toward Bobby slowly. Bill held him tightly, and Tim connected with Bobby's nose so hard the crunch echoed in the desert.

He thought of Ruby's wrist, her bruises and her fear. He hit Bobby over and over again.

"Tim! Tim, hold up," Bill said.

"Not done yet."

"No, someone's here."

Tim looked behind him and saw the twin headlights approach. Shit. If it was the cops, he was through. If it was the Chicago boys, they were dead.

"You see anyone tailing us out here?" Tim asked.

"I wasn't looking!"

If Bill could walk, they'd be able to run, but with his bum leg they were in hot water.

"I bet you regret shooting me right now," Bill said.

"Shut up."

Bill dropped Tafani on the ground. He didn't make a sound.

The car pulled up, the headlights blinding them. Tim kept his hand at his back, aiming to go for the gun if he had to.

The engine died, and two men he didn't recognize got out and stood in front of the car, cutting some of the light. The two men wore suits and bolo ties. No badges. No visible guns. From the look of them, not cops. Shit.

"Can I help you boys?" Tim asked.

"A mutual friend has a score to settle with Mr. Tafani," one of the men said.

A mutual friend.

Wyatt.

Relief flooded Tim's system.

"I was having words with ol' Bobby," Tim said.

The men approached.

"We have some words as well."

Tim didn't move and watched them haul Bobby off the ground. He was coherent now, looking from one suit to the other.

"What is this? You with Moro? These guys, they fuckin' kidnapped me!"

The two men hauled Bobby toward their car.

"Where're you taking him?"

"Our mutual friend thanks you for your help in locating Mr. Tafani. But he has to atone." The muscle turned to Bobby. "Robbing people isn't very nice."

Bobby's eyes went so wide Tim could see the whites from where he was standing.

"Look, that was a one time thing, alright? Look, Chicago boys get wind of this, and you're all dead! All of you!"

"You think these guys would do anything without the okay?" Tim called out. Bobby looked from Tim to the suits and struggled. They yanked him toward the back of the car.

The trunk opened, and Bobby was shoved inside.

A gunshot roared, the muzzle flare bright in the dark desert.

"Shit," Bill said.

There was silence from the trunk.

"If you wouldn't mind bringing Mr. Tafani's car to McCarran Field, where it will be found in the morning, it would be appreciated," one of the suits said.

Tim nodded. "Yeah."

"Jesus Christ," Bill mused quietly. "Tim . . . "

"Shut up."

The two suits got in the car, then floored it out into the desert. They'd probably never find Tafani. The mob didn't like scaring the tourists away with dead bodies popping up in Clark County.

Tim knew Sam Wyatt was a mobster, an old school kinda guy, but Jesus. He'd not only taken out a guy, but he did it with them as witnesses. Just in case, Tim supposed. No way they could squeal on Wyatt without risking the same end, and insurance for Sam if anyone ever threw his name into the ring as being responsible. Not that they could—it'd be their word against his. He had two nice patsies set up right here.

Tim let out a breath. He had to admire Sam.

Bill looked over at Tim. "I take it back. Maybe you aren't the one that needs professional help."

"You take Pete's car, go back to the warehouse, and get cleaned up. I'll ditch this car and meet you there."

"You're gonna do it?" Bill asked. "Who's to say the sheriff isn't waiting there."

"One, we have no choice, and two . . . not Sam's style," Tim said. "It'll be cool."

"You gonna tell the boys about this?"

Tim shook his head. "Far as I'm concerned, Bobby Tafani never existed."

Tuesday, May 31, 1966

Ruby woke up early Tuesday morning. She hadn't slept well last night; Jake had shown up the night before, back from Amarillo, and spent the night with Darla upstairs. It was a mix of laughter, sounds Ruby tried to block out with her pillow, and low voices in argument which turned to loud ones. She didn't fall asleep until the wee hours of the morning.

She got dressed and went downstairs.

"You heading out to the stable?" Everett asked.

"Don't I every day?" she asked.

Ruby moved behind the bar with him and stacked up some dirty dishes on the bar. Everett reached underneath and brought out a gun.

It wasn't the gun from before. This one was a Colt with a shorter barrel. She stared at it for a minute, wondering when Tim slipped it under there and waiting for Everett to say something.

He spun out the cylinder—it was full of bullets. He snapped it back in, turned the gun over in his hand, then grunted his satisfaction and put it back under the bar. Ruby stared at him.

She sighed. Tim said he'd get a better gun. And he would have, since that would ensure Everett's silence on the matter.

Raised voices drifted downstairs. Ruby rolled her eyes again, then cringed as a door slammed and heavy footsteps descended the stairs.

Jake walked into the room, wearing nothing but low slung jeans and his cowboy boots, a shirt tied around his waist. He walked behind the bar, grabbed a beer, cracked it open and drained half of it in two great swallows.

"You gotta pay for that," Ruby said, seeing Everett watching out of the corner of his eye. She was content to let Jake drink the entire bar if it meant he'd leave her alone.

"Fuck you," he murmured.

He walked into the pantry, and Everett followed.

Everett protested, but Jake stalked out of the room with a six-pack under his arm and some bottles in his hands. The screen door banged shut, and it was blessedly silent.

Quieter footsteps were on the stairs, and a moment later Darla appeared. Her clothes were a little rumpled, but she had her lipstick on and perfect curls in her hair. Ruby had no idea how she managed it first thing in the morning.

She gave them a tight smile. Ruby noticed the red-rimmed eyes. She couldn't picture a girl like Darla crying, but maybe Jake had that effect on people.

"Bye, Everett," Darla said. "I'll see you, Snow White."

Darla turned to leave, then turned back to Ruby.

"Don't listen to anything Jake says," Darla told her. "You remember that."

"Okay," Ruby said. She had no idea what Darla was talking about. "Bye."

The screen door banged shut, and Ruby grabbed the car keys and headed toward the El Camino. She could look forward to a night with Tim, and that'd take the edge off of the irritation she felt at Jake for disturbing her sleep.

Hollis showed up later that afternoon, and Ruby learned Bill Pearce had appeared before the classification board and had his status change to 4F—unable to serve. To celebrate this fact, she figured he must have gathered every person he had ever met in his life and sent them all to Everett's.

She was pouring a beer for Tim when the man walked in.

If she thought the decibel level dropped when Tim came in a room, this man made it quiet completely.

He looked unassuming, maybe in his late-fifties, and was wearing a bolo tie and Stetson hat, which he took off and hung on a hook inside the door. He spotted Tim and approached the bar.

"Timothy," he said. "Nice to see you."

Everett came out of the back room and froze in place.

"Mr. Wyatt," he said. Well, stuttered was more like it.

"Mr. Gordon," Wyatt replied. "I think we need to have a chat."

"You're Sam Wyatt," Ruby said, speaking before she thought much of it. "Tim told me you're from Texas. I came here from Abilene."

"Was born in Sweetwater, myself, but the family moved over to Odessa when I was school-aged. I take it you're Ruby Gordon?" he asked.

She wasn't too surprised he knew her name. She nodded.

"I guess you're here to tell Rett off for opening this place at all hours and driving me to distraction," Ruby said.

"Ruby!" Everett hissed.

Ruby glanced over at Tim, who hid a smile behind his glass of beer.

"As a matter of fact, I am," Sam said. He took a seat at the bar. "I see he's got lots of spirits here, and a couple of one armed bandits in the back."

"I can explain that," Rett said.

"I'm sure you can," Sam said. "Why don't we go talk about it in that back room you hold poker games in?"

Rett had paled. "I was about to go out to the stable, I got a doc coming, and my stable man's out for the night."

"I'm sure Ruby can handle that, can't you Ruby?" Sam asked.

"Sure," she said.

"I saw you at the rodeo, you ride real well," Sam said. "You like the spread out there?"

"Out where?"

"My ranch."

"*Your* ranch?"

Ruby looked over at Rett.

"I'm sure I mentioned that I was renting that place from Mr. Wyatt," Rett choked out.

Ruby stared at Everett. "Oh, I'm sure you didn't."

She noticed Tim looked surprised as well.

"Everett," Sam said. "Why don't we go have that talk?"

Rett swallowed, gestured at Ruby to get lost, and went into the back room.

"He ain't gonna hurt Rett, is he?"

"Don't think so," Tim said.

"Good, I'm gonna do it later. Telling me that was his ranch. Jesus, Rett has some nerve."

Ruby took the El Camino keys out of the register.

"Want some company?" Tim asked.

"Stay," she said. "Enjoy the party. I shouldn't be too long, Doc Jenkins had an emergency earlier, said he'd stop by tonight instead."

Tim nodded and took a sip of his beer. She slipped out the door, glad to be away from the noise of the bar and drove to the ranch.

Doc Jenkins had just arrived and hoisted himself out of the car. He joined her inside and went about his job quickly, giving each horse their shot.

"How was that boy I stitched up?" he asked, sweating, even in the cool night air. "I kept meaning to ask you about him."

"Fine," she said. "It healed real nice. He still has some stitches in, but it looks good."

Doctor Jenkins nodded, looking pleased. She paid the doctor and bade him goodbye.

Midnight Bandit was kicking up his heels in his stall, and she wondered what was agitating him so much. He wasn't usually this restless when it was quiet, and he hadn't acted up with the doctor.

"Calm down," she whispered. "The vet's gone. Nothin's gonna happen to you."

The horse bobbed his head, and she brushed his forelock out of his eyes. A groan punctuated the eerie silence.

"W-Who's there?" she called out. She grabbed the stall rail, wishing she brought the gun.

"Shut the fuck up," came the reply.

Ruby rolled her eyes and opened the gate to the empty stall.

"Jake, what're you doin'?" she asked. He was propped against the left side of the stall, sitting on a pallet of hay, a bottle of Jack Daniels in one hand. He looked two sheets to the wind.

"Drinkin'." He held up the bottle up and took a swig to prove it.

"What are you doin' here is what I meant." She crouched. He didn't look good. She hoped it was the light in the barn, but his face looked pale.

"It's as good a place as any for some rest." He was slurring his words a little. The bottle was almost empty. He looked awful, and she saw the bloom of a black eye and a cut by his lip. He'd gotten in some kind of fight. She looked at him, and her anger melted away. He was a mess.

"This stall ain't no good," she said. "Come on back to Everett's, I'll find a room for you."

He shook his head. "Too fuckin' loud."

"Well ... then come with me, I'll let you in the barn," she said. "The hay's clean in the loft, Wick's not here tonight."

Jake looked up and slowly struggled to his feet. He reeked of booze, and she saw him sway toward her. She held out her arms in case he fell.

"Are you gonna be able to make it over there?" she asked.

"Fuck you," Jake said. "I can walk."

She said nothing and walked slowly to the door, Jake following behind her. She was afraid of him when he was like this. He scared her so many times when he drank, and she never knew what to expect. One day he gave her compliments and fought three guys off of her, and the next he pushed her into walls and threw glass bottles around.

"You have any cigarettes?" she asked.

"One left," he said. "Why? You gonna take up smokin', too?"

"Smoke it now," she said. "I ain't lettin' you in there with any cigarettes or matches, you're liable to burn the place down with you inside. As much as you annoy me, I'm not eager for them to wheel you out on a stretcher."

He looked down; his smile was eerie in the artificial light from the stables. Ruby walked over and turned the lights off, then shut the stable door and locked it. When she returned to Jake he was leaning against Everett's car, trying to light a match. It took him six tries before he got it.

"Tim wants you to drive to Los Angeles tomorrow," she said. She watched him smoke his cigarette. "Are you gonna be sober enough to do it?"

"Why the fuck do you care?" Jake asked.

"Well, that truck needs to go back to its owner in one piece," she said. "Tim promised he'd stay here, and I'm aimin' for him to keep that promise."

"I can do it." He blew a plume of smoke toward her. "Relax."

"Jake, why do you do this to yourself?" she asked.

"Do what?"

"Drink yourself into a coma," she said.

"I ain't in a coma, darlin'," he said simply.

"You're gonna be if you keep this up."

"You ever thought of minding your own business?" he asked. "What do you care anyway?"

She looked at her white tennis shoes, glowing in the moonlight. "I never said I did."

She could feel his gaze burning into her.

"You lie as bad as Kelly does," he said, his voice soft. She looked up at him and was surprised at the look on his face. For once it didn't hold the harsh, bitter smile, or the vicious glint often in his eyes. He looked tired and sad, and it made her sad.

He took another drink of the bourbon, and Ruby worriedly looked at the dwindling alcohol. He'd be in a world of pain the next day. If Tim had to go on the run because Jake was still drunk, she'd bury him in the pasture.

He ground his cigarette out a few minutes later, and they walked toward the barn, Jake weaving slightly as he moved. Ruby opened the large doors, and they went inside. It was pitch black.

"Hold on a second." She held her arm out so Jake wouldn't walk past her. "Wait a few minutes until your eyes adjust, it's blacker than a coal miner's lunch pail."

"You ain't got lights in here?"

238

"No," she said.

A few minutes later she walked forwards, hoping Wick had cleaned the barn up and she wouldn't step on a rake or pitchfork. Jake's steps shuffled along with the swish of alcohol in the bottle.

"Gimme that." She grabbed the bottle and set it on a nearby haystack. "You're gonna need both hands to climb."

She pulled him gently by the arm toward the ladder that went up to the loft. Jake hesitated a moment before climbing. Ruby went up right behind him, not knowing what good it would do. If he lost his grip or footing, he'd take them both down.

She left the bourbon below on the haystack. He didn't need any more.

Jake made it up to the loft and promptly smacked his head when he stood. "Shit!"

"Sorry!" She scrambled up the rest of the ladder. "I forgot to tell you the ceiling's low, you can't stand."

"Christ," he spat. "You tryin' to kill me?"

"I said I was sorry," she said. She took his arm and crouched under one of the beams. "Watch it here, there's a low beam."

They made it underneath and moved toward a small window at the end of the loft. She let him go for a second and collected up some of the loose hay into a bed of sorts.

"Go sit down, I'll find a few blankets," she said. She left him alone, praying he wouldn't go exploring and pitch right over the edge. She found two horse blankets, shook them out, and brought them over. She could see better over here; the moonlight poured in the small window and coloured everything silver.

She put a hand on his shoulder, grabbing the collar of his jacket. She was nervous so close to him; if she said the wrong thing he was liable to send her flying over the edge and onto the ground. He looked back, confused about what she was doing.

"Come on, help me out a little," she said.

He shrugged out of his jacket and Ruby took a good look at it—a brown leather bomber jacket with a Nellis Air Force base patch on it. She'd seen Darla wearing the jacket more than once. She glanced at his finger—the Air Force ring was back on it.

She paused and felt stupid she hadn't realized it sooner. His anger, the way Darla and him fought ... her goodbye that morning and warning to her. She had said she was leaving on Tuesday—and here it was. Ruby sighed and looked at Jake moving unsteadily around the loft. Maybe he was already in a world of pain, and the bourbon was his answer to it.

Jake settled clumsily into the blankets.

"Hey, where's the bourbon?" he asked.

"Nowhere close to you, you've had enough," she said.

"Don't go tellin' me what I've had enough of," he said irritably.

He closed his eyes, frowning deeply. He massaged the bridge of his nose, then dropped his hand and took a deep breath.

She crouched beside him, reached over, and tentatively brushed a hand against his forehead.

"I guess Darla left, huh?" Ruby asked quietly.

Jake opened his eyes. They were dark and pierced her with an intensity she had never felt before.

"Who?" he asked, his voice harsh, and his eyes holding nothing but hatred.

So that was how it was, then. Ruby couldn't decide who she felt more sorry for, Darla or Jake. She remembered what he said about his mother leaving and felt a pang of sympathy for him. She knew just how he felt. She just hoped he wasn't about to turn on her. It would be easy for him to shove her off the hayloft and break her neck. She brushed her hand across his forehead.

He grabbed her wrist, and she inhaled sharply. It was the same one Bobby Tafani had twisted so badly.

"Stop it." His voice was low. She bit her lip, and he let go of her wrist slowly. She yanked it away and held it to her.

"You gonna run and tell your boyfriend?"

"No," she said. "You're drunk. And whether you want to admit it or not, you're feelin' sorry for yourself."

"Why do you always gotta be a fuckin' bitch about things?" he asked.

"Why do you always have to play Mr. Tough Guy?" she asked. "Why can't you admit you're upset she's gone? It ain't like I'm gonna tell nobody. You boys are crazy! You hurt and hurt, and you don't ever say a damn thing about it. You ever think it might not hurt so much if you let it all out once in awhile?"

"Ruby," he said, his voice tired. "Get the fuck outta here."

"Jake, I'm just tryin'—"

"I said get lost!" he exploded. "Just go! Get the fuck away from me! You got no idea what she did! What they always do! You tell anyone I'm here, and I'll fuckin' beat the shit outta you."

Why did she bother trying to help someone like him? He didn't care, and he never would.

She stood slowly, careful not to hit her head on any beams. She thought of something to say that would hurt him, but she couldn't bring herself to do it.

Jake watched her with his cold eyes, taking pleasure in the fact he upset her.

"I'm sorry," Ruby said.

"What?" he asked, confused and surprised.

"I'm sorry she left," Ruby said. "I know what it feels like to be left. It ain't fair."

She moved toward the stairs, unsure if she'd been talking about his mother, Darla or something else entirely. She heard a low "fuck you" and ignored it. She climbed down the ladder and headed for the door, sliding it shut.

She got in Everett's car, started the engine, and tore onto the road. Never in a million years did she think she'd feel bad for Jake Wheeler. But he reminded her of the way she felt when her mother died, and the way she felt every time her father left her in another town, with another relative. It really wasn't fair.

All she tried to do was make Jake feel better. She shouldn't care that he didn't appreciate it.

She slowed as the road blurred and wiped tears off her face.

23

All was quiet for Ruby over the next few days.

Everett was in a good mood seeing as Sam Wyatt was allowing him to operate whenever he liked for a stake in the profits and ownership of the slot machines. Ruby thought her brother got off easy on that one. She hadn't forgiven him for lying about who owned the ranch. Knowing Everett rented the place made her mad.

She was glad Jake had gone on the run to Los Angeles on the first of the month like he promised Tim.

She was behind the bar waiting on Jed to arrive, and a pretty good crowd had assembled, including Ray Roth and a few of Tim's other boys. She noticed Roth's gaze following her as she bustled around the bar, and she hoped he wasn't going to cause any trouble. She had no doubt Tim would crack his head open if he did.

"You got any Old Milwaukee hiding behind there?" Ray asked.

"Sure." Ruby got one out the fridge and placed it on the counter.

Ray looked her up and down.

"Don't start, Ray," she said.

He backed off and turned to Jimmy Lewis. "Heard Tim got hauled in by the sheriff."

"What?" Ruby asked.

"Just for questioning, Ruby," Jimmy said, giving Ray a look. "He's out, it wasn't nothing."

"Yeah, Tim wouldn't have the guts to make Bobby disappear."

"What?"

Ray turned back to her, wolf-like. "Bobby Tafani's up and disappeared. Found his car at McCarran Field, and no sign of him. Found a gun in the car, too."

"A gun?" Ruby asked, feeling sick.

"Yeah, they think it was the one he shot Bill with."

She spotted Tim and Bill coming in the front door and got beers for them.

"What's up?" Tim asked.

Ruby cocked her head toward Ray.

"He giving you any trouble?" he asked.

"No," Ruby said. "He said you got hauled in by the police."

"Just wanted to talk, no big deal," Tim said.

"They said Bobby Tafani's missing."

"That's what they're saying."

Ruby stared.

"Don't look at me. He probably ran off, scared I was coming after him for what he did to you."

She wiped the bar, unsure he was telling the truth.

"Jake back yet?" Tim asked.

"Haven't seen him," Ruby said. She hoped she wouldn't have to, either.

But speaking of the devil usually brings him, and a few minutes later Jake sauntered in the door.

"How was it?" Tim asked him.

"They want you there Monday," he said. "Something about Topeka. Don't ask me to do it, I got a rodeo in Denver, a big one. I'll make more money doin' that than helping you. Get me a beer, will ya, Ruby?

He wasn't in a mood, so she went in back and came back with a Budweiser. She handed it to him, and he nodded. She wondered if he remembered the other night in the barn. That would teach her to be nice to him.

After awhile the crowd dwindled, and Tim took Ruby upstairs. They were tangled in her sheets, the breeze from the open windows cooling their bodies.

"I gotta do a run, leaving Monday," he said, his fingers running up and down her arm. "We'd get back maybe Thursday or something, I'm not sure."

"We?" she asked.

"You and me," he said. "If you can come, that is."

"I don't have to ask no one," she said.

She lay her head on Tim's chest and listened to his heartbeat, sounding in time with her own.

Monday, June 6, 1966

He picked Ruby up early Monday morning, Everett giving him the eye from the front porch.

The ride was uneventful, and they pulled in at the ranch at noon. There was a lot of activity going on. Tim noticed Ruby eyeing the stables longingly.

Insane Wayne came out of the barn with the Mexican girl behind him. She looked at Ruby, smiling insouciantly, and Tim grinned at Ruby's angry expression.

"What's up?" Tim asked. People were moving things, and it looked like chaos.

"Folding up the operation for now." Wayne nodded a hello to Ruby. "We'll pay you half of this run up front, mail you the rest."

"That wasn't the deal," Tim said. There was no way Wayne would get away with stiffing him on this job. There was no way he was spending hour upon hour driving that truck and coming away holding nothing.

"If you ladies would excuse us," Wayne said. He and Tim walked toward the barn, leaving Ruby and Rosa. Tim stopped and made sure he was in viewing distance—he felt the impending storm. He listened to Wayne with one ear and strained to hear Rosa and Ruby's conversation with the other.

"He is yours?" Rosa said, sidling up to Ruby.

"Yeah," Ruby answered. He laughed at the hesitation in her voice, like she wasn't sure she should be claiming him. He was surprised to find he didn't mind the idea of her saying it as much as he thought he would.

"He is not nice," she said. "He is too rough."

He saw Ruby bristle at her comment, and Tim was poised to walk over and give Rosa a piece of his mind if she tried insinuating anything had happened between them.

"He ain't rough with me," Ruby said, her voice stronger.

"You do not excite him, maybe." Rosa sounded too-sweet.

"I'm more exciting than a Juarez whore," Ruby said, smiling politely. "Tim don't like to get his hands dirty."

Rosa's face clouded over, and she looked at Ruby with a measured glare. Tim nodded at whatever Wayne said and cocked his head toward the girls to get Wayne's attention.

"Vete a la mierda!" Rosa said.

"Puta la madre, puta la hija," Ruby shot back, to Tim's surprise. He shouldn't be too surprised she knew some Spanish, but he had no idea what she said to Rosa.

"Ladies!" Insane Wayne said, walking toward them. "Let's not fight now. We're all friends here, aren't we?"

"No," Ruby said pointedly.

Ruby walked toward Tim and fell in step next to him, and they all walked to the barn, where they were loading up a mint condition black muscle car.

"The car's going to Topeka," Wayne said. "It's cherry, huh? A 1966 Dodge Charger. It was bought legal, too."

Wayne turned to Tim and handed him the paperwork.

"It's all there," he said. "The buyers in Topeka already paid in full."

"Yeah, and when do I get paid?" Tim glanced over at the car they were loading. He'd look good driving around Las Vegas in that. "You keeping your eye out for some wheels for me?"

"I'm working on it," Wayne said. "Maybe in lieu of paying you the rest on this job and for those parts you brought last time, I'll get you one cheap."

Tim nodded. "We'll see. Don't go thinking I'm gonna forget about all this."

"It's a long drive to Topeka," Wayne said. "You'll need to be there by Wednesday night to meet with our contact. I can find you a map with truck stops on it."

"That's okay," Ruby said, speaking up from behind Tim. "We'll be fine without one."

When the car was loaded and secured, Tim took the paperwork and walked toward the cab of the truck with Ruby. He didn't miss the self-satisfied smirk that Ruby threw at Rosa.

They left Los Angeles late, and Tim drove on past Las Vegas. It was nice being with him, no one in their way. But Tim was quiet and moody, and it wasn't at all what she wanted.

"What's wrong?" she asked him.

"This whole thing hasn't been what I thought."

She froze for a moment, wondering what thing he meant. He must've seen her expression, because he grinned. "Not you, kid. These LA boys."

"They do seem kind of disorganized," she said. "But you can drive a truck now. That'll get you places."

He shrugged. She bet he wanted to make more money, and maybe he would if those Los Angeles boys weren't so badly organized. She didn't ask any more questions, but did her best to talk Tim out of his bad mood.

Then sun had set by the time they stopped past Richfield, Utah. He said they'd stop in Denver the next night, then go on to Topeka for Wednesday night.

The sleeper area in the truck was pretty small—it was about three-quarters the size of a double bed, and there was no bunk bed in this truck. It would be a fairly tight squeeze, but she didn't mind that. Tim pulled the vinyl curtains across the front and side windows and turned on a light inside. Ruby felt a familiar feeling of being home, ensconced inside the truck.

Tim sat on the edge of the mattress and hung his head down, then rolled his shoulders.

"You never told me how much driving hurts," he said.

She climbed onto the bed and slid in behind Tim. She tentatively placed her hands on his shoulders. He didn't flinch or make any move to shrug her off, so she kneaded the muscles in his neck and shoulders, watching as he rolled his neck to get the kinks out. She snaked her hands over his shoulders and down his chest, then gathered his shirt up in her hands and pulled it off him.

She leaned over and kissed the side of his neck, then behind his ear. She slowly moved her lips, tracing along his skin until they reached the back of his neck. He tensed up as her hands ran across his shoulders. She let her hands rest on his shoulders for a moment, and she kissed the back of his neck. His breathing changed, becoming shallower and quicker.

She let her lips fall to the top of the first scar on his back.

He moved forward, and she held him still with her hands.

"Don't," she breathed. "Please."

"Ruby," he said, his voice strained. Her heart almost stopped at the sound in his voice.

Fear.

He was afraid.

"I'm not going to hurt you," she whispered.

He was still, her words giving him pause. She slid her hands slowly between his shoulder blades, feeling the scars scattered on his back. He was holding his breath, and she kissed his neck again while her hands moved slowly.

"Trust me," she said.

He took in a shaky breath. She let her fingertips brush across his back, the scars barely concave against his skin. They were old and had healed long ago, growing with him. She hesitated, her lips pressed against the skin over his spine. She could feel the vertebrae move as he breathed.

This had happened when he was a child, and it couldn't have been an accident.

His breathing became faster, more laboured. She moved her hands slowly and carefully down to his lower back. Then she moved them slowly up again, bowing her head to kiss her way down his spine. She stopped at every scar and let her lips touch every one and pretended she was taking all the pain from them.

It's all here, she thought, feeling his heated skin beneath her fingertips. All his anger is here.

She stored her own anger in her feet and her hands, kicking at things when she was angry and balling her fists when she was upset. Tim stored it here, along with whatever horror had brought these scars, and there was no way for him to shake it off.

"Does it hurt?" she asked, her voice so low it sounded far away.

"No," he said.

"Do you want me to stop?" She settled her palms against his shoulder blades.

There was a long pause.

"No."

"Tell me what happened," she asked.

Tim felt sick.

Her hands felt like velvet on his back, but everything was so mixed up. One second it felt like fire snapping across his shoulder blades, then the memory would fade, and he would feel the softness of her breath, her tongue flicking against the skin. He didn't want it to end.

He closed his eyes.

"Tell me," she said again.

Her hands were gone for a second, and he wanted to cry out. Fabric rustled, then her hands were on his skin again, tentative at first. She kissed the centre of his neck and let her hair fall around his shoulders, and he breathed in raggedly. She had taken off her shirt, and her skin pressed against him, warm and smooth.

He wasn't sure he could form the words. He had told no one. Ever. The only people who knew what happened that day were there.

He arched his back as her hands slipped down his sides, then ran up his spine. She circled her arms around his shoulders and neck from behind, and she held him, the bare skin of her chest cool against his back.

"It was September." His voice sounded pained to his own ears. "Di was seven. I was almost fourteen."

Her lips landed on his collarbone.

"Di was home sick, and she got it into her head to use dad's booze bottles to make music with, you know, filling them with water? She dumped them all out and had them set up on the kitchen floor. It was hot out that day."

He paused, remembering the images all too clearly.

"The old man came home drunk and went crazy," he said. "I heard him yelling from down the block, on my way home from school. I started to run."

She said nothing; the only thing he heard was her breath in his ear. Why was he telling her this? He spent so much time trying not to remember.

"I got in the door, and he had smacked Di around. He had a coat hanger ..."

He closed his eyes again; the feeling of the air choking out of him was overwhelming. Ruby must have sensed it, because she moved her hands to his shoulders and kneaded the muscles again. As he relaxed, he opened his eyes, and she kissed his shoulder and rested her cheek against his back.

"I told him it wasn't her fault, she was a kid and didn't know better," he said quietly. "He wouldn't listen. He was about to hit Di with the coat hanger when I ran over and jumped on him."

He paused again, hearing the rage in his father's voice that day.

"I was a scrawny kid. Couldn't do much. He was so pissed he said he'd beat the shit outta me for getting in his way. So he did," Tim said. "I took it as long as I could. Figured I had to or he'd go for her next. He got so tired he didn't even get to her. My mom came home and found him passed out drunk in a chair, Di crying and trying to mop all the blood off me. I was barely conscious."

Ruby kissed his shoulder again.

"What did she do?"

"Nothing," Tim said flatly. "Didn't wanna risk the police showing up and losing our rent if he went to jail, so she bandaged me up, never took me to the hospital."

He was quiet again.

"I hate him, Ruby." His voice was bitter. "I hate him. He's spent years hurting everyone around him, drinking up our rent, and all I've wanted to do since that night was kill him, but I can't. My mother loves the son of a bitch. I can't get Diana outta there. And if I do, that leaves my mother as his punching bag so I need to get them both out. I hate him, Ruby. I kill him, I go away, and my mother and Diana have to fend for themselves. Diana's walking a tightrope as it is. I can't do shit, and it's killing me."

She circled her arms around him from behind, then circled her legs around his waist.

"You saved her life," she said softly.

Tim nodded. He had known that the first time his father had made contact with his back with that hanger. His father would have beaten Di to death.

"Does she remember?"

"A little," he said. "Not much, I hope."

He breathed easier when she let go and ran her hands across his back. Somehow, it didn't feel like it used to. It didn't make him think of it like it used to. In fact, the feel of her hands and the feel of her breasts brushing against him turned him on instead of making him remember past horrors.

He turned toward her, and they both moved so they were lying side-by-side in the bed. He looked at this strange girl, who was too pale, asked too many questions and let everyone in the world see how she felt, and he felt grateful to her. She had done something just now, but he didn't know what. Everything had changed.

Tim rolled on top of her, and Ruby moved sensually underneath him. Her eyes were deeper blue than he'd ever seen them before. Usually they were pale grey and ghostly. Her cheeks were flushed, and he could feel the heat radiating off her body, as if she'd been left in the sun all day.

She arched her back, and he closed his eyes, buried his face in her hair and brought them both over the edge.

He kissed her, tried to say thank you with his lips and with the way he cupped her face, knowing he couldn't trust himself to say it with words.

He was pretty sure she understood anyway.

24

Ruby awoke early. They had a seven hour drive ahead of them to Denver, and she wanted to let Tim sleep a bit. She was used to being up when the sun was, only right now she couldn't see if it was sunny from the inside of the truck. Tim was curled around her, his arm across her chest, and his face pressed against the back of her neck.

She had never heard such a terrible story before.

She hadn't met his father, and now she understood why. Tim did what he always did, protecting her. Protecting everyone but himself. She felt sad, knowing what Tim went through, but a larger part of her was proud of him. He was almost killed protecting his sister.

She sighed and placed her hand over his arm, then turned over in the small bed so she was pressed against his chest.

Tim tightened his arm around her.

"Did I wake you?" she asked, tilting her head up to look at him. She always marvelled at how wide awake he looked first thing in the morning, as if he could go from sleeping like the dead to being completely aware of everything, just by opening his eyes.

"No," he said.

"Liar," she teased.

He smiled one of his real smiles, then pulled the blankets up close around them. She slipped an arm around his side and ran her hand up his back, and she was relieved to see he didn't flinch or make any effort to move away from her touch.

She closed her eyes and rested her forehead against his chin. She thrilled when he kissed her forehead.

"Come on," he said. "We better get up."

"No," she, pressing herself tighter against him.

"We can get breakfast before we leave," he said, his breath whispering along her hairline.

"I'm not hungry," she said.

Tim looked down, his eyes dark and inviting. She touched his cheek and ran her fingers across his damaged face, and he brought his lips down to hers gently. She arched her back, trying to make him kiss her harder, but he matched her movements, and his lips were always just out of reach.

"Tease," she breathed.

He paused before rolling them both over, and her body was covered by his weight. His mouth explored hers, and the truck rocked with their movements.

Tim started up the truck and pulled onto the road, heading out of Utah and into Colorado. It was a tight squeeze sharing a bed that small with Ruby, but it was worth it.

He watched Ruby's mouth as she spoke to him and watched her hair fall across her shoulders. She was so unaware how unlike other girls she was. She didn't dress like they did or act like they did. His gaze rested on the fading bruises on her wrist, and he smiled grimly.

The cops thought Tafani took off since his car was left at McCarran. The Chicago boys were denying they ever knew him. Tim doubted he'd ever be found.

They drove through the day, reaching Denver in the mid-afternoon.

"I've always liked Denver," Ruby said. "Of course, I've never been in the winter."

"You miss Abilene?"

She shrugged. "I miss the little ranch. That's about it. Abilene wasn't good to me."

"I figure on getting a motel room for tonight," he said. "I have to meet with this contact of Wayne's about something."

He found a cheap motel on a quiet road and they checked in.

"I'll be back in awhile," he said. "Don't get yourself into any trouble when I'm gone."

She grinned. "Double for you."

He smiled back and walked down the street to the bar he'd be meeting this guy at.

Tim returned before dinner, and they ate out. Awhile later, Ruby's head rested against Tim's bare chest. Her fingers traced the sparse hairs, then travelled to the stitches across his stomach. He shooed her hand away, like he did every time, then scratched at them himself.

"I'm gonna pull those damn things out before long," he said. Ruby grabbed his hand.

"You'll open them up again if you keep scratching like that." She brought his hand up to her lips and kissed it.

She rolled over slightly and propped herself up on her elbows, looking into his face. He looked with barely contained curiosity.

"What?" he asked.

She shook her head, maybe too shy to speak.

He reached up and slid a hand around the back of her neck, pulling her to him. His lips were insistent and searching and left her gasping for air.

"I love you," she said breathlessly, the words escaping from her like she had uncorked a wine bottle.

He froze slightly. He moved his fingers through her hair. He couldn't believe she said it. But it was Ruby; of course she said it. She said whatever came into her damn head.

He saw the shadow pass over her face, and the hurt in her eyes when he hadn't responded. Shit, he knew she couldn't leave it all alone; he knew she'd come looking for more.

She said nothing else. She put her head down on his chest, but he felt as if she were a piece of bone china and she'd shatter at any moment. He couldn't think of anything to say. He couldn't say that. He'd never said that.

Shit. Why couldn't she be happy with what they had? The night before had drained him of any emotion he may have held. Christ, he'd practically skywrote how he felt about her the night before, why the hell couldn't she see that?

He took in a breath and felt her body tense.

"We'd better get to sleep," he said. "We'll need to be out of here early."

She nodded, slipped out of his arms quietly, and rolled over in the bed. He considered circling an arm around her, but in the end, he couldn't.

Wednesday, June 8, 1966

Ruby didn't think she slept much that night. The events of the night tumbled over and over in her mind. Maybe she shouldn't have told him she loved him. The look on his face had said as much, even though he hadn't.

But what else was she supposed to do? She couldn't exactly hide it forever.

She thought he might feel the same way. She felt so close to him on this trip, like they were connected. The night she broke through those barriers and he told her about what happened to him, that felt like something. They had made love after that, and she had known it was different than any other time they slept together. Maybe he loved her in that moment.

Maybe she was wrong.

The mattress moved, and she closed her eyes as Tim got out of bed. She watched from beneath her lashes as he moved around the room, not wearing a stitch of clothes. Her stomach flip-flopped as she watched his lithe form. She ached to have him come over to her side of the bed, sit down, smooth her hair and tell her he loved her. But instead, he grabbed some clothes out of his bag and headed into the bathroom.

She tossed the covers off when she heard the running water, then dressed quickly. It was already hotter than Hades out, despite the clouds. It was a muggy heat, and it made Ruby nervous.

The sun rose in the distance, the light soft. Tim came out of the bathroom and watched her as she packed up her bag.

"You gonna be like this all the way to Topeka?" he asked.

"Like what?" she asked, her hands on her hips. "Tim ..."

She stopped, unsure of what she wanted to say. She was screaming inside, and she wanted to yell at him until her voice was gone, but she knew it would have no effect on him.

"What?" he asked.

"Nothin'," she mumbled, turning back to her bag.

Tim approached and gently took her by the elbow, turning her around to face him.

"You're mad," he stated.

She tilted her head. "Why would I be mad?"

She tried to read his expression, but he kept it in that oh-so-perfect mask.

"You're mad because of last night," he said.

"You can't even say it!" she exclaimed. "You don't even want to think about it. Good Lord, I don't know why I bother."

She tried to turn back to her bag, but he had taken firm hold of her arms.

"Ruby, you remember me telling you not to box me in, and I meant it," he said.

"That ain't what I'm tryin' to do!" Her voice sounded oddly desperate to her. "What does that mean? You want to be free to ... to screw anyone who comes along? Fine, you're free."

"Ruby," he said. He ran his hands, still closed around her arms, up a little higher. "Dammit, Ruby, that isn't what I want, and you know it."

His eyes were dark, and his brow was furrowed, like he didn't know what to do or say.

"Ruby, we've got something good here, let's not mess that up."

"I'm not messing it up." She looked him dead in the eye. "I can't help how I feel."

Maybe he couldn't help how he felt, and that was the problem. He felt nothing for her, and she felt everything for him.

"You look like you wanna pretend it never happened, like I never said I love you," she said, trying to will the tears away that were forming, watching his face change when she said the words. "Fine. Go on and pretend."

She turned away and tried to hide the fact she was crying.

Jesus Christ.

Tim wanted to put his fist through the wall.

It wasn't what she said; he could handle that. It wasn't like Carolyn had never said it. Of course, he knew she never meant it, being either drunk or plain happy she was in someone's bed instead of alone. But it was different this time.

It was Ruby saying it to him.

His heart damn near stopped when she said it. He couldn't recall the last time he heard those words, and it sent his mind reeling and made him feel panic in a way he never had before.

Now he was on the verge of blowing everything to hell, all because he couldn't say it back. He never said it to anyone, and she shouldn't expect it from him. It frustrated him to no end that she did. After all they'd been through, how come she couldn't see for herself?

He sighed, not knowing what the hell he was doing, and that part scared him. He always knew what to do and what to say. This was something altogether different.

If it was anyone else, he could—and had—lied through his teeth about how much he cared. But he couldn't do it to Ruby. Did that mean . . . ?

He felt disgusted with himself that he couldn't finish the thought.

Ruby felt better as they got into the truck, and Tim started the diesel engine. He hadn't said he loved her, but he also hadn't said he didn't. He was always straightforward with her, and she couldn't understand why he couldn't come out and say how he felt, whatever it was.

Lewis had told her so many times. He loved her, and he'd always love her. It never occurred to her then that the words had always come before they slept together and never afterwards. She wondered if it was better to hear them, even like that, than not hear them at all.

They rolled along the highway in silence for the most part. They left the mountains of Colorado into the flat plains of Kansas, and the sky got stormy.

A flash of light startled her.

"Was that lightning?" she asked, her voice wavering.

"I dunno," Tim said. She saw him glance at her a few times. He probably expected her to jump half out of her skin if thunder rolled, but she wouldn't give him the satisfaction.

She was quiet, watching the horizon, when another flash lit up the sky and startled her. Tim looked over again.

"You gonna be alright?" he asked.

"I'm fine," she said.

"You can't lie worth a damn," Tim said.

She watched his profile, his eyes darting to the side, trying to look at her without taking his gaze off the road too long. The rain began to fall in big drops, splashing against the windshield. A few minutes later it poured, and the rain drummed on the nose of the truck. Tim had the wipers on, and she tried to lose herself in the rhythm.

Being in love was supposed to feel good. Well, this felt like horseshit.

"Ruby." He steadied the truck as a gust of wind blew so hard she could feel it herself. "I trust you. Let that be enough right now."

She couldn't stop herself from crying, and she tried to convince herself it was because of the thunderstorm. She wiped the tears away quickly and cringed when another flash of lightning lit up the sky.

"You want me to pull over?" he asked.

"No." She shook her head. "I wanna get outta here."

"The storm's moving north, we'll be past it soon," he said.

Tim accelerated more, frustrated as hell with Ruby. He couldn't tell whether she was crying because she was mad at him or afraid of the storm they were in. He was itchy in his own skin. Once, this would have been his worst nightmare, a girl in love with him. He decided he wasn't upset about it. He could tell her that.

But he kept his mouth shut.

A flash lit up the sky to the left of them.

"I hate this," she said, stifling a sob.

He tightened his grip on the steering wheel. She was crying again, and he didn't think it had anything to do with the storm.

"What do you want from me?" he asked. "I told you, I'm trying, Ruby."

"I know," she said quietly.

He pushed the truck into the next gear.

"You take everything so goddamn personal," he said.

She was silent, and it made him angrier.

"Girls like Carolyn, they don't make me half as crazy as you do," he said.

"Maybe you should go have some fun with her, then," Ruby said, her arms crossed protectively. "Some fun this is."

"I told you before," he said tiredly, his headache going full blast, "it's not them I want. You gotta know that."

Ruby looked over at him and was about to speak when the siren blasted the air, and the blue and red lights flashed on behind them.

"Shit."

Ruby clutched the side of the seat with her hands. Tim stopped the truck on the side of the highway. She looked through Tim's side mirror and saw a Kansas Highway Patrol cruiser parked behind the trailer. The officer climbed up on the running boards.

"License and registration," he said. "I'll also need your log books and any Bills of Lading."

Tim handed him the license, then took the registration papers from the visor overhead. Ruby handed over the other paperwork wordlessly.

The officer took them and disappeared for a few minutes.

"What're we gonna do?" Her voice was barely above a whisper.

"Nothing yet," he said. "Don't look so scared."

She couldn't help but be scared. Insane Wayne had said the car was legit, but how much could you trust a fake cowboy?

Tim looked over. "If they haul me in, you stay out here and wait."

"What?" she asked, startled by the instructions. A flash of lightning lit up the sky, and Ruby swallowed hard.

She didn't have a chance to ask him what he meant. The officer stepped back up on the running boards.

"I'm gonna need you to step outta the vehicle," he said. "No sudden movements please. Young lady, if you'll stay there until I ask you to come out."

She swallowed hard and watched as Tim's expression changed.

"What's the problem?" He hadn't reached for the door latch.

"Your license isn't in the system," he said. "But I ran your name."

"And what did you find?" Tim asked, his voice bored.

"You've got quite the record," he said. "We're running you for any warrants."

"Don't have any," he said.

"Is that so? Well, we'll see," he said. "Step outta the truck, don't make me come in there and get you."

Tim held his hands up in mock surrender. "No need to threaten, officer. You might wanna let the lady go."

"Step out of the truck," the officer said again.

Tim opened the door and slowly stepped down onto the pavement. He cuffed Tim and searched him. The thunder rolled overhead, and Ruby squashed the tears. She wanted to throw up.

256

"Switchblade. No, scratch that, two switchblades," the officer said, laying them on the running boards.

"For protection," Tim said. "You wouldn't believe the kinds of people you find in truck stops."

The officer turned to her. "Step out the driver's side, Miss."

Ruby slowly got out, imagining Everett's voice when she called home asking for bail money. He'd probably leave her in jail to teach her a lesson about Tim.

He asked for her identification, and she handed over her driver's license. He scrutinized it, then used his radio to call into his dispatcher. As he was by the car, another flash of lighting lit up the dark sky and Ruby yelped.

"Keep it together, Ruby," Tim cautioned.

"I can't," she whispered. Her breath came in gasps. She held her breath for a moment as the police officer made his way back to the car.

"What're you doing with this guy?"

She looked at Tim, then at the officer, not sure what to say.

"Don't know her," Tim said laconically. "Picked her up at a gas station, hitchhiking."

Ruby looked at him, hurt.

"Right," the officer intoned, clearly not believing him.

A flash lit up the sky, followed by rolling thunder, and she bit her tongue, biting on a scream.

"You can ride into Brewster with me if you like," he said. "I'll be taking him in."

Ruby froze. "What for?"

"Possession of a weapon, driving without a license," the cop said. "I'm sure more charges will come when I get that report back on his warrants."

"You're not arresting me?" She hoped he would. At least then she wouldn't be stranded in the truck in the middle of nowhere during a storm. She couldn't stay here. She'd die if she stayed here.

Tim looked with blank eyes.

"I'm not arresting you," the policeman said. "But you'd best come into town with me, it's dangerous out here."

"Ruby, stay with the truck," Tim said.

"What?" Her throat was so dry.

"I need you to stay with the truck."

"But, I can't!" Bile rose in her throat as the lightning flashed.

"Stay with the truck!"

Tears welled up in her eyes, and she struggled to blink them away. A crack of thunder burst in the distance, and she jumped.

"Tim," she said, her voice a pathetic whimper.

"The judge won't be in until tomorrow afternoon," the officer said.

Ruby paled and looked at Tim, who was blank-faced in front of the cop. She wished the man would walk away and let Tim talk to her.

"Tomorrow?" she asked. "Please, do you have to take him in?"

"Sorry Miss, rules are rules," the officer said. "Your friend here likes to break them. There's nothing I can do."

Ruby looked wildly over at Tim as another rumble of thunder sounded in the distance. She was terrified, and her hands shook. Tim's face was a mask with no expression. Anger bloomed in her chest. He couldn't break his perfect mask in front of anyone, and now she teetered on the edge of losing her mind. All she needed was some words from him, and they never came— would never come. Everything else was always more important.

She had no idea how she would get through the night alone during this storm. She shuddered and watched the police officer walk Tim to his car.

He put Tim in the backseat and got in the driver's seat. He did a U-turn near her, and she locked gazes with Tim. The look on his face didn't change, and she turned away, tears falling. The clap of thunder made her jump.

She climbed into the truck, shut all the curtains up, then flung herself on the bed and cried as the storm crept upon her.

25

Tim sat in the holding cell, the only person there on the dreary day. He made his one phone call and settled in. The judge wouldn't be in until tomorrow, and there was nothing else he could do.

Ruby's face as he left her at the side of the road haunted him. The terror was plain in her eyes, but the cop wasn't going to let him stick around to make sure Ruby didn't go into hysterics. He couldn't reassure her, he couldn't stop the storm from coming, and he couldn't let that truck sit there unguarded.

He needed the money from the run. That truck was a sitting duck on the side of the road with no one in it. At least with Ruby there, things had a chance of staying together.

He pictured her shivering against the storm. It was obvious they scared her in a real way, no matter how much he told her it was air and noise and rain. She'd linked it in her mind to her mother's death, and he couldn't undo that. He hoped she'd calm down enough to huddle in the truck and wait.

Things were going to be a pain in the ass when he got back to Las Vegas.

Hopefully by then she'd be calmed down from the storm and see there was no other way. As for what she wanted from him ... maybe when they got back home she'd realize things were okay. He wasn't going anywhere; didn't want to. Maybe it would come in time. Maybe it wouldn't. She would be okay with that once they were home.

He settled his head on a flat feather pillow and closed his eyes, listening to the storm and hoping Ruby was making it through.

Ruby cried until the thunder was gone.

She was curled up around a pillow that smelled like Tim's aftershave. It made her miss him and it made her feel sick, all at the same time. She kept putting her nose against the fabric and inhaling his smell, then crying about how messed up everything was.

Maybe he was trying to punish her for telling him she loved him.

She rolled onto her back, and a tear slid down her temple and into her ear. She couldn't imagine Tim being so cruel as to leave her somewhere he knew she'd panic to death. But he had looked so different when she said she loved him; his face had changed, and she was unable to read his expression. She would give anything for a clue to whether he was happy or angry with her.

She supposed she should be happy she loved him. Maybe he would come to love her in time, if he kept her around that long.

She wished she could drive the truck and go back to Las Vegas on her own, but her past experience at it told her she'd ruin the transmission in no time.

Maybe she could flag another car and get the driver to take her to the police station. Tim would be mad, but she was close to not caring, as long as she didn't have to spend the night alone during a storm. She was homesick for Everett's.

She looked at her watch. It was noon. Her head hurt, and she was hungry. There was no food in the truck, and she'd be damned before she would go to the bathroom on the side of a well-travelled road. She couldn't believe Tim had left her like this.

A second later she almost jumped out of her skin when someone rapped on the driver's side window.

She crept over and held the curtain back slightly, hoping she'd find the policeman back to arrest her. She was surprised to see Jake Wheeler standing there.

"Open up for Christ's sake," he said when he spotted her looking out the window.

She flung the curtains back and unlocked the door. Jake climbed up into the truck and into the driver's seat.

"How did you get here?" She was shocked to see him sitting there. "How did you even know?"

"So I'm in Denver, getting ready for my saddle bronc ride and someone says I got a call." Jake lit up a cigarette. "What do I hear on the other end? Bill Pearce ruining my day. He said Kelly got busted and needed me to come take the truck over to Topeka tonight."

"They're not letting him out?"

"He's such a fuckin' asshole, doin' this to me. I didn't even get to ride. I'm gonna lose my pay, and it ain't like he'll cover it."

"How did you get here?"

"Guy dropped me off," he said. "Now I gotta miss one of the biggest rodeos of the season to take on this shit. Kelly knows how to piss people off, lemme tell you. Tim said you'd know what was up, he said all the paperwork was in the truck with you."

She burned with anger toward Tim. All he cared about was getting the money for this stupid job. He could have at least told her he was going to call Jake so she wouldn't be afraid, but he didn't. She sat back in her seat and crossed her arms.

Jake looked over from the driver's seat.

"What the hell's got into you?" he asked irritably, starting up the diesel engine.

"I'm not going," she said.

"Yes, you are." Jake put the truck into gear and pulled into the nearly deserted highway. Tim was right; Jake knew what he was doing behind the wheel.

"Just let me out, and I'll hitch my way back to Las Vegas," she said.

"You been cryin'?" he asked.

"What if I have?"

"You're mad ol' Tim got picked up, huh, darlin'?" A smile tugged at the corners of his mouth.

"No," she answered.

"Well, get used to it." Jake took one last drag of his cigarette before tossing the butt out the window. "Me and Tim got matching cells down at the City Jail. I think he's beating me on overnight visits though."

Ruby rolled her eyes and looked back at the road. The storm was passing, and she felt a little better since Jake arrived. He was someone to talk to, which was better than nothing if the storms started up again.

"You look like shit," Jake said.

"You sure know how to charm a girl," Ruby said sarcastically.

"Go lie down or somethin'," Jake said. "I'll wake you up when we get near Topeka."

She wondered what kind of game he was playing, and he looked over and met her gaze.

"You look like you could use a rest," he said simply.

She felt bad breaking her own self-imposed rule about being awake when the driver was, but she was bone-tired all of a sudden. She moved into the bunk and climbed into the bed, circling her arms around a pillow, letting the rhythm of the road rock her to sleep.

She woke up hours later; it was past four thirty in the afternoon. The sky looked dark and foreboding, and the air was muggy. She moved up to the front passenger seat. Jake was watching her.

"You look better," he said. "Your eyes ain't all puffy at least."

"Where are we?" she asked.

"Outskirts of Topeka." He lit a cigarette. "Looks like there's gonna be a hell of a storm."

She shivered and rolled up the passenger window. The roads were slick with rain, and she could feel a sense of foreboding; the air didn't feel right.

"I figure we'll crash at a motel tonight," Jake said.

"Why can't we deliver this stuff tonight and head back to Las Vegas?" she asked.

Jake looked over, and she caught the flicker of annoyance cross his face.

"What, you so eager to get the hell away from me?"

"That's not it," she said quietly. "I hate storms, I don't wanna be here."

Jake had a curious look on his face as he alternated between watching the road and her. She felt uncomfortable under his gaze.

"Tim said you knew how to drive trucks," she said, hoping to distract him.

"Yeah, what of it?"

"Nothin'," she mumbled. She felt exhausted. He couldn't even hold a decent conversation. "I meant you look like you know what you're doing. Who taught you?"

"The United States Air Force," Jake blew a few smoke rings. "But I'd taught myself before that when I lived in Alabama."

"My dad's a driver," she said.

Jake nodded. "I heard that around. Where's your mom?"

"Dead," she said. She was silent for a minute. "You mentioned your mom before. What about your dad?"

He shrugged. "Shot himself in the head three months after I enlisted."

She stared, shocked at the casual way he said it.

"I'm sorry," she said.

He didn't reply, and she watched his hands work the shifter as he changed lanes.

"Why do you hate storms?" he asked.

"I just do." She didn't want him knowing about that hellish ride to her mother's deathbed. He'd probably think she was stupid for caring about her mother, since he wasn't fond of his own.

"So why are you all hacked off at Kelly?"

"Who said I was?" she asked.

"No one had to, it's all over your face," he said.

"It's none of your business."

She felt his gaze on her.

"I bet a million folks told you not to go fallin' in love with him and look at you now," he taunted.

She felt dangerously close to tears. "Shut up."

Jake laughed coarsely.

"Shut *up*." She swiped at a lone tear that escaped.

"No matter how much you try and pull him into it, he ain't gonna fall in love with you," he said, his voice serious.

"Why not? You fell in love with Darla." She knew she was skating on thin ice. "If you can, anyone can, I guess."

"I never loved that broad. Two-timing snake," Jake said. "Should ask Tim about that, you'd drop him pretty fast."

His hand clenched the gear shift as he forced the truck into another gear, speeding up on the slick roads. His face looked darker than the storm clouds above them.

She didn't want to think about what he was trying to insinuate. He was trying to make her feel worse.

As if that was possible.

The storm began minutes later.

Ruby gripped the sides of her seat as the first flashes of lightning streaked across the sky. The thunder rumbled loudly, even over the sound of the diesel engine. When the third lightning strike lit the sky up to their left, she gasped at how close it was.

The crack of thunder was so loud the vibrations shook the truck.

She squeezed her eyes shut, waiting for the loud rumble to pass and cursing herself for not being able to hide her fear better. She could see out of the corner of her eye that Jake was watching her.

She screamed when the next flash came.

"What the hell's got into you?" Jake looked at her like she had two heads.

"I just hate storms," she managed to gasp out, wishing she could shut the sound of the thunder out of her head. Instead, she started to cry.

Jake muttered a string of curses that made her blush.

"Look, I can't control it," she sniffed. "I just hate them, I wanna get outta here!"

"Well, where the hell do you expect me to go?" he asked.

The rain fell so hard she could barely see out the windshield. Jake had floored it at first, but the rain forced him to slow the giant rig down or risk turning it over. Jake was cursing the truck, Tim, the job, the weather, and God, all at once.

"We'll find a motel and get inside for awhile," he said. "I don't like the looks of the sky."

He was right about that. It was dark and ominous, and the clouds moved in a swirl of blackness.

Jake got off the highway and drove up Southwest Topeka Boulevard, pulling into a motel with a big parking lot. He manoeuvred the truck into the lot and shut the engine down. The rain had let up, but the clouds were dark and thunder was in the distance.

"Where are we?" she asked.

"Dunno," he said. "The address you got for these guys who get the car is over on Southeast Tenth. It won't take no time to get there tomorrow."

"I still think we should go tonight."

Ruby grabbed her bag and hurried after Jake toward the office.

"Wait up!" she cried out, hurrying to catch up to him.

He looked back, then slowed so she was walking alongside him, and she felt grateful for a gesture that would have been second nature for Tim.

Ruby's nerves were on fire as she stood in the small office, hearing low rumbles in the distance. She paced the small room until Jake got a key.

"We're not having two rooms?" she asked weakly.

"Do I look like I'm made of money to you?" he asked. "We're gonna bunk together, sweetheart."

She scowled at his back and followed him to the door of their room at the end of the motel block. She was relieved when he opened the door, and the room had two double beds inside.

"We'll rest up a bit, then go grab some food. I wanna be outta here early," he said.

"Fine with me," she said. "I'd rather be outta here now."

"Can it, Ruby," he said. "If you're gonna whine all night, sleep in the truck."

She sat on the edge of one bed and tucked her bag into the corner. She felt safer inside the motel room as the thunder rumbled in the distance.

She hoped Tim regretted leaving her. He knew it was storming, and he knew she couldn't stand it. Her eyes burned with tears, but these ones were born out of anger instead of fear.

"Jesus Christ, you'd think you'd never seen thunder and lightning before," Jake said, flicking on the small black and white television and lying on the other bed. He kicked his boots off and let them fall on the floor.

Ruby got up and paced the room. It was darker out now, and the air felt electric and wrong.

"I wanna go home," she said miserably. "Jake, I wanna go back to Las Vegas!"

He was incredulous. "We ain't goin' nowhere until we get this shit delivered. How the hell does Tim stand you cryin' like this all the time? Christ."

Ruby exhaled sharply. "Maybe he doesn't."

Jake looked curious.

"Maybe it's like you said, and he doesn't give a damn." She wished she smoked or something. She needed something to do with her hands before she went crazy.

"Don't ever get attached," Jake said. "That's the rule."

"Your rule or Tim's?" she asked.

Jake's gaze flicked over to her. "It's a good rule, is all."

The thunder cracked overhead, and Ruby screamed and clapped a hand over her mouth. The tears came in earnest this time.

Jake muttered curses again.

"I do Kelly a favour, and I get saddled with this," he said. "Ruby, you think you might be able to shut the hell up and not go all hysterical on me for maybe five minutes, so I can relax?"

She wanted to punch him. At least Tim was willing to try and calm her down. She doubted Jake would do anything if she went hysterical. He'd let her go crazy until she died, then he'd thank God for the quiet.

Ruby jumped at the lightning. She braced for thunder, but instead heard a siren.

"Oh no," she wailed.

"It's just a tornado siren. You must've heard a million in Texas."

The sky was an odd colour, and it was very still. There was no rain, no thunder, no lightning. It was as if someone had switched off Mother Nature.

"Ignore it," Jake said. He got up and opened the door. "See? No tornado."

He left the door open and went back to the bed, idly watching the end of the six o'clock news. Ruby paced, feeling in her bones that something was wrong. She was going to go stir crazy with Jake; she knew it.

She couldn't stop the tears from overflowing.

The news switched to a weather report, and Ruby turned up the volume. Jake got up and stepped onto the cement sidewalk outside the room.

"Jesus Christ," he said.

She was about to ask him what was wrong when the newscaster on television spoke.

"For God's sake, take cover," he said. The power cut out a second later.

She rushed to the doorway and saw the giant funnel cloud before Jake shoved his way back inside.

26

Ruby froze.

She had never seen anything so massive in all her life. The huge black funnel looked as if it was standing in place and posing for a photograph. She barely registered it was real until she saw the swirling outer edges.

"Shit!" Jake swore again. "Come on!"

Ruby's legs weakened, and for a second she was sure she was going to pass out. She grabbed the door frame and held on, staring at the tornado bearing down on them in awe.

"Ruby!" Jake said. "Move! Come on!"

She turned her head and saw Jake standing in the doorway to the bathroom. There was no way she could make it that far.

"Fuck!"

Jake strode toward her. He grabbed her arm tightly, kicked the front door shut and pushed her ahead of him and into the bathroom.

He shut that door, too, and turned around in the small room.

"Get in the tub," he said, as the wind rattled the windows.

She still couldn't move.

He grabbed her upper arms and bent over so he was looking in her eyes.

"Hey!" he shook her. "Move it, this thing is comin' whether you want it to or not!"

He stared for a split second longer as she tried to say something. No words came out.

He swore again, then pushed her toward the bathtub.

"Get in, lie down," he instructed, speaking loudly over the wailing wind. She crouched into the tub, but it was hardly long enough for her to lie down in.

Jake yanked the plastic shower curtain off the rod and covered himself with it. Just as he moved to lay down on top of her, a sound like a freight train roared in her ears.

Jake's weight settled over top of her, and she circled her arms around his waist as tightly as she could. She opened her mouth to scream as the deafening roar sounded all around her, and the air was sucked from her lungs.

Debris was flying and things hit her, even in the tub. She sucked in air and screamed, then tried to move, to get out of the tub, out of the bathroom, and out of the hotel. She wasn't going to die here.

As she raised her head she was smacked in the forehead by something and startled. Her mind blurred and things went dark for a moment. Jake's hand was on her forehead, holding her down, then a trickle of burning hot water fell onto her head from the faucet.

The roar of twisting metal, devastating wind, and breaking glass filled her ears. She tried to scream, but no sound came out.

She tightened her grip on Jake, praying for the end, and praying that if she had to die it would be quick.

It was silent.

Ruby trembled beneath Jake, hardly daring to believe she was alive. She opened her eyes slowly. Jake was looking at her, his eyes wild and disbelieving. The shower curtain had disappeared, and Ruby saw glass in Jake's hair. His brow wrinkled as he stared.

"You're bleeding," he said, his voice hoarse.

She tried to swallow, but her throat was so dry. She couldn't believe how utterly quiet it was, as if the tornado had never happened. She looked up and saw the small frosted glass window was gone and beyond it was clear sky, of all things.

She was so confused. This was like a nightmare.

"Holy shit," Jake said, slowly getting to his knees. The sound of broken glass and debris falling into the bathtub as he moved made her feel sick. He stepped out of the tub, glass crunching under his feet, and he swore under his breath.

He held a hand out to her. She took it, but could barely pull herself up. Jake frowned again, then leaned down and picked her up under the arms, like a baby. He tried to set her on the floor, but her legs were so weak she could barely stand. He sat her on the toilet.

"Come on." He grasped her with one arm and shook her, as if it would solidify her body. "Ruby, come on."

He hauled her up, then dragged her to the bathroom door, which was set off its hinges. He bumped against it with his shoulder and it flew open. He pulled her into the other room, an arm around her supporting her weight.

She inhaled sharply when she saw the room.

Some of her things were scattered in the room, but her bag was gone. The entire room was glittering, covered in glass from the big picture window. The television was missing, lamps were turned over, and the bedding was gone. A hole in the upper left corner of the room was dripping with water. Everything was still.

Jake pulled a mattress over and sat her on it. He found his boots, one jammed under a table and the other in a closed closet. She noticed the bottoms of his socks were bloody as he pulled the boots on.

"Anybody here?" came a voice.

"Yeah!" Jake yelled back. A second later their door was forced open, and the manager from the small office was poking his head inside.

"You folks alright?" he asked.

"Yeah, we're okay," Jake said. "She could use something for her head."

"Will do," he said. "I'll check on the other rooms, see if there's one in better condition for you, but the end of this place is gone, and there ain't a window left here."

"Just bring a broom and dust pan," Jake said.

"What?" he asked.

"Just do it." He nodded her way.

The manager wandered off, his voice echoing outside as he called to people.

Jake came over and crouched in front of Ruby.

"How many fingers?" he asked, holding two up in front of her. Ruby saw them fine, but she was so exhausted she wouldn't have been able to say a word if there was a gun to her head.

Jake sighed.

"Alright, kid," he said. "Stay here."

Ruby's eyes widened as he moved for the door.

"No!" she screamed, bolting up from the bed.

Jake looked back, then walked back over to her.

"I'm gonna get a bandage, darlin'. You're bleeding like a stuck pig," he said, touching her forehead. She was surprised to see her blood on his fingers.

"Don't leave me." Her voice was hoarse and strained. "Please."

Jake sighed, then steered her toward the bed again and made her sit.

"Alright, I won't go nowhere," he said. He looked around the room and found a pillowcase. He brought it over and held it against her head. She gaped at all the blood. He pressed against her head, which ached, and she looked at the floor. A child's doll was laying in the middle of the carpet, and a hubcap was next to it. Nothing seemed real.

"Probably got cut by flying glass. Does it hurt much?"

She shook her head. She didn't know she was cut. Her head felt fine. In fact, she felt so good she was ready to go home.

A moment later the manager came back inside, handing Jake a broom and dustpan.

"Everybody here's accounted for. I heard this thing is out at the airport now," the man said, wiping his thin brow with a cloth. "I ain't never lived through anything like that in my life. I got a first aid kit up at the office, I'll be back with it."

"Can you sweep?" Jake held a broom out to Ruby. "Come on, you can sweep some glass, right? It's easy."

He was trying to distract her. She was aware of herself and where she was, but she couldn't trust herself to talk. If she opened her mouth, she'd scream forever. She wasn't going to forgive Tim for leaving her to this. Maybe if he'd been here it wouldn't have happened.

Even she knew that was stupid.

She took the broom Jake was holding and swept debris into a pile on the floor. The rhythm of the broom occupied her thoughts; she imagined the glass was glittering diamonds, and she was a giant collecting them.

She didn't hear the manager return, but awhile later Jake sat her down and put something on her cut forehead that made it sting, then stuck a giant bandage on top of it. She would have looked at herself in the mirror, only it had shattered into a million pieces in the bathroom. That was seven years bad luck.

"You folks go on," the manager said. "I'll tidy up some before you get back."

She looked over at Jake in confusion.

"Come on," he said. "We're gonna deliver that car and get the hell out of here."

Ruby protested, but Jake maintained that she either stay in the room alone or come with him to the truck. She followed him out wordlessly, but was relieved when he walked slow enough that she didn't have to hurry to keep up with him.

"Holy shit," he said.

Whole areas were levelled. Part of the motel was gone, reduced to nothing but a cement slab. A few blocks away Ruby could see what used to be a house; now there was a foundation. Wood, bricks, pieces of garbage, peoples' belongings ... it was everywhere. The part of the motel they were in looked untouched compared to the opposite end. People wandered in the streets and looked around in confusion.

She was amazed at how light it was. It had to be nearing eight o'clock but the sky was as clear as if nothing had happened. She slowed a bit, then was prodded along by Jake's hand against her back.

They both stopped short. The truck had moved all the way across the parking lot and was sitting on the foundation of what used to be a house.

"Jesus Christ." Jake looked at the truck. "Let's hope it still runs."

He couldn't get in the driver's side, seeing as it was pressed up against a tree, so he unlocked the passenger door and got in, and Ruby was shocked when he turned around and offered her a hand inside.

She took his hand gratefully, glad to feel another person's touch. She had to hang on. She couldn't lose it here. She willed herself not to cry.

Jake started the truck up, and she sighed in relief that the engine was still running. She cringed as the truck and trailer scraped against the tree, making a noise that was far too close to the sound of the tornado for her liking. After ten minutes of manoeuvring, Jake got it free. He moved the truck through the debris and managed to park it closer to the motel. He turned the engine off.

"Let's walk, so we can make sure there's nothin' on the road. I don't wanna get stuck in this thing."

"Walk?" she asked.

"Yeah," he said. "It'll be okay. There's lots of people out, see?"

There *were* quite a few people on the street.

"Gimme a second," she said. She took a few deep breaths. If it came back and came at her again, she was not going to survive it. She looked around for any sign of where it had gone.

"Ruby, it ain't comin' back. Tornados ain't like that," Jake said, his voice close to being reassuring.

"How do you know?"

"Isn't my first rodeo," he said wryly. "One came through Birmingham when I was twelve or thirteen."

She nodded, trying not to cry. He had an unlit cigarette hanging out of his mouth. His gaze flicked side-to-side, looking for unseen trouble. He was so mean to her so many times, but the second she needed his help, he was there.

He had no reason to come back for her. He could have climbed into that tub and protected himself and let her get sucked right out the door and into the tornado. But he had come back for her, he covered her body with his. She could see bruises forming on his arms, which were marred with what looked like cuts and pin pricks. He had shoved her back into the tub and prevented her from escaping when she'd about gone crazy.

He saved her life.

This wasn't rescuing her from a group of men and getting in a fight to protect her. He honestly saved her life.

"Thank you," she said quietly, looking over at him. He was staring, and if she'd known better, she would have thought he looked worried about her.

"For what?" he asked.

"Saving me," she said.

He shrugged and looked forwards again. He said nothing more, and neither did she.

"Come on," he said. "Let's go find this place and tell these guys we've got their car. We can unload it here when we find 'em, and they can come get it themselves. Then let's get the hell outta here."

The streets were a hazard, filled with danger. Power lines lay like fat snakes on the cement, lights were out, and people filled the streets. Some were trying to drive cars, but not getting far. Jake was smart not to take the truck.

He walked quicker now, and Ruby struggled to catch up to him. She felt like she'd run a marathon and wanted nothing more than to crash into bed and wake up a week from now, safe in her own bed at Everett's, Tim next to her.

She wondered if her father was worried about her; he had no idea she wasn't in Las Vegas, anyway. Everett knew they were headed east, that was it. She wondered if Tim had heard. She felt awful for hoping he was worried, but she did. She hoped he was going crazy in his jail cell with worry for her.

"Come on, this way," Jake said. It was hard to find the right building. So many buildings were damaged and destroyed, they could barely see the numbers. Jake slowed as they approached a building and he saw the numbers.

It looked like a warehouse.

"This is it," he said. "Come on."

He went to open the door, and it pulled right off its hinges. He shrugged and lifted it out of the way, placing it to the side. He stepped inside and coughed.

"It's okay," he said.

She was shaking. She would have stayed outside if she could, but there was no way she was going to be alone anywhere. She wished Jake would turn around and go home. They could go back to Las Vegas, and Tim could bring the car here once he got out of jail.

They moved inside the building, and Ruby stayed as close to Jake as she could, bumping into him a few times as they moved.

"Kid, you wanna watch it," he said, his voice not as harsh as usual. "I ain't goin' nowhere, calm down."

He hollered a few times, calling the name that was listed on the Bill of Lading. No one responded.

"I'm gonna look over here," Jake said.

She nodded, tears welling in her eyes.

She pushed her way through fallen boxes and drywall dust that was everywhere. She called out a few times, if only to make sure Jake heard her. She could hear his voice bellowing all over the place and it made her feel better.

She tripped over a small machine that had tumbled out of a box onto the ground. She stepped over it gingerly, then froze when she saw it.

A hand.

She screamed and didn't stop until Jake was at her side.

He threw boxes out of the way and cleared the fallen machinery off the man. Ruby closed her eyes and did her best not to throw up. The man's head was severely injured, blood pooling onto the cement and snaking down a drain in the floor.

"He's dead," Jake said tonelessly.

The bile rose up in her throat, and she turned away from the blood pool and the man's dead eyes. She couldn't block out the sound of the blood dripping into the drain.

"We better get outta here," Jake said. "This guy won't be drivin' shit."

She was too tired to be irritated at his attitude toward the dead man.

"What are we gonna do?"

"Go back to the motel," he said. "It's dark. I don't wanna drive around this place in the dark. There ain't no streetlights or stoplights, power lines are down everywhere. It's a mess now. We'll have to leave in the morning."

Ruby was quiet the entire way back to the motel. Their room was tidied more and someone had left a sleeping bag on one of the beds. Ruby moved around the room with the dustpan and broom, sweeping up more glass fragments and depositing them in a trash can.

She cleaned out the bathroom and swept all the glass up. The window was blown out in there, too. When she was finished, she found Jake and the manager hammering up a sheet of plywood over the gaping window and plastic sheeting over the hole in the ceiling.

"I ain't got enough for all the windows, this'll do for all the rooms folks are in," he said. "It'll be a little dark, but I got candles in this box here, you can use 'em for tonight. If you don't wanna stay, the Red Cross is setting up a shelter at a primary school down the road."

Ruby picked up the small box, sat on her bed, and held the candles in her lap.

When Jake finished hammering up the wood over the window, the room was as dark as a cave. She remembered him drunk and sad in the barn and wondered if he remembered that night.

"Gimme the candles," Jake said.

She handed over the box and watched as he set them on the desk. He lit a few and stuck them on the night table between the two beds. It would have been pretty if it hadn't been caused by such a terrible thing.

Ruby clutched at her legs, felt her control slipping, and struggled to keep her composure.

She saw Jake straighten up and look at her. She averted her eyes from his gaze, which was so intense she couldn't stand it.

"What?" she asked, looking back again. He was staring with a strange expression.

"You okay?" he asked.

"I'm fine." Her voice sounded anything but. Before she could say anything else, she broke down in tears. "Can we find a phone?"

"Ain't none workin' around here," he said. "Lines are down, darlin'."

She cried harder. "I wanna go home."

She wanted nothing more to be in that dirty roadhouse, serving drinks to bikers and hoods and gamblers. She wanted to feed carrots to Bella and ride until she couldn't remember this storm.

"I wanna go home!" She was crying so hard she couldn't see the floor. She was barely aware the high pitched wail she heard was coming from her.

Jake grabbed her arm, and she twisted, crying a banshee-like wail that scared her. She was going crazy, she could feel it. She was going to die here.

"Ruby, calm down, it's okay," his voice was saying, sounding like it was coming from far away. "You ain't gonna get hurt, alright? I promise."

How could anyone promise that?

She didn't move away when he took hold of her shoulders. His voice was soothing and low. Her tears slowed as she listened to him.

"Come on, don't cry." He pulled her toward him. She crumpled against him like paper. Her tears began again in earnest when he folded his arms around her and held her tightly. She circled her arms around his waist, remembering the feel of his weight on her body as the storm roared above them. She remember how he saved her, and she held onto him for dear life.

He brushed his hands over her hair, down her back, and across her arms, still speaking in a low voice, trying to soothe her. His heart beat loudly, and she tried to control her spasming breath as she buried her head against his chest. His hands smoothed her hair down.

"You're okay," he said again, kissing the top of her head. She raised her head up, and he kissed her forehead once, then twice. She tilted her head further, and he kissed her nose.

His lips were gentle when they reached her mouth.

She cried as he kissed her, and he ran his tongue over her cheek, tasting her tears. She ran her hands up to his face and pulled him to her, kissing him.

She felt alive again and glad for it.

She didn't protest when he pulled her to the bed.

She shut her eyes as his lips fluttered across her lashes, and his hands slid up her back. She felt momentary panic when they stopped, and she tilted her head back, eyes still shut, willing him not to leave her.

His hands caressed her shoulders and gripped the back of her neck. She pushed the thought of how different his kisses were out of her head and concentrated on not being alone. He moved over her, his body pressing her into the soft mattress. Her eyes flew open as she remembered the bathtub, the roar of the wind. She closed her eyes to the blind panic and gasped slightly, pushing at his shoulder lightly.

He understood her panic; his voice was low and soothing again, whispering that she wasn't going to be hurt, everything was okay, and he'd protect her. Nothing would happen to her.

She could feel the heat radiating from his body. His arms were bare and covered in small nicks and cuts. She opened her eyes slowly and pulled his face to hers, kissing him. He was battered because of her; he was injured because of her.

His lips brushed against her neck and the hollow of her throat. He slid the thin fabric of her shirt up her ribcage, and his callused hands moved softly against her side, then slid up to cup her breasts. She closed her eyes again, let him pull the shirt off, and toss it to the floor.

He kissed her, harder this time, his mouth exploring hers, and she felt only the weight of him, his belt buckle pressing into her stomach. The weight of his body felt like the only thing tethering her to the earth.

She pulled his shirt off, his skin hot and deeply tanned. She clutched wildly at his hair, soft between her fingers. She was desperate to feel him respond to her. He was still as she kissed him and touched his face and his chest. She felt as if she was in a vacuum; nothing existed, nothing lived. Her lips trailed along his cheek, her forehead against his. She pulled back, but he pressed his mouth to hers, and she felt a gratefulness at being alive.

He slowly came alive as she did, his hands rougher, and his kisses more forceful. Her hands avoided his back and clutched only at his hair and the back of his neck. She was in a frenzy; needing him like she needed air. He rubbed a thumb across her mouth and pushed her further into the blankets. His eyes watched her carefully, an intensity in them she couldn't place. He kissed her again, his body bucking as she circled her legs around him. She couldn't make out what he said, his face buried against her neck, but she suspected the name on his lips was not her own.

She was barely aware she was crying. If he noticed, he paid no attention.

27

Ruby woke up and froze as she saw Jake next to her in bed. He was awake, staring. She looked away in horror.

He stood, lit a cigarette, and tossed the match into an ashtray. She grabbed at the covers, pulling them against herself, nausea roiling her stomach. This wasn't real.

"I guess Tim ain't too crazy to be bedding you every night, after all." He directed the plume of smoke toward her. He had a self-satisfied smirk on his face. "You ain't bad. You'd give Carolyn a run for her money, that's for sure."

She shook. What in God's name had she done?

She pulled the covers around her, feeling slivers of glass grate across her skin. It had felt right, she'd felt safe and protected before, like she would be okay and survive this, like nothing was wrong. Now she felt sick.

She had slept with Jake Wheeler.

He was looking with an amused expression, a smirk on his face.

"I'm gonna enjoy seeing Kelly's face when he hears about this," he said.

Her blood ran cold. She scrambled out of the bed, taking the sheets with her to cover herself. She felt disgusted.

Jake laughed at her sudden modesty—or at least, that's why she assumed he laughed. Jake pulled on his jeans then laid down in the bed she vacated.

"You can't tell him."

"What, Little Miss Perfect is gonna lie to her boyfriend?" he asked, raising an eyebrow. "I can't believe that."

She would have to tell Tim. She couldn't hide this if she wanted to. One look and he'd know what she did. She tried to imagine his face, what it would look like and what he'd say. She shivered.

"I want to tell him myself," she said. "Oh God, what've I done?"

Jake scowled. "Yeah, poor you, jumpin' into bed with me, oh the horror. You know, worse things could happen to you."

"Stop it!" she said. "Stop tryin' to make me feel bad for you, you used me!"

"I didn't see you pushing me offa you, honey," he said contemptuously. "No, you were pretty damn into it, if I remember right."

"Stop it." She closed her eyes and shook her head. Her eyes stung with tears.

"Tim should've thought twice before he asked me to come out and rescue you." He took a long drag of his cigarette. She wanted to take it and burn holes in him. "He'll learn once and for all it's an eye for an eye out here."

"Jake, please," she said. "Let me tell Tim."

He looked triumphant at her begging and studied the cuts on his hands. "I dunno."

"Jake," she said. She wiped her cheek with the back of her hand. She could feel the cut skin sting from her salty tears.

She watched him smoking and trying not to smile. He thought this was funny. A joke.

"Please," she said again. It only made him smile more.

"I dunno," he said. "What'll you give me for it?"

He looked over seductively and stared so intensely she felt naked, despite the covers. She blushed, feeling ashamed, wearing only a sheet in a motel room with another man.

"You bastard," she whispered. She picked up her clothes and tried to pull them on without dropping the sheet. "You did this on purpose."

"So what if I did?" he asked. "You shoulda seen it coming, I say. Guys like me only want one thing, right? You gotta learn sometime, the world ain't fair, darlin'."

"Fair? I never thought the world was fair, it wouldn't have taken everything from me if it was!" she screamed. She paused. She was not going to tell Jake anything more.

"I did you two a favour."

"A favour?" she asked incredulously.

"Yeah," he said. "You've gone and fallen in love with a guy like him. He couldn't keep his hands off what was mine, and sooner or later he had to know it was coming back at him. And you gotta learn to spot the wolves when they're wearin' sheep's clothes."

She stared.

"He never would've done anything with Darla, you know that!" Ruby said. She remembered Darla's words. Don't believe anything Jake says. She knew this was coming, but why? Because something had happened?

"You're a gullible little thing, take off those blinders, darlin'." Jake stared. "You're better off."

"It's no wonder Darla left you."

She saw Jake's face harden, the smirk fade. Jake sat up and pulled on his boots.

She finished dressing in the bathroom, then went outside—it still looked like a disaster zone. She walked on shaky legs toward the truck, hearing Jake follow behind her.

She got in the passenger seat without a word.

"You gonna ignore me the whole way to Las Vegas?" he asked.

"Just drive," she said.

He didn't say anything, and slowly pulled out onto the road. There were wires across many of the roads and trees were down, debris scattered every-where. Once Jake had cleared the devastated areas, it was a lot easier to drive. Soon they were on the highway, headed to Las Vegas.

They didn't speak for the first few hours. Ruby stared at the plains, the farms, the land, trying to figure out what to do. She tried to lie down in the back, but she could smell Tim in the sheets. She returned to the passenger seat and stared out the window.

"I won't tell him," he said.

Ruby looked over, not sure she heard right.

"What?"

"I won't tell Tim," he said.

"Thank you."

It didn't make her feel much better, in truth. She still had to tell Tim. She briefly considered not telling him, but he'd know right away something was up. She couldn't count on Jake keeping his mouth shut forever, either.

They had to stop in Grand Junction. Jake got her a motel room and slept in the truck. Ruby cried, alone in the motel room, feeling like her entire world was ending.

The next day, as Las Vegas rolled closer, Ruby got a horrible headache. As they cruised down US 93, she got more and more nervous.

When they pulled into Everett's place, she knew she was going to be sick. Tim was already there, waiting.

Tim was relieved to see the big truck and trailer roll up. There was damage to one side, but everything was intact. That meant Ruby was intact, too.

He let out a breath when she climbed out of the cab of the truck.

She was a mess. Her hair was tangled, her face was red from crying, and her eyes were so swollen from the tears it looked like someone had punched her. She had a large bandage in the middle of her forehead, and he spied more than one bruise and a few superficial cuts on her arms. He couldn't imagine what Jake had dealt with. If she had freaked out like she had over a thunderstorm, a tornado must have been something else.

She stopped short before she reached him, and he figured she wondered if they were still fighting. He remembered how she looked when he hadn't been able to say 'I love you' back, and he thought she probably felt as lonely as she looked. He stepped toward her, reached a hand out, and she rushed into his arms.

She was crying so hard her whole body shook.

He kissed the top of her head, then she raised her face to him, and she kissed him desperately. Tim broke the kiss gently.

"You okay?" he asked, sounding much more gruff than he meant.

She shook her head, holding him tightly.

A minute later Everett came out of the house, and Ruby rushed over to him; Tim had never seen her so glad to see Everett. She was shaking like a leaf, and Everett led her over to the stairs and sat her down.

"Jesus, I was hopin' you weren't in Topeka, but I can see clear as day you were. I've gotta go to the stables quick," Everett said. "I been on the phone all morning with highway patrol trying to find out where the hell you were, I haven't fed the horses. I'll be back before the hour is up, alright?"

Ruby nodded. Everett went to his car, his eyes on Tim and Jake.

Ruby had barely spoken, and Tim was worried. It looked like someone switched a light out in her eyes.

"We brought the car back," Jake said. "Guy that was to get it is dead."

Tim looked over at Ruby, wondering if she'd seen it. That would explain why she looked so shell-shocked.

"Good," Tim said, thinking it over. Wayne shorted him on that last run, and he figured the car was now his payment.

"When did you get out?" Jake asked.

"Late yesterday. Hitched back. They only fined me, anyway." Tim turned to Ruby. "I'm gonna get Jake to help me get the car out of the trailer. Then I'll take you for a drive."

She smiled. She looked so damn sad, and he had no idea why. He tucked a loose strand of hair behind her ear. He paused for a minute, watching her. He hoped she didn't need a hospital or anything.

He and Jake got ramps out of the trailer, and he got inside and unwrapped dozens and dozens of furniture pads off the car and started it up. The engine was loud and throaty.

He drove the car out of the trailer and parked it. He grinned at Jake's sour expression.

He watched Ruby stand up, rubbing her arms as if she was cold, even though it had to be over ninety degrees out. She looked so exhausted.

"Jake, you wanna let me and Tim alone?" Her voice was thin and unsure.

"What? Eager to get rid of me?" Jake asked.

Ruby glared at Jake like she wanted to shoot daggers out of her eyes.

"What's up?" Tim asked them.

He looked at Ruby, then Jake. He studied Ruby's face and felt uncertain. Something was wrong here.

"Nothing," Ruby said.

"I wouldn't say nothing," Jake said, leaning against the stair railing.

"Stop it," Ruby said, her jaw clenched.

"What's going on?" Tim asked.

In the days after, there were moments where he wished he never asked.

Ruby stared at Jake in trepidation. Jake had that dangerous look on his face, and her eyes stung from tears forming. Dammit, she shouldn't have any left after all the crying she'd done.

"Well?" Tim asked, looking at them both.

"Go on Ruby, tell your boyfriend," Jake said, his voice jeering and mean.

"Jake, go away," Ruby said, tears spilling down her cheeks. "Why are you doin' this? You promised."

"What's going on?" Tim asked again.

"Come on, Ruby," Jake said. "Tell your boyfriend how upset you were. Tell him you were so upset you had to jump in bed with me."

Ruby was shocked. He had promised.

She looked over at Tim quickly, who was eyeing them both, his brow creased. As he looked at her face, his expression changed.

"What's he talking about, Ruby?" Tim asked, his voice low and serious.

"I'm talkin' about how your girl was so eager to forget you on this little trip, that she decided fucking me was a good solution," Jake said. "Not that I minded, she wasn't too bad in the sack. Fair's fair, Kelly."

Ruby couldn't breathe.

"Stop it!" She turned to face Jake. "Just go away, you've done enough damage!"

She turned to Tim and saw an expression she had never seen cross his face for a split second before he became blank again. Jake must've seen it, too, because he laughed.

"Jake, I think you better get the hell outta here," Tim said, his voice even.

"Tim, please," Ruby said. "Let me explain ..."

"Nothing to explain if what he's saying is true," Tim said, looking her in the eye.

"Let me explain," she said again.

Jake gave a course laugh. "Ain't nothin' to explain but how easy it was to get her in bed."

Tim flicked his switchblade out and went for Jake.

Ruby screamed as Tim sliced at the air; Jake jumped back in time. Jake grabbed Tim's arms and slammed Tim back into the building, causing him to lose the switchblade. Tim punched him once in the face, and as Jake got tripped up in the soft dirt, Tim kicked him once, then kidney punched him. Tim hit him in the face again, and Ruby saw the blood spray from Jake's mouth.

"Get the hell outta here," Tim said, holding Jake's shirt by the neck. "I'll finish you off later."

Ruby wiped away tears. She was so confused. She was glad he was upset because it meant he cared, but it also meant he was upset with her. There had to be a way to fix this.

Jake stood and spat blood on the ground.

He looked over at Ruby, his eyes triumphant again.

"See you around, Ruby," he said.

"Stop it!" she cried. "You bastard!"

She ran to him and shoved Jake as hard as she could, but he barely stumbled. She hit him, feeling blind rage when he laughed.

"Just because she left and you're miserable doesn't give you any right to make everyone else miserable," she said as Jake walked away, a smirk on his face. "It doesn't give you the right!"

He continued down the road like he didn't have a care in the world.

She turned to Tim.

"Please, let me explain," she cried.

"What he said's true?" Tim asked, his eyes cold.

"You don't know how it went, it was—"

"Is what he said true?" he asked again, his voice colder.

The air was as dead as it was after the tornado passed.

"Yes," she said in a small voice.

Tim turned and headed for his car.

"Tim, please!" she pleaded, running to him and grabbing his arm. He whirled around and shoved her.

She stumbled back into a post on the porch and hit her head on the wood before she hit the ground. She sat up in shock, put a hand to the back of her head, and came away with blood. Tim looked shocked himself, then his face turned blank as she scrambled to her feet.

"Tim, I wasn't myself," she said, crying. Her head was throbbing dully. "I was so scared, and you weren't there."

"And you thought you'd get yourself a substitute?"

"No! That wasn't how it was!" she cried. "We found that man dead, there was blood everywhere, and I wanted to go home, I wanted to be outta there, and Jake was bein' so nice to me ..."

"I'll bet," Tim said sarcastically.

"I felt so alone, and I didn't think about what I was doin'," she said. "I know it's no excuse, I know that."

"Sure as hell isn't."

"Tim, I'm sorry," she said crying. "Please don't hate me. I love you."

Tim looked up at the sky and laughed. "You love me? Pretty damn nice way of showing it. When you told Lewis you loved him, did you go open your legs for his friends after that, too?"

Ruby staggered back as if she'd been slapped.

"I didn't mean it," she cried. "God, if I could take it back, I would. He did it on purpose, Tim. The stupid bastard'll never admit it."

"Don't go blaming it all on him, Ruby," Tim said bitterly.

"I'm not," she said miserably. "Tim, I'm so sorry."

"Sorry's not gonna cut it, Ruby," he said.

She was quiet, not sure he was saying it.

"Tim," she said, her voice pleading.

"I never told anyone about what happened to me," he said. "No one. You were the only one. I trusted you, Ruby. I . . . "

He didn't finish the thought, but it came through loud and clear.

He loved her. He loved her, he just hadn't been able to say it.

And now she'd done this.

She cried harder and tried to go to Tim, but he held her away from him, gripping her arms and trying to keep her at a distance. She wanted to hold him, she wanted him to feel how sorry she was. She struggled vainly against him.

"If I could change it, I would," she said. "Please, Tim, don't."

He shoved her back again, lightly this time, and turned toward the car. He opened the door, got in, and started the engine. Ruby cried again and put her hand around the door handle and tried to open the door, to make him stop and listen.

He drove off, and she lost her grip on the handle.

"I'm sorry!" she cried out as the dust kicked up, and the car left the parking lot. "Tim, I'm sorry!"

He tore off down the road.

She waited and waited, but he didn't come back.

28

Friday, June 10, 1966

Tim fired the gun again, breathing heavily when the last shot rang out. He didn't know how far out of town he was. All he knew was that he had to get out of there before he exploded.

He hunted up Pete Malcolm and got a rifle off of him, then hightailed it out of town. He opened the car up on the road, wishing he could enjoy how well the Charger handled. He would've given anything to be cruising Fremont, letting all of Las Vegas see his new ride. Only the victory tasted like sawdust in his mouth.

Jake fucking Wheeler.

He should've known Jake would try something—hell, he did know. He never thought in a million years that Ruby would fall for Jake's false charm. She didn't drink too much, so she was never out of her mind that way. He didn't doubt the tornado had messed her head up; the news was saying it had killed sixteen people and destroyed most of downtown Topeka. The Las Vegas morning paper had shown houses levelled, neighbourhoods gone, and total devastation. A huge black funnel cloud was the headlining picture.

He snapped the magazine in place, then took aim at the defenceless rock face about forty yards away. He fired until the magazine was empty.

He took in another breath and leaned back against his car.

She'd probably been scared out of her mind.

Jake would've seen that; he was nothing if not observant. Since Darla had left he was acting worse than usual. Insane Wayne said Jake did something he shouldn't have with Rosa. Carolyn had up and turned the other way when Jake had wandered into the Round-Up a few days ago.

Maybe he shouldn't have left Ruby with the truck. She could've stayed with him, slept in the police station or got a motel room and let Jake tussle with the tornado by himself.

She would have been vulnerable. She would have been seeking comfort.

It still didn't make it right. The damn broad should have some self control.

He threw the rifle in the trunk and slammed it down. He was going to level Jake. There was gonna be no question after this, Jake Wheeler would stay away from any girl Tim looked at.

He got in the driver's seat and cursed when he noticed his hands shaking.

He thought she was different. Maybe no such thing existed. He trusted her, for Christ's sake, and that didn't come easy with him. She tossed it aside like it was nothing. All she had cared about was he couldn't say "I love you." He turned the engine over. She should have known how he felt, she should have realized.

His head pounded with another headache. He remembered her face as she tugged on the door handle, begging him to stop. He remembered her face when she saw blood on her hands, blood he put there. He hadn't meant to hurt her. He wasn't like his father, there was no way. He hadn't meant to shove her so hard. She was so small, and he was so angry ...

He shifted into first and drove. He pulled off on the Strip and hunted up a liquor store.

He went straight for the bourbon.

Tim rolled over on the bench behind the Calypso. It'd make a decent place to sleep, but right now, it was a damn fine place to drink.

The streets were quiet for Las Vegas. No one found him hidden away here. He left the car at the warehouse and walked. He didn't want to see anyone—it would likely be all over downtown and the Strip the next day anyway. Jake would open his fucking fat mouth and tell the whole town he got Tim's girl into bed.

He took another mouthful of bourbon. It made him nauseous to taste it, but it was a fast way to get plastered.

He wondered how Ruby would take it when everyone talked about her. The folks that wanted to be in good with him would treat her like shit, thinking they were taking up for him. She'd get a lot of attention from guys she wouldn't look twice at. Hell, maybe she would look at them, apparently he didn't know much about what kind of girl she was.

He slid down on the bench seat and leaned his head back, then thought better of it when the sky started to spin. It was pitch black out, and he had no idea how long he'd been there.

He drifted off to sleep and woke up to the sound of an engine. He spotted the car circling around the alley slowly. A moment later a lone figure limped through parking lot. Bill sat next to Tim with some trouble.

"Di is screaming bloody murder," he sighed. He took the bottle from Tim's hands and took a swig. "She heard what happened from a friend, she's itching to claw Ruby's eyes out."

"That makes two of us," Tim said. "I guess Jake's telling the whole fucking world?"

"Pretty much," Bill said.

They sat quiet for a minute.

"Wheeler's telling everyone you and Darla made it, and he ran her out of town because of it."

Tim sat up.

"I know, I know," Bill said. "It's a pile of shit, but that's what he's saying."

Tim wondered if Ruby believed it. Maybe that was why. Jake would've flung that in her face.

"I gotta say, I didn't take her for the type to two-time," Bill said.

"She's not, really," Tim sighed. "I know Wheeler manipulated her for all it was worth."

"You gonna take her back?" Bill asked.

Tim laughed wildly. He didn't miss the alarmed expression on Bill's face.

"You gotta be shitting me," Tim said. "I don't wanna see her face again."

"That'll be hard to avoid," Bill said, shifting on the seat, "seeing as how we're at Everett's all the time. You wanna a find another place we can get beer that cheap?"

Tim thought it over. He was going to have to see her whenever he showed up there. He pictured the sad little face she made when she was upset, and it angered him already. He wondered if she'd be able to stand seeing him at Everett's.

"Come on," Bill said, struggling to his feet. "You can crash at my place."

"Brenda there?"

"Nah, she's at Warner's place," he said.

It took Tim a few tries to get up and longer to get to the car. Bill laboured to get him inside, then shut the door and took his sweet time getting in the car himself. Tim started to laugh at the craziness of it all.

"You know I'm sorry I shot you," Tim said to him as they drove.

"I know," Bill said.

"I'm sorry I ever met her, too," Tim said sleepily. It seemed like Bill lived awful far away.

"No you're not," Bill said softly.

"Yeah, I am," Tim said.

"You just think you are," Bill said.

"You'd argue with a fucking stop sign, Pearce," Tim sighed.

They pulled up to Bill's house, and it took forever to get inside, what with Bill's leg and Tim not being able to feel his feet. He fell onto Bill's couch and realized he lost the bourbon somewhere along the way.

"You think she believed you slept with Darla and that's why she did it?" Bill asked him.

Tim stared at the carpet and sighed. "No. That's the thing. I don't think she believed it."

Tim turned over onto his back and stared up at Bill's ceiling.

"I trusted her," Tim said quietly.

Bill was looking at him carefully from the other couch.

"I know, buddy," he said. "I know."

Saturday, June 11, 1966

Ruby was miserable.

Everett hadn't asked her what was wrong since she got back, although she caught him looking worried over dinner the night before. He grilled her something awful about the goose egg on the back of her head and all the blood. She had lied told him it was from the tornado.

She was pretty sure he heard the rumours by that morning. He watched her with an even more worried expression, but he still hadn't said a word. It suited her fine, she didn't want to talk.

Just this morning she tried to go over to Tim's house after she went to the stables, but he hadn't been there. Diana answered the door and told her she better not show her face around again or Di would rearrange it for her. She had no doubt the little wildcat would, either.

She hoped Tim would show at the bar tonight.

After dinner she took Everett's car to the stables and rode Bella forever, through the scrub to the dried up stream bed. She had cried, and Bella understood she was sad. She was on her way back to the barn when she spotted Jake in the distance.

"Damn him." She kicked Bella to speed her up. She got to the barn and put Bella in the stall quickly.

"What the hell do you think you're doing here?"

Jake glanced over, looked her up and down and raised an eyebrow.

"Doin' what I always do, ride horses," he said. "From what I've seen, you like to ride, too."

She grabbed the broken handle of a pitchfork that was lying against one of the stalls. She got a good grip on it and swung as hard as she could, aiming at Jake's head.

At the last second he ducked out of the way, and she angrily followed him, swinging blindly. He grabbed the handle with a free hand and wrenched it from her.

"What the fuck's the matter with you?" he asked incredulously, like he couldn't believe she tried to bean him. He better get used to it.

"Get out!" she exclaimed. "I don't want you anywhere near this place."

"You ain't got no say, darlin'," he said.

"Stop calling me that, and get the hell out of here," she said. She tried to stop them, but the tears overflowed. "You had no right, Jake."

"I can do whatever the hell I want," he said.

"Why?" she asked, crying. "Why do you want to destroy everything you touch?"

She saw his face flicker with some kind of emotion before he caught it again.

"I get that it bothers you," she said. "But just because Darla left you doesn't mean you have to even the score with everyone else. I was happy!"

Jake snorted with laughter. "Happy? You bitched the whole way up to Topeka that he don't care none about you. You cried so much I didn't think you had a fuckin' off switch."

"So you thought you'd swoop in and save me?" she said, her tone jeering and mean, like his could be. "I don't think so. You didn't want to save anybody, you only wanted to hurt us."

"Hey, I got somethin' out of it at least," he said with a smile. He looked her up and down, leering.

Her breath caught.

"You save my life one second, then ruin it the next," she said.

"Hey, you helped me out plenty on that last one," he said with a smile, as if this was all some funny joke and not her entire life.

"You planned it."

"Believe whatever you want, darlin'," he said.

"Stop calling me that," she said.

"I was evening the score," he said with a bitter smile. "Havin' a little fun."

"Just like you were havin' fun the night Darla left? You remember that, Jake?" she asked. "Do you remember being so drunk I took care of you? I felt bad for you. You know Darla never would've cheated with Tim. Dammit, Jake, I saw how much you were hurting. I felt sorry for you."

He threw the broken handle across the barn, and it clattered against an empty stall, making Midnight Bandit jump and whinny.

"Fuck you," he said. "I don't need no one feelin' sorry for me. The bitch left because I wanted her to go, alright?"

She stared. He believed every word he said.

"You loved her, I get it," she said. "And I love Tim . . . and Tim loved me. I know that now. You had no right to take that away from us."

"I didn't take away shit," he said. "And, for the record, I didn't love that sneaking broad, either. As for me takin' things away, you were there same as me."

"You didn't do it for any reason than you wanted to hurt me and hurt Tim, because you can't hurt Darla."

"You don't know shit, Ruby," he said. "Maybe I did it for kicks, huh?"

She sighed and looked resigned.

"You can lie to yourself all you want, Jake Wheeler," she said. "But I was decent to you, and you took advantage of that. If you ever wonder why you're miserable at the end of the day, don't go lookin' at Darla leaving. You're miserable because you like it."

She turned, left the barn and had no urge to turn back.

Ruby got back to Everett's and showered, then changed into a fresh pair of blue jeans and a western shirt. She hoped against hope Tim would show up at Everett's tonight. She hoped Jake would stay the hell away.

As people started trickling in a few hours later, she felt the stares as they came up to the bar for drinks. Ray Roth showed up and lewdly propositioned Ruby so the whole bar could hear. She tried to drown out the laughter that followed.

The girls looked over like she was nothing more than a piece of trash. She burned under their gazes, wondering why they were judging her so badly when almost every one of them had come out of one of Everett's rooms with someone they shouldn't have at some point.

Ruby thought about that, then got the keys from the register. If anyone wanted upstairs tonight, they'd have to go through her. No one would bother her if they thought she might rat them out for talking about her.

She spent most of her time in the kitchen at first, until the bar was in full swing, and the room was packed with people. Jed ushered her out to make drinks. She spotted Hollis Warner and wondered if he'd speak to her again.

She brought more beer mugs into the back for washing, then returned to her post behind the bar. It wasn't long before Hollis came up for a refill.

"How's it goin', kid?" he asked.

She shrugged and tried to smile. "It's been better."

"I heard," he said.

"Yeah, I guess all of Las Vegas has by now," she sighed.

She refilled his glass and turned toward the door when the din of the bar hushed a little. Tim and Bill walked in.

Her stomach turned over at the sight of him.

Even though he had a black eye and a bandage wrapped around his knuckles, he looked good. She watched him, hoping he would come over to the bar to talk with her, but he didn't glance her way and headed for the big table in the far corner. She wondered if he was watching her through the window, like he used to.

She looked back at the bar, then Hollis. "Do you think ..."

Hollis looked at her. "I wouldn't get my hopes up, kid." He took his beer and disappeared into the crowd.

A few minutes later Bill Pearce came up to the bar.

"Hey, Ruby," he said.

"Hi," she answered, her voice catching. She didn't want to cry in the middle of the bar, she'd never live it down.

"Two Buds," he said.

She took out two Budweiser bottles from the fridge and took the caps off before placing them on the bar. She didn't let them go.

"He didn't sleep with her. If you're wondering," Bill said.

"I know." She looked at Bill. "Do you think he'll ever forgive me?"

Bill looked sad. "It'll take another lifetime before he does, Ruby."

She looked at the bar forlornly.

"He knows Jake had a bigger hand in it than he says," Bill said. "Hell, *I* know he did. Jake's talented at starting trouble."

She looked up at Bill hopefully.

"But it doesn't matter, Ruby," Bill said. "He can't forget it. I told you once that trust was a big thing with Tim Kelly, and that wasn't a lie. He don't take kindly to people breaking it."

"What if I talked to him? Tried to fix things?"

Bill shook his head. "It's best to leave him alone right now. Especially now."

"But—"

"Ruby, I know him," Bill said, cautioning her. "He doesn't wanna look at you right now."

She looked at the bar, and one of her tears plopped onto the wood.

"For what it's worth, Ruby, I'm real sorry," Bill said. "For the both of you."

She managed to distract herself the rest of the night by serving beer, breaking up a couple fights and shooting the guys meaningful looks when they came to ask for room keys. The girls had worried expressions on their faces, like she was going to get loose lips and spill her knowledge all over Las Vegas. If they kept looking and talking about her like they were, she sure as hell would.

She watched Tim every chance she got.

He sat with a group of his boys, Ray Roth standing off to the side and watching Tim like he was disappointed Tim wasn't falling apart. Ruby knew better. Even if he was mad as hell, he'd never let anyone see it.

She debated going over to talk to him or taking him a free beer, but just as she screwed up the courage, someone put "Runaround Sue" on the jukebox. She saw people looking at her, snickering, and whispering behind their hands. Someone said something to Tim, and he laughed. Her face burned.

A moment later the mood changed. She looked over to the doorway and was dismayed to find Jake standing there.

He looked horrible. His face was bruised and swollen, he was limping slightly and favouring his right side. People were gawking, and he ate up the attention.

He sauntered right over to the bar, and she imagined everyone was looking at them. She was too scared to check and see if they were or not.

"Gimme two beers," he said.

She looked up at him, and he smiled. "Come on, I'm a payin' customer, you can't refuse me."

She put two cans of Hamm's on the bar. He took them and disappeared into the crowd for a second.

The crowd parted, much like it did when Tim moved through the bar. Ruby saw Jake heading toward Tim's table and held her breath. What was he up to?

She was shocked to see him clap Tim on the shoulder and hand him one of the cans. Tim looked at Jake, then took it and nodded. Jake disappeared into the crowd.

So he and Tim were settled up, just like that?

Ruby watched Tim, confused. He could forgive Jake, but not her. She wondered how on earth that was possible. Bill said Tim knew Jake started it all and yet here he was accepting a beer from the guy.

Ruby kicked at the floor and stubbed her toe against the bar.

A few minutes later, her heart leapt as she saw Tim walking toward her. He caught her gaze and didn't break it as he approached. She moved over near the register, and he walked up to the bar.

"I need a room."

"Okay," she said, her nerves jangled. She walked around the bar and took the set out from her pocket.

"The one facing front, base of the third floor stairs," he said meaningfully.

It was the room they had often ended up in, the one right under her own bedroom. If he stayed the night, there was a good chance they'd get an opportunity to talk when the crowd thinned.

She took the crumpled bill he offered her, then found the right key on the ring and started up the stars.

"Penny, come on," Tim said from behind her.

She turned around on the staircase and saw Tim take the hand of a golden-haired girl Ruby knew from around the bar. He slung an arm around Penny as they passed Ruby going up the stairs.

Ruby stood frozen to the spot.

"Sometime tonight would be nice," came Tim's voice from the second floor. Ruby found her legs and moved up the remaining stairs. She looked at the floor as she unlocked the door and handed Tim the key. Penny slid past her, and Tim did the same. She raised her head slightly to look him in the eye as he passed.

"Thanks, Ruby," Tim said, his voice casual.

Ruby ran up the stairs to the third floor and slammed the apartment door. She paced the small living room, kicked the couch and spotted an ugly ceramic candy dish. She dashed it against the far wall. It made a satisfying noise as it shattered.

"Whoa, whoa, whoa!" Everett said as he opened the door and ducked to avoid flying shards.

"I hate him!" Ruby said, tears streaming down her face. "I hate him!"

She paced, then grabbed a small vase off the table and dashed it against the same wall. Water and glass puddled on the floor.

Everett shut the door.

"Oh, Ruby."

She cried in earnest, and Everett came over and enveloped her in a bear hug.

"I tried to tell you, I really did," he said. "I ain't sayin' I told you so . . . I'm just sayin' I wish you'd listened."

"You have no idea what he did ..." she said.

"I got a pretty good one," he sighed. "I saw Kelly bring that girl upstairs right in front of you and the whole world."

"Kick them out." She looked up into Everett's eyes pleadingly. "Get rid of Kelly and his boys, kick 'em out."

"Ruby, I can't," he said.

"And while you're at it get rid of Jake, too," she said. "Make sure he ain't never around that barn again, Everett."

"Ruby." He gently extricated her hands from around his waist and led her over to the couch. He got her a glass of water. "Don't go throwin' that, alright?"

She managed a tiny smile, for his benefit.

Everett shook his head. "Ruby, I can't fix this. Tim's a paying customer, and he's in good with Sam Wyatt. This place'd go under if he wanted it to, and it's all I got."

"It ain't fair," Ruby said, her voice small. "Get rid of Jake, then."

"I can't do that, either," Everett said. "He put in a word with the stock company, gonna take all the foals when they're ready. He could shut that down real quick, and I can't burn that bridge cuz of what you've done."

She cringed at his words. "You know it all?"

"Just what I heard," he sighed. "You sure got yourself into a mess of trouble."

"I ruined everything with Tim," she said crying. "Not that you care."

"I won't deny I thought he was trouble for you," he admitted. "But I can see your trouble came in the form of Jake Wheeler. I wish I'd warned you better about *him*."

Ruby put her head in her hands and cried, for how long she didn't know. Everett did his best to comfort her, which must've been a stretch considering he likely never had a hysterical girl in his apartment before.

"When I talked about broken china, Ruby," he said, "I didn't mean china, you know that. I meant broken hearts. I don't mind sweeping up broken dishes and glass, but it's damn near impossible to fix someone who's been hurt so bad."

Ruby laid her head against his shoulder.

"I can't sleep in there tonight," she sniffed, looking toward her room.

"I know," Everett said. "I saw the room he took. Bastard."

Everett handed her a tissue, and she blew her nose.

"Pop called here again last night, he's been pretty worried about you since the tornado," he said. "He's comin' into town in a couple days. Why don't you take off with him for a week or two, get away from town for a little while?"

She nodded, but was wondering if she'd ever feel comfortable in a truck again. "I guess I could. Do you not want me back?"

Everett laughed. "'Course I want you back. I ain't never ate so good in my life since you showed up. Ruby, you got a home here no matter what."

She looked at her brother, who didn't even look drunk when he'd said it.

"Thanks, Rett."

"You know, you might wanna think about going back to the high school in the fall," he said. "Do your senior year, graduate. You'd meet some folks, and not ones that spend their days around here."

"Maybe," she said. She didn't know what she wanted.

"The foals'll be coming in a few weeks, and that'll keep you busy, too. Come on now, you can lie down here on the couch and watch the new television," he said. "I'll shoo these folks outta here before too long."

Everett covered her with a blanket, turned the television on, and shut the lights off as he headed back to the bar.

Ruby slept fitfully.

29

Ruby spent two weeks on the road with her father, going from state to state. Her father laughed and joked with her like he always had. She figured Everett hadn't told him anything about what was going on, only that she was traumatized beyond belief from a tornado. Her father's jokes and stories were small comfort when she felt like she was dying inside.

She sat on the sand at Fort Walton Beach in Florida, staring out at the blue ocean and missing Tim. She knew Bill was right—nothing would convince Tim to talk to her again. He had to do that in his own time.

She wouldn't be able to win him back. He had too much pride, and she had too much to make up for. It was her fault this had all gone to ashes. As much as Jake was part of it, in the end, it was her choice that Tim was angry with, and for good reason. The proof was in how he forgave Jake.

Maybe forgive was the wrong word. He wasn't the forgiving type. Maybe he tolerated Jake because being a jerk was what Jake did best.

Las Vegas was familiar and homey when her dad dropped her off at Everett's, with a promise to call on Sunday. She wasn't angry this time, and she wasn't bitter he was leaving. She couldn't turn bitter like Jake. There was no way she wanted to turn into the kind of person he was, someone who found joy in hurting other people.

She went into her bedroom and was surprised to find a shirtwaist dress, plaid skirt, and a blouse with a matching sweater lying on her bed.

"Everett, where'd these come from?" she asked him.

"Thought you might like them for school," he said gruffly.

"How'd you know my sizes?" she asked.

"Looked in your closet," he shrugged.

She hadn't the heart to tell him that she hadn't seen a single girl in a shirtwaist dress in all of Las Vegas, but she appreciated the gesture. He was right—school would give her something to do in the fall.

She made sure to tidy up the small apartment, clean behind the bar and change all the sheets in the second floor rooms, because Lord knows Everett wouldn't have done it while she was gone. She realized she liked it here, despite everything that had happened.

Friday afternoon she headed to the stables for the first time. One foal was born while she was gone, and the other mare was due any day. The little colt had comically long legs and followed its mother Luna around the yard. She named him Trooper.

Bella greeted her like an old friend, and Ruby went over every single move and worked on every routine. By the end of their practice Bella wasn't angry with her anymore, and Ruby felt close to happy for the first time in weeks.

Her good mood faded when she saw Jake moving around inside the barn. At every turn she expected a wisecrack or a lewd comment, but aside from looking over when she came in, Jake didn't speak a word to her. He scowled and looked like he wanted to say something, but he never did. That suited her fine, but she told Everett about it when she got back home.

"I may have had a few words with him," Everett said slowly.

"What did you say?" Ruby asked, trying not to smile at the thought.

"I told him if he gave you any trouble I'd turn him out of the barn and make sure none of the other ranchers would hire him. I wasn't sure he believed me, but I think he took me seriously," Everett said.

Ruby hugged her brother.

She prepared for the bar to open, cutting up lemons and limes and organizing the beer. Hollis Warner strolled in late in the afternoon, the first partygoer on the scene.

"You're back!" he said. "Everett told me you're thinking of going to school in the fall. Is that right?"

"I dunno, I guess." She poured him a beer from the keg.

"Marilyn Harrison, Bill's girl, she'll be a senior at Rancho High."

"Does Diana Kelly go there?" she asked.

Hollis grinned. "No, she goes to Las Vegas High. You're safe."

"Well, maybe I will go back," she said. She didn't mention that it would be the one place she knew she wouldn't have to worry about running into Tim. Her hands were sweating thinking about it.

At least she had something that would keep her occupied. Only it was a long way until the end of August.

Tim walked into Everett's, took a quick look around, and was surprised to see Ruby back behind the bar.

He heard she'd taken off on the road with her old man. He hated to admit that he wondered if she'd come back. But here she was, behind the bar slinging drinks again. He remembered walking in and seeing her that first time, and it'd be a good thing if he could go back and replay that night and never speak to her. Maybe none of this would ever have happened.

The thought made him sad, and he tried to push it out of his head.

He walked over to the big table and sat down. Carolyn was lurking around, a knowing look in her eye when his gaze met hers. He nodded, guaranteeing himself a night with some company, but he'd bring her to the warehouse. At least he always knew where Carrie was going.

The thought didn't bring him much comfort.

He watched Ruby's reflection in the window. She served drinks and chatted with people, like she used to. Maybe that trip away had done her some good. She didn't look so haunted anymore.

His anger flared. He didn't want her to ever forget what she'd done.

Then he remember what her face looked like as he and Penny headed up to the room, the one he and Ruby had slept together in, the one right below her bedroom. He felt sick satisfaction that night when she looked at him like he'd shot her in the gut. He was almost ashamed of how he tried to make so much noise that night that it would carry up to her room. He wanted her to feel the betrayal the way he did.

But her eyes. He dreamt about them sometimes; the way she looked at him. He always woke up twisted in the sheets and covered in a cold sweat.

He shouldn't feel guilty about giving her what she gave him.

Bill had bothered him about settling things with Jake.

"You'll forgive him and not her?" he'd asked.

He hadn't really forgiven Jake, but he brokered a peace with him at least. Jake was always gonna be Jake, no matter what. He'd try and jam any girl he ever picked up, just to annoy him and prove he could.

Jake Wheeler was a fucking bastard, and he always would be. He expected it outta him. Hell, he would've died of shock if Jake hadn't tried something with Ruby.

But he never would've guessed that Ruby would cave and give in.

Maybe he underestimated Jake's manipulation, or Ruby's fears. But at any rate, it hurt more that she'd done it. He would never utter those words to a soul and did his best to cram them out of his mind.

"You gonna hook up with Penny again?" Adam Barnes asked. "Heard she's been askin' about you."

Tim shrugged. Penny was a means to an end.

An end he hadn't seen coming.

Ruby watched Irene shuffle in behind the bar.

"Kelly's table wants beers. Keg for all but Tim and Bill," she said. "They want bottled Buds."

Ruby went in the back for the bottles while Jed and Irene served up the glasses. She paused in the kitchen and grabbed a Pearl and a Lone Star from the fridge instead.

She walked over to the table, her nerves on edge. She put the Pearl in front of Bill and the Lone Star in front of Tim.

"Irene's on the way with the rest," she said, her gaze lingering on Tim for a second. He raised his head slowly and looked her in the eye. He nodded slightly, and she managed a tiny smile.

She walked back to the bar feeling lightheaded.

"You alright?" Hollis leaned in to the bar and spoke quietly.

"Yeah," she said. "He looked at me, at least. That's something."

She wiped the bar and looked at Hollis thoughtfully. "You know, I see Jake at the ranch, and we don't say more than two words to each other. I never thought I'd miss how it was before, but I do," she admitted. "I hate the feeling of hating someone, but I can't forgive him, Hollis."

"Jake's acting like an A1 jerk right now," Hollis said. "What he did was shit, but it wasn't about you. Rumour has it Darla was cheating. Everyone's saying . . . well, that it was with Tim."

"I'll eat my hat if that's true. I never wanna be like him, Hollis. I never wanna be so angry and so hurt that I lash out at everyone else."

"Like you did to Tim." He took a sip of his beer.

She thought on that. "Like I did to Tim. I never thought he slept with Darla. I was upset at him for another reason. Then the tornado hit, and I was so scared . . . when Jake kissed me, it was like Band-Aid. Maybe I was tryin' to hurt Tim, deep down somewhere, but I hate to think I was."

She looked at Hollis, wondering why he was bothering with her. None of the girls so much as talked to her now, Brenda included.

"How come you still talk to me?" she asked. "It's not like anyone else does."

"Shoot," he said. "I know what it's like to feel lower than dirt. And I know what it's like to do something and not know how you got there. We're friends Ruby, what goes on with you and Kelly isn't gonna change that."

She smiled at Hollis. She had no idea how she managed to find a decent friend like him.

She watched Hollis look over his shoulder at Kelly, and Ruby looked as well. She felt Tim watching her in the reflection in the window.

"You think we'll ever be okay?" she asked, her eyes on the glass.

"I think you'll talk, make like acquaintances. I think that's the best you should hope for, Ruby," Hollis said. "I'm not saying it to be mean."

"I know," she said, resigned to it.

Tim stayed at Everett's until three in the morning. Ruby was still working hard behind the bar. She did her best to stay away from them ever since she brought the beers. He was glad he looked her in the eye, though. Maybe she'd stop haunting him now.

Tim headed for the door, and he paused when Ruby laughed. He felt like someone was scraping him across the chest with a sharp knife. He remembered kissing her in the barn, waking up next to her in the morning, and the feel of her hands on his damaged back.

He would never be able to stand another woman touching his back the way she had.

He remembered the creases in her brow when she was upset, the way her eyes looked when she was happy. He remembered her face when she said it was true, she slept with Jake. That one moment that erased all the good ones before it.

He opened the door.

Then he turned around and found her staring at him. They locked gazes, and Tim felt a sad longing for her.

"Thanks for the beer," he said, as if he had never met her.

"You're welcome," she replied.

He nodded, then walked out into the night, alone.

If you enjoyed this book, please leave a review on Amazon and/or Goodreads.

Acknowledgements

There are so many people I need to thank for helping me get this book to this stage.

The biggest thank you goes to my editor Summer Wallace Minger, who is always there to harass me to edit one more paragraph by holding treats for ransom. Your editing made this book way better than it deserved to be, and your treats meant I finished it. Thanks for Ray Roth, Carl Hamilton, Jimmy Lewis, Adam Barnes, backstory galore, the best summaries in the world, and for being the sounding board to a thousand story ideas.

Thanks to Tally Blackman for her in-depth character analysis. Your comments were invaluable. Nobody analyzes a character like you!

Which leads me to my early beta readers at 731 for all of their comments over the years—thank you to Allison Boyer, Ashleigh Pullen, David Cross, Elizabeth Royer, Emily Rebro, Erin Bucknell, Haley Kelsey, Jen Gobes, Jennifer Mathieu, Kailey Shelton, Katie Sawyer, Katie Kuhn, Kimberley Jayne, Kori Upp, Laura Schibinger, Lindsay Schneider, Maggie Bechtel, Mariko Conner, Maryse Valiquette, Magen Holdway, Meaghan McCans, Michelle Weagle, Nicki Keating, Olivia, Pam Gray, Racquel Capo, Samantha Collins, Sarah Chrzanowski, Steph, Taylor Hitchings, Teegan Thorpe, Tiffany Haendel, and Whitney Renville. I know there are many I forgot, but know I appreciated all of your comments and suggestions.

Thank you to the National Museum of Organized Crime and Law Enforcement (The Mob Museum) in Las Vegas for the wealth of information and amazing exhibits that helped colour the 1960s Las Vegas in this book. Also to Frank Cullotta, formerly an associate of the Chicago Outfit, for his recollections about criminal activity in Las Vegas in his talks at the Mob Museum and his books, which were amazing resources.

Thanks to my mom Carol Samson for the roof, Heather Samson for the cat, and Jasper Jax Samson for being the cat.

Read on for an exciting peek at the next *Sin City* novel, *Tilt* by Jennifer Samson and *Sin City* co-author M.B. Miller:

Tilt

From Chapter 2

It was well after 1 a.m., and Darla was tired down to her bones. One of the girls had gotten sick, and she ended up dancing the dinner show and the late show. It was extra money, but her legs felt like rubber. She couldn't wait to sink into a hot bath all the way up to her chin. After that, she planned to sleep for solid eight hours, then go somewhere nice for brunch.

She left the Slipper by the service entrance, trying to remember if she had bubble bath as she stepped outside. She didn't hear the soft footsteps behind her at first. When she did, a cold finger traced its way down her spine. A tail was never a good thing in this town.

Darla kept her eyes on the neon lights casting a riot of colour over the Strip and her pace steady, but her mind worked frantically, calculating the distance between her and the far side of the parking lot. It was a maze of automobiles, and plenty of dark places the streetlights didn't touch. Too far; much too far.

She spun around, hoping to startle them.

"Jesus, Darla! Give a guy a heart attack, will ya?" Eddie Demarco held his hands up to show her they were empty. Eddie was a valet over at the Desert Inn, but he'd worked up and down the Strip. Everybody knew Eddie.

"What the hell are you doing, Eddie?" He scared her, and she didn't like it one bit. She hated feeling helpless, cornered. "I thought you were . . . "

"You thought I was what?"

"Up to no good, that's what!"

"Geez, Darla, I'm sorry." He looked abashed. "I just thought you might want somebody to walk with—you shouldn't be out this late by yourself. How come you're not with the other girls?"

"They went to dinner, and I'm too tired to eat." Usually she would grab something to eat or go for a drink with the girls after a show, but she was so exhausted the idea gave her nausea.

"I'll walk you home, okay?" Eddie said.

"No need, fellow." A tall, slender man stepped out of the shadows, followed by short, stocky guy. If they didn't look so grim, the difference would be comical in a Mutt and Jeff way. They wore suits with the narrow lapels that Dean, Sammy and Frank had made popular. These suits only aspired to that quality and didn't look nearly anywhere as good on these two lugs. "We'll be happy to see Miss Redmond home."

Eddie stepped forward and Darla shook her head slightly. They might get rough with a woman, but they would beat the shit out of a man interfering with their business.

Eddie was on the edge of everything—street gangs, jobs, the Outfit. He was a guy who could get things or knew people. He had the connections to be a made guy, if he wanted, but Eddie didn't have a mean bone in his body. These guys would grind him up and spit him out.

Darla sighed; this was why she didn't date nice men.

"You two want to leave me be? I've got a boyfriend," she said.

"We know." Mutt grabbed her forearm, pulling her toward him.

Darla had planted her feet, and she stumbled when he yanked her arm. "Ouch!"

Eddie took another step toward them, anxiety and uncertainty written all over his face. Darla shook her head again, more urgently. "If you know I have a boyfriend, then you know who he is and you know what a dumb move this is," she said.

"Sweetheart," Jeff said with a smile, "do we look like we're scared of Jake Wheeler?"

"I wouldn't have pegged you for stupid, but . . . "

That got her a sharp smack from Mutt, and she tasted blood. Fear settled in her stomach like ice. Of the guys affiliated with the families, only Johnny Moro, that son of a bitch who handled things for Chicago, was prone to put the squeeze on a guy's loved ones, and Johnny was a hand's-on guy. These two weren't mob guys, and that was bad news for her.

"We have a message for Wheeler, and you're going to give it to him," Mutt said.

"Go talk to him yourself," she shot back. "I ain't Western Union."

He shook her hard. "Your boyfriend owes us money."

"Do I look like Parry Thomas or the Bank of Las Vegas to you?"

"That mouth is going to get you into trouble," Jeff said.

As if she wasn't already in trouble—all thanks to Jake and before she said a word.

"You're coming with us," Mutt said, pulling her along.

"Hey!" Eddie surged forward, and Darla's heart jumped up into her throat. "You leave her alone!"

She bit her lip. They would hurt Eddie, and he didn't have a blessed thing to do with anything. He just was trying to be a good guy and see her home safe.

"Shuddup." Jeff opened his jacket to flash the gun under his arm. Like Darla hadn't known it was there—the cut of his suit wasn't good enough to hide it.

"You should take your own advice." Jimmy Lewis stepped from behind a black Packard, a Saturday night special levelled steadily at Jeff's face. It was only a .25-caliber, but Darla bet it was mighty big when looking down the barrel from less than five feet away.

"Don't say a word, don't make a move," Jimmy said. His voice was cold and distant, and the expression on his face was strange. It took Darla a moment to put her finger on it: Jimmy wasn't smiling, and Jimmy ordinarily was happy-go-lucky. He didn't look like himself when he was serious.

"Let go and take a step away from her or I'll put a new hole in your buddy's face," Jimmy said. The gun never wavered.

"Do it." Jeff swallowed.

Mutt released Darla, and she skipped back two big steps. She was touched when Eddie positioned himself between her and the two thugs.

"The two of you are gonna walk out of here, and you're going to leave her alone. You don't look at her, you don't talk to her, you forget her name. You do that, and we won't have any problems."

"We know who you are, Lewis," Jeff said.

"Good," Jimmy said. "Then you know I'll do what I say." He didn't look or sound like himself. It scared Darla. Jimmy wasn't Jimmy without that go-to-hell grin.

Mutt and Jeff backed away, and Jimmy advanced on them, the gun still pointed at Jeff's right eye. "Darla, get in the car. Start it up, Eddie. Keys are on the seat."

Eddie guided her around the car, and Darla got in the back seat. Eddie climbed in the driver's seat and started the engine, throwing the car into reverse and backing out. Jimmy kept pace with Mutt and Jeff, and he would be out of sight soon.

Darla leaned over the front seat. "Follow Jim."

Eddie nodded, and put the car in gear. He was pale and beads of sweat stood out along his hairline. "You keep some strange company, Darla."

"Some good company, too." She squeezed his shoulder, and he glanced over his shoulder to give her a wan smile.

When Mutt and Jeff figured they were close enough to the street that Jimmy wouldn't risk shooting them, they made for the sidewalk as fast as their legs could carry them. Jimmy watched them go, holding the gun down near his leg, hiding it in the fold of his slacks, but not stowing it.

Eddie pulled up alongside, and Jimmy got in, slumping in the seat and bracing his knees against the dash. He gave Eddie directions, and Eddie nodded, pulling into traffic.

Jimmy stared out the passenger window, brooding, and no one spoke for several minutes.

"Thank you," Darla said. "I don't know what I would have done if you two hadn't shown up."

"It was Jimmy who got the drop on them," Eddie said. He was more confident behind the wheel. Driving was something Eddie understood and did very well. Word on the street said he was the getaway man in a score or more of robberies.

"You were holding your own," Jimmy said. "But what was that all about?"

Darla sighed. "Jake owes them money. They wanted me to give him a message for them."

"More like they wanted you to *be* the message," Jimmy said.

"Scum," Eddie said. "Laying hands on a woman. Things have changed around here, and not for the better."

"Still changing," Jimmy said absently. "The Families are losing ground." He held the gun semi-concealed in his lap. They better not get pulled over.

"Jimmy, how did you come to be there?" Darla said. "I'm glad you showed up, but I didn't expect to see you."

"I was at the burlesque show at the Slipper," he mumbled.

She laughed. "You weren't looking for me, were you, Jim?" she teased. She didn't dance burlesque—not yet. Burlesque would kill any hope of an acting career, and Jake's head would explode. Of course, Blaze Starr and Tempest Storm made piles of money, and the older dancers said they were sweethearts when they were at the Slipper.

Jimmy blushed. "Only if I wanted Wheeler to beat my head in."

"Those two guys, they knew they could find Darla at the Slipper," Eddie said. "Not at the Burlesque Room, though," he hurried to add.

"Darla, you better stick with people from here on out," Jimmy said. "I got a place that's safe, if you want to lie low for awhile."

"That's awfully nice of you, Jim, but I think it'd be better if I didn't."

Jimmy's eyes were dark and his face closed off. "Pull over here, Eddie." He pointed to the curb in front of the most disreputable, dingy warehouse Darla had seen since she left the Rust Belt. A sign advertising "Cade Meat Packing Co." still hung across the front, albeit with a drunken lean.

"This is the place." Jimmy nodded toward the warehouse. "You got trouble, Darla, you go there. Tell 'em I sent you."

"That looks like the set for a horror movie, Jim," she said doubtfully.

"Well, it doesn't look like much, but it's out of the way and secure. Even the Outfit and the Syndicate don't know about it."

"I'm flattered to be taken into your confidence, Jim, but does Tim know you're giving me an engraved invitation to his hideout?"

"It isn't a hideout, Darla," he said. "It's . . . a place of business. Besides, I know you can be trusted. Eddie, too."

Eddie was one of the most reliable sources of information about what everyone else on the Strip was doing. Hopefully, his better angels—and a healthy fear of Tim Kelly—would keep his mouth shut. Otherwise, everyone and their cousin would know about this place by next week.

"If I need somewhere to go, I'll keep it in mind, Jim," she said. "Now, I had better go see Jake and let him know what's what."

She didn't relish explaining it to Jake. Not at all.

About The Author

Jennifer Samson (she/her) is the author of the coming-of-age *Sin City* saga (currently at four full length novels and two side novellas) and co-author of the dark comedy/thriller *The Final Cut*, the first in the *Billie and Diana* series. She has been published in the literary journals *Thursday* and *The Lyre*, as well as the BoldPrint book *Friends*. Her work has been featured in the Brookline TAB, Toronto Star, Ottawa Citizen, and Edmonton Sun.

She enjoys fine-nibbed pens, Hilroy loose leaf paper, corner store candy, adorable cats, and beating her Goodreads Reading Challenge every year. Being Canadian, a love of hockey goes without saying.

She is a member of Gamma Xi Phi, a predominantly African American, anti-racist, non-hazing, all-gender professional fraternity for artists and creators where she currently serves as National Secretary. She is also a member of Alpha Phi Women's Fraternity.

She currently lives on the unceded traditional and ancestral territory of the Sḵwx̱wú7mesh (Squamish), səlilwətał (Tsleil-Waututh) and xʷməθkʷəy̓əm (Musqueam) Coast Salish peoples.

You can find her on Goodreads, Bluesky and Pinterest. She's probably there instead of editing.

* * *

Sign up for my newsletter and receive free ebooks and information on new releases - https://tinyurl.com/arieswriting

Arieswriting - www.arieswriting.com
Goodreads - www.goodreads.com/jennifersamson

Jennifer Samson Book List

The Sin City Series
(Crime/Love Story Saga)

Piece of Work
Sin City
Tilt*
The Dead Woman
Neon and Tinsel*
Bayou Bound

Coming Soon:

Under The Gun

*With MB Miller

The Billie and Diana Series
(Comedy/Thriller)*

The Final Cut

Coming Soon:

Curtains

*with M.B. Miller

Join my newsletter at https://tinyurl.com/arieswriting for free ebooks and news on my latest releases.